HELLFIRE

What is Hellfire?
Is it being critically injured in a warzone?
Is it living through the worst bushfire of its time?
Is it being so successful that you have everything you want, except love and contentment?

Tony L Hennessy

Tasmania weaves its magic through the lives of people from diverse backgrounds in this saga of frustration, and love, and bitter hate, but an enduring love of place.

ISBN 978-1-7637342-2-7

The moral right of the author has been asserted.

All rights reserved

HELLFIRE

A novel based on real life events in 1967.

All characters, except for those of historical significance are totally imaginery, but showing references to recorded history of the times, especially in relation to the Vietnam War and the Tasmanian Bushfires. None of the actions involving historical characters are based on recorded facts but reflect opinions at the time.

The hatred of Harold Holt among those drafted into the Army was real. The imagined behaviour of Harold Holt has no basis in fact, but was common talk among those who despised him because of National Service.

The author, as a Physiotherapist of fifty years, has cared for one Veteran of the Boer War, at least twenty from the Great World War, hundreds from the Second World War and uncountable numbers from the Vietnam War. Unfortunately the numbers from the Gulf War, the Iraq War and the Afghanistan conflict continues to add names to a very sorry list of human suffering.

Some servicemen and women have coped well after their war service, but I am yet to meet one that has not been scarred; some physically but every single one, mentally.

So the hatred that Marcus had for Harold Holt is written as fact, and his imagination as if it was real.

Tony L. Hennessy

Acknowledgements:

Writing a novel is a solitary endeavour, but it never happens alone.

The following people have been essential to the development of this novel.

Those early teachers that instilled a love of reading, and encouraged creative writing.

To Helen, who consistently encouraged me to keep writing, even when it seemed pointless; to the early proof readers who offered constructive criticism and even those who were concerned about my sanity.

To all of those hundreds of war veterans who trusted me with their stories and their nightmares; I hope that these have been treated respectfully and that this novel provides some empathy for those who have struggled through life to cope with the scars that war always creates.

To Lazlo Biro, who has been an inspiration to take a rough manuscript to a printable novel. The assistance with editing and formatting has been appreciated for what it has been; the difference between being ready to print and never being so.

To my brother, Rod, who read the manuscript many times and added valued criticism at every stage.

To all those friends and associates who may recognise a bit of themselves in characters in this book; you have been an important part of my life and some of the characters and events in the book are based on real experiences. Hopefully you will feel I have treated your memories with respect.

Tony L. Hennessy

FOREWORD:

The late 1960's is a turbulent time in Australia with the Vietnam War, the deadliest bushfire in Australian history, the disappearance of the Prime Minister and a young country trying to establish its place in the world.

This a story of human endurance seen in the lives of people from all walks of life, some of whom go through incredibly difficult experiences during these turbulent times.

Forces drag a disparate group into one location in the Cradle Mountain National Park; an isolated area that can be highly dangerous if the weather turns treacherous and where tempers can become frayed, and people become exhausted.

Marcus Pigeon, a very troubled young man, arrives in Vietnam as a conscript; he chooses to join the Tunnel Rats although he knows the life expectancy of that group is near zero. Marcus survives serious injuries before being repatriated to Australia and a long process of rehabilitation in Tasmania. He physically recovers with long-term mental issues, many of which relate to his life before Vietnam.

In Hobart, a senior Teacher is struggling with his physical health and dealing with an arduous Outdoor School Expedition.

In London two hard driven business executives, Jane Hampton, and James Pattinson, have decided to leave their stress filled jobs and take a sabbatical.

In Belgium two young women, Katrien and Marine, plan to have a year away from their studies, knowing that once they qualify in Medicine that there will be no holidays for many years.

In Melbourne two young University students, Elizabeth and Alison are planning their summer break.

The lives of these people intersect, in some cases for the better. None of them are aware of the forces that bring them together on the Overland Track in the Cradle Mountain National Park.

1: SHOT.

'Fuck' -he screamed into his brains as he bit
down hard on his lip.

The pain was beyond anything he had been
prepared for. Away in the distance there had been a slight
flash of light and then this feeling like he had been
skewered on a red-hot barbeque fork that was ripping his
guts apart. 'Don't make a noise, just get out of there. The
Gooks know these tunnels inside out. If you are caught
you will be dead, and it will not be pleasant. Not after what
you have done.

Get out and find a hiding spot and then just hope
your mates find you before they do.'
He wanted to run for the entrance and escape, but he
knew the soldier that had shot him was waiting for any
movement, any sound. He had managed to get behind the
bend in the tunnel. The Vietnamese were clever bastards -
the Viet Minh had built these tunnels with right angle
bends to prevent blasts penetrating the main areas of the
tunnels when they fought the French, and the Viet Cong
had made them bigger and more complex. Now that was
the only protection that Marcus had. It meant that the
fellow who shot him had to wait and listen and hope that
he was dead.

The normal rules of warfare did not work down here. There was no point firing off a machine gun because they could not hit anyone outside the short piece of tunnel the shooter was in. And anyway, the percussion would deafen whoever fired the weapon. This was a place for old, underpowered guns from the Viet Minh era or knives. Marcus was struggling to keep alert and not scream in pain. If the Gook came to the corner only one was going home, and at the moment he wanted it to be himself. He could feel the blood slowly trickling through his shirt, but he felt like his guts was sloshing around in a bucket of water; except it hurt like it was in battery acid.

He sat still until his eyes fully adjusted to the light. He knew that if he stayed where he was that he would bleed out or go unconscious. He did not want to wake as a prisoner. He had heard how they treated prisoners, and he knew that they hated the tunnel rats more than anyone else. No sense denying what he was, the tattoo on his arse would guarantee a slow painful death.

Marcus pulled out the service revolver and checked it was fully loaded. He had been trained to do that in total silence. If he could get a clean shot and kill the bastard on the other side of the bend, he might survive; but the chances are that he would be deaf. His pistol was designed for shooting outdoors and even then, the percussion hurt the ears. He took his knife and cut two small slices off his shirt. He stuffed these into his ears as hard as he could and crawled to the corner. He had his head on the ground as he looked around the edge.

At the other end of the tunnel, maybe a hundred foot away he could see a boy with a very weak torch, checking his gun. He quietly aimed his pistol, about eighteen inches above the head to allow for the bullet to lose height. He squeezed the trigger and just watched the head explode like a watermelon that was hit with a sledgehammer. Funny thing that: a clean head shot was weird. The fellow fell straight forward, like a puppet that just had the strings cut. No sound from him at all. The head jerked back, the body tipped forward and he went headfirst into the dirt.

Marcus knew that the place would be swarming with Viet Cong in seconds. He raced backwards along the tunnel until he found a ladder. 'Christ.' he said to himself, 'I hope I come up somewhere near where I entered. Too many Rats have been shot by friendly fire when they come up near a group of bloody Yanks who don't know we are down here.' Every step on the ladder was a new level of pain. 'Don't scream! One noise and you are a dead man'. He reached up to the next rung and the pain in the chest was extreme. As he lifted his leg it felt like the bucket of acid was again pouring through his guts; he pulled himself up a rung, but the pain caused him to almost black-out. He knew there were about two hundred steps with the Viet Cong running around in the tunnels below.

His head hit against the tunnel trapdoor. He just leaned his head into it and pushed. He wanted to yell out that he was Australian, but he knew that the soldiers below would fire every weapon they had up at him.

He also knew that as his head popped out of the trapdoor there was a fair chance that a trigger-happy Yank would shoot him without checking.

He pushed the door up just far enough to take a furtive look. This was not the bunny hole he had gone down; there was no-one around. Marcus decided that it was time to hide because the area would be swarming with Gooks in a few minutes.

His memory was fading in and out as he listened for any sounds that the Viet Cong had come up through his tunnel. How did he end up here under these palm fronds hiding in the root system of a bloody big tree? He remembered that it looked like a Moreton Bay Fig. The huge roots sat out of the ground in large gnarly lengths. There was a space he could lie down and cover himself with the fronds and hope he would not be noticed. Hell, what day is it? It must be about the twenty second of June. Marcus remembered writing in his notebook that they were going out to Long Phuoc near Nui Dat on the twenty first. The whole place was riddled with Viet Cong and the orders were to clear the vipers out.

The whole village was destroyed by the Australians. It took a while to realise there were tunnels everywhere and the Viet Cong seemed to evaporate into thin air as they disappeared down the tunnels. The Australians cleared the village house to house, tunnel to tunnel and then burnt it to the ground. He followed Harry's rule. If it was Vietnamese, kill it.

He watched about ten Viet Cong go down a tunnel at the edge of the forest. He waited long enough to allow them to feel they were not being followed then he entered the tunnel. Marcus waited thirty minutes in total darkness to allow his eyes to pick up enough light to silently move along the tunnels. There was no sound anywhere as he inched forward, making sure he did not step on a twig or a booby trap. He had no idea where he was when he came across a ladder in a shaft. As he lifted the cover, he could see he was in the middle of a clearing with about ten Gooks close by.

He raised his pistol and shot two of them before dropping down the tunnel and moving as quickly as he could by touching the walls and trying to remember where he had come. The short amount of time in daylight had effectively blinded him in the tunnel.

There was still no sign that anyone in the tunnel complex was aware he was there. He must have moved to an unoccupied section of it. Hopefully, he was not going to stumble into one of the training camps or hospitals that were down there. Only a few days before a few of the Rats were talking about some of the things that had happened in recent months. Three soldiers had come across a rudimentary hospital ward with camp stretchers and about twenty Viet Cong wounded. They threw three grenades and raced away. The percussion had deafened the three of them for weeks. They had scrambled back to Nui Dat with blood oozing from their ears.

They had a few weeks recuperating in Saigon, but the hearing was gone. The three of them returned to Nui Dat to collect their stuff and were evacuated to Australia. They were the lucky ones. Tunnel Rats knew that there was not much chance of going home, even in a body bag. Most of them died in the tunnels and the bodies were never returned. Those who were captured were tortured and eventually executed.

Harry Jackson was their mentor. He had fought in World War Two in the Pacific, in Korea and in Vietnam. He told them there no such thing as a nice war, and that the only rules that mattered were the ones that kept you alive.

"These are Harry's rules, soldiers. They have kept me alive for thirty years in war zones. If you want to play nice go ahead; I'll come to your funeral. If you want to stay alive these are the only rules that count.

- Don't trust an Asian
- Everybody in a uniform is likely to kill you.
- Anybody not in a uniform is likely to kill you.
- If they are in a South Vietnamese uniform, there 50:50 chance they are from the North and will kill you if they can.
- If you are not sure, kill them first. Dead Gooks don't count.
- Don't let them know where you are
- Don't make any noise, especially if you are hurt.
- Learn to walk so gently that you don't disturb the insects.

- Rub your boots with Lanolin until there is no leather squeak from your boots, no matter how much you twist them.
- Cover your footwear to leave no identifiable tracks.
- If they associate with the enemy, they are the enemy.
- Does not matter if the enemy is young or old, male, or female.
- If the tunnel comes up in a village, then they are all Gooks.
- Kill as many as possible and then vanish down the tunnels.
- Train to scream into the brain. "You make a noise you're dead,"
- Harry said. Scream as loud as you like, so long as you don't make a sound.
- Practice with sharp spikes and blades.
- Never fire more than three bullets before you reload.
- If they hear six rapid shots, they know your magazine is empty.
- You won't get time to reload.
- Do not use a torch. You may as well put a target on your forehead.
- If you see a flashlight coming your way fire as much as you like. You are already a dead man.
- Your eyes will adjust after a while, no matter how dark so you can see enough to get around.

- Respect respect. A leader deserves respect unless he proves to be untrustworthy or hopeless in the position.
- Failing to follow the leader will kill you and others. Following a hopeless leader will kill everybody. Gallipoli proved that.
- Learn to breathe like a butterfly no matter how hard you are working.
- Make no sound, make no tracks, and leave no trace. Move like a ghost. Make sure that not even a tracker dog would know you had been around."

Harry wanted his men to survive, although the chances were slim. At least if they followed his rules their prospects improved. He gave them his usual lecture, knowing that most of the tunnel rats would be only half listening.

"The Vietnamese hate the Tunnel Rats. They reserve a very special, slow painful death for us if they catch us. So, no badges, no markers, just your Greens. They know the Tunnel Rats do not fear them and are the most effective combatants in South Vietnam. You will be their trophy if they kill you."
Harry told them that the tunnels have been there since the French controlled Vietnam and were still a bit of a mystery. He was a student of war and devoured every bit of information he could find. When the first information about the tunnels was found he poured over them with a French interpreter to make some sense of it.

"The size of the tunnels are hard to believe, and the underground infrastructure is beyond comprehension. The Vietnamese had been fighting forever and the tunnels have developed over more than a century. But in recent years they have become extraordinary.

The first tunnels were discovered in early 1966. As far as we can tell the Cu Chi tunnels were developed by the Viet Minh during the French Colonial Invasion. They led to a massive underground complex that was 14 miles long. The entrances were covered by wooden hatches. The tunnels had multiple right-angle turns to absorb blast shock.

They housed barracks, ammunition dumps, food depots, hospitals, clinics, and serious intelligence stations. There were several training-camps underground. The main areas were fitted with ventilation shafts. The Viet Cong can hide in the tunnels during attacks and reappear behind the lines when their enemies have passed. They could stay underground for months if necessary."

He explained that explosives were not effective down there so the "tunnel rat" was born. Small, fit and extremely brave they entered the tunnels armed with a torch, a handgun and a knife and an occasional radio headset connected by wire back to the waiting troops.

"Using the torch is not a good idea, and firing the large service pistols in the confined space will cause instant deafness. The best weapons down there are the small underpowered pistols of the Viet Cong if you can get one or small calibre pistols that are not Army issue."

Harry told them that the tunnels were often booby trapped with snakes or dangerous pits filled with water or gas. They were incredibly small and tight but opened up to large spaces where needed.

"Be bloody careful when you come out of a tunnel. You are likely to be shot by a bloody trigger-happy Yank as you try to leave it.   Too many of our boys complete their work only to be shot by friendly fire as they leave the tunnel.

When you are in the tunnel you are on your own. Assume you are not coming out alive. Do as much damage as possible.

If anyone comes out of the tunnels what we need most is information. We need to know what is down there, and how we reach it. If it is important enough, we will take it out, even if that results in the loss of our Rats."

Harry's rules had kept Marcus alive, but only just. He knew that he was not safe till he was back at the base and somewhere that a medical team could put him back together. In the meantime, he needed to hide until he could be rescued. He was slipping in and out of consciousness when he heard movement near where he was hiding. As he opened his eyes, he looked into the face of a wild boar that nudged his shoulder with its wet nose. He was too frightened to scream out, even if he was about to be eaten by a pig. Marcus thought it was ironic that they often said they were fighting the pigs and now a real one was likely to kill him. He closed his eyes and for the first time in a long time he started to repeat the prayers he was taught as a young boy.

The boar jerked away and collapsed. Marcus had a sudden warm feeling around his face and chest. It smelled like blood; it tasted like blood. 'Well, something has ruptured, and I am about to die', Marcus thought. He closed his eyes and just breathed quietly. 'I will go to my death with some dignity'. In the confusion he could hear laughter and American voices. He slowly focused on the Army uniforms, as one of the soldiers said that the cook would be making roast pork for dinner.

God, he hoped that someone would not shoot him as he moaned out a weak cry for help. He dared not move so as not to frighten anybody. A Yank with a gun in a war zone is a dangerous beast, old Harry had told them. Instead, he just whispered that he needed help in the most Australian accent he could pull together.

The soldiers pulled the fronds away and Marcus smiled very weakly as he repeated that he needed help. All they saw was a fellow covered in blood. The pig had been stabbed in the throat and the knife ripped sideways, severing the arteries as he dropped. It had squirted blood like a fountain. The sergeant called in the radio operator to get a helicopter to get Marcus out. "And hey, we've killed a giant pig for dinner. Can we get that on the chopper as well?"

His mates had seen him go down the tunnel and heard the gunfire. They had waited for two hours but when Corporal Marcus Pigeon did not come out it was obvious that he was dead.

They knew that the enemy would wait for rescuers, and they would be ambushed and killed as well if they went down the tunnel looking for him.

Harry was blunt. "We can't afford to lose soldiers trying to retrieve the dead. It happens everywhere else, but it can't happen in the tunnels."

There were only a hundred Tunnel Rats and they died at a rapid rate. They knew that statistically only 15 out of a hundred would go home and most of those would be severely injured. It was a full-time job getting volunteers; they had to be little blokes but as brave as hell. Most of them came from troubled backgrounds and the "Couldn't give a rats arse" motto was pretty apt.

They often joined up after hearing from home that girlfriends had found someone else, the loving wife was pregnant, but they had not been home for quite a while or family and friends had been killed. Sometimes families had gone broke because the business was not viable without them at home to help.

They joined the Rats and went to work. In the early days they called themselves the ferrets, because they were chasing rabbits through their burrows. But once the team joined up with the Americans and the New Zealanders the name changed, and they adopted their motto and the Rat motif.

Marcus was flown to Vung Tau Evacuation Hospital, but the medics told the troops that there was not much hope. His pulse was barely palpable.

He was ashen white and hallucinating between episodes of unconsciousness. All the vital signs they could test were in the process of shutting down. It was unlikely that he would be alive in the morning but at least the family would get a body to honour and bury.

The surgeons at Vung Tau rushed Marcus to theatre; they were surprised that there was a small entry wound and no exit wound; there was a large blood stain on the clothing but not much else and he had been shot at least 48 hours earlier and was still alive.

He appeared to be comatosed, but as they removed his clothing and started to clean him up for surgery, he quietly asked them if they had found the form. The head surgeon asked him what he meant, and he said in his call up papers there was a paper for his mother to sign to give permission for anaesthetic if he was injured. He had not bothered his aunt with that because she would just be terrified. The surgeon shook his head and told Marcus he was a surgeon, not a bloody public servant and he did not give a stuff whether they had the form or not. Marcus nodded and went to sleep.

Over the next few days, he had vague recollections of doctors and nurses, injections and tablets and drips being put up and taken down.

He saw the kids he killed when he popped up from a tunnel and hurled a grenade at a group of Viet Cong, only to realise they were far too young. He saw the young woman on a bicycle who smiled and waved at a group of Americans before she rode her pushbike into their midst as it exploded.

He saw the soldiers he killed in open battle but then he saw their wives and children in the photographs on the dead bodies.

He saw his mates who were blown to pieces by jumping jack mines, which leapt up when triggered and exploded a couple of feet in the air, cutting those near to the blast into pieces. He saw the day when his platoon had to pick up pieces of human beings and sort them into enemy and friend and then to try to put as many pieces together as possible into boxes so they could be sent home for burial. He just hoped that families accepted the advice to not open the caskets.

Gradually he started to return to the land of the living and became aware of what was happening around him. A young army doctor was checking him one morning and told him that they felt he might defy the odds, that he was probably going to live. Over the next few days, he spent more time awake than asleep, and he kept asking what had happened. Dr Rory Jones came to see him and told him he had a long way to go but he was doing well. " Marcus, you still have serious medical issues. We can't get you out of here yet, but when it is safe we will get you back to Australia.

"I am not sure if you were extremely unlucky or the luckiest man alive. The bullet that hit you was fired from an old, poorly functioning pistol. I would not be surprised if it was a leftover from the war with France. It punctured your anterior abdominal wall and bounced around inside you, hitting your liver and spleen, both kidneys and your bladder. It nicked your bowel but did not perforate it.

It ripped your gut in a few places and broke a few ribs from the inside. When we got you most of your blood was in your abdominal cavity and you were full of infections everywhere. How you did not die I don't know. We did the best we could, but we did not expect you to make it. We will keep you here till you are well enough to move then you are off to Saigon for some further surgery and hopefully home as soon as possible."

Marcus told them that he was officially Victorian but the only family that mattered was in Tasmania. Dr Jones said they had a good Repat Hospital in Hobart so he would almost certainly go there. Marcus drifted back to sleep but woke up as he got another jab in the buttock. The injections never ceased. That was the first time he realised there were women in the hospital. Mary told him she was there on a six-month tour of duty that would end in two months.

"What is that tattoo on your buttock, Marcus?" It looks somewhat official."

"One of my stupidest decisions. Drunk as a Lord in Saigon back in January and I decided to get my bum decorated with that. It is the symbol of the Tunnel Rats. He was supposed to have a pistol and a torch, but I deleted the torch and had him drawn with a bloody big knife because a torch will get you killed. And the beautiful Latin means something like 'Couldn't give a Rats Arse.'
That was how I felt at the time, but had I been caught in the tunnels that would have been my death warrant."

"Well Corporal Marcus Pigeon, you are lucky to be alive."

"Well maybe, Nurse Robertson, and maybe not."

"I am happy to talk whenever you need to, but it is time for sleep now."

Marcus closed his eyes as the medication kicked in. For the first time in many weeks Marcus slept without nightmares. He woke in pain and got another injection of Christ only knows what and faded off to blissful nothingness. The next day Mary was there again. "You worried me last night when you said that maybe being alive was not lucky. Do you want to talk about what is troubling you?"

"It hardly matters but my life so far has been a long way less than good. That bastard Harold Holt oversaw National Service when they called up my father in 1941. He was wounded in Europe and came home for recovery. He spent almost a year in the Heidelberg Repatriation Hospital in Melbourne. He was returned to service in Europe in June 1944 without knowing that Mum was pregnant with me. He was killed in August, and we never knew whether he was aware he was to be a father again. I was born on New Year's Day 1945. Ain't that just perfect? Harold Bloody Holt and his conservative mates reintroduced National Service with the first call up being for men turning twenty between January the first 1965 and June the thirtieth. If I had been born one day earlier, I would not have even been in the call-up. The only raffle I ever won was the Lottery of Death; one of the first dates drawn was January the first.

As if Mum had not had enough to deal with Dad's death. She had managed to get a job at the Government Aircraft Factory in 1945, the only concession she seemed to get as a war widow was a hard job in a brutally tough factory to support her family of four kids.

She had to go to work to keep them alive during the war, even though that meant leaving them home alone for most of the day.

She was a riveter. They were promoted as seriously tough women and even though the rules stated that the female staff can do everything a man can do but are not allowed lift more than 25 pounds, it did not really matter.

" Great, the panels weigh thirty pounds, so we can do SFA without a male off-sider and there aren't any." His mother said over a cup of tea with a neighbour. "The only way the job gets done is to ignore the rules. We spend every day lifting the panels and riveting them to the frames." Every night she went home too sore to do much for the children. Marcus muttered, "No one could claim that the Government was very helpful to war widows in those early years."

Mary could see his eyes were closing and his speech was slurring. She told him to have a sleep, and she would talk to him later. She reported to Dr Rory Jones that Marcus was much more alert, but she was concerned that he was struggling to cope.

The next day he told her the rest of his family history. His sister, Elizabeth, was born in 1930.

She became pregnant to an American serviceman in 1945 when she was only fifteen and went to USA looking for him in 1948. She had contacted Marcus once from New York; she had not found her man but was still looking. She was working in a clothing factory in Brooklyn, New York. Her son was six and about to start school. He had lost contact with her and had no idea if she was still alive. His oldest brother Johnny was born in 1934. He was uncontrollable after the death of his father and spent most of his life drunk or fighting, or both. He was killed in a car accident in 1954 when he was too drunk to stand up. Robert was born in 1936. He refused to go to school most of the time. He was allowed to leave school in 1950 to go to sea as a fisherman. He came home once every year for a couple of weeks but was swept overboard in 1955 in the Great Australian Bight. His body was never found.

By 1945 Margaret was a broken woman, physically and mentally. She was incarcerated at Kew Lunatic Asylum in 1955, leaving Marcus effectively as a 10-year-old orphan. Kew proudly boasted that it was one of the largest Asylums in Australia and was designed for lunatics, inebriates, and idiots. The Administrators at Kew made it clear that it was in nobody's best interest for a child to visit his mother in a facility that was full of the insane. Marcus had no-one else so it was decided that maybe he should live with his aunt in Tasmania.

"So, you can see Harold Holt and his mates killed my father, indirectly killed both of my brothers, and made my sister disappear to God knows where.

And thanks to his bloody lottery that he fought so hard to get back, he has got me here with my guts shot to hell. How could those stupid bastards make him Prime Minister? He caused the death of my father and the complete physical and mental wreck that used to be my mother." Marcus sobbed as the drugs kicked in and he drifted off to sleep again.

Mary was somewhat relieved that Marcus had let down his guard and told her of much of his early life. She assumed the drugs had relaxed him enough to get him to talk. At least now she had a better idea of why he became so angry with minor provocation.

Marcus had been up for short walks a few times and was slowly improving physically. He could walk a few metres with assistance but was often in a wheelchair when he needed to be moved any significant distance.

On the 18th of August he was told that if he wanted to, he could go to see Little Pattie and Col Joye, who were putting on a concert for the troops.

'Who in their right mind would send a seventeen-year-old girl into a war zone with thousands of young over-sexed males who had not seen an available white woman for years', he thought. Well, she was at no risk from him at least.

The concert had barely started when rifle fire could be heard over the noise of the performers. The Australians at Nui Dat had been sent out to check out a rubber plantation at Long Tan when all hell broke loose. There were Viet Cong everywhere.

Eighteen Australians died and twenty-seven were wounded in one of the fiercest battles of the War. The local hospital at Nui Dat was swamped with casualties so anyone who could be moved was put onto a Huey and moved out.

Marcus was sent to the Rehabilitation Unit in Saigon but even that was stretched by the injuries at Long Tan, so it was reluctantly decided to send him home for further care. Marcus was delivered to The Hobart Repatriation Hospital, accompanied by two nurses. Mary had volunteered to go with him. Her tour of duty was up anyway but she knew that Marcus would feel safer with a face he knew. He was small when he arrived in Vietnam, but he was powerful. He had a body that was hard packed muscle. Now he was thin and weak, struggling to walk and looking old and tired.

He joked that he would not even know the place when he got home. "Bloody Hell; I left spending pounds, shillings and pence and I am returning with dollars and cents. I'm glad I won't be buying groceries any time soon; I would not have a clue what things should cost." Mary told him that he would have plenty of time to adjust to that and all the other changes. There would be months in Hospital with increasing periods of time out with staff.

Nobody was made aware of his return or the extent of his injuries; he just arrived after dark and was in bed in the Repat at eight o'clock on August the 28th 1966.

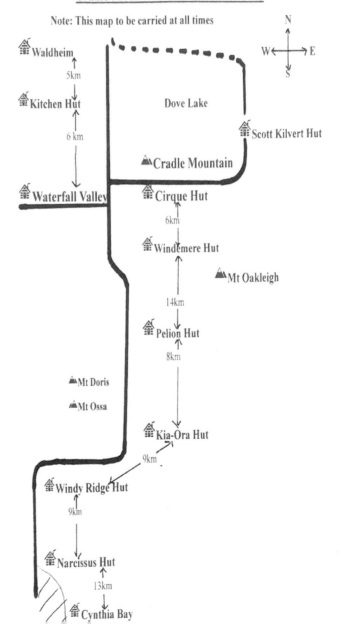

Cradle Mountain National Park 1967

Note: This map to be carried at all times

2: The Knee.

"Good God, this knee is absolutely killing me."
Andrew muttered

"Your face is no picture book either, Sir."

"Thanks Marilyn, I value your opinion".

Andrew was sitting on a rough-cut bench at the Echo Point Hut on the Overland Track with his teacher mate, Pete and eighteen students.

"You are getting too old for this, Mr Carruthers?" Billy Jackson said.

"No, I just twisted it on the track, Mate. It could happen at any age."

"Maybe, Mr Carruthers but you have been limping around the school for weeks."

Andrew had hoped that had not been noticed. The knee had been sore for a while. His doctor had told him he might have to do something different, as Physical Education tended to have a relatively short lifespan. Andrew told him that he had thought of that and had been doing a new degree in Science, so he could change over if his body started to tell him he had to. But he was a sports addict.

He played cricket in the summer and footy in the winter. He swam in the ocean when he could, and he and his mates went bushwalking when they could find time.

When he was eighteen, he was picked by South Melbourne as a recruit in the VFL. They paid his costs to go to Melbourne Grammar to finish his University Entrance Exams. He stayed there playing footy in the seconds, before deciding to return to his home state of Tasmania to go to Teachers College. Phys Ed was the only option considered. He had no wish to teach academic subjects, but his broken body was starting to tell him otherwise.

He was quickly realising his doctor was right, but he had another year and a half before he would be finished his studies and could limp off into a classroom to teach physics and chemistry. So here he was on another "Homage to the Mountain" with a bunch of kids who had volunteered for an adventure, with little knowledge of what was ahead of them. It was different every year.

The School Group had arrived at Cynthia Bay on Lake St Clair quite early, considering the long bus trip in from Hobart. The road was not easy, and it was subject to snow and strong cross winds, so the group were on the bus before sunrise. They had stayed together at the school camp grounds the night before and Andrew had forced them all to unpack their bags for his personal inspection. The instructions had been non-negotiable. If the pack was not complete, the student went home and not on the walk. They all had to have proper hiking boots and three pairs of woollen socks.

They were not allowed to walk in cotton or denim clothes. When it became wet it was deadly in the freezing Central Highlands. They had to have a walking outfit, which included a warm shirt, trousers or shorts, gaiters, and a jumper. A dry set of clothing was wrapped in a water-tight bag and double looped with a rubber band. Full waterproof jacket and trousers were mandatory. A hat was essential.

In summer, a broad brimmed hat was essential because the sun could be intense, but in winter a close-fitting hat that covered the neck was better. And sunglasses! When the sun came out on snow it would blind you if you did not have dark sunglasses. No pretty little things with pale blue or light brown lenses. The darker the better, was the rule.

"One change of underclothes girls, and no make-up!" was the catch cry every year, usually associated with continuous complaints from the girls, who claimed they did not want to look horrible.

"You might get a chance of one wash over the next fortnight, and you may not. Anything you carry in; you will carry out.

You will all have a small plastic spade to make your toilet. You will carry twelve ration packs; one for each day and two extras in case we get trapped. Everything will be freeze dried or dehydrated. You will include a small pack of nibbles for each day that will include nuts, and dried fruit with chocolate. You will need a Dixie to eat from and some camp utensils.

You will have a Trangia to cook with. You can share this with one other person if you wish. One can carry the stove, and one carry the metho fuel.

Your backpack will be lined with a large plastic bag which will be closed over in a double loop at the top and fastened with a strong rubber band.

Remember, put your sleeping bag in another plastic bag and seal it. If you don't you will learn the pleasure of sleeping in a wet sleeping bag. I don't want anyone dying of hypothermia on this trip."

The year before, a teacher and a student from Riverside High School had died in a blizzard in the park and the Education Department had made a complete equipment check mandatory for all teachers taking students on trips through the Cradle Mountain National Park. Andrew Carruthers was taking no chances. They all had the list, but he intended to make sure they all had everything required.

"Bloody Radar will know if we have left anything at home" one of the boys said. There was a general laugh among the students. They called him Radar because he always knew what was going on. "One thing for sure, he will know if we try to get into the girls' tents. Last year two boys got expelled just for trying that stunt." When all the checks were done, he got the school's tents and divided each tent into two equal amounts and gave them to the students to attach to the top of the back packs.

"Oh Sir, can I share with Marilyn? John snores."

"I would rather share a tent with a pig than you." Marilyn said instantly.

"Hey Johnno, Marilyn wants to share with you."

"OK Cut it out. Once your kit is checked, repack your bags. We will have dinner soon and an early night. You will have a chance to have a decent sleep on a bed tonight and a good wash down. Take the opportunity; it will be ten days before the opportunity comes back again. The next morning began in the dark and the bus rolled into the Cynthia Bay parking area at nine thirty-five. Everyone had ten minutes to get the boots and gaiters on. The waterproofs stayed in the bag as the morning was fine. The temperature was only two degrees, but everyone would warm up after a few minutes of walking up the western side of the lake. The track was covered in leaf litter. It was all damp and clung to the boots and gaiters. If everyone stopped, the leaf litter moved slowly as the leeches crawled around looking for something to latch onto.

Andrew and Pete Smithies, the other teacher, had walked the Park many times and knew most of the difficult areas, but it was different with students. This was the third time he had done "The Homage to the Mountain" as he called it. Every year was different. The first time in '64 had been easy. The students were all keen to learn, and Pete was a geology teacher so he could do a bit of subtle teaching as the days went on. The weather was cold but kind; there was little wind and only slight flutters of snow a couple of times.

The students were a typical bunch of eighteen-year-olds but basically well behaved. They left the Park, having faced a tough ten days but elated that everyone had covered the distance unharmed and without any concerns, other than a few blisters.

Last year had been different. Andrew and Pete made a pact that they would never let that happen again. That meant that the first few days would be governed by strict adherence to the rules they had set over the last two months of talks and training.

It was all going to plan until Andrew trod on a tree root in the leaf litter and that bloody knee had wrenched sideways. The pain ripped up his leg, his knee buckled, and he went down like a bag of spuds. He landed face first on a rock with blood pouring out of his nose, and a cut above the left eye. Pete had his backpack off in seconds and got out his first-aid kit that he carried at the top of his bag.

"Mr Carruthers, you look worse than Ian and Scotty last year after the trip."

Pete told the boys to go and get the billy on for a cup of tea. "We will get Mr Carruthers patched up and we will carry on to Echo Point. There is a very basic hut there so will stop for lunch. Mr Carruthers will be OK, but we may have to take it a bit easy today."

The knee was swelling, so Pete got the compression bandage from the kit and put it on tightly in the figure of eight pattern he had learnt at the First Aid course. "I guess we can dispense with the ice treatment Andrew. It is so bloody cold today that we don't need that."

Andrew muttered that he hardly needed reminding about the two boys last year. It had almost cost him his job, and probably would have done if not for Sergeant Garry Rogers from Search and Rescue. Garry had organised the medal for bravery just in time to shut down the school investigation.

Seven days into the trip in 1965 the party was between Pelion Hut and Windermere in very exposed country when a fierce storm blew through. It was carrying sheet ice and winds of sixty miles an hour. Students were getting blown over and there was a real risk of losing the track and getting lost. People die in those conditions.

Andrew had ordered everyone to stop, get into their pairs and put their tents together.

"Remember to create a little channel to make the rain go around your tent. Cover the edge of the tent facing the wind with a small amount of soil and bunker down.
Get your dry clothes on and if you feel cold get in your sleeping bags.

"If you were smart enough to bring a book then time to get it out. I do not want to be rude but if you need a toilet break, be quick. Find some shelter and do your business. But remember that part of your body can freeze quickly."

By the second day Andrew told them to reduce their food packs so that they created Day 13 rations just in case.

By the fourth day everybody was stir crazy from the time in the tent with nothing to do except shiver and talk to the same person for the fourth day in a row.

Ian and Scotty called out that they were getting dressed and were going to get help. Andrew told them to stay where they were; they had no idea where they were, and they would get lost and die like Scott and Kilvert had four months before.

"No we won't Sir. We were both Boy Scouts and we are in the Army Cadets. We know what we are doing."

"Boys, stay in your tent. You will not be told again."

"Sorry Sir, but we are going for help. You might be OK, but the girls are frightened, and they have been crying for hours."

They stepped out of the tent into a roaring ice-blown wind. Andrew roared "I told you to stay in your tent" before he hit them so hard that they were both knocked out cold. "Hey, you two over there watching, get over here and put these two clowns back in their tent."

"But Sir, they both have got blood noses."

"Better than being dead; take their boots off and give them to me so they won't try that stunt again. Put them back in their tent and then the rest of you get back in your tents and warm up."

A short while later, both boys could be heard muttering about reporting bloody Radar for hitting them. Scotty said he thought his nose was broken when Janice called out that it would probably improve his looks.

The boys went quiet when they realised they were not getting much sympathy.

The weather started to ease as night fell, so the students were told that it looked like they could probably start walking again tomorrow but they would need to be careful as snow would obscure the track and every step would be in heavy snow. It would be difficult.

At daybreak the sky was blue, and the wind had dropped to a light breeze. "OK kids, time to get back into your wet walking gear. Yes, I know it stinks but so do you, and I know it is cold, but it will warm up soon after you start walking. Get your gear on and everything back in your backpacks. Make sure your sleeping bag and dry clothes go back into their bags and sort out your food for today. We will have something to eat but I want us walking in an hour."

One of the boys called out to the girls to see if any of them had smuggled in some makeup. "I think Ian and Scotty need something to cover those black eyes". "Shut up" they both said. Scotty said that this was not finished. He was going to report it to the school and Radar will be looking for a new job next week.

Four hours later Sergeant Garry Rogers and a six-man group from Search and Rescue came down the track from the North. They had estimated that the group was somewhere between Windermere and Pelion Ridge from the track notes the school had lodged. Garry and the others had come in on a side track, to shorten the search time.

"Bloody glad you were not on a sidewalk. We probably would not have found you. We are going to go back to the Arm River Track and walk out.
We have an Ambulance and a fleet of vehicles to get you out of here. We will advise the school not to wait for you up at Dove Lake once we get to the police radio."

Scotty called out. "Hey, are you a policeman?"
"Yes, I am. Why?"
"Mr Carruthers hit Ian and me so hard he has given both of us black eyes, and I think he broke my nose."
Garry sat and listened to their story before he went to Andrew and said, "Is that exactly as it happened?"
Andrew agreed the story was pretty accurate. Sergeant Garry Rogers turned to Andrew and told him his care for his students was exemplary. He told Ian and Scotty that one day they would be grateful that their teacher had been so forceful. "Otherwise, we would be looking for two dead bodies. Now listen to me, if you make trouble for your teacher, I will make trouble for you. You got that?" They both nodded.

On the second day back at school Andrew was advised that he was under investigation from the School Commission for assaulting two students. The story was in the newspaper the next day, and Andrew was told to take some leave while the whole thing was checked.
Andrew decided that gave him some time to do some intensive study, so he headed off to the University to do a block full time.

If the Schools Commission were too tough, he would change to a straight academic Science degree and pursue a new career in private industry.

He was called in to school after two months; all investigations had ceased after Sergeant Garry Rogers told them that Andrew Carruthers would be receiving a Medal of Bravery from the State Governor in honour of his ability to get his students away from danger. Janice had asked, on behalf of the students, if it could include his nickname of Radar on the Medal.

Andrew as not sure whether the "Homage to the Mountain" would happen again after that incident. But if it did; the parents now knew that Radar would keep his students safe even if he had to beat some sense into them. Now here he was on day one with a nasty injury and no real way of getting help. He just needed to look after his knee and do the best he could. He found a limb of a tree on the ground and broke it to make a walking pole. He could stand up and walk with care. Pete suggested he could go back to Cynthia Bay, but it was not safe to have that many students with one teacher. He decided he would get to the other end of the track one way or the other. Anyway, with the walking pole and the bandage it came good quickly.

At his now restricted pace Andrew knew the walk to Narcissus would take longer than first planned. He felt a little sorry for the kids because he would need to create reasons to allow him to rest his leg. Pete understood and agreed that they would use a few diversionary tactics.

Pete told the kids that as the weather was very clear he would take them over to Lake Helen so they could have a look at Mount Olympus.

As the track to Mount Helen was quite steep and not well marked, he told them they had better stick together. "The mountain is spectacular, and it is often covered in cloud or fog so this will be an opportunity you may not get again". As he headed off to the left to told Andrew they would be at least two hours. "You might want to kick your boots off and wade into the water. The lake is bloody freezing but that would certainly stop your knee from swelling".

By the time they got back Andrew had been for a walk in the lake, dried off as best he could, reapplied his bandage and put his boots and gaiters back on. The knee felt much less painful, probably because it was frozen to complete anaesthesia. The weather was kind, and the kids were very caring as they knew Andrew was uncomfortable, but keen to let them experience the walk. They offered to carry some of Radar's pack to help with his knee, but he told them he would soldier on. The plan had been to walk to Windy Ridge and hope for enough space to lie down in the old hut, so they did not need to set up the tents. By the time they got to Narcissus, Andrew had walked as much as he wanted to that day. The boys decided they would set up the tents and the teachers and the girls could sleep in Narcissus Hut as it was rather small and not meant to be overnight accommodation. They managed to collect some wood and light the fire. The sun was setting as they finished their meals and hot drinks.

They were all asleep before anyone thought of lighting a candle. Andrew's knee throbbed for a couple of hours, but he fell off to sleep. There is no shortage of sleep hours in winter in Tasmania. Only two of the boys were awake before sunrise. They collected some wood and had the fire going when the rest started to stir.

The boys got water from the lake and added milk powder till it looked about right and heated a billy full of milk for breakfast. Teachers and kids rolled out of bed fully dressed in their dry clothes and beanies, woollen gloves, and unlaced shoes. "Make sure you only eat today's ration kids, or you will get awfully hungry on the last few days."

"Not a problem, Radar; we will probably have to leave you behind soon, so we will pinch your food."

Andrew laughed. 'These kids were all right. A bit cheeky to call me by that name directly, but I guess they are using it with respect, so it's OK'.

Thank God the walk to Windy Ridge was reasonably flat and the weather was great. It was only about five degrees but when you are carrying a sixty-pound pack you warm up quickly. Andrew liked to walk from the South for many reasons. It was the easiest access for a group from Hobart. It took many more hours to drive to the North of the state and then come in near Devonport to Cradle Mountain National Park. Not so bad going home, as everyone was exhausted and slept on the bus. The second reason was that the bag became lighter as the food was consumed and the walkers became fitter.

The northern end was much steeper and required a vicious climb, whether the walkers kept to the west of the lake and climbed Marions Lookout or went to the East over Hanson's Peak and up the Goat Track.

The third reason was that most people went the other way, so it was more interesting to meet different people each day. The walkers were from all over the world, although not many Tasmanians walked the Overland Track. It was a cultural experience to sit and talk to adventurers from around the world.

It only took about three hours to get to Windy Ridge and even Andrew's knee was no real problem. There was enough room for everybody to put their sleeping mats on the floor and lay out their sleeping bags before anybody else arrived. On occasions there were no other people in the huts, but on occasions they were full. There was no way to know how many would come through the door, so it was always wise to stake out a space with your sleeping bag and backpack.

"There was a little nook behind the fireplace where you can have a little modesty time for a light wash with a rag and get into the warm clothes from the bag. I don't care who you are, there is no excuse to look to that area unless it is your turn to get changed. Respect everybody's privacy and yours will be respected too. Just tell everybody that you are going to the modesty corner and when it is available for the next person."

"Listen up kids, there is good cover away from the hut. Best to do the toilet duties before getting changed into dry clothing.

Go out of sight from the hut but close enough not to get lost and remember to dig a small hole and cover it in before you leave. Then come back for a wash and get changed for the evening."

"Hey girls, are you happy you are all sleeping with me tonight?" one of the boys said.

"In your dreams, buddy, in your dreams."

"Yep, you will be."

"OK, you can stop that now." Pete decided the conversation had gone far enough. It was time to get the fire going and put the billy on for tea. There was enough bench space to set up the little metho burner stoves and get the meals going. One dixie was used to heat the freeze-dried main meal and the other to make up the Deb instant potato. It was made quite moist and then freeze-dried vegetables were added. It was hot and filling and after a gruelling day walking in the wilderness it was like a dinner in a restaurant.

Pete reckoned he had never seen any person get food poisoning in the mountains. "It was too cold for the bugs, and no one would want diarrhoea in that environment, so it just doesn't happen."

The knee was doing surprisingly well but Pete suggested that Andrew take a break at Du Cane Hut the next day. He wanted the students to see Cathedral Falls and he would do a little practical Geology while they were there. There were bench seats in a small enclosure in the old timber slab hut, but it was not meant to be anything other than emergency accommodation.

Andrew threw down his sleeping mat on the bench and put his head on the backpack. That is how the students found him when they got back. Sound asleep and snoring peacefully. In his earlier days he had explored Pine Valley and climbed the Acropolis and Mount Massif.

On this trip he was struggling to climb onto a bench seat, but he planned to get through to Waldheim to meet the bus. Last year was a bitter disappointment that they only managed half the walk because of the blizzard.

The students were keen to tell him what he had missed that day and he listened to every story, although he had been there with Pete on many occasions. He was impressed how Pete could teach Geology without the kids realising that they were learning anything.

It was time for a warm drink and a light amount of food and then a pleasant easy walk to Kia-Ora.

The weather can change rapidly on the Track. The blue sky turned blue-black in ten minutes. Andrew and Pete knew the signs: it was time for everybody to get the wet weather gear out of the backpacks and get the gloves on. Within half an hour the wind was howling, and the sleet was coming straight onto their faces. It was like ice needles around the eyes. Pete told everybody to get their sunglasses on to protect the eyes from the ice.

"We are going to head to Kia-Ora Hut. It will take less than an hour, but this weather is not going to improve. We get a hot drink and food when we get there but we are not stopping. If you are feeling tired, get up the front with Mr Carruthers. I want a couple of boys to stay at the back with me. Please keep an eye on each other.

We don't want to lose anybody today in this weather," Pete said to all and sundry. This was not a time for negotiation.

The wind blew a couple of the lighter students over but there were no injuries.
Inexperienced walkers struggled to get back up with heavy protective clothing and heavy backpacks. They thrashed around like turtles on their backs till someone helped them to stand. Vision was down to a few yards when Andrew said they were almost at the Kia-Ora Hut. The old slab hut was quite large, but others were there already. They had the fire going and were in deep conversation when the school party arrived.

It was not difficult to read their minds; they were hoping for more room and less noise than sharing the hut with a group of school kids.

The girls found an area to put their gear and started laughing about the struggle when they had been blown off their feet. It was like a circus act with clowns falling over, and others trying to help but falling as well. The boys were of minimal help, but Pete found a solid tree branch to help them get up without two much concern.

Andrew asked them to quieten down but there was not much change. The boys were loudly bragging of how well they had managed the conditions outside, and the girls were laughing about how silly they felt when they fell and could not get up.

"Good day for it," came from an older fellow with a very British accent. "Where have you come from?"

Andrew told him they were walking from South to North and they had walked from Windy Ridge that day.

"How far is that?"

Andrew told him that they had a few side excursions, but it was about three hours south.

"Well fellows, we should head down there before the day closes in. I'll be buggered if I want to spend the night with a pack of Gigglin' Gerties and smart-arsed lads. Who wants to walk to the next hut?"

A half a dozen put their backpacks on and headed out the door. One of the boys said, "Don't worry Captain Scott. Oates has just gone for a walk."

"Good to see you were paying attention in History class, Tim. But maybe a bit harsh. They will be lucky to get to Kia-Ora before dark."

The weather blew through, but everybody was asleep by nightfall. The slats did not really block the wind; just slowed it down. A few of the girls managed to get to sleep on the bench seats but the rest were on the ground. Most people ignored the sign on the wall and slept on their backpack but next morning Andrew told them "the next hut, Pelion, is notorious for rats. In that hut follow the rules and hang your bags on the hooks from the roof otherwise the rats will eat into them and get your food. You will need to roll up some dry clothes and put them in your sleeping bag cover to use as a pillow."

The wind was howling, and the temperature was below freezing the next morning. The walk across Pelion Gap was always tough but that day was excruciating.

The ground was boggy, which annoyed Andrew's knee, but the twisting caused by the wind made it pinch every few minutes.

Andrew and Pete had climbed Mount Ossa twice, but not this time. They pointed out to the students that Tasmania's highest peak was off to the left but there would be no point going there. The cloud cover was too low to see it and the track would be too dangerous to climb.

It was a four-hour slog in the conditions, but they arrived at Pelion Hut by early afternoon. The old hut was still standing, but they were early enough to get into the new hut with the pot belly stove and a lot of space. Everybody found a place to get changed. They had given up the full modesty thing and just did the best they could. Frankly, they were too bloody tired to think of much other than food and sleep.

Again, the weather cleared overnight and gave everybody the view of the magnificent face of Mount Oakleigh; its razor tooth silhouette unmistakeable. Andrew made sure they all knew that that view was the middle of the park. "We are now heading home kids.
We are not moving on tomorrow. We are staying here. Mr Smithies will take those who wish to go across the plain to Oakleigh and he will climb with you up the safe ascent. Those who wish to stay here and rest can look after me."
Eight of the boys and six of the girls were happy to climb Mt Oakleigh with Pete. He explained that the weather could change quickly so everyone had to carry the full backpack.

He could not guarantee that they would get back to the hut before nightfall, so they had to have their tent and all belongings.

Temporary pairings were organised, as were the matching tents. They were back in late afternoon, excited by the achievement of having climbed the mountain with exaggerated stories of slipping in the scree and near-death experiences. Andrew and Pete knew the next part of the track involved crossing Frog Flats. The Flats would be wet and boggy and demanding work. Best to let everybody have a relaxing day before tackling that. It was probably the longest day with a lot of climbing and descending and it would be uncomfortable in mud. Hopefully, it would not be raining, or it would prove to be a day of tears.

"Oh, Thank God for that." They woke to a dry and sunny morning. Still freezing cold but a great day for walking. The terrain was long and arduous because the track had to follow the contour lines of the ranges and valleys. It went down in the base of one of those valleys where everything turned to mush. At times ,the mud was knee deep and thick and sticky. Today it was over the boot tops but kept out by the gaiters. But each step felt like weightlifting in a gym. The boots were sucked down as the body tried to lift them up. It was strength sapping and a mind-numbing slog to the other side. Some of the boys looked grimly determined but others just said they had had enough. Most of the girls cried but Pete and Andrew just kept telling them the bog dried out and the ground became easy in a few hundred yards.

It did about an hour later and they all stopped for a hot drink, and a feed from the trail packs. "We have a bit of climbing to do then it flattens out to a doddle.

The good news is that there is a beautiful lake where we stop at Windemere tonight. If you are game, you can hop in and have a real wash. The girls can go first, and we will take the boys out of sight. When you are all out and dressed, we will bring the boys back for their turn. It is freezing cold, but water never felt so good as after you have crossed Frog Flats," Pete told them.

Lake Windemere is a beautiful sight at any time, but that day it was glistening in the sunshine. The girls were told to get their soap and hop in with their walking clothes, minus the boots.

"Give yourself a good scrubbing and clean your clothes as much as possible.
Take off as much as you want and then get back into it to run to the hut. Get yourself dry and dressed in your dry clothes. When the last one is finished, come and tell us and we will bring the boys back over."

There was lots of squealing and laughter but when the boys came back the girls were much cleaner and flushed pink from the freezing water.

"OK Girls we are going to shut the doors. Please start with lighting the fire and getting things ready for dinner."
"And if you look out the window you will be made to go back in the lake with the boys."

Most of the boys stripped to their underwear and got as clean as they could, but Jack de Nuit threw his singlet and underpants up on the edge of the lake and made a great show of lathering up and duck diving with his bare arse at the sky.

The opportunity was too great. One of his mates scooped up his underclothes and took off with them till Pete latched onto his ear and made him take them back.

The girls were shepherded away, and the boys got dry and changed before everybody came back to the hut for hot drinks and dinner.

Fortunately, they had the hut to themselves that night and did not need to put up the tents. The pot-belly stove was glowing a light orange and threw out enough light for everybody to sit around and have a talk for a while. Within an hour everybody was asleep. Andrew's mantra to make them too tired to think about anything else was working a treat.

Andrew had decided that when he got home ,he was going back to the Orthopaedics Department at the Royal to have a serious discussion about this knee; it was too disabling to allow him to have an acceptable life. He could not envisage a life where he was so disabled. There had to be something wrong that could be fixed, or something that would allow him to be more functional with whatever was wrong with the knee.
But there were still several days to go to finish the "Homage to the Mountain ."

If there was nothing that could be done with the knee this might be his last one with the students. Pete would do it but no one else in the school had shown the slightest interest and the trip required at least two supervisors.

Convincing the group in the morning to put on the very wet clothing from the lake the day before was a battle.

"Look we told you not to wear cotton because when it is wet it stays cold. You all have clothes that will quickly warm up when we start to walk. Trust us, we have done this before."

There was plenty of complaining about being wet and cold, but after ten minutes all the noise ceased. It was easy terrain with waterfalls and lakes just off the track. Andrew's knee was much better after a long soak in Lake Windermere. He was glad he already had three kids; he had serious doubts he would ever have any more after that prolonged cold spell in the water. He joined Pete and the students as they went to Lake Will and Innes Falls and was pleased how well the knee stood up to it. By the time they got to Cirque Hut it was early afternoon. It was going to be a long day and night if they stopped at that stage, but it made sense to have a good meal and maybe something easier and light in the evening.

In the mid-afternoon a couple came in that helped them decide. She was giggling about consummating the relationship on top of Barn Bluff, and Cradle Mountain and Marion's Lookout. It was obvious that Cirque Hut would be on their list that night.

Andrew had overheard enough to decide that they should move on to Waterfall Valley Hut. He told the students that the view of Barn Bluff from there was unique, and sometimes in the early morning it was breath-taking. He told Pete later that he was concerned that if they stayed at Cirque, it may have been breath-taking as well. And anyway, that would give them a better start to climbing Barn Bluff the next morning.

The Waterfall Valley Hut was down in the Valley next to a lovely running stream. The water tasted like nectar of the Gods. It was so pure and ice cold that it should have been sold by the glass.

The hut was small, so most had to put their tents up, but eight girls got to sleep inside. The pot belly stove was gorgeous and extremely warm. Several people hung their socks up to dry near the stove, so the place smelled like a bear cave, but the girls were not giving up their bunk spaces for a tent, no matter what the socks smelled like. And in the morning Andrew proved to be right about the view. Everywhere else in the park, Barn Bluff looks like a Turkish Fez, but from Waterfall Valley it looks like a broken diamond tip; the clouds intermittently obscuring it. One minute it was there in all its glory and then it was gone, then a few minutes later it was back. It was one of those times in life when the lucky ones who saw it knew they were blessed. It was a magic spot; the students agreed this was the best place on the Overland Track so far. Barn Bluff was standing like a sentinel in front of an azure blue sky when they left the valley and climbed back up to the Cirque.

Andrew was pleased with his knee. It had caused no trouble for more than a day so he decided he would lead up Barn Bluff. Three of the students were tired and asked if they could give it a miss, so Andrew suggested they stay at the bottom of the climb and protect the backpacks so everyone could climb without them. He made sure everybody had their water-bottle, which he insisted they all filled at Waterfall Valley. It was about a five-hour return trip, so time was tight. They climbed up, had a look across the beautiful valleys and came down to retrieve their packs and get to Kitchen Hut. Melissa rolled her ankle on the snow-covered rocks near Kitchen Hut. It did not seem broken, but it was very swollen; Andrew took the bandage off his knee and wrapped her ankle in the same figure of eight pattern. He handed her his stick and told her it was her turn to be the school cripple. They pitched their tents around Kitchen hut and used it to have dinner and a hot drink. They decided that Melissa and her tent mate could sleep in Kitchen Hut, so they did not have to put up the tent with her damaged ankle.

The next morning, everybody except Melissa and Andrew set off to climb Cradle Mountain. Andrew had done it several times, but he still regretted not being able to do it with the group. Melissa was heart-broken. This was the one thing on the whole trip she really wanted to do; she had teased her brother who had "chickened out" in 1964 when everybody else did it. He got halfway up and could not go on; the fear of heights just bit him hard, and he had to sit and wait to be helped off the mountain when the school party came back.

There was no point thinking his family did not need to know. As soon as the family picked him up from the bus, they were told he was a piker. "When we got two feet up the side of the mountain his legs went to jelly, and he just sat down and shook till we came back for him."

Now he would tell everybody she faked an ankle sprain to avoid climbing the mountain.

The snow was light from the base of the mountain to Marion's Lookout. The walk was easy, but the descent was scary. Walkers had to face the wall to have something to hold onto, so it was necessary to look down between the feet for the next footholds. One slip and it was a long way down, and with a heavy backpack trying to topple the climber backwards, it was frightening.

Everybody managed to get down without further concerns. Melissa's ankle was sore, but she was holding up well and Andrew's knee was swollen but otherwise Ok. It would bend half-way, so he had to ensure that his good leg did the holding as he stepped down, but he was getting used to being a "bloody cripple' so he was coping.

They walked to Waldheim Chalet and decided to set up camp. They were ahead of schedule by one day because of not staying at Cirque so they planned to do some short walks the next day along the marked tracks around Waldheim. The bus arrived at 3.00 pm to take them into Devonport. Everybody had clean clothes in the bus, and a hotel booking in Devonport. A hot shower, a proper meal and a real bed was a fantastic way to finish ten days of exhilarating torture.

3: The Consultation.

Mr Harris-Smith, the senior Orthopaedic Surgeon at The Royal was furious.

"I thought I told you to go easy on that knee. What the bloody hell have you been doing? Your knee is black and blue and swollen to hell and back. You are struggling to walk, and you are as pale as a ghost."

Andrew had decided it was time to give up the pretence. He told the surgeon about the school trip and the initial fall.

"Look, I am sure it would have been all right if I had not taken that fall. I really thought I had broken my leg and ruined three months of preparation for the walking party." He explained about spending time in the icy water of Lake St Clair, the bandage as applied by his colleague and the walking pole. He outlined the ten-day struggle to get to the end, but the joy in finishing the trip.

" I suspect young man that you have completely stuffed your knee. It was not good four months ago when we spoke, but it was perfect compared to now. If we decide to do anything with this knee, you will be given instructions to follow. If you fail to follow even the most trivial thing I tell you, then you will be on your own.

I don't like wasting my time with bloody fools who ignore my advice."

The X-Rays confirmed there were no bones broken but Harris Smith told Andrew that it felt like the cartilages were catching and the knee was quite unstable. There was surgery available, but removing the cartilages was a horrendous operation that put the patient on crutches for six weeks and usually meant the end to most physical activities.

"Certainly, no sport, and no bloody tramping around in the bush for weeks on end."

The instability was a major concern.

"There is a growing belief in orthopaedics that you have ruptured some support structures in the knee but there is bugger-all knowledge about how to fix it. You heard of Polly Farmer? A colleague of mine in Melbourne is looking after his trick knee. They have made a brace that is keeping him on the footy field at Geelong. We expect he will have a useless knee in a couple of years but that does not matter much. He is a blackfella so once the footy is finished he won't do anything much anyway. Probably go bush with his tribe and not be heard of again.

My colleague is keen to try it on a few normal fellows and see if it helps with normal daily activities. I will send you to the Physios with a note. If the brace is of interest to you, they will take some measurements and get started. The Melbourne team developing the brace are keen to do some testing, so if you wish we will get the brace for free.

You will have to see the Physios every week for six months and they will monitor your progress and report back to Melbourne.

If the Polly Farmer brace is not of interest to you, I have nothing else to offer. The joint will be completely stuffed by Christmas, and you certainly will not cope with being a Phys. Ed. teacher for much more than another year.

Your call. Do you want to try the brace and the rehabilitation?"

Andrew knew that of two choices, only one gave him any hope. He opted for the brace.

"OK. Go home and get off your bloody leg. The staff at the front desk will notify you when the Physios can measure you for the brace. Make sure you attend the fitting and all the rehab, or you will be on your own. I get annoyed with timewasters. We don't bother with second opportunities.'"

'He might be a good surgeon' Andrew thought. 'That statement was uncalled for. Polly Farmer is a very good football player and a genuinely nice fellow. He has already shown that he is more than capable of accepting his celebrity status without doing anything stupid. He is a mentor for young Aboriginal players in Melbourne and will have a future at Geelong for as long as he wants it'

Andrew knew he was going home to another browbeating. Julie was fed up with his knee injuries. They had met in 1960 when Andrew returned to Tasmania. He was tall and athletic 'and gorgeous to boot' according to Julie.

He was studying to be a Phys. Ed. Teacher, and she was studying Music in Hobart. She planned to be a music teacher until she could build a career as a folk singer; Andrew could support her once he had his teacher's ticket. She knew Andrew had played footy at South Melbourne and was showing promise of making the seniors when he decided to come home to study. As a kid he had always supported North Hobart, so he went along to training and was immediately given a contract: new boots, jumper, and shorts and ten pounds a week to play.

He quickly became a key player at Centre Half Forward and helped win a premiership in his first year, and then repeated the win the following year. In the third match in 1963 he landed awkwardly from a high mark and felt his knee give way. There was strong pain and a lot of swelling, but the X-Rays were clear, and there was not much bruising. "You've sprained your knee Sonny" was the word from the Head Trainer. "Go home, wrap it in Lectric Soda and sit out a week. We will see you back here in a fortnight for training." Six weeks later he was still struggling to walk, and the surgeon told him his season was over. The team never made the finals, so he returned in 1964 but lasted only two games. The knee buckled again, and he was back on crutches. The surgeon told him to retire.

"You are thirty-two years old and in good health, but your knee will be an issue in a few years. You need to look after it now. Do something else."
Reluctantly he retired.

Four years too late, according to Julie. He reminded her they had a nice house and a good car because he played football.

"And you have got a buggered knee because you played football. And your kids haven't had enough time with you because you play football, and…".

"OK, I get your point, leave it alone."

Now he was going home to tell her the surgeon had told him he would have to wear a brace all the time and the knee was going to become a major concern very quickly.

The future might hold some hope, but the crystal ball was foggy; and as far as anyone could guess he was on a downhill slide to a severely arthritic knee before he was forty. He also had weekly sessions of Physio for the next six months. Please God, not on the night the girls had music lessons, or his son went to cricket training.

'Could have been worse. Had I been born four years earlier I would have been off to the war and probably dead or severely wounded. Julie would not have liked either of those options' he thought with a smile.

He got halfway through telling Julie what the surgeon had said when she burst out crying, dropped the plate she was wiping and told him she was going to see her parents. "I may or may not come back."

Julie was gone for a few hours, but his nerves were rattled when she returned.

He told her he was going to make his leg strong so he could get out of the brace as soon as practical, and he was not taking any further risks. His family and career were too important to jeopardise.

The phone call to measure the brace came four weeks later. He had one choice; do you want a pull-on stretch panel or one with centre lacing. He decided that the second option made it more likely that he could make it fit as he built up his thigh muscles, so he opted for that. It turned up a few weeks later. There were leather straps top and bottom, with leather covered hinged steel bars on the side and lacing through leather strips up the front. The Physio bent the steel side bars to the shape of Andrew's leg, and they started the exercises with weights, pulleys, and bikes. The brace was tweaked a little but once it was set, Andrew felt for the first time in years that he could exercise hard without fear. It was a nice feeling. He attended the Physiotherapy Department every week for a while and then opted for a private clinic that provided better equipment and hours that suited his schedule. He bought a bike for home and some leg weights. And he studied Physics and Chemistry in every spare moment. He made two commitments to his family; his interest in football was over and he would give that time to his kids. Every Saturday afternoon was for the family unless he had work commitments that he could not avoid.

The leg became stronger and felt much more stable. The swelling was gone, and the withered appearance of the thigh gradually returned to normal, with well-defined thigh muscles and hamstrings.

Andrew could sleep comfortably without the brace and knew that he could get away with a lot of activities without it, but he was not prepared to. His leg bulked up so that the laces were on full stretch when he went back for a review from the surgeon. A bigger brace was ordered, and he was encouraged to continue to strengthen the leg.

"The good news, Andrew, is that research has found the culprit. You have broken one of the cruciate ligaments. The surgical research body at Stoke-Mandeville in Britain are convinced that it can be repaired eventually. In ten years or so you may be able to get the function back if you look after it properly in that time," Professor Harris-Smith told him.

"However, it is essential you do no further damage. If your knee is full of arthritis, or the cartilages are shredded, then no amount of surgery will repair the joint."

Andrew planned to transition from Phys Ed to teaching Science in 1968, providing he could get the degree by then. In the meantime, he had a family to support, so he planned to stay at Hobart Matric. College as a Phys. Ed. teacher for one more year and hopefully find another teacher to lead the Overland Track excursion for future years.

If the "Homage to the Mountain" project was to continue it would probably require his participation for at least one more walk. He knew that with his brace and his structurally stronger and more stable knee that would not be the same issue as the last time.

He just had to convince Julie to let him do it again.

"If you have to do it, why don't you take the kids in the first term when the conditions are much better, and you are less likely to have problems with the students and less likely to fall and hurt yourself again?" Julie asked.

"Honestly, we are trying to give these students a challenge that will be one of the strongest memories of their school years. The summer is too easy, and the kids are more likely to misbehave because they will be comfortable and not particularly tired. I want them to experience the biting cold, the powerful winds and the fear of the Mountain when it is angry. They need to learn the power of nature and the need to prepare for the worst; to overcome fear and to beat the elements. They can only do that in winter."

"Andrew for God's sake, think. A teacher and a student died up there doing exactly what you do with the kids. Why do you want to do that?"

Andrew looked away into the distance and then said quietly, "Because people die up there."

"What the bloody hell did you just say? You do it because people die; for Christ's sake. Andrew, you are one really sick bastard. I stay home with three young kids while you go off playing glory boys and now you tell me it's because you might die in the bloody mountains.

This time I am leaving, and I am taking the kids. You want to kill yourself, go ahead, but I am not waiting here to get a message that your dream has come true, and you have died in the Highlands."

"Julie, listen to me; that is not what I said. Why do people do the Sydney-Hobart Yacht Race?

There are quicker, warmer, and safer ways of getting to Tasmania from Sydney? Why do people race motorbikes, why do people climb mountains? It is because these events are inherently dangerous, but if you are careful and plan for all scenarios then you return unscathed. That is the challenge, that is the raison d'etre. I don't plan on dying up there, I am teaching the students if you plan properly, if you mitigate the risks, if you follow the rules and respect nature you come out stronger and better. It prepares these softies for life, Julie."

"You won't win me over with throwing rubbish at me. You do it because it fits your macho risk-taking attitudes that destroyed your knee and is destroying us."

"Bugger it Julie, people do these things because they are dangerous. If yachting was as safe as having a bath, then no-one would go yachting. I want these kids to understand that if you do your preparation, if you follow all logical precautions, you mitigate the risk. You win."

"And if you don't, or one of your students doesn't follow the rules, what then? You die and maybe half the kids as well.

Do you think that Scott and Kilvert did not plan to go home after their walk? Well, they went home, in bloody coffins Andrew. We have three children, and I don't want to raise them alone.

"Julie I will only be doing this one more time. Pete Smithies is going with me, and the school has demanded the girls have a female teacher go as well. New rules to please the bureaucrats.

Well, Sonia Johnstone has volunteered to go. She is an experienced bushwalker; she has walked to Base Camp in the Himalayas and she has tramped over much of the British and Scottish Highlands. She takes no crap from the girls at school. She will probably be the team leader after this year."

"Oh, I see. You are going bush with a young woman for ten days. That should make me feel really comfortable."

"Oh, for Christ's sake, woman. Is that how much you trust me? I have never given you one reason to think I would be chasing any other woman in any circumstances. I have not and I would not. That comment is just stupid. I have worked with her for five years. The Mountain is too harsh to think of anything but survival. I am certainly not planning an affair but if you are so bloody worried, get yourself fit and come with us."

"I just might do that if I can figure out how to get the kids looked after."

'Well, she was welcome to join the walk if she wanted to do it. She would learn it was no doddle in the park. She would have the same rules as the teachers and the students. She would have to prove her fitness and be prepared to be one of the leader group. She would carry her own pack and be self-sufficient in the same way as everybody else. There would be no privileges and no exceptions to the rules.'

He loved the frisson caused by having a mixed party of girls and boys. There was always sexual tension, both sexes wanting to prove their strengths and he knew that he needed to be vigilant. There was always the possibility that two students could end up in bed together, no matter how smelly and tired they were.

He loved the drama of seeing these soft, pampered kids gradually become hardened as they fought the elements. And he relished their triumph when they finished the walk and proved they could measure up to a hostile environment and beat the bastard. He loved giving that feeling to young people just before they had to be adults.

Andrew knew he would miss the Homage when he gave it away. It had given him solace since the end of his days of football and. it wasn't an accident that "The Homage to the Mountain" was in September every year. It enabled him to get away from the radio when the Grand Final was on. There is no radio reception up there and he banned any student taking any radio just in case. He just did not want to know if North Hobart was winning, or his old team in the VFL was doing well. His days as a Swan still were filled with guilt and loss. He had used their scholarship and then packed up and returned home without repaying them much at all. In his darkest moments he felt like a thief and a fraud.

4: Rehab.

"How long have I been here?"

"Three weeks according to the notes, but I have been supervising you for ten days. I am here on rotation from the Royal."

"Where the hell am I? The last thing they told me was that I was going to Tasmania."

"You are in Tasmania. You are at the Repatriation Hospital in Hobart. We move all veterans to here when they are stable. You came in from Vietnam seriously unwell but not requiring any further emergency surgery. If your specialist decides that surgery is required, it can be done here, or you might be taken to the Royal. It will be the choice of the surgeon where he does it. It usually depends on theatre rosters.

The Repat had a great surgeon in Douglas Parker, but he hung up his stethoscope last year. He used to be here most of the time. But it does not matter which hospital the surgery is done in; we share the surgeons as needed." The young doctor was still in training and working under supervision.

He was vitally interested in Marcus because his birth date had been called out in his ballot, but his call-up was deferred till the end of his studies. That was in a little over two years. He had jokingly told his mates that he had to study hard so he could fake an illness to get tossed out of the Army. He had heard that if he told them he was a homosexual he would be instantly dismissed but one of his mates told him if you made that claim they arranged for you to be interviewed by one of their civilian workforce, who was bent. He was apparently very good at getting nashos to drop that pretence.

"The head Urologist says that he needs to perform one more operation. The bullet ripped a gaping hole in your bladder, and it had a temporary repair because of the incredible number of internal wounds you suffered. He now wants to do the final repair. Providing you get no further complications we hope to allow you home in the next few weeks. You will need to come back every month or so for us to keep you under observation, but we now expect a full recovery. Believe me Marcus, that is not what any of the medical staff thought when you arrived here. We thought we would be lucky to keep you alive.

The Army records have indicated that you were shot with a round of ammunition that was made in about 1948. They are assuming the gun was a leftover from the war with the French and that the gun was about the same age. It had a fair bit of rust on it so they think it was restricted in power. Probably why you are still with us, mate."

Marcus was still in a lot of pain, but he had been trained to live with that. But he was struggling with nightmares. He had killed a lot of people; to him that was his job and he accepted that was the conditions of employment. But he struggled with the images of dead children. When he closed his eyes, he saw the little head in the tunnel explode as his bullet slammed into the space between the eyes. And the image burned into his brain.

He was certain it was a child of about ten. 'The Gooks are small' he kept telling himself, but he knew that he killed a child. He knew the child had shot him and would give him a second bullet if possible, but it troubled him. Wars that made little children become soldiers were immoral. He remembered, rolling a hand grenade into a small house, and seeing only dead children in the ruins. He silently entered a Viet Cong threshold in a village outside Nui Dat and cut the throats of every person he saw. He knew how to do that, so they never made a sound. Another three children went to whatever God they prayed to. It was easy to justify on the basis that he would not get away if children were left alive. But his nightmares did not listen to the excuses; they just kept putting the faces filled with terror in front of him.

And the faces went on and on. The Doctors had given him Serepax to help him sleep, but that only added confusion to his already fragile state. The doctors asked him to give it time, it was only a new drug, and he needed some adjustment time. After two weeks he refused to take it; he was just feeling worse, and the nightmares had elements of paranoia.

He decided to try to tough it out and hopefully get through it with time. Marcus woke as a nurse gently rubbed his forehead with a damp towel. Mary said, "How do you feel, Marcus? You were trembling and sweating a bit." He told her he was just having a bad dream, but he would get over it. Mary told him that his severe nightmares were mentioned in the hospital notes.

"Anything you want to talk about? I have been with you from the beginning, so I've got at least a start."

"Mary, my nightmares are from before I met you. And I am not sure that it would help me ,or you, if I told you. I am damn certain I wouldn't see much of you again if I told you too much detail."

Mary said she knew he had seen and done things that were not part of normal life. He told her that he was confused. He went to Vietnam because it was necessary to protect Australia, but he did not see anything that was related to Australia. He was now severely injured and probably did not have much of a future. He questioned everything to do with his time in Vietnam.

"So tell me Mary, who is winning? I don't think it is us. How the hell would we know. The Army tells us lies and the government does not tell us anything. They certainly have not told people here anything of worth about the war. They think it is a little skirmish.

How are we supposed to fight an enemy we don't see, and we don't know? They are not in uniform; they are absolutely no different in appearance to any other people in Vietnam.

How can you kill a woman before she kills you? She rides down the street on a pushbike and leans it on a fence while she gets dumplings. It blows up and she vanishes. Three of your mates die. Should you just shoot every woman on a bicycle?

We were on patrol and a young woman with a baby covered in blood screams out for help. The first two that ran to her aid trod on jumping jacks and were ripped to pieces. She just turned and walked away.

Two weeks later we were patrolling close to the same area and a woman with a baby was calling out to us. Not falling for that again. A carefully aimed bullet killed her and the baby in one shot. We called in the sappers to clear the land mines. There weren't any.

A young Yank just rolls a hand grenade into his officer's tent. They both die. He was high on something he got in Saigon, but there was no known problem between the two of them He just snapped under the pressure.

So tell me Mary, are we winning? Because I don't think so."

Mary tried to divert the conversation by asking what he planned to do when he got out of hospital; he said that he was going to try to forget all this shit, but I doubt whether that will be possible for a long time.

She checked his drug sheets and sorted out his pain medication for him, staying with him till he drifted off to sleep.

She was struggling with this; maybe she should go back to the Royal.

Dealing with Marcus was becoming extremely difficult as she knew she was making his care a bit too personal. She had been there when everybody was sure he would die and now she was seeing him struggle mentally during his recovery.

Marcus awoke feeling better. He had slept relatively peacefully and as far as he knew he had not had any nightmares. After breakfast he was off to Physio to be tortured for two hours. They were good at their work. They stood him up and made him walk. He lifted weights and rode stationary bicycles. He did leg exercises till he was blue in the face. And he listened. There were four of them, all under thirty and they spend the full two hours complaining. He heard them saying, "We do not get paid enough for the level of study; We have to start at 8.30 in the morning so we are constantly in peak traffic. It takes 10 minutes from downtown to the Repat at that time. If we started a half an hour later, it would be less than five minutes. The food in the cafeteria is awful, the uniform is uncomfortable, there are not enough parking spaces on the hospital grounds". It went on constantly for two hours.

Marcus felt like screaming at them and telling them they were pampered princesses. Go to Vietnam, get a bullet in the guts, be too crook to eat anything, let alone what was in the cafeteria and then have a job that pays you next to nothing. You poor little selfish bastards.

But he didn't.

Sometime in their pampered lives they would realise they were living a fantastic life; in the meantime, let the little pricks whinge all they liked; one day they would get their comeuppance.

The Anglesea Army Barracks were next door to the Hospital, senior staff would wander through occasionally and talk to the injured soldiers. Of course, most of the beds were filled by Old Diggers from the Second World War or Korea. Many of the beds were now occupied by older females, since the Government decided war benefits would extend to widows. Funny that, they would not give them a dollar while they were supporting their severely injured husbands but as soon as the men died the same women were worth a pension.

An officer spoke to Marcus and said they had noticed he had enlisted in Victoria so why was he in Hobart. He just said that he was born there, but went to school in Tasmania, went back to see what Melbourne was like before he was called up but his only relative was a Tasmanian. "Okay then young man. Well, get strong so we can get you out of here. You'd be better out in the real world as soon as you can cope."

He knew if he could get well enough to get out of hospital, he would be better at facing his demons but that seemed a long way off. Marcus had to think for the first time about what he wanted to do once he was released. The only home he had was not really home.

After his mother was locked away in the Kew Lunatic Asylum he was sent to Aunt Doris. She was a very wealthy woman with a beautiful Merino Stud property at Cressy.

Doris was lovely and kind but had no idea about raising children, and even less knowledge of caring for a boy mourning the loss of his complete family. She would be even less likely to cope with a severely injured young man with his guts blown out who woke up every night screaming his lungs out.

He gave a half a thought to asking Mary if she was married. Maybe he could rent a room from her and pay her a bit of his repat pay to look after him till he was well enough. When Mary came in the next time, he asked her what Mr Robertson does for a living?"

She told him that her father was a motor mechanic. He was the only Mr Robertson she knew. Well, Marcus had his answer, she was single and not at all concerned to tell him.

"If they get my gut working half-well when they release me, would you let me buy you dinner as a thank you for your care.?" Mary laughed and said that as his nurse that would not be viewed as professionally appropriate. "Well, when I am discharged you won't be my nurse, so that would not matter." She blushed a little and told him that would have to wait. He had to get well, start sleeping without nightmares and get back to being physically strong.

She was about the same age as him and at least she understood something about Vietnam. She was small and slim with the most piercing blue eyes and dark wavy hair to the shoulders. She spoke very quietly, but that was probably because she worked around people who were critically ill. He noticed though that she listened carefully. He never heard her ask anybody to repeat anything, she was attentive to a fault. "Well, she never said 'No' so there was a chance."

He drifted off to sleep and woke up as dinner arrived. The young woman plonked it in front of him on his bedtable." Best of luck with that", she said. It looked all right to him, but she told him she would rather starve than eat that crap. 'No, you bloody well would not. Try living on Army rations for two weeks where you eat everything cold, dry, or raw. If you try to cook it, the Viet Cong have got you by the short and curlies before you get the meal anywhere near your mouth. It would be wonderful to see all you ungrateful pricks just have a few days of misery to make you appreciate your pampered existences' Marcus thought. She saw a wry smile on his face and asked him what was tickling his fancy. "Starting to have naughty thoughts are you soldier boy. You must be getting better by the day."
'If only you knew, you overweight lump of lard.'
        The Physios had told him to get up and go for a short walk whenever he wanted to. He ate as much of the dinner as he needed, then slipped on his dressing gown and wobbled his way to the door.

He braced with both arms on the door frame and took a few breaths and then headed out to the passage. He had been doing that for five days and he could see the improvement. He could walk around the ward and have a look out the windows. He could see the people coming and going up Davey Street. In the distance he could see the top of the buildings in Hobart. For the first time he thought that if he were well enough it would be great to go to a pub and have a beer.

He had just finished his lunch when one of the wardsmen called to collect his crockery and cutlery. He asked Marcus how he was going. He said he was satisfied with his progress but was looking forward to when he could walk downtown and have a beer.

"Mate, don't bust you boiler over that. They only have that Cascade stuff here. It is horrible. I just love to get a beer in Melbourne or Sydney but here I resort to bottles.
Not as good as over the bar, but better than that cat's piss." Marcus bit down on his bottom lip to prevent him saying what he was thinking. 'If you had spent the afternoon picking up body parts to send back to Australia, you would drink Cascade and love it. Christ, is everybody in Australia convinced that their life is horrible? Why doesn't Harold Fuckin' Holt shuffle all these ungrateful bastards off to Saigon to get shot at. They would shut up and eat the food, and drink the beer, and gain some common sense.'

The nightmares were easing, and Marcus looked forward to seeing Nurse Mary Robertson when she was on duty, and she made a point of visiting him every day. His moodiness lifted and he seemed much more settled. The repair of his bladder had healed, and had returned to normal function. The nurses had given up measuring his urine volumes, it had been perfect for weeks. The pathology tests were clear, so they were no longer necessary. The Physios told him he was ready for civvy street, and the doctors told him to prepare to go home. He asked Mary to walk him to the door. She took his small bag of belongings on a trolley to the front door where he expected Aunt Doris to be waiting. As they passed through the door he said, "Mary, you are no longer my nurse, so, would you go to dinner with me?"

"Well Mr Pigeon, I would be honoured."

"I am not going back to Cressy at this stage. I might have to if I can't cope, but I thought I would stay in Hobart for a few days. I have found a boarding house in Argyle Street, so I thought I would try for two weeks and if it proves too difficult, I will go back to Cressy then, unless I get a better offer."

"She thought that might have been a veiled hint, but she let it pass. When do you want to try this dinner date, Miss Robertson, and where is your favourite place?" Mary told him that there was a good hotel in North Hobart that had a great counter meal. Mary told him that one of the doctors has said that the roast beef was sensational. She was free that evening and the pub was close to where she lived.

"Just get a cab and get them to take you to the Empire Hotel. They will know where that is."

He went into the bank to get some money and was shocked when the teller filled in his passbook. He had not touched if for more than a year. There was more money in his account than he had ever seen in his life. Then he remembered it was dollars, and they were only worth ten bob each, but hey, it was still a lot of money. 'My God, I have got enough money to buy a new car.' He had read about the new HR Holden with the X2 racing motor while he was in hospital. 'Now that would impress young Mary Robertson.' He imagined turning up to the pub in that. That wasn't going to happen because he did not have a driver's licence, he was not well enough even if he did have the licence, and there was a three month wait for that model with the big racing motor. He decided to have a look at the car in the next fortnight and see what it was like in reality, but it sure looked impressive in the magazine.

He had the taxi take him to the Empire Hotel for his dinner date with Mary and arrived just on six o'clock. Mary was waiting in the Ladies Lounge. She gave him a light kiss on the cheek and told him that this was the start of a whole new chapter in his life. He could start planning his future now and as his health returned there would find some great opportunities. The dinner was wonderful; he could not remember when beef tasted so good, certainly not in the hospital and even more certainly, not in Vietnam. And Cascade beer was wonderful.

He only had the one as his bladder surgery was recent and he did not want to put any pressure on the system. That idiot wardsman had obviously never drunk Vietnamese beer or he would not criticise Cascade.

Mary talked to him about her life as a nurse. She had started training when she was sixteen. She had lived at the Royal's Nurses Quarters and studied hard. She was a fully qualified Nurse after three years. She was only twenty when she started some work at the Repat and became a theatre nurse. When one of the surgeons received a posting to Vietnam, he asked Mary if she would go. "I need someone that I know I can work with. Trauma is hard enough without having to deal with staff you don't know."

She said that it was weird, but she arrived in Vietnam on her twenty-first birthday. Marcus realised Mary was about the same age as him; and had seen some terrible injuries in her time. She was small and beautiful but very tough.

Her father had a little garage in Launceston and her mother had died when she was five. She had no brothers and sisters, so like Marcus she had no real family other than her father. They kept in contact but were not really close.

The weird shifts made any social life difficult, and whenever she seemed to have a social occasion organised, she would get a phone call to return to the hospital as an emergency had occurred and she was needed in theatre. That was the first time he realised that she worked as a theatre nurse; he had only seen her on the wards.

She said, "Marcus, I was in the theatre in Vietnam when you were brought in. I have no idea how you survived; you were torn to shreds. But you are one tough fellow, and I am so glad you got through it."

The light was streaming in through the window when he awoke. He had slept peacefully for the first time in months. He did not even remember heading back to the room on Argyle Street until he realised that Mary was alongside him and it was not his room. She told him that he had become very tired ,so she had taken him home. He realised he had not been dreaming, that he really was in her bed. "Marcus, I am not sure how this happened, but we made love last night. I was concerned about hurting you, but you were fine. Your nurse reports that all parts are working fine, Mr Pigeon. Do you feel OK?" Marcus told her he thought he was dreaming, and it was not the first time that he had dreamed of making love to her. "I will have to try it again sometime when I am awake."

"That was my plan too," she said.

5: Albert and Doris.

Albert Beech-Jones inherited a fortune before he was twenty.

He grew up in Wales where his father owned a coal mine. Albert was a swashbuckling character with Hollywood good looks; he was of average height, with a lean athletic body, and neatly trimmed moustache. He always wore a black trilby hat, slightly cocked to the side. Albert was an intelligent, well-read young man with a desire to see the world while he was young enough to visit all the exotic locations he could imagine. He enjoyed a care-free life of wandering the world on one ocean liner after another and chasing all the pretty women that he could find. He had no particular wish to live his life in the bleak winters of Wales. His fortune had come on the backs of coalminers, but he was embarrassed to see the health damage mining did to the workforce, including all the young boys who worked in his mines. The industry was booming, and even small collieries made the owners very wealthy. His father had hit a rich seam of coal in the Cynon Valley and was able to find willing workers to haul the coal out of the ground.

His father left the colliery to him in his will and as an only child there was a fortune to be had.

He had no interest in running the business; he had paid lackeys to do that. His interest was in having a good time, and spending as much of the money as he could prise out of the business.

He was in Scandinavia when he received a telegram advising him that there had been an explosion in one of the mine shafts and more than fifty workers had been killed. Albert knew that the mine was not very safe; he had planned to get as much coal out as possible and then sell the mine to one of the big companies buying up the smaller ones. He had already turned down two offers. He now wished he had accepted the offer and walked away from Wales with the money and not the guilt.

When the offer did come the price was heavily discounted because of the deaths and loss of workforce, as many of the survivors moved on to mines that were safer. Many of those mines were expanding so they took the opportunity to entice the workforce away. Albert really did not care any longer. His heart had never been in coal mining; he just enjoyed the income so long as he did not have to look at the poor forlorn souls coming and going from the shaft every day. He had inherited a fortune and then earned another one in a ten-year period. The sale topped up his financial assets, which along with his home and investments made him one of the wealthiest young men in Wales.

He set about selling up his investments, his home and property and left for Australia. He arrived by boat in the Australian winter of 1912.

Albert knew that Europe was heading for war, and he did not want to be part of it. He decided that Australia was about as far as he could go before he started coming back, and Tasmania was as far as possible from Britain and Wales as he could go and still find people who spoke English.

The new country was keen for anybody from Britain to become Australian citizens, but he was quick to note that the talk was that Australia would join the war effort. He chose to remain a British citizen in Australia so that hopefully he could avoid military service in both countries. He quietly slipped into Tasmania and found a beautiful sheep stud for sale in Cressy. He immediately bought it, along with its stock of fine Merino sheep and rams. He kept the manager on because he had no knowledge of sheep. In fact, he had no knowledge of farming, but he loved the property. He decided to call it 'Cynon' and just like his coal mine he decided to leave the day-to-day work to his experienced staff.

He was forty years old when he arrived in Tasmania and settled at Cressy. It was idyllic, with a large farm producing some of the best Merino wool in the world and good, experienced staff who did all the work. It nestled on the Macquarie River with excellent water supply. The summer was beautiful and temperate, and the winter was quite pleasant when compared to Wales.

Albert was almost forty-five when he met Doris, who was working in the Greengrocer store in Cressy. Doris was working hard in the store as a distraction.

Her beloved Joe had died in France in 1915, 'fighting for God only knows what' and she had decided that she could not face another romance that would probably end in death on a battlefield somewhere. Every man she knew was either at the front or likely to go there soon. Doris had a long string of admirers who bought food they didn't need, just to have a conversation with her. She was slim and stunning in the fashions of 1916. Her hazel eyes and auburn hair seemed to make any outfit sparkle and she knew it. The clothing was somewhat austere due to the war, but she added a ribbon or a bow and transformed the ordinary to the beautiful. She managed to cover her grief with a pleasant smile and conversation that endeared her to the customers, who regularly told her boss that she was a treasure that he needed to protect, or some dashing young lad would sweep her off her feet and he would lose the business's greatest asset.

Then Albert turned up. He was a handsome fellow with a very worldly nature. He had travelled all over the world before buying one of the best properties in the District, and he had no intention of going to war. He was wealthy beyond any level she had ever imagined. Albert made it very clear he was interested in her; When she said that she was only twenty and far too young for a man of his stature in the community, he said, "young women entrance me.

I find them exciting, and playful, and more than ready to help me spend my money. As soon as that damned war is over, I will take you to Paris and marry you in the Notre Dame Cathedral."

Three months later she was officially the housekeeper to 'Cynon'. A love affair blossomed, and Doris became the subject of gossip through the farming District.

"Goodness me, he is old enough to be her father. She will live to regret it when he is old and doddery." That may have been true but in 1919 they did go to Paris, or what was left of it after the Great War, and they married in the Cathedral. The word was that the service cost a fortune, but he owned several fortunes and was not concerned to spend one to get his beautiful wife. He took her to all his favourite places in Europe, but most of them had been devastated. Eventually they decided to come home.

Doris used to tell her closest friends that Albert had learned a lot when he was young, especially about how to make her happy. She and Joe had had a fling, as she called it, but he was very inexperienced, and she thought this sex thing was not much to get excited about. But Albert was different. He seduced her with presents, and his time, and his voice and when they did go to bed together, he showed her a world she could not have imagined. He turned her into a passionate woman that adored him. She would blush when she thought of how they behaved privately, but all she wanted was more of the same.

He told her that he had never met anyone like her and that he had known enough women to recognise a treasure. "There will be no other women in my life" Albert told her, and he meant it. He doted on her and told everybody that he adored the ground she walked on. Doris was his Queen.

Albert loved his farm; he loved his sheep, and he loved his Doris. As the years went by and no children were born, they reconciled with the thought that they would be childless. She was only thirty-nine years old when Albert took a massive heart attack. It was obvious that another World War was about to start in Europe and Albert was worried that his idyllic world could all come crashing down. There were no signs, he just went out to check the sheep and did not return. He died in a paddock close to the house, loading bales of hay onto a trailer.

Doris was suddenly an independently wealthy woman, with a very productive farm and absolutely no idea of how to run it. She had been through enough grief after the death of Joe in the war; this time she decided she would make herself too busy to grieve. She studied her Merino flock and developed strategies to improve the quality of the fleece. She quickly became an expert in the husbandry of the Merino. She had enough money to travel overseas to visit the best animal research facilities and to share her knowledge. In 1938 she became the first female judge of the breed at the Royal Sydney Show and was a sensation because of her knowledge and her beauty. Of course, she was flooded with invitations from wealthy farmers with large sheep stud properties to visit them and help with improving the flock.

She was aware that most of the invitations were from single men, and she had no intention of another long-term relationship. Occasionally she accepted a dinner date and stayed overnight but she made it clear that there was no future to any affair.

Albert had satisfied every need she had in marriage, and she was sure no one else would get even close. Better not to bother.

Doris made 'Cynon' the best producer of fine Merino wool in the Southern Hemisphere. The great tailors of Saville Row in London kept Cynon cloth for the landed gentry of Europe. It was frightfully expensive; the cloth of choice in the House of Lords. The King used the cloth for his regular suits. Doris kept a little box in her study with the details of her most important clients. The tailors happily sent her the names, providing she kept giving them access to the wool. She would send it to them in bales and they would forward it to the finest woollen mills in Italy where it would be made into cloth that was exclusive to the tailor. Each tailor had subtle differences in their signature pin-stripe cloth.

Doris had received notification from the war office that her brother, Jonathon Pigeon had been killed in France and his wife was expecting another child. She kept making plans to visit her sister-in-law, Margaret, but never found the time. Occasionally she would send ten pound to help out, but she never received a thank you note so after a while she stopped sending money.

Her brother had gone to Melbourne as soon as he left school and was married before he was twenty. She had visited once but there was not much in common, and her sister-in-law seemed to be struggling. Doris offered to help with the education costs of the three children after Jonathon was killed, but was told not to bother.

"They go to a Government School, so it does not cost me anything; and anyway, I don't want to be beholden to you."
Doris left after telling Margaret that she would help with anything that was required, and to just let her know.

Doris was fifty-four when she received an official letter from Kew in Victoria, advising that Margaret had been placed in the asylum and there was virtually no likelihood she would ever be released. Her young son was currently being cared for at the Kew Orphanage as there were no surviving family members in Victoria. Margaret's Medical Records had listed Doris as next-of-kin. The letter was to advise that Marcus could be placed for adoption but as next-of-kin it was her decision.

Doris immediately arranged to go to Melbourne on the steamer to meet the little fellow and see what she thought was best for him. She found a shattered ten-year-old boy, who was grieving for his Mum. All he knew was she was sick, and he was not allowed to visit her.
Doris decided to take him to 'Cynon' as a trial, but with an understanding from the Orphanage that he was told he was going for a holiday.

If it proved to be acceptable, she planned to look after him but if there were problems she would take him back there for placement with adoptive parents. It was mid-winter and Cressy could be quite cold, but Marcus settled on the farm and loved helping with the animals. He went to Cressy Primary School in Grade 2. The teachers told Doris that Marcus was quite bright and was doing well at school.

He seemed happy enough on the farm so Doris sent an official letter to the Victorian Department to advise that she would remain as foster–mother to Marcus and that he would not be returning to the Orphanage.

When he finished Primary School, Marcus was doing well academically, but Doris felt he was under her feet and that she was not feeling comfortable as a mother. She decided she had the resources to put Marcus in the best boarding school she could find. She quickly ruled out the schools in Launceston; they were too close, and she did not want to be involved on a regular basis. She wanted a school that was full time boarding, with school holidays and Easter at home, but the rest of the year at school. She wanted an academic school and one that instilled personal discipline and self-reliance. She felt that Marcus had been subjected to enough trauma in his life. She wanted a school that would teach him to be comfortable with himself. Hopefully, that would allow Marcus to grow into a strong young man with a future. She chose the Friends School with its twin objectives of silent reflection combined with pacifism. Doris decided young Marcus needed that influence; his life has been too turbulent.

The Friends School was operated by the Quakers and as far as she could tell the Hobart College was unique in Australia. The school had a record of academic excellence with many of the past students being doctors, lawyers, and university lecturers. She loved the fact that it was co-educational from its founding a hundred years before. She knew that her early life was restricted by education that limited girls to house studies and not much else.

She thought that Marcus would become a much better man if he had contacts with girls from an early age.

Marcus again felt he was being abandoned but the school was good for him, and he quickly settled into the boarding environment. His first nickname was "Chook" but it did not stick. Then one of the boys called him Carrier for a while but that was a bit too clever. When one of the older boys made a noise like a pigeon near him, he got annoyed. He was branded Coo-Coo and he hated it, but it stuck. Eventually he did not care and often used the name himself.

He had never worn a school uniform before. In fact, he never had any new clothes. The blazer was weird, and the tie felt like he was being strangled. Beneath the pocket was a motto 'Nemo Sibi Nascitur'. He quickly learned that was Latin for 'no-one is born for self alone.' He wasn't sure of what that was about, but he agreed that he had spent too much time alone and he did not like it.

There was a rhythm to Boarding School that Marcus liked. Everything happened to a timetable.

He knew exactly what was happening today, tomorrow and the next day. There were jobs to do around the school, and there was regulated study time. For the first time in his short life, he had teachers who challenged him, and he relished the challenges. He was studying mathematics and science; he was reading Shakespeare and Joseph Conrad, and he was very competitive at tennis. He gradually became less reserved and started to make friends; an extremely useful thing to do at that school as the parents were very influential in the city of Hobart.

Aunt Doris offered to fund University studies if his grades were good enough, but he knew that was probably because Doris had a new man in her life. She said that no-one would replace Albert, but Tom Swinson was different to her usual suitors that she found easy to love and dump.

Tom came to Australia from Scotland to drive in the Formula 1 Grand Prix at Longford. It was about ten minutes' drive from Cressy to Longford, so she went along in 1954 to the first race for a giggle and to catch up with some friends. They were all wealthy landholders in the District, so they organised dinner trackside and settled in for an afternoon of drinks and gossip. Tom was invited for some after-race drinks ,and they quickly struck a friendship. She was a bit older than Tom but not enough to matter and he was a notorious flirt. There was a two-week break between races and Tom spent the two weeks at 'Cynon'. Cressy was alive with gossip, and with good reason; Tom and Doris were seen all over the town and it was obvious that it was not platonic.

Tom went to the next race in Monaco but was back at Cressy in less than a month. In the off-season Tom returned and announced that he would have one further year on the circuit and then retire. He said he was too bloody old for this racing game, and he was coming back to Doris permanently at the end of the next season.

Marcus was in senior school at Friends; but felt like he was in the way. He stayed at Cressy over the summer break but made himself scarce till he returned to school. Tom and Doris were like a pair of lovebirds.

Even from the other end of the house he could hear her squealing during the night, and during the day she talked about Tom continuously. When Tom was in the house Marcus had to look away. They spent most of their free time groping each other. Marcus was embarrassed; and decided one Christmas break of that was one too many. He had another year to complete his High School certificate and Doris suggested he should take a year away in Europe before settling into university. He extended it for an extra six months. Marcus was furious because he was just about ready to go to university when 'that bloody Harold Holt drafted me into the Army, and before I knew what was going on, I was on my way to Vietnam.'

6: Friends for Life.

"For God's sake Jane, what do you want me to do?"

" You work in an office full of hard driven young men You turn up here dressed in the most provocative clothing and make-up as if you are going to work at the BBC Production Company, and you are complaining that the fellows are noticing you."

"They are not 'noticing' me John, they are groping me. For weeks there has been an increasing number of staff that have been bumping into my breasts or finding reasons to touch me on the back. Twice I have my buttocks touched and on one occasion I was firmly smacked on the bottom. When I told him to cut it out, he told me it was a love tap; that I should take it as a complement."

"Jane. Listen to me. You wear those bloody stilettos that sit your arse up in the air for everyone to see, what do you expect? If you continue to wear the short skirts and crop tops, you can hardly complain that you are being noticed. That is what you are buying them for, isn't it?"

"No, it is not why I am wearing them. I am wearing them because they are the fashion ,and I don't want to look like a frump."

"Well, you keep telling yourself that if you wish, but it isn't true. You have been separated for a year, and you are feeling your oats. You are hanging it out for everyone to see and you complain like a fucking nag when people notice."

Jane threw the submission on his desk and walked out in tears. That was not true, she kept telling herself. She had no wish to ever have another relationship, the last one nearly killed her when she realised her husband had another woman. He wasn't even the slightest bit repentant; he just told her he was sick of her spending all her time at work and coming home too tired to want to go anywhere and too tired for him.

She exploded when he said that. "I am not too tired for you. I am sick and tired of your selfish attitude. I work sixty hours a week in a high-pressure job and you work forty in the public service where you do very bloody little. You finish work and go to the pub with your work-mates; and expect dinner when you get home. Then you think that after you watch soccer on TV, I should be ready for two minutes of sex before you go to sleep. I am not too tired for you; I am bloody sick and tired of you."

"Well fuck off then. I will see you later."

Four hours later he returned, smelling of alcohol and sex. He told her that he had decided that he would move out. He had a far better relationship with Jackie in the office anyway and at least she didn't work herself to death.

His passing comment as he went to the bedroom was that Jackie was good in bed and it lasted for hours. Sex wasn't boring with her. He told her she had become an old hag that he shagged to use up his sperm, so he didn't blow it all over the bedding. "Other than that, you are a waste of space."

He threw some clothing in a suitcase and grabbed the car keys. "I'll arrange to pick up anything else I need tomorrow. Speak to your fucking lawyer mates about the divorce. I will fight you for everything and I will win. You earn the money; I will play the victim and the judge will give most of the assets to me. I will even ask for the cat, just to annoy the shit out of you. Good riddance."

He jumped into the car she had bought, spun the tyres for a hundred yards and left.

Jane went back to her desk. She was a Litigation Lawyer at Smith, Clyde, and Farrow in the Temple District of London. She had been there for twelve years and had risen to the management circle of Commercial Litigation. She had an expert knowledge of copyright law and was equally as useful prosecuting Copyright Infringement as defending companies being sued for potential infringement. The Partners loved her work; she won a disproportionate amount of the cases she was involved in; she worked whatever hours that were required but because she was a female her remuneration was seventy five percent of the males who were not nearly as successful. The directors called her Jane, the money train.

She looked at the pile of work on her desk and thought that she had been insulted enough for the day. She phoned down to the front desk and said she would be out of the office till the next day. She had an appointment to go to and would not be available to take calls at home. She planned to be in early the next day so write a message list on her 'to-do' sheet and put it next to her pad and pen on her desk. "Anything urgent, give it to John in my Department. He seems to not have much on his desk today."

She picked up the phone and rang the Switchboard; she asked to be connected to the Bank of London, Central Business District Branch. The operator at the Bank asked her who she needed. She decided there had been enough people in the phone call already and she could not be bothered with dealing with a senior Secretary, whose job it was to block or divert calls to senior Managers.

"Put me through to James Pattinson please, in Corporate Finance. This is Jane Hampton, senior Litigation Lawyer for Smith Clyde, and Farrow."
That usually worked, like throwing a ferret down a rabbit burrow. The Secretary immediately put the call to James' desk.

"I hope this is a friendship call and not to tell me that we are being sued over something."

"James, I need a friend to talk to that won't turn into an arsehole. I checked my Rolodex and you are the only one I know.

Is there any chance we could catch up for lunch or just a talk. I need someone I can trust for a serious discussion.

James suggested they meet for a light lunch at the Red Lion in Trafalgar Square and Jane readily agreed. It was fairly close and very public. No-one would be accused on any improper behaviour in such a popular place.

Jane arrived a couple of minutes before him and ordered a Gin and Tonic. She had no intention of going back to work, so an afternoon drink was not a problem. "Just don't drink alcohol and return to work" was the first rule of socialising with clients at Smith Clyde and Farrow. She was looking at the empty glass when James arrived. He summed that up quickly. "Bad day, hey"

Jane got up to shake his hand and he said, "Jesus, woman, you look good enough to eat."

"James, I asked for a friend, not another sleazebag. I have had enough of that to last a lifetime."

He apologised, "Sorry Jane, you looked really unhappy, and I tried to lighten the moment. Looks like I misjudged that badly. Can we start again. Hi Jane, you look like you have been having a bad day. Can I help?"

Jane unloaded it all; the unwanted touching, the crass comments and the inappropriate rubbish from her immediate Manager.

"James, on top of that, I am the most successful Litigation Lawyer in the office, and they pay me twenty five percent less because I am a female."

James looked like he was about to comment when she said, "And don't bother about the skirt. I know it is short, and no, I am not looking for a new husband. I have been treated like dog shit for the last decade and I am sick of it. The Company can accept me as a vibrant young woman or they can send me packing, I really don't care."

"Look Jane, I am not looking for a fight, but I am unsure what you are telling me. Are you about to leave the Firm?"

"Maybe, maybe not. I thought I might take a six month sabbatical and go to Africa or Australia, or somewhere and then they can see if they can maintain the earnings I bring in."

James told her that he understood what she was thinking. He suggested she should talk directly to the Partners. Tell them her grievances about behaviour in the office and the unfair salary issue. He told her to tell them that she was taking a sabbatical for six months, while she decided if her future was with that company. He told her to be forthright and tell them if she returned, she would receive the same salary and conditions as the males on the same tier or she would seek employment with another company. "Just let it be obvious that was not negotiable." Jane and James had renewed a friendship from University days when they commenced Law at the same time. James moved to Economics and Jane stayed with Law. They were buddies, totally platonic and never a couple. "We are too good as friends for that shit," she said, and James agreed.

He told her to think it over carefully and not to do anything until she had calmed down completely. No decisions when angry, was good policy for the private life as well as the business one. She told him that she would let it percolate for a while and she would discuss it with him before she spoke to the Company.

"Who knows, maybe I will come with you when you decide. I spend all year handing out hundreds of millions of pounds to all kinds of charlatans and carpetbaggers to make the shareholders wealthy. I get a good salary, but the Directors get more than me for meeting once a month to ratify my decisions."

Jane felt more settled. At least she had vented, and he had listened. He gave her a smile as he said, "Keep your chin up lovely lady. And just let the boys know that the next unsolicited touch will be met with a karate chop to the gonads. I have it on good authority that you only have to do it once to stop repetitions."

James had to hurry away. He had a late afternoon appointment with a financier for a new Office Block in the square mile of the City of London. He needed two hundred and fifty million pounds to finance an impressive building to rival Manhattan in New York.

He had read the plan and had a close look at the prospectus and the pre-signed contracts for office space. It looked like the City of London would use a large part of it to house much of its public servants. *'Gold plated tenants'* according to the Book of James.

'Christ, she looked good. Bloody angry, mind you, but lovely. She has been a friend for so long, and a married one, so out of bounds. But that has changed, and I have been divorced almost forever. There are worse thoughts.' James mulled over the possibilities as he quickly went back to the office. 'I might have a look at what accrued leave I have got, maybe a few weeks in some far-flung Colony with Jane would do us both the world of good. Well, me at least,' James thought.

James had never regretted changing career paths from Law. The constant conflict was not to his liking, and he concluded that the belief that Lawyers were extremely bright was extremely wrong. They were glorified Clerks who could use an index, choose a precedent, and try to convince a Judge who was usually old and vague. They charged inordinate amounts of money whether they won or lost and were usually so frightened of previous clients that they kept their home address, and their after-hours interests a complete secret. In Corporate Banking, you received a bonus for a great loan book and a complete shellacking when loans went sour. Playing for two hundred- and fifty-million-pound prizes required just sound financial management and a bit of luck. It was nerve racking but very rewarding. There was no playbook, but the judgement was clear. A good decision resulted in a good return to the bank. James had not had a really bad one to know how bad the bank's reaction could be.

James lived out of the City at Henley-on-Thames and had a small townhouse to bed down through the week. The property at Henley was close to the river and its value had grown dramatically since he bought it. Some very well-known people had bought great houses nearby, it was a beautiful place to take female company to impress them. There had been many, but James saw no future with any of them. They were fun, but usually he concluded they were vacuous dolls; great for showing off till they joined a conversation and proved that they were not terribly bright. However, they were not invited to Henley-on -Thames for the conversational skills.

Maybe he could invite Jane to Henley for a weekend before she met the Partners. He could help her with some briefings and maybe some role play. He had interviewed hundreds of staff at the bank for annual reviews. Some were good and some were not. It was a fine balance between appearing appropriately affirmative and aggressive. Any senior staff member looking for a better financial package had to understand the process, have all the facts and just the right level of affirmative negotiating skills.

'Anyway, she is single, I am single, and there are some fabulous restaurants and pubs around home. Henley-on-Thames is gorgeous in the Spring, with flowers along the riverbank, and flowerpots hanging all around the town. It would be a great place for Jane to have a bit of R&R if she is considering her future.'

Jane spent the evening quite confused about her future at the Firm. She sometimes felt like meat at the London Markets, being pushed and poked and spoken about as if she couldn't hear. But it was a fabulous job that suited her perfectly. Did she really want to jeopardise that over some off-colour behaviour, or should she just let it ride? And even James could not meet her without making a sexist comment, even if he was just trying to calm her down when she looked upset. She decided that she would give it a fortnight before deciding. Sleep was difficult, she felt lonely, frustrated and a little afraid.

Jane arrived at the office twenty minutes ahead of schedule to see if there were any messages from yesterday that had to be prioritised. There were a couple of phone calls that could wait, but there was a note from John, her office manager. He was annoyed that she was not in the office; there was an important case to discuss and there was no obvious meeting away from the office that she needed to attend. He was fed up with her being a grump over a bit of office banter and he wanted to see her before lunch to sort it out.

'So maybe this won't require a fortnight', she thought. 'I will see him and listen to his issues and then tell him to arrange a meeting with the partners in a week's time.'

"Okay John, I have a half an hour before a client appointment. You wanted to talk so fire away."

"I was genuinely concerned yesterday that you left this office and threw your paperwork on my desk.

You obviously did not like my answer to your statements about your colleague's behaviour. Is that a fair assessment?"

"John, that is accurate, but you were a million miles from fair. I do not come to work to be sexually compromised; I don't come here for you to suggest I am husband hunting when I am not, and I do not come here to be the biggest income earner for the Firm in the Litigation Department, and yet be paid less than the half-wit males who would not understand a litigation case if they tripped over it. Accurate, John, yes. Fair, no."

"Well, I have spoken to one of the Partners about your attitude, and it was not received well."

"Fine, John. I will make a time to meet all the Partners and I will make sure you are invited to the meeting. I will place on record my requirements to stay here or I will move "my shapely arse" to a chair in one of your competitors Offices. You got that, John? Maybe you would like to tell your pet Partner, that unless I am provided with protection from sleazebags as well as fair remuneration ,they will see a reduction in billings for this Firm of several million pounds. Maybe you should get accounts to provide you with a record of the gross billings for each person in Corporate Litigation so you can brief the Partners in relation to my usefulness in this Company. So, anything else, John before I go. No? Good. I will let you know when the meeting is on.

By the way, my contract is for forty hours per week. I am guessing I have at least six months accrued leave for unpaid overtime.

I am planning on taking it soon. I will have the details of that in writing for the meeting. You might need to advise the Partners of that as well; Oh, and find someone to do my job till about May next year, I am likely to be overseas. Have a great day, John."

She stormed out and went back to her office for long enough to organise her desk and make sure her Secretary knew she was away for the afternoon.

She placed a call to the Executive Office to advise that she required 20 minutes at the next Partners Meeting for an urgent matter. "You will be made aware of the content of the discussion in time for distribution to those attending."

She arranged a telegram to James to be delivered to him in a sealed envelope. "I am going back to the Red Lion. If you want to catch up, I plan to be there all day. I should be drunk by midday. Best wishes, Jane."

Jane had settled into a corner and was quietly drinking a pleasant cold chardonnay and eating some very greasy fish and chips when James came in.

"Jesus, woman, you know how to get my attention. What the bloody hell happened?" She gave him a detailed account of what had happened from the time she arrived at work till she left two hours ago.

"So when are you meeting the Partners?"

"They meet fortnightly, so it should be in the next few days. I will get my planning done and deal with it as it occurs. I am sick of the crap James, so this will be a serious crossroad.

Things will change or I will be gone."

James invited her to Henley-on-Thames for the weekend. "The Crooked Billet is a lovely old-world pub next to Friar Park where we could eat, and we would have time to get your plans sorted. If you need some role-playing I am sure I could be half convincing as a Partner with attitude."

Jane was surprised with the invitation, and it must have shown, but James told her they had been friends forever and now she needed someone she could trust implicitly. He wanted to make sure she was ready for the Partners Meeting as it would probably get rough. Having a dress rehearsal was a good idea, and she needed someone who was used to the cut and thrust of no-holds-barred meetings. He assured her they would have a great meal and wine after their make-believe Partners Meeting, but he was going to try to make her cry and he intended to make her hate him with a passion.

7: Two Smart Women.

"I still hate dissection."

"I can handle most of this course with ease, but. Surely there must be a better way to learn human anatomy than cutting up an old fat man," Marine said.

Katrien laughed as she said, "My group was allocated a withered up old woman. God, it is hard to believe that we will end up looking like that."

"Well at least you don't have to try and work with a willie looking at you all day."

"Won't matter after week sixteen. That is the week you cut it off and record it in your workbook and then toss it in the bin under the dissection table."

"I will leave that to someone else in the group. I have enough nightmares just from the normal stuff. That is just barbaric."

"I agree; but once you have dissected part of the body, the anatomy is ingrained in your brain, it is so much easier to remember it than just stuff you read in the textbooks."

Marine and Katrien were the best of mates, against all the odds.

Katrien grew up in Antwerp in the Flemish Dutch section of Belgium and Marine was the daughter of a French couple from Brussels. Belgium had been overrun by foreign armies so many times that everybody hated everybody. The Belgians spoke three versions of Flemish Dutch, plus a dialect of French and German. Virtually everyone born after 1945 spoke English fluently. English was the binding agent for the country, as the Flemish speaking people hated the Germans and the French, The French hated the Germans and 'The Dutchies" as they called the Flemish speaking section and the Germans disliked everybody except visitors.

Marine and Katrien both wanted to study Medicine and they were both offered placements at Leuven University. The Medical School used English as the base language to avoid the need for translators but textbooks were available in all three languages as well as English. The four languages were deemed essential to be a Doctor in Belgium as a normal caseload would involve people from all backgrounds.

They were in the second year of study and enjoying the challenges. They had both been Exchange students, with Katrien in Britain and Marine in Boston, Massachusetts. Their English had a very British sound, with Boston residents sometimes sounding more British than the local Londoners.

Both were twenty-two years old, healthy blonde girls with typical Nordic features of blue eyes and porcelain skin, slim athletic bodies, and sparkling personalities.

They were the first generation to have a normal upbringing after the Second World War. Belgium had been severely damaged by the German invasion and occupation and then even more so by the liberation. They had seen much of the Medieval Ancient cities restored from rubble to near perfect reproductions of how the cities looked before the two World Wars. Belgium had quickly restored its economic and educational status as a powerhouse of Europe. Against all the odds Belgium quickly became wealthy and both Marine and Katrien were lucky enough to have well educated parents with good incomes.

Both girls accepted entry to Leuven University because of the reputation of the town as a University City and the University being well recognised as an educational institution. Both had experienced international travel and believed they would like to work overseas. They became good friends despite the enmity that tended to exist because of the differing heritages.

Leuven was a wonderful city, with the old town centre restored to its pre-war appearance, with the magnificent Guild Halls and open cobblestone Town Square. It had a vibrant youth culture with arts, theatre, and music. The city was a magnet for the best bands of Europe, as well as those from England and the United States.

In the first year University break they took their bicycles to Ireland for three weeks and had a wonderful holiday together. They drank Guinness and sang rebel songs and fell in love with Irish Culture.

Maybe when they graduated, they would return to Dublin and work there for a while, they told their parents, but they wanted to travel further during their breaks. They were lucky; university in Belgium was cheap and the parents fully supported them anyway. They did not need to work summer jobs.

Both girls were excelling in the studies. As summer of 1966 approached, they completed their second year of university study. The exams were tough, and everybody knew that year was brutal. The University needed to reduce numbers to what they could place in Clinical training in the hospitals in and around Leuven, so students tended to become insulated from their colleagues; your best friend could be the reason you were dismissed from your studies. They studied together, they played together, and they travelled together. They planned to work together after graduation, so they had a pact to make sure they both passed the exams.

Other students struggled but for them the exams were a breeze and they both passed easily. They were free for eight weeks, so they set off to Cologne in Germany to see The Rolling Stones in Concert. It was an easy trip to organise with a regular train service from Leuven to Cologne. They took a trip to Paris to shop, and Nice to try their first attempts at surfing. They decided that they would go surfing at the end of the next year. "It might be California, or Sydney or even South Africa," Marine told her mother.

"We will ask at the University to see where the best surf is, and what is the best place to visit in summer."

"If you are planning on a trip like that, Katrien, you had better look for a summer job. We can provide you with some help, but you will need the money for airfares. And internal travel when you get there. There is plenty of summer work for young people in those countries, but you need your airfares organised in the next six months. And don't forget that it is winter in Australia and South Africa"

"Oh Mum, Dad said he would look after the money till I graduated."

"Yes, he did, but I am sure he was not planning on trips around the world, princess. You will need to get some of that money yourself. We will talk to your father tonight, but I am guessing he will be able to find someone who needs a short-term worker over the remainder of this break."

"Marine, Mum has told me that if we are doing that trip next year, I have to get a summer job to pay for the airfares and some of the spending money. I know that Lien is starting University next year, but Dad promised he would meet my expenses. I won't be able to do any more travel this summer unless I can convince Dad to do what he promised."

"I haven't mentioned the trip to my parents yet because they were unhappy with our trip to Cologne and Paris.

Dad said that I was wasting too much money, and I needed to save some, it because we would have more travel to our placement hospitals this year, and they were finding it a bit of a stretch." Marine said with some concern.

" Any idea where you are going to work?"

"I want to be an usher at Rock Concerts."

"Best of luck with that. They don't have ushers and you know it. We have been to enough concerts to know how that works."

"Well then maybe I can be a Front Desk help at the Hilton Hotel. With some luck I can get to meet a rock star or a movie actor."

"Maybe you can be on the cleaning staff and get to clean their toilet!"

Why don't we have a look and see if there is anything that would be fun. Maybe at Christmas time we could get a job in the Alps at one of the ski lodges. Lots of gorgeous young men with lots of money. Maybe they would take us overseas."

"If they took us anywhere they would be looking for some compensation, and it would not be paying for lunch."

"That would not be so bad, if they were young and gorgeous. I could think of worse ways to pay for the trip."

"Oh for God's sake Marine, don't let your mother hear you talking like that or she won't let you out of Brussels."

She just laughed and said she guessed her mother knew she was no virgin, but Mum and Dad encouraged her to respect herself and make sure she was not involved in anything she would regret later. Remember, they would tell her, as a Doctor, people will look up to you. A bad reputation would seriously damage your career.

Marine was very French in her tastes. She loved good food, and fine coffee and great chocolate cake. She loved to dress elegantly and wear stilettos when going to a high-class restaurant. She demanded people pronounce her name properly. She would tell that it was MAR - RINN; she was not an American soldier.

Marine loved casual day wear, but it was always close fitting, to show off her trim figure. She had a radiant smile and teeth that gleamed white. She refused to join her friends smoking cigarettes because it would stain her teeth, and although she loved coffee she carried a traveller's toothbrush and paste so she could clean her teeth as soon as possible after she drank it. She was gorgeous and she intended to stay that way.

Katrien spoke with a soft Dutch accent. She was stunningly good looking, immaculately groomed with long straight blond hair to her shoulder blades. Her whole face lit up when she smiled. She had a disarmingly quick wit that helped her win most arguments. She would stop a disagreement with a male student by totally flagellating every aspect of the discussion and then turning to him with a beaming smile and ask coyly, "But you still love me, don't you?" Katrien and Marine attracted attention everywhere they went.

They made out they ignored being stared at, but they deliberately added a minor attention seeking accessory, so they stood out. In Leuven Med School, girls were outnumbered five to one by males, but that was a problem they were happy to have. It meant they had plenty of choices for University functions, even before they considered the other faculties. On their own each was stunning, but together they were the dynamic duo. They literally stopped traffic.

"Let's go to the Students Office and see if there is any work available for us for the next three weeks till the start of term. Unless I can save some money, I think our next trip might be just back to Ireland. It would be nice to go somewhere exotic for a couple of months, but it looks like Dad is becoming a bit of a Scrooge." Katrien was annoyed; Dad promised to support her through University, and this was the last chance for a real holiday. She knew the heavy Clinical years would start after her planned trip and as a trainee she would have to work long hours with no breaks at all so if she missed the opportunity to go overseas, it would be at least another three years before she could consider it again. "Parents can be greedy," she said to Marine.

The university Students Office did not have much to offer. All the good jobs had been taken at the start of the break when the girls went to Cologne. There did not seem to be anything on offer in the ski fields and they were not prepared to work in a shop.

Marine said, "Maybe in a French Boutique or a good jewellery shop." She was surprised when she was told that those jobs took specific training, "and as highly trained as you are, I don't think Medical School has classes in fashion. At this stage you might get some work in a Department Store or a café. There is not much else. You need to come see us two weeks prior to the next term break if you want any chance of a better offer."

They decided to see if the parents had any better ideas; they socialised with a large number of business-people, so they probably knew somewhere to get some work for a few weeks.

Eventually they went to a new supermarket in Leuven and applied for work but were rejected because there was not enough time to put them into training before University resumed. The best offer they could get was as cleaners in the city. They complained about working in the banks and insurance companies, but when they were told they were scheduled once a week to clean at the hospital where they had been gaining some clinical experience they resigned.

Katrien decided they should go to the ski fields in the French Alps and try themselves. They were lucky enough to get work as housekeepers in a five-star ski lodge that catered for wealthy Americans and a few from Britain. Well at least they were not going to be recognised and ridiculed as would have happened at the hospital, and there was always the chance of hooking up with some wealthy fellow who would take them overseas.

"Both of us, with the one fellow. Not likely!" Marine was drawing the line at that thought but Katrien laughed and told her not to be silly. It was a case of being seen and see what happens.

Well nothing did, other than eight hours a day of hard work. When they finished cleaning the cabins and suites, they were put to work cleaning and gardening outside. The temperature was freezing so the first week's income went on appropriate clothing. But at the end of the third week when they had to head home to get ready to return to University, they had some money in the bank accounts.

Then they took the opportunity to talk to the young men at the lodge, they realised most of them were ski instructors, who were not going to break their circuit to spend a few weeks with two gorgeous girls. There was plenty of choice wherever they worked; their income was good, but if they broke a contract they would never get it back.

Marine's father told her she had about twenty percent of what she needed. She should look for some work on Sundays and then work full time through the next term break. Providing she had the money to travel wherever they planned to go, then he would provide a stipend for the time away. If she wanted to really enjoy the trip, she needed to earn some extra spending money.

Katrien was surprised when her father told her the same thing. He told her that he took the liberty of speaking to Marine's parents because he was concerned that the two of them were spending too much time having a good time.

He was pleased that Marine's parents told him that the Dean of the Medical School had said they were doing well, but it got progressively more difficult from next year and they would have to not lose focus.

"You spoke to the Dean about us?"

"Well actually, I didn't, but Frederick did. He wanted to be sure that Marine was studying hard, as the two of you have been doing a lot of travel.
Frederick told me of his arrangements with Marine about a big trip next year, and I agreed that in fairness the same should apply to you."

"What? You are not going to pay for my trip? Look Dad, as the Dean said, it gets more difficult from next year. This will be our last chance to have a relaxing break for years."

"I am glad you understand that. So, you will need to save that money in your bank account and keep adding to it. Depending on where you choose to go, you are going to need a lot more money."

8: Hobart.

Marcus and Mary were living at the same address in North Hobart.

Technically he was renting the spare room and paying fair rent. In reality the spare room was a dressing room for him, and he and Mary were together in the main bedroom. He was not sure why they were playing this game of subterfuge. They were not doing anything illegal, and the romance had not started until after he was discharged but somehow, they both were more comfortable keeping it secret. He felt unusually settled when Mary was around. She made him feel complete in a way he had never felt before. They talked about everything, and she helped salve his demons. When she came home from work at odd hours, he had her dinner ready. He loved her voice and her smell, and he loved their time together in their bed. She was playful, but careful because she knew he still had serious pain at times. She knew that his dreams were disturbing him often as she heard him crying in his sleep, and watched as most nights he left the bed for extended periods to sit near the window and stare at the darkness.

Sometimes she would leave him there but often she would sit with him and hold his hands until he stopped shaking. She would lead him back to bed and gently make love to him. Often the bed was filled with sweat, even on the coldest Tasmanian nights, as the horrors invaded his space and gave him a mental thrashing. But gradually he became more settled.

"I only do that to trick you into jumping on to me," he said, but she knew that was not true.

"Tell me what is causing the dreams Marcus. Talking about it will help." Marcus told Mary he was talking to the psychiatrist at the hospital, but he did not want to tell her.

"Mary, if I told you half my life-story you would have me out the front door in an instant."

"Listen to me, I was in Vietnam too. You are not the only soldier I looked after. Some of them told me about the patrols, and the deaths. You were doing your job, honey. Whenever you are ready, I will listen. I won't be judging you; you were keeping us safe."

"One day I will tell you about my life as a child and if that doesn't rattle you too much, I will tell you about growing up with Aunt Doris. I might even take you to meet her. You would like each other. She is getting up in years now but by God she enjoys life. Unfortunately, you can't meet Albert, because he died years ago. They were the most marvellous couple. I was sure Doris would be on her own till she died but gradually she pulled herself together and started getting out and about.

I was old enough to know she was having a fling or too, but none of them lasted long. She was having a good time though. Sometimes she was so noisy that I could hear her from the other end of the house.

Tom Swinson came into her life a few years ago and has been there ever since. Albert was much older than her and he treated her like his little girl. She loved it. But Tom is about the same age as her. From the first time I saw them together you could see something magic was happening. She blossomed almost overnight. They have been overseas together many times and when she is home she dresses beautifully, plays the piano and sings. She has enough money for a housekeeper and a gardener, so she has become the lady of the house. Tom was a race car driver, so he was extremely fit. I heard her tell her friends that Tom was a raging bull in bed, and even in their more advancing years it was obvious they were still very active in the cot."

"You know, my love, that is probably the longest little speech I have ever heard from you. I want to hear everything about them, and I would love to meet them; it would scare the daylights out of me, but I want to share everything with you Marcus. I love you and I hope that when you are ready you will feel comfortable to share all your life with me."

"Mary, I haven't been to see Aunt Doris since I went to Vietnam. When I was in the hospital, she phoned every Sunday night and promised to come to the hospital to see me, but between her passion for the Merino breed, and her passion for Tom she never actually turned up.

I never told her that I was here with you so she may have given up trying to find me."

He had a long way to go before the Army would consider his return to service, but his pay continued on a regular basis. He was told to keep working on his recovery. If he failed to reach the markers by June 30, he would be provided with a Veterans Service Card and a reasonable pension. His medical bills would continue to be paid, and he could get some help with accommodation. Every day he went to the Rehabilitation Section of the Repatriation Hospital and spent five hours working hard in the gym and the hydrotherapy pool. The rest of the time he spent in the Library downtown, or in the bookshops. He was fascinated with magic and was learning a few tricks to amuse Mary and a few of his mates at the Repat. They were simple card and rope tricks, but he was getting slick and he was able to fool his audience most of the time. He was doing a couple of lovely switch tricks at the Hospital when one of the Doctors told him he did a bit of magic as well. He took his cards and ropes and mesmerised everybody.

"Here is one just for you, Marcus." He took a large surgical dressing and formed a small bag with it in his left hand. Then he took a piece of rope about a foot long and poked it between his fingers into the bag. He did the normal hand gestures and silly noises and flipped open the cloth. In his hand he had a live pigeon. He walked over to the window and let it go. "See, Mr Pigeon, it is possible to fly again even if you feel stuffed."

Marcus wanted to learn how to do that and any other trick and begged the Doctor to teach him. He agreed on one condition; that Marcus go to Bernard's Magic Shop in Melbourne, where they would teach him ten tricks for a modest investment. If he proved he could do those professionally he could buy his magicians hat, wand, and cape, and importantly he would be inducted into the Magic Circle Club.

"You bring that certificate to me, and I will teach you some amazing tricks. My name is Doctor Bill Adams, but I worked the stage when I was a student under the name of Doctor Slash. Did all my tricks in a dissection coat, blood stains and all. They will remember me. I spent a fortune in that bloody shop. I have a contract here till June next year; after that I have no idea where I will be, so I am happy to teach you a few tricks providing you get started before I leave."

Marcus was waiting when Mary came back from work, and he told her what had happened with the pigeon, and the offer that Dr Adams had made to teach him.

"Well, you are probably safe with Bill, but all I hear is that he is good at making nurses undies disappear. He is a total playboy and seems to use his card tricks to get young women to follow him home. I was warned about his behaviour, so I bought a cheap ring and made out I was married. At least he was honourable enough to tell me I was obviously out of bounds, and he has never even shown me his card tricks, let alone offered to show me more at his place."

"Pleased about that, or I might have had to treat him like a Gook."

"Don't even joke about that Marcus."

"I am not joking," was all he said as he went to get a coffee.

"I wasn't trying to make you jealous, Marcus. He is a devil with the nurses but good luck to him. I have my man Marcus, and I promise you, you are all I need and all I want."

"Good. Would you like to go to Melbourne with me?

We could drive up to see Aunt Doris and Tom and then fly to Melbourne for a few days, and I would love to learn those tricks. I have sufficient money for the trip. I am not sure whether my mother is still alive, but it would be worth checking. I know she was locked away in the Kew Lunatic Asylum because Aunt Doris tried to contact her once. Even if she is still alive, I doubt that I want to dredge up those memories. But if she has died, I would like to go to her graveside and just say a prayer, if I can remember how to do that."

"She had a terrible life, Mary. It would have driven the strongest woman insane, but they gave her no help. They could see she was struggling, and they just left her till she fell to pieces, then they locked her in that prison and told everybody to forget about her. That bloody Harold Holt took away her husband, and when he was killed the family disintegrated. Holt is one bastard that the world could do without."

Mary asked him if he wanted to talk about it and he just nodded. They sat in the sunlight on their front verandah and he rambled through his memory bank for more than an hour. He cried often. Mary just pulled him close till the weeping stopped and he could start again. When he finally went quiet, she cradled him till he went to sleep in her arms. She sat on the verandah for another hour letting him sleep peacefully. It was getting cold, so she helped him up and tucked him into bed fully dressed.

Marcus slept for ten hours and never moved all night. Mary slipped into bed next to him and smiled when she felt his boots in bed. 'Well, the bedding needed changing anyway' she thought as she snuggled up close to him and felt his body warmth on her back.

It made her smile to think she was lying in bed with a fully dressed man who was wearing his jacket and boots; and he was more peaceful than she had ever seen him.

9: Melbourne University.

Elizabeth Ainsworth absolutely loved Melbourne University.

It was massive, with beautiful architecture that just screamed culture. Its beautiful old-world buildings around the Quadrangle in the Law School and the Students Union facilities were beyond anything she ever expected to be part of. Lizzie, as her father called her, went to Port Melbourne Public School. It was typical of a school in what was one of Melbourne's most underprivileged areas. It was a slum where the wharfies lived in tiny little terraced houses. The suburb was controlled by the communists on the Australian waterfront. There were several groups, but the Waterside Workers Federation and the Painters and Dockers had fought for years for control of the wharves; the money in graft and corruption was massive and the right to steal anything that came across the wharf made the leaders very wealthy indeed.

Gus Ainsworth lived with his wife Faye, in Ross Street, only a couple of blocks from the Wharf. Behind the row of terrace houses was a cobblestone laneway.

The lanes allowed the night-cart to collect the toilet cans without having to deal with traffic and cars parked in the way. Gus had a woodshed just inside his back fence that was never locked. It was a transit shed for stolen goods from the wharf. Wharfies would deliver a box load of Tonka Trucks in November that had gone missing from a shipment destined for the big toy stores in town, and a few days later they would be collected and sold in the pubs around town. They were better than stolen five-pound notes because they were untraceable. Gus got a regular dividend and Faye turned a blind eye. If she said anything, she got a smack in the face and told to mind her own business. There was always a free beer at the pub or a pound of sausages from the butcher, providing they were kept on the list to buy some cheap stuff from time to time. Gus wasn't real bright but he knew to be quiet and just accept the dividend and freebies as a side benefit to the job.

Lizzie spent much of her school life worrying that her father would get caught and go to gaol, or worse; get murdered by the rivals on the wharf. Wharfies vanished with regular monotony, and many others were found on the street dead from a hit and run or an attempted robbery. The local police considered it garbage collection and did not look too hard for the killers. Occasionally a worker that was not in on the game had something fall on them from a great height. A crate dropped from a crane would do one of two things; kill the mongrel or frighten him so much that he would be no further problem. The more they killed each other the less the police had to deal with.

Lizzie worked hard at school and had her mind set on being a teacher at a Private School. She wanted to meet a nice man and live in a good suburb, like Kew or Balwyn or along the Bay.

Lizzie stayed at school when most of her friends left, and she graduated in 1964. She was offered a Teachers Scholarship to Melbourne University by the Victorian Government with an agreed bonded time working in a Government school. As far as she was concerned that was perfect; money while at University, no fees, and a guaranteed job when she finished. After her four years with the Education Department, she would probably have enough experience to move to a good private school in a nice area of Melbourne.

The University was huge, and the Arts buildings were relatively modern buildings on the Grattan Street side of the University. They were close to the Medical Building and the Engineering faculty. There were students everywhere, but as she spent most of her time within the Arts Faculty that was where she developed her circle of friends.

She met another girl in the first week with a similar family history. Alison Jamieson lived in the rough and tumble suburb of Fitzroy. Her father was a boilermaker welder at a Workshop in Reid Street, only a couple of blocks from her home on Nicholson Street. Alison had decided in Year 9 that she wanted to be a teacher. Her mother encouraged her to become a hairdresser, but she worked hard and won a scholarship to Melbourne University.

Her father reckoned she was wasting her time. "By the time you finish you will be pregnant, and you won't work a day in your life. Some poor bugger will have to support you and a bunch of kids. You'd be better to follow your mother's advice and get a job and some money before you end up knocked up and housebound."

Alison and Lizzie became study buddies and thought they might join a share house, but home was cheaper and some of the scholarship money helped the family budgets.

Alison's brother, Jack, trained with the Fitzroy Football Club. He was only seventeen ,but he was tall and wiry and he had an amazing leap when he went for a mark. He quickly picked up the nickname of Jumpin' Jack and the staff at Brunswick Street Oval were keen to develop him as a future senior player. They kept him on the players list for six quid a week and in the off-season, they found a good job for him as a groundsman at a local golf club. Well not actually in Fitzroy but at Northcote, where there were people who had the time and money to play the game. It was a public course and quite new, so Jack was signed to an apprenticeship, which was sponsored by the Footy Club in association with the Golf Club. He was living at home but was away most of the time, so Alison usually had the house to study when she wasn't attending classes.

Alison and Lizzie often studied together and pushed each other hard. They both wanted a second scholarship to take the pressure off the family finances and to allow them to find somewhere to live away from home.

"When all is said and done this is supposed to be the Swingin' Sixties and we haven't done much swinging yet," was Lizzie's answer when friends asked why they wanted to leave home when they lived almost close enough to the University to walk there.

Alison and Lizzie welcomed a new member to their little friendship club when Anne Fraser joined for lunch in the second week of term. She lived at Janet Clarke Hall on the University Grounds. It had excellent tutors and study areas as well as private living spaces. It was expensive, but her parents were landholders near Ballarat with a significant farming operation. Anne was never short of money, and she was happy to occasionally help out if the budget was tight for Lizzie and Alison. Her parents owned a holiday house at Cheviot Beach, near Sorrento and they allowed Anne and her friends to use it, providing it wasn't being used by the Frasers or their friends. Anne had her own car so when the weather was good, she could take the girls to the beach for the weekend.

There was a collection of surfboards and wetsuits at the house. She said that they could set a target of two hours study a day and then as much fun as they could cram in.

Anne told them that though the beach was lovely, and the surf was excellent, sometimes it got a bit intimidating. The Prime Minister liked to swim at Cheviot Beach and there always were security guards around. Anne laughed and said that Harold Holt used to tell the security fellows to go to town for a coffee and come back and get him in a few hours.

He seemed to have a string of young women around him and often they would vanish for a while into the sand dunes. She said he was notorious, but everybody knew that while he was playing up with the young women, his wife was playing up with anyone that was available. It seemed like they both liked a lot of sex, just not with each other. Anne went to the Student Union building and used the red phone to call her mother at home. She seldom went out except to major social occasions at night. "Ballarat is a significant city and Mum and Dad are quite well known so they get invited to a lot of events," but she knew that it would be likely that her mother would be in the kitchen making the evening meal when she called. Her mother confirmed that they were not going to the beach for four weeks, so it was okay if Anne and her friends used it. Her mother reminded her that the neighbours were permanents and did not enjoy their peace being interfered with by noise from next door. "They will call us if you can be heard at their place, and the old lady will be quick to call the police if you don't quieten down."

"It only takes twenty minutes for the Police to travel from Sorrento, Missy, so tell them to shut up or the police will shut them up!" was her gentle way of letting the Frasers know that the people in their shack were too noisy.

Anne told her mother they planned to study and surf, so there would not be any noise. She said that they had not brought any of the LPs with them, and she doubted they would be listening to Mantovani or Perry Como from her father's beachside collection.

"Now be nice, Anne. One day your kids will laugh at your choice of music. The Beatles and the Rolling Stones will be a source of humour for your children, even if you think they will last forever."

The girls went down for the weekend. They studied hard for an examination in English Literature, and they surfed. Anne was good at surfing, but Lizzie and Alison were novices. Cheviot Beach faced Bass Strait just outside the heads to Port Phillip Bay. The water was cold, so the wetsuits were necessary. Alison struggled to get one to fit and when she did, she struggled with the long zipper up the back to the neck. She had injured her shoulder at training for Thai kick boxing and it was still a bit stiff and sore. Anne helped her get the wetsuit on, and then told her to get used to it because she wasn't going to help get it off. She laughed and said that after some surfing the sand and salt gets up your bum and drives you crazy. Of course, after a couple of hours in the water the girls helped her out of the suit. They washed them out and hung them up to dry. They were sitting on the front verandah watching the waves when the Prime Minister turned up for his swim. He liked to swim early, but if work interfered, he went later in the day. Unless it was really cold, or he was planning on some spearfishing, he never wore a wetsuit.

Wearing just his speedos so people could see he was still quite fit, and carrying his beach towel, he walked from his car near the dunes down to the middle of the beach. He headed out for a swim and before long a group of four young women joined him.

They splashed water at each other like teenagers, and swam around, just slightly too close.

 Harold was duck diving between their legs and lifting them out of the water and throwing them back in. It looked like fun but somehow inappropriate.

"Who are the girls?" Alison asked.

"Just some local tarts that play up to him and he throws some money their way to help them get by. They say he is very generous."

The weekend came and went with sunshine, swimming, surfing, and studying. One night the girls went into Sorrento for some pizza, but most of the time they just enjoyed the peacefulness around the pristine beach and the silence.

Late on the Sunday they piled into Anne's car to head back to Melbourne. Alison needed to be back in Melbourne for Monday kick boxing practice. She had started it as a bit of a joke, but she found it quite invigorating to know that she could defend herself if she had to and that there would be very few people who could hurt her unless they had a weapon; and even then, she would probably disarm them before they had a chance to use anything other than a gun.

Lizzie was quiet for quite some time and then asked, "How far do you have to go with Mr Holt to get some of the money he throws around? It looks easier than working in a café and the hours look better!" Anne told her that the word around the place was that he shagged one or two of them every time he came down to the Beach.

"He is not kinky, and he is not aggressive. He is certainly not my cup of tea, so I don't plan to find out exactly."

"That is okay for you; you have a family that provides you with a lot more than we get. Sometime when we are down here, I will ask those girls what the deal is."

10: The Cradle.

"You have to be kidding me."

"It's a friggin' blizzard up there and it has been like that for three days. Come on, you are setting me up, right?" Garry Rogers yelled down the phone.

Sergeant Garry Rogers from Search and Rescue had just been informed by the Park Ranger that a couple of walkers had just struggled out of the Cradle Mountain Overland Track seriously unwell from hypothermia. They had made it to the Rangers Hut just in time. Both were hallucinating and one was drifting in and out of consciousness. The Ranger was trying to locate one of his assistants so he could get both to the hospital on the coast. Their preparation had not been good enough. They had been sleeping in wet sleeping bags for three days and they had not eaten for two days.

He now had them in dry clothes and in super-warm sleeping bags and lying on air mattresses in a warm room but well away from the fire. Since the death of Scott and Kilvert everybody was aware to warm hypothermic walkers up slowly. Don't let them near the fire or they are likely to die of gas embolism.

"Garry, the more lucid of the two told me that there was a fellow on the Track just before the blizzard started walking the track in a dinner suit and black patent leather shoes. He was dragging a rucksack on a little trolley. He reckoned the walk was piss-easy and was doing it on a bet. Obviously, we are not sure, but this fellow with me is adamant. Always possible that it is an hallucination, but he has too many facts. It sounds like that clown that we rescued last year that got as far as Kitchen Hut in bloody thongs before we forced him back."

"Fair dinkum, if it is that stupid bastard, I am going to give him a spell in Derwent Park. A few weeks in the nut-house will shake him up and stop this shit. We are going to lose good people looking for this arse-hole, if we are not lucky."

Garry was based at Police Headquarters in Hobart but had a depot in Glenorchy, where the rescue vehicles and equipment were housed. Garry asked the Secretary to call his team that had trained for the Mountain and tell them there was an emergency on the Overland Track. They all had a kit of essentials ready to go. That included their weatherproof clothing and their boots and gaiters. Between them they carried a lightweight stretcher and emergency rations and a basic medical kit. They had warm clothes and a high-quality sleeping bag in a waterproof bag. Of recent times they had started carrying a space blanket; a thin aluminium-based sheet that acted as a thermal insulator when wrapped around a freezing casualty. They all had First Aid training ,as well as the new techniques of dealing with people who were hypothermic.

They trained together regularly and were all very fit. However, they knew that did not make any rescue on the Track safe. At times it was brutally dangerous.

The list of deaths was extensive; and some of those people who had died were very experienced in the highlands of Tasmania. Several fatalities involved walkers who had walked in the Himalayas and the French Alps. It was easy to be complacent because it looked peaceful and in relatively low altitude. But sometimes it bit like a rattlesnake. And it was certainly like that now. Garry briefed his crew, saying this idiot might even hide from them.

"Fellows, let's get this straight. We are all coming home to our families with or without this clown. I will call off the mission if it is too dangerous. You know the rules, keep an eye on your mate in front and behind you. Walk from snow pole to snow pole and watch for areas you can fall through the snow. If you lose sight of the party, stop, and look for the marker on top of the snow pole. Use your whistle if you need to attract attention. For Christ's sake, don't just wander about trying to find the rest of us. You will all be issued with new heavy-duty plastic whistles. You can put your standard police issue whistle away. They stick to your bloody lip and cause some horrible ice burns in these conditions. Take them out of your bag and keep them for footy umpiring or give them to your kids, but don't take them with you. Actually; keep them for your normal police duties. The commissioner will not be impressed if you give them away."

Garry went through a briefing session with his crew. He decided he would take two groups of five experienced walkers. Because of the amount of time from when the idiot was seen, Garry assumed he had to be somewhere around the middle of the Track. They decided to take two Toyota Troop Carriers and head to the start of the Arm River Track. They would walk in to meet the Overland Track near Pelion Hut and split with one group heading South and one heading North. If they found him, they would use the walkie-walkies and meet back at Pelion to stabilise him if necessary, and then decide what they would do with him. That might be to get him to a hospital, take him to Derwent Park for psychiatric assessment, or just lock the silly prick up before charging him with a pile of offences related to public nuisance.

Garry knew that the mission could take days, so he arranged for caterers to bring hot meals to the depot for everyone, and some hot-pots to take on the road for another meal before leaving the carpark. There were four thermos flasks with tea and coffee and a chiller with some milk. As well, they had Army ration packs and portable stoves in case they were in the mountain over an extended time. They needed tents, sleeping bags and heavy wet weather gear. Their backpacks averaged fifty-five pounds; but the rule was to take everything that might be needed. There was no way to get something that had been left behind.

"The Arm River Track is relatively short, but it is not well maintained. It is steep and in these weather conditions, it will be bloody slippery.

We don't need heroes, so be careful." Garry knew his men, but nevertheless he reinforced the obvious.

On a good day it took experienced walkers about an hour and a half to walk the three and a half miles through rugged bushland, but in the blizzard, with rain, ice, and snow, it was likely to take double that.

Conditions were terrible, with fierce southerly winds blasting freezing air and ice into their faces as they struggled through broken ground. The snow was just thick enough to cover the rocks, making it impossible to walk quickly. Ankles were wrenched as rocks moved underfoot, but at least they all had solid boots on that prevented ankle sprains.

Their faces were being lashed by sharp branches of shrubs that were being whipped around by the strong gusts. After almost three hours they reached Pelion Hut and sought some shelter to get some food and a warm drink.

The hut had been there for years. It had been built from rough-cut local timbers with gaps that could be seen through, but it provided some protection for regular bushwalkers. Today it was shelter for the Rescue Team to have a bit of food and drink before splitting up to do the serious search. Everybody had a map and a compass. The map had marked spots to make radio contact, so the two groups did not lose contact with each other. The plan was to search till an hour before darkness, and then bed down in the nearest decent hut to sleep, unless they were lucky and found him quickly.

"If we find that this fellow is playing a game, he will be lucky to get back home in one piece. I have had about enough of hippie shits thinking they can survive up here on their crappy food and meditation." Garry wasn't talking to anybody in particular, but they all felt about the same. This was the third time in four months that the team had been called to the Track to search for people who had not used basic common sense before heading into the wilds. Often, they were mainlanders that had been advised in their own state that the dangers were exaggerated and a pair of firm tennis shoes, jeans and a woollen jumper was enough. The problem was that sometimes it was enough. On other occasions walkers were at risk even if they were dressed like Scott of the Antarctic.

Sergeant Garry Rogers and his team of four experienced rescue people and one Advanced First Aid Officer headed north, and Sergeant Trevor Keating and a similar crew headed south. They agreed if they found him, they would call on the walkie-talkies but if not, they would seek shelter by 4.30. "Let's search the area between here and Windermere to the north and as far south as Windy Ridge. Keep in contact."

Garry and his crew set off across Frog Flats. The weather had turned it to a bog. They set up a system, one person calling and everybody listening for a response. After seven hours they reached Windermere Hut. They were freezing cold, covered in mud, and had not seen one person on the track. Trevor had used his personnel to search several side-tracks without any result.

They decided to stop at Kia-Ora Hut as it was starting to get dark and there was no chance of getting to Windy Ridge in daylight. Both groups settled down for the night eating Army rations cooked on top of the wood fired heaters in the huts. A cup of tea tasted like nectar of the gods in that environment. They decided to continue looking the next day with Garry and his team heading towards Cirque Hut and Trevor searching as far south as Windy Ridge. If they had not found the fellow by one o'clock Garry said they would try to contact the cars at the bottom of the Arm River Track and ask for them to go out to a phone to get another party to start at Waldheim and a fourth at Cynthia Bay. "If we don't find the silly prick in the next two days, we should call off the search."

At midday Garry tried to reach the crew at the cars with the walkie-talkie but they were out of range. From the top of Cradle Cirque there was just enough contact to get the other two crews into action as soon as they could be mobilised. In the late afternoon a rucksack was found abandoned near Fury Gorge, but there was no indication where the walker was. A quick search of the bag showed there was no food or wet weather gear in it, but the black patent leather shoes and dinner jacket were in it.
Hopefully, that meant he had wet weather gear and boots on. Unless he was completely stark raving mad, in which case they would be bringing a body out, or nothing at all.

There was nothing around Benson's Peak at the back of Cradle Mountain, with visibility less than twenty feet. Garry stood at the precipice of the gorge and called out.

Three people thought they heard a weak response from down in the Gorge. There was a rough track down, but it was incredibly difficult and dangerous in low visibility and slippery conditions. Three of the most experienced crew set off down to the gorge. The walker was found fifteen minutes later, buried under leaves and bracken that he was using for shelter. He was barely coherent, passing in and out of consciousness with hypothermia.

The rescue group decided to get him out of Fury Gorge where he could be assessed and basic First Aid done, then get him on the stretcher and head for Kitchen Hut. Garry called Trevor and asked him to try to reach the cars by walkie-talkie or get someone down the Arm River Track as soon as possible. "We need a helicopter to Kitchen Hut as soon as possible. We will try to stabilise him and start to get him warmer here, and then we will head back to Kitchen Hut and wait for help. We won't return to Pelion; it is too far. With a bit of luck, they might ferry us out on the chopper, or else we will walk to Dove Lake. Your team should get back to Arm River, otherwise see if they can send another chopper for you fellows."

The walker told them he was Sam Others from Melbourne. He was a Medical Student at Melbourne University and started the walk as a dare from the Mr University Competition. He was challenged to do something really stupid to win the prize from the Students Union.

"Well Sam, you probably will win, and as a memento you will get a free trip to court and a certificate from the magistrate that should be worth several hundred dollars. You will have no trouble proving you did it," was Garry's summation of the event. "You have tied up the time of ten highly trained police officers and thousands of dollars of public money. I would not be surprised if the magistrate puts you in prison for a while as a public lesson for other idiots who think this is a toddle in the park. And who knows, maybe the University might decide that Medicine needs people with at least a minimal amount of common sense and turfs you out of the course. We can only hope!"

The Mercury newspaper carried the story but made light of it.
"Young Doctor gets some of his own medicine in Cradle Mountain," was the headline.
Marcus showed the headline to Mary; he asked her if she would inject the silly prick with something really painful to put some common-sense into him. "Mind your language, Marcus. That might be all right to say to your mates, but I don't like it. Anyway, I doubt if my registration would cover that."
"Well, someone needs to knock some sense into him, I am glad I did not have that idiot looking after me a couple of months ago."

11: Snug.

Colin Anderson was an institution in Hobart.

He appeared on Channel 6 through the summer, telling people of the fire danger and asking them to be careful. He had been in the Fire Service for thirty years; from when it was a group of volunteers with an old truck and a few hoses, through its development as a professional service to becoming one of the first responders to accidents and emergencies.

Hobart has always been an enigma. The mainland view is that Hobart is wet and cold, the grass is lush green and the whole state has enough rain to not have to worry about droughts or bushfires. He regularly told people that Hobart was the driest State Capital in Australia, that it had the longest summer days in Australia, that it had the most blue-sky days and in summer if was often one of the hottest places in Australia. Drought was an absolute curse, with the land often cracked from lack of water. Colin had already advised the State Government that the summer of 1966-67 was looking particularly dangerous.

The state had dried off in September and it was already having days with temperatures in the high seventies. The grass had grown rapidly through the wet winter and was now golden straw. Colin had put his Fire Chief hat on and gone down to Parliament House to speak to Premier Eric Reece about his concerns. Eric was a practical man that had developed much of the hydro-electric system for Tasmania. He wasn't called Electric Eric by accident, but he was frugal. He believed that Governments spent other people's money, so it needed to be spent wisely. He was quick to say that he had worked as a lowly paid manual worker, and he never liked seeing governments take his money as taxes and waste it.

Colin was concerned that the city was increasing in population and that many of the new areas had low pressure water supplies. The locals loved living among the trees and being in a natural environment. Many did not want lawns as that was artificial; They wanted bush-blocks with natural grasses and trees, not English Shrubs. Colin kept telling them at public meetings that it was beautiful, but that they needed to keep the areas trimmed, and the grasses short. "The gums are explosive in strong fire. The oil in the air burns like petrol. It explodes and can jump for hundreds of feet." He was most concerned about the foothills of Mount Wellington because houses were being built everywhere in steep locations. They were in amongst the trees, with only tanks to store water. In a major fire there were no high-pressure outlets for the fire trucks to hook up to, and the trucks had only small onboard storage.

Colin was keen to see an integration of the Fire Service into a state-wide body so that resources could be moved to the areas of most need. He wanted bigger trucks, with much bigger on-board storage and he wanted water bombers. They were being used overseas as fixed wing and helicopter aircraft and could unload massive amounts of water into the middle of a raging inferno in relative safety.

Colin put his case as Eric ran his fingers through his curly hair; "Colin, that is a good plan and we will put it into our forward estimates, but there is no money for it this year. We will have to deal with what we have now." Colin pushed his case as hard as he could, and Eric realised his concern. "Look how about we put a bit more in your budget to get your men out there to do some clearance burns. We will call for some volunteers to clean up the worst, and if necessary, we will provide you with compulsion powers to make some of householders clean up the most dangerous areas." "That is good Eric, but the real problem is that many of the worst offenders are highly educated people who want to get back to nature. When we tell them to clean up, they tell us to leave them alone or they will get their lawyers to keep us off their properties. Many of them are lawyers, and doctors with plenty of resources. That problem is all over the State. We have attracted a whole lot of new residents from interstate who are coming here for the peaceful lifestyle and the beauty, but they just don't get the danger. Eric, some of them sit in your bloody Parliament as well, so we are having some concerns."

He left the Parliamentary offices with a sense of foreboding that they would not be re-equipping the service quickly enough. It was good to know the Premier was listening, but that would not put a fire out if the warning signs all proved true. He called the coordinators for the Southern Fire District to a meeting for some planning and to advise they were basically on their own. It was good to know that the Government would compel people to comply with the safety orders but that would not happen immediately. It needed legislation through Parliament, and that would take weeks to draft and months to legislate.

The whole state was a tinderbox; idiots with matches could cause havoc, but lightning strikes in summer were common and the effects could be devastating. Back burning and fire trails were implemented, and Colin told everyone in his command that overtime could be used as needed. "Make sure you are getting real work done. Eric will not tolerate us wasting money." Brigades were ordered to back burn around the known flash points of Hobart, as well as down the Tasman Peninsula and the Highlands where possible.

"We lost Port Arthur to a fire in the past. Absolutely nothing left standing after it ripped through there. If we had a fire like that in Hobart, we would be counting deaths in the hundreds, and property losses beyond thinking," Colin said. "I need a written update every two days so I can keep the Government informed.

I will start using my segment on TV to warn everybody of the dangers and let them know of the precautions we are taking. If you have any other ideas that we should do to keep everything safe, then get it to me as soon as possible. And nothing is silly! Don't keep a good idea to yourself; let us all know."

"Please give me a rating of the current danger in your location before Friday. Let me know if you think we need to introduce fire bans now, and if not, when you think they will be needed. And if you have people with any idea of the highlands then get them to assess those areas. I will talk to Garry Rogers from Search and Rescue for his opinion of the flammability of the Cradle area. He will know the current position without even going up there."

He went home to his property at Snug. He thought 'how ironic that I criticise the idiots who live in the foothills and don't look after their property, while I live here, and am too busy to trim my own trees and keep the grass down.' He made a mental note to use his next few days to clear away the rubbish, clean his gutters and get tree branches away from the house.

He started to put together a list of essentials to get to the car if a fire started. He put aside a packing box to put important stuff, like insurance policies and photo albums, just in case. Colin decided to talk to Linda and the kids tonight about what they wanted to take with them, and to talk about an escape plan. The biggest concern was that they lived at the end of a leafy road. There was one way in, and only one way out. If a serious fire occurred, they would have to get out early.

'The house is well insured. It can be rebuilt, but I am not risking my family over possessions.'

His brother lived in open country on a sheep property at Hamilton. It was unlikely to burn as there were few trees and the winter snows kept the soil moist. He decided that once he had spoken to the family, it would be best to take their dogs up there on the weekend. They could keep the cat at home, and if worst came to worst, they might have to leave the chooks behind. The cat could be kept in a cat cage if the fire risk became worse, so it could be quickly put in the car. The cat was easily spooked and would be impossible to catch if it was roaming when a fire approached.

Colin started to write some notes, to detail his thoughts. That would make for a practical presentation on TV and might just spook a few people to take the danger seriously, he thought. He decided that his short TV segment should be called "Fire Safe – or Fire Victim. Your choice." He could go back to his "Fire Services Report" format in Autumn when the main danger has passed.

The reports started coming in and the situation was not heartening. The East Coast from St Helens was dry, the whole South-East danger level was already extreme, and the inaccessible south would be impossible to control with a lightning strike. Hobart, the jewel of the Derwent, looked sublime but Colin knew that the city would be lucky to avoid a major blaze over the next few months.

'God help us, it would be easy to fix with some water bombers scooping up from the Derwent, but it will be a bloody inferno if we have to rely on old trucks and garden hoses.'

Colin spent the night with Linda and his two kids, putting together a list of what they needed to save. Of course, Jasmine had to save Teddy, so she was told to keep him out in the open. Don't tuck him into bed during the daytime. Colin bought them a little suitcase and told them to pick their favourite clothes and whatever they wanted, so long as it could fit in the case. That gave them at least a feeling of some independence.

He went on television on Sunday before the evening news. He planned to explain his decision to have an escape plan and make sure the family, even the little ones had some idea why they were doing it. He would unpack the box of essentials and ask people to write in with the list of what they had in their emergency box. He emphasised that they should pack a week of their medications and all prescriptions in the box, and a copy of their will wrapped tightly in a fire blanket. He showed what his two little ones had packed, to demonstrate that everybody has their own definition of what is important.

He had called in the TVT news crew to film his backyard, to show that even he had been less than sensible with the maintenance of the property, and he showed the simple things he did to reduce the fire risk. He asked for volunteers to help the elderly in their street to tidy up their properties and reduce the fire risk for everybody.

The Fire Service spent the spring cutting fire breaks and doing back burns for maximum protection of the properties as well. Each member had an area to personally visit to convince people "to be fire-ready."

Colin waited for a disaster but prayed it didn't occur.

12: Melbourne.

Marcus had improved physically.

He was comfortable driving his car, although it was heavy in the steering and hurt his chest wall when turning it at slow speeds. It was a brute of a thing, but he loved its raw power. He could spin the rear wheels from stopped, facing uphill in second gear. The X2 motor made people stop and stare. It growled at low speed. The motor, coupled with the four on the floor gearbox was built for the Bathurst Racetrack and it felt like it. The clutch was short and stiff; it hurt Marcus when he pushed the clutch in, but it was a good pain. He had bought the Holden with the leather luxury pack as reward for his recovery.

He asked for a month's break from rehab at The Repat Hospital. He just needed some time away from the hospital. He planned to go to Melbourne and get his Magic Circle licence, and he wanted to call in to Aunt Doris on the way to the ferry. He needed some idea of what had happened to his mother; he just hoped that somehow she had found peace.

Mary took leave from the Hospital, as Marcus had insisted that she go with him. He was a tough mongrel, but without Mary he felt vulnerable.

They packed their bags for the sea voyage but there was no need to be totally frugal. The luggage travelled in the car and was only taken out as needed. Mary allowed enough for three weeks, but Marcus had next to nothing. Mary noticed a little canvas bag and asked him what it was. He told her it was his first aid kit. "It looks rather small," she said. "I have everything I need. A retractable scalpel, some betadine, a small roll of gauze, a small pair of tweezers, a roll of gaffer tape and a compression bandage, a needle, surgical thread, and two tubes of superglue."

"OK Marcus, you are having a lend of me, right?"

"No, I am not. If things need cleaning up a scalpel, tweezers and betadine with gauze is enough. If a wound needs closure, superglue is better than stitches on small wounds. Infections won't get through it, and gaffer tape can hold anything. You can make a splint or even a stretcher with gaffer tape and some small tree branches. It worked in 'Nam and it will work here."

He sent a letter to Doris and just hoped she was home, because if she wasn't, he would not have time to wait around. He had left Cynon as a little boy to go to school and had virtually no time there before he was sent to Vietnam. It was a strange feeling to drive up the tree-lined driveway to the house. Doris and Tom must have worked tirelessly on the property; it looked like the grand houses of England in some of the books in the school Library. The gardens were manicured, and the plants were trimmed beautifully. The house was freshly painted, and the upstairs verandah was fully restored.

It was accessed through the sitting room next to Aunt Doris' bedroom, but the door had always been locked because the flooring was rotten.

Now it looked magnificent. He tried to remember why the house looked so impressive; then he realised that it looked like Tara from "Gone with the Wind." It was beautiful.

Aunt Doris was waiting at the entrance, with a huge smile. She was considerably older than he remembered, but then again, so was he. Aunt Doris took one look at Mary and threw her arms around her. "Thank you, Mary for looking after my boy. I can see why he fought so hard to survive." She kissed her on the forehead before taking Marcus in her arms. She was sobbing uncontrollably, and as she held him close, she hurt his ribs. He did not complain, he had never felt such total love from anyone other than Mary; he could put up with the discomfort.

"My goodness Aunt Doris, the home is spectacular. You and Uncle Tom must never stop working on it." She told him that she and Tom were too busy gallivanting around the world for that.

"The merino stud is now world renowned, and Cynon has become its own brand. Our wool is making us very wealthy Marcus. We employ housekeepers and garden staff these days, and we have a team of highly skilled farmhands that supervise the breeding of our flock and the shearing of our sheep. Our wool is now so valuable that we only use the same shearers every year. We pay them well to be extremely careful. Our top rams are now worth more than many houses in Launceston."

She asked about his health, and Mary and their plans. She told him to be sure to come up and spend some time with them to learn about the farm and how it works.

"You see Marcus, Albert and I had no children, and Tom and I got together when it was too late to have kids. Didn't stop us having all the fun, but we knew we were past rearing kids. You are my boy, and we plan to pass this property to you when we both leave this Earth. We are having a grand time, but honestly the farm earns money quicker than we can spend it."

She told them to make sure they created the kind of bond that only comes with love "but don't worry too much about money, you will have plenty of that."
Mary was enthralled by Tom; he was such a great character. He had lived a fantastic life, and then found Doris when he was ready for a settled retirement. He told Mary that he and Doris adored each other and were a perfect match.

Tom said that he wanted her and Marcus to stay for a couple of days, "but we will put you at the other end of the house; then you can do whatever you want, and you won't hear us making noises like teenagers on heat." Mary smiled when she saw them holding hands all the time and sneaking a kiss every few minutes; she watched as they snuggled up on the couch to watch Television.
Tom loved BP Pick-a-Box; and often beat Barry Jones to the answer. He loved that Barry Jones often told Bob Dyer that the answer was wrong, and later proved it.

He sat next to his set of Encyclopaedia Britannica and would have a one-sided argument with the television, reaching for the Encyclopaedia to argue his case with the flickering screen.

Doris would laugh as he would say, "Beat the smart-arsed bastard. Again!"

Marcus and Mary were booked on the boat the next evening, so they left around midday and headed to Devonport to catch the Princess to Melbourne. Aunt Doris gave him two hundred dollars and told him to stay at the Windsor. "About time you got used to a few luxuries young man."

Marcus went to get the car and Doris stayed talking to Mary. She told Mary that she hoped that Marcus would buy a European car, but Mary said that you would not get him out of his car with a crowbar.

"Aunt Doris, he loves that car. It is a brute of a thing, but he enjoys the power and the throaty engine. He says it would beat a Ferrari on an Australian road. He doesn't care if that is true, but he loves to say it."

Tom laughed; "Maybe we could test that some time. A fair bit of the Longford racetrack is still open, and I reckon I could make a donation to a Police Charity for them to supervise a race". Tom had a Ferrari parked over in the stables, and Doris bought a gold Rolls-Royce to annoy the daylights out of all the old biddies, who spend every waking hour talking about them. "Mind you, we give them plenty to talk about. They complain all the time that he holds my hand when we go shopping.

Good thing they are not in our house after dark or they would really have something to talk about."

They drove to Devonport on the North Coast for a night trip across Bass Strait; by reputation one of the roughest ocean crossings in the world, but they were blessed with one of those evenings when the Strait was a millpond. They stood on the top deck where they could feel the engine rumbling, and watched the moon rise over the ocean. It was an idyllic way to travel to Melbourne. They had a nap in the cabin, but it was hardly comfortable. It did not matter because they were in their car for disembarkation before sunrise. They arrived at Williamstown and drove the few minutes to the Windsor Hotel in the city. Doris had phoned ahead, so they were met with a welcome reserved for the special guests of the hotel. Doris had arranged the payment for the Hotel, including meals, so the cash was to enjoy the city.

It had been a long night with minimal sleep on the Boat. Mary decided she needed a nap on the luxurious bed in their room and asked the concierge to arrange a wake-up call for two o'clock. She had a soaking bath and was asleep as soon as her head hit the pillow. Marcus lay down as well, but he felt restless, so he chose the bed in the other room so Mary could rest. It was strange being back in Melbourne. He had left there as a child and his family history certainly did not include the Windsor. His rest was a bit disturbed, but he drifted off to sleep. When he awoke Mary was in his bed, sound asleep and with the slightest smile on her face.

Just before two o'clock there was a knock on the door as the bellboy delivered a cup of tea. It was exactly as she had requested from Aunt Doris' kitchen staff. She must have organised that as well.

The Windsor was beautiful; they catered for wealthy Victorians when they came to town from their country estates as well as people from all over the world. It was reasonably close to walk to the city, but they chose to hop on a tram and enjoy one of the features of the city. The tram conductor provided them with return tickets, which he clipped as he advised them that they were all-day tickets so they could be used until midnight . They could be used all over the city, but not the suburbs. Marcus asked for directions to Bernard's Magic Shop. The conductor laughed as he told them to get off the train at Elizabeth Street and walk towards the train station. "You will see it on your right as you head down Elizabeth Street. That shop makes a fortune selling trinkets to the gullible. But they are good at it. Everybody leaves there with a smile on their face."

They walked into the small entrance area where there was a full wall of things in bags with signs saying, "Disappearing Golf Balls" "Magician's Playing Cards," "Magician's Baton", "Magician's Cape" and hundreds of other dubious items. When Marcus said he wanted to learn serious magic and join the Magic Circle Club they invited him into the area behind the shopfront. "Look, I don't mean to be rude but if your beautiful friend wants to stay, she will have to pay the training fees as well.

Magic is all about illusion; it is about deception and teaching you how to do things that people don't see."

Mary said that she would enjoy being bamboozled by Marcus, but she did not want to learn to do it herself.

"Ok. Well, the first session will take two hours. You might like to wander up to Bourke Street and visit Alders. That is a great store, and I am sure you will easily be able to walk around there for two hours."

The magician could see that Marcus was pretty good at basic tricks. He told him that he would easily trick many people, but even amateur magicians would see through his tricks. "Today you will learn how to apply distraction to the tricks you already know, and we will hone your skills to make them far better."

The two hours were gone in an instant. He arranged for another lesson the next day and hurried away to find Mary at Alders. "He is an absolute master, Mary. That fellow is amazing. I can't wait for the next lesson."

Marcus had lessons every day for two weeks and became proficient at card tricks, rope tricks and learning to undo knots behind his back, as well as picking locks. He was told to practice for a week and then return for a further week of lessons. If he could complete all those tricks without detection by a selected audience, he would become a member of the Magic Circle. "You will learn very complex tricks when you are able to spare the time, and the money. The big tricks are fifty dollars a lesson, but we will teach you to do these so well, no one will know how you are doing them."

Marcus was taken aback, that was about two weeks wages for most of the fellows he knew. 'What the hell, in for a penny, in for a pound,' thought Marcus.

He booked his first lesson in the advanced programme and went looking for Mary.

Marcus told Mary he was going to have a day off and go out to the Kew Lunatic Asylum to see what had happened to his mother. Kew was quite close, so they took a taxi to the hospital. After speaking to Reception, they were asked to wait for the head doctor on duty. When the doctor came to them, he was carrying a small file of paperwork. The black cross on the top right on the manila folder was ominous. He told Marcus that his mother was very unwell when she arrived at the hospital. It was before his time, the doctor said, but she had died eight years ago. We can arrange for you to talk to one of the psychiatrists if you need a detailed history.

Marcus said that he did not need that, but he wanted to know where she was buried. All they found out was that Tobin Brothers had arranged a funeral for her, so they collected a business card and went there. Tobin Brothers said that there were many people who were buried without relatives. They arranged for one of the staff to take them to the plot in the company's service car. "Thank God it is not the hearse," Mary said as they left the offices.

The plot was untended, with a simple wooden marker that was faded to a level that was difficult to read.

Marcus could make out her name, and the date indicated that she died a few months after he went to Aunt Doris. He hadn't known, and he wasn't sure if Doris had either.

He and Mary went back to Tobin Brothers and arranged for the gravesite to be concreted, and a headstone in black marble with gold lettering to be erected.

He asked for it to include her name, and the name of her husband and her children.

"I wish I had known you better, Mum -Love, Marcus and Mary."

He looked at Mary and asked her if that was OK. She told him she would be honoured to have her name with his. Marcus paid them cash for the work. He said "I will be back next year to visit Mum but please send me a photo when the work is done. Please include a close-up photo of the headstone."

With that they went back to the Windsor for dinner. They cried themselves to sleep, but for Marcus it felt somewhat cleansing.

Mary spent the week falling in love with Melbourne. She visited the Markets, and the shops downtown, she went to the Zoo and the Botanical Gardens. She went to the Melbourne Exhibition Buildings and all the gardens and parks. She loved the trams and the trains.

Marcus stayed at the Windsor most of the time. He practiced the repertoire of magic tricks to qualify for the Magic Circle Club. He loved the illusion of making things appear and disappear.

He wanted to be able to make a pigeon magically appear so he could release it and let the pigeon fly free. By the time he went back to Bernard's Magic Shop he could conjure up a teapot but was a long way from a bird or an animal.

"Marcus, you are a natural. You have been working this for less than two weeks and you could mesmerize a group of very observant people already. You have obviously qualified to join the Magic Circle Club. I will give you your card shortly, but I have a challenge for you to practice. I want you to be able to do all those tricks with four people around you. And they must be close enough to touch you with their outstretched hands. That will make you a real magician, not just an amateur. Start with your Mary standing in front of you so that you could reach out and touch her. When she is unable to work out what you are doing, put another person behind you, and eventually one off each shoulder. When you can do that, come back, and see us for a full month of instruction; at the end of which you will be a Master Magician. You will be so good that I could guarantee you a paid spot on 'In Melbourne Tonight.' Phone us before you come back. I will need to be sure we have enough staff to get you to that standard. It will be hard work, but you will be able to do it."

He checked the price, and almost backed out. It was half the cost of the X2. He decided he could afford it, but that he could not afford the regret if he did not do it. He told his teacher he would be back once he had completed the rehabilitation.

Marcus walked to the Princess of Tasmania's booking office in Collins Street and arranged the trip home. He and Mary had another two days together in Melbourne; walking and talking and falling in love over and over. Then they went home.

Marcus went back to hospital with a new-found determination to be strong and pain-free. He spent every spare minute in the gym or the pool. He decided that he would allow himself to be discharged when he could run at full pace from The Hospital on Davey Street to his home in North Hobart and arrive with no more than a light sweat and no sign of breathlessness. When he left for Vietnam, he was a sprinter, and he promised himself that was what he would be on discharge from the Hospital. He was not going back to the Army; he had been discharged from active duty before he went to Melbourne, having exceeded the mandatory number of days away on injury induced leave.

When Dr Bill Adams came to see Marcus, he was amazed. Marcus was practising illusions that had taken him four years of hard practice to master, and Marcus was doing them expertly in less than two months.

Every day that Bill was rostered on to the Repat, he set aside an hour with Marcus to teach him new illusions. He laughed when he suggested that it would be fantastic when Mr Pigeon could make a pigeon appear from nowhere and have it fly away. Marcus learnt the trick with a fake bird. That was easy. A self-inflating realistic looking bird would fool most people, but it certainly could not fly away.

Bill promised him that when he could fool four nurses with a fake bird, he would teach him how to work the trick with a live one.

They started exercising together and going for a run after work. Marcus was often given invitations to join Bill when he went out socially, but based on what Mary had told him, he felt that it would be better to diplomatically refuse the offer.

Marcus felt he was ready to leave the hospital for Christmas. He decided to follow his own test, running at full pace from the hospital to his home. When he arrived at home he would not have made a candle flicker with his normal breathing, but could blow it out from sixteen inches away when he wanted to.

Dr Bill told Marcus that he was ready for the master illusion when he came to his room with a trained pigeon and a homing box. He placed the box outside the window with the door open and showed Marcus the technique of revealing the pigeon without anyone being aware he had it. As promised; Marcus could learn the secret because he was a full member of the Magic Circle Club. Marcus performed the trick for the staff, and then went home and performed it again for Mary. As much as she begged, he refused to tell her the secret. "If you are not a member of the Magic Circle Club, I can't tell you." It led to their first argument, but she accepted it eventually.

Marcus told Mary that he needed to look for work; it was essential he got back to being productive.

He went to the Commonwealth Employment Service with a knowledge of how to do some magic tricks and how to kill people very quietly. Probably not the best CV they had seen that week. Marcus had his payments from the Department of Veteran's Affairs and was surprised when he was told that he would lose those if he earned much money. He was advised to become a volunteer for a while, as it was much harder to get his military pension back than it was to lose it. That annoyed the living daylights out of him. 'Why would they make it difficult for an injured soldier to work himself back to a productive life? That is just plain dumb.' He checked at the Repat, but they told him he could not be a volunteer, as the Public Service would go on strike if they believed a job was being done by someone who was not being paid. The same applied at the Museum, and every other public building in Hobart.

He could have some work at Port Arthur, among the remains of the convict settlement, but the place was not very busy, and it took hours to drive there. People could wander around as they saw fit. There was no entrance fee and no budget, so he was told they could not help with petrol money. If he wanted to, he could spend a day a week there but there wasn't much to do other than on Saturdays. "Tasmania is embarrassed about the convicts, so we don't promote it much," they told him at the Employment Centre.

Marcus was directed to the National Trust, who had some historic sites to attract visitors to Hobart. The town had very little to interest visitors once they had been to Mt Wellington and Cadbury's, but they hoped people might find some of the old buildings in and around Hobart interesting. He volunteered to help tidy up the disused gaol on Campbell Street to make it more appealing for visitors. It had been there through the convict years and had only been closed for six years when the prisoners moved out to a new prison across the River Derwent at Risdon Vale. Well at least it was something to do, and it helped keep him fit, but it was sporadic, as work details had to be approved from head office.

He was much younger than all the other volunteers, but he got on well with his work crew. He just got frustrated when they stood around for days, waiting for someone to tick a box on a sheet of paper to enable them to work in a new area of the gaol.

He read in the Mercury that the local Fire Chief was looking for volunteer fire-fighters for the Northern Suburbs of Hobart; that uniforms and training would be provided. There was potential that the volunteer position could eventually become full time paid employment, but there were no guarantees. It did not take long to get to the station, where he met Colin Anderson.

Colin was surprised that such a fit, healthy young man said he could be available at any time and even more surprised when he heard as much of the Vietnam experience as Marcus would share with someone he did not know.

Marcus was quickly made aware of the imminent dangers of a major blaze over the summer and the need for many new recruits. "With your age and military experience, I would expect you will become a brigade captain out here in the north. The training can start tomorrow if you wish."

13: Henley on Thames.

Jane woke with a blinding headache.

She usually drank small amounts of alcohol occasionally, but last night she had used up her quota for about two years.

'John can get stuffed. I am not going to work today,' She thought and then remembered it was Saturday. 'Well that gives me time for some rational thinking before starting at the office Monday. She thought about the offer from James, and decided the opportunity to have a practice before meeting the Partners was a smart idea. She could hone her skills and work through a few issues that might be difficult but were necessary. She was not planning on going to this meeting and being negotiated into submission. They would accept her employment on her terms, or she would work for their competitors. She knew she was good enough to get any job she wanted, and she was sick of being treated as second rate because she was female.

'Now is that the totality of the suggestion from James? Well frankly my dear, I don't give a damn.

It has been a long time since I had a wild night in the sack, and I could not care less if he respects me in the morning. If it looks like he wants a root he will get one to remember.' Jane realised that made her just a little more than excited. 'Maybe if he doesn't make a pass, I might just tell him that I get cold at night and I plan to sleep in his bed.'

She phoned James at home and was surprised when he picked up the phone. "I am planning on telling the senior Secretary that I need a meeting with the Partners as soon as possible to discuss my future with the Company. On Monday I will write out a comprehensive overview of my grievances and the employment contract I demand.

Then I am going to tell them that they have plenty of time to think it over, because I am taking a year off to wander the world and destroy my reputation.

If they argue they will get my resignation forthwith. So, is that offer of some practice still available?"

James was stunned. "Christ, woman, you just blew me out of the water. Yes, of course it is available, but when?"

"I thought this weekend. I could come up on Friday afternoon and drive back on Monday, with a planned start back in the office at eleven o'clock. If that is okay, I will try to clear my desk with some long hours this week so if they give me the shits, I will tell the Partners to shove their fucking job and leave."

"Jane, calm down. The objective of the sessions at Henley is that you do not get angry, and you do not burn your bridges.

You must leave them with some wriggle room, so that once they see how much work does not get done if you are not there, they can come back and give you what you require, or even more than that."

Jane agreed to drive up on Friday and meet James there. Her plan was simple. 'Let's go to dinner somewhere on Friday evening and start the serious devil's advocate sessions on Saturday. Repeat it till every potential issue has been discussed and a plan has imbedded in my brain. When I am comfortable that I can tackle every issue they throw at me without giving ground, then we will cease the training programme and see what happens then. There is potentially Saturday and Sunday night for fireworks if that is the way it goes.'

She made the call on Monday at ten o'clock, and she was given a maximum of thirty minutes at the Partners Meeting on Wednesday of the following week. 'Perfect. Long enough to get ready for it and not long enough to panic and back out.'

She sat down and wrote out her issues to be dealt with; her specific grievances, and the details of what she required in the future.

She stated that she was planning on taking some leave and that final negotiations could be completed on her return. She did not indicate when that would be.

She did not want to forewarn anyone, so she never handed it to the legal secretaries to type. She wrote it neatly on a legal notepad and hand delivered it to the Senior Secretary of the Partners.

She then returned to her desk and started ploughing through the stack of notepaper and files in front of her. She made a list of clients to call in on Wednesday and Thursday morning, leaving enough time to update notes or commence action so that she could get out of the office on Friday at two o'clock. "Hmmm, that's rather weird, I feel quite aroused. I have not felt like that in years. James might be in for a surprise; or maybe not,' she thought.

She never got her desk cleared because new stuff kept getting put in her in-tray. 'Well, that is proof of the pudding. Whose in-tray will it go in when I am away? Poetic justice if it is John's.' She smiled as she thought of the panic in the office among the slackers, when they were told she was going to be away for up to a year. 'A few of them might have to do something. That would be an alarming thought.

She put in long hours to clear the desk but was finished for the week and one way or the other it would be an interesting weekend. She knew that James would not be there for a couple of hours, so she could have a quick drive by the house and then come back to the beautiful Main Street. There were a couple of magnificent old pubs near the bridge, so a bit of Dutch courage might help make the evening go smoothly, she thought to herself.

She drove past his house, but it was locked up and there was no car in the driveway, as she expected so she returned to the pub. She chose a scotch on ice and sat near the window to gaze at the gentle life passing the window. She looked at the old one-way Bridge, where everybody knew their turn.

There was no need for beeping horns; the traffic moved calmly, nobody seeming rushed. The ends of the bridge were adorned by a profusion of beautiful potted flowers as the Thames moved at a leisurely pace. She wondered what the flowers were. Where she lived in the city, flower gardens did not exist. She had time for work, eating and sleeping and not much else. Maybe that is why that arsehole of a husband had moved out. 'Must do something about finalizing the separation and divorce. I would not have him back if he came begging,' she thought. He phoned once and asked for money. She told him to look in the girlfriend's bra, "That's where cheap strippers put their tips." He hung up.

At six o'clock she drove around to his house. The lights were on, and his Jaguar was in the driveway.

He opened the door as she approached the front entrance and invited her in. She could smell that he had started cooking dinner, which was something of a surprise. She thought that like most of her bachelor friends, once they got past the toaster and the kettle, the rest of the kitchen was redundant.

"Wow, what are you cooking?" she asked.

"Chicken Provencal. I hope you are not vegetarian." She assured him that she was not.

She guessed he was a little late because he had been buying fresh produce at the markets. She watched him in the kitchen; this was nothing new to him. He moved around with ease, barely glancing at any recipes. He said that he knew it had been a rough week so had decided they should not go out to a restaurant.

She could kick off her shoes in front of the fire and he would get her a drink. Dinner would be at least forty-five minutes so they could have a talk, "but not the stuff for the discussions tomorrow. Tonight should be about getting to know each other again. There has been a lot of water under the bridge since we left Uni full of hope and ambition."

He told her he was earning more money than he ever imagined possible, but most of the time he felt miserable and believed life was passing him by. "When I die there won't be much except a brass plaque on the grass, unless I get on with it," he said.

She told him that during the past week she had used part of her free time to write up a balance sheet of life. She concluded she had a great education and a high paying job. She spoke to her mother on Mother's Day and Christmas Day and usually forgot her birthday. She had no family, no children, and no real interests outside the doors of Smith, Clyde, and Farrow. She felt she was a shallow, hard-driven law bitch that would not be missed if she died tomorrow. "Well," said James, "Don't leave me guessing, will you. I thought you were a very successful lawyer in a prestigious law firm in Central London. I guessed you had friends and lovers all over town and your biggest concern would be fitting all the requests into your social diary."

"I wish."

"You said you were going to take some time off work no matter how the meeting went; what are you planning to do?"

She replied that as she was not short of cash she wanted to wander. I have been to Scotland, Wales, Ireland, and France a few times. I went to a conference in Germany last year, but that is it. I would like to go to the USA, Africa, and Australia for a start. Maybe New Zealand, who knows? I just want to wander aimlessly and live frugally. I might look for some work in pubs and clubs like we did during our university years, but I certainly have no wish to do any legal work.

"How long do you think you would go for?"

"At this stage, I don't know. I would probably buy an around-the-world open ticket and come home when I have had enough. I really don't care if the job closes, as I know I have the skills to pick up at any one of fifty firms in and around London. Who knows, I might discover heaven somewhere and just stay there for a while.

I am not sure of the rules, but I think the ticket allows you to have as many stops as you like, providing you don't turn back." Jane said.

I haven't checked whether you can choose clockwise or anticlockwise, but you either get back on the plane where you got off or further along in the direction you were travelling. So long as you do some planning you can do a lot of travelling on one ticket."

"Gee-zus, Lady Jane, that sounds like liberation. Have you made a mental list of your must-see places at this stage."

"Haven't thought it through really.

I would like to see the Statue of Liberty, and Disneyland, and ride on a riverboat in Tennessee. I would like to go to a Lion Park in Africa and a Tiger Park in India. I would like to see the Taj Mahal, and maybe the Ganges. I would love to go to Australia and climb Ayres' Rock, swim in the Pacific in Australia and California, visit the Great Barrier Reef, and see some of their blackfellas in the wild. I want to see some kangaroos and experience a hot summer. Not sure what else. I would have to do some study. Anything that does not include sitting at a desk in cold old London deciding who is using whose product without permission."

They talked until dinner was ready. James had gone to some trouble; he had fresh beans and potatoes, with peas and carrots and the most magnificent chicken Jane could remember. She did not know the wine, but it was French and obviously expensive. It was not a style she was used to. It was a something-or-other Grigio that was perfect with the chicken.

He had cooked French crepes with fresh berries from the markets and very thick cream.

The meal was sensational. 'No wonder he did not take me to a restaurant. There would be little likelihood of a better meal in Henley anywhere, and they had many fine eating houses. If he is planning to get into my pants, I think the elastic let go a while ago,' Jane thought as she gave a little smile.

James caught a glimpse of the smile and said, "Penny for your thoughts."

"You really don't want to know. Just that at the end of a rough week this has been lovely."

"Well, the week is not over yet, so let's see how the rest pans out."

James told her a bit about himself. He met Maureen in Ireland. She was stunning, and sang like an angel. They toured Ireland on pushbikes and made love in the freezing waters of the Irish Sea. He travelled to Ireland three times before she moved to London to be with him.

They married after eighteen months, but her parents were devastated. Maureen was marrying and Englishman and a Protestant at that. She did not care; neither of them went to Church and she did not have a hatred of the British like her parents did. They lived in a lovely area in a semi-detached house in London, not far from James' work. He was in a suburban branch but had been told he would soon move to Headquarters in Central London.

James adored Maureen and told everybody how lucky he had been to find her, but he was troubled by his long hours and her loneliness for Ireland. Two years later he came home to an empty house. She left a note and said that she could not handle the loneliness any longer and had gone home. It was a few months later that he discovered that she had met someone else whilst he was at work, and they had actually relocated to Devon.

James said, "I have never met anyone else that makes my toes tingle and I doubt I ever will. In fact I have done everything possible to make sure I never do. I enjoy life on my own."

Jane told him a bit more about her marriage, but it did not take long for them to decide to talk about the future, not the past. Her marriage collapse was recent and devastating, if not unexpected, and his was years ago. But it still gnawed at his soul.

They finished a lovely meal and settled in front of a raging fire with another bottle of the French wine and a large packet of marshmallows with some fondue forks. "Do we follow the fondue rules if I drop a marshmallow?" Jane asked, slightly inebriated from the earlier scotch and the wine. By the end of the next bottle, she knew she would not be in control of anything much. 'What the hell; let's see how the evening works out.'
They drank the wine and ate the marshmallows and they talked for hours. She gradually fell asleep on the sofa in front of the fire and woke up several hours later quite disorientated. It took a few seconds to realise where she was. She was in a bed in a side room. Her jacket and skirt were hanging up, but she still had the rest of her clothes on. It did not take long to realise that James had done nothing inappropriate when she was vulnerable. She wondered if she would have been as honourable if the positions were reversed.

She looked at her watch. It was three o'clock. 'How would he react if I went and climbed into his bed?' she thought but decided better of it. He had chosen not to pursue her last night, and she should respect his decision. She went back to sleep and woke at daybreak as the sunlight streamed through the windows.

"Good morning sleepy head" he said when she wandered into the kitchen. It seemed odd to get out of bed and then put her pyjamas on, and he laughed when he saw her. "You were ready for work when I tucked you into bed last night," he said. She smiled and told him she was grateful he looked after her.

He already had Eggs Benedict on the table with both tea and coffee ready to pour. She had known this man for years and now she realised she did not know him at all.

"After breakfast I want you to have a long hot shower and then we will start the Grand Inquisition. I plan to be ruthless, so I must be extremely nice to you before that or you will run away, and I don't want that."

Did she just notice a naughty little smile as he said that, or did she just imagine it?

"James, I need to be up front. You know my marriage went west recently and it has really screwed with my mind. I suspect that part of this trouble at work stems from me being unhappy personally, and I have become far less tolerant of the behaviour of colleagues in the office.

Last night was remarkable. I didn't know you could cook like that, and every part of the night was romantic in a lovely way that I have not experienced before. I am grateful that you put me to bed like you did.

You are a real gentleman, so thank you for your consideration.

I plan not to be weak today and I want you to go as hard as possible. Try to break me mentally and emotionally. I know the Partners will try that, so I need the practice to be strong and not intimidated.

I will have a shower, and I plan to dress in the same way as I will for the meeting. Be as tough as possible, I need the practice."

She returned 30 minutes later in a smart business suit; a two- button jacket with a mid-thigh skirt made from a beautiful Australian Merino wool. The wool was very light, with a fine pinstripe on the deep blue cloth. She had it tailored in the city from Cynon wool, a rare cloth woven in Italy from wool grown in Tasmania. "You know you asked yesterday about my must-see items. I want to go to Tasmania to see these sheep; this cloth is just extraordinary.

The tailor told me he can only get enough cloth for ten outfits in a year, and if the wool merchants get just one legitimate complaint the tailor is permanently prohibited from buying it. This is the Rolls-Royce of cloth."

"Where is that? Are you sure you have the name right?"

"It is in Australia. It is an island I think, but I will check with Australia House before I finalise my plans. It is in the Strand; I've seen it several times when I have walked from the Office to the West End."

"Ok, you look fantastic. We can go to my study and mock-up the Inquisition for you."

The study was massive. James said that he often held meetings in that room with his divisional managers. Some stayed at his place, and some in the town. There was a huge banker's desk in the middle of the room with a double green banker's light in the centre of the desk.

There were twelve mahogany chairs where his work colleagues sat. He moved one of those to the middle of the desk, directly opposite him. He turned both lights on and placed a yellow legal pad in front of her. He was nothing if not thorough.

"Right, Miss Hampton, please feel free to check any notes you want as we talk. I will advise you that our two most accurate stenographers will be here to record this meeting. Later this afternoon you will receive a transcript of the meeting and so will we. You will have the opportunity to correct any transcription errors, but they will only be changed if the partners agree that an error has occurred. The final transcript will be signed by both of us and two witnesses, and it will be sealed and locked in our safe.

For the sake of the record, please state your name, your age, your marital status, how long you have worked at Smith Clyde and Farrow and your current position."

"My name is Jane Hampton, I am 34 years old and I have worked at this firm for 12 years. My position is Litigation Specialist in Corporate Law, specifically in relation to Copyright and Trademarks. I have been separated from my husband for several months. It is irreconcilable and a divorce will be issued in due time."

"Really, Jane. At which University did you do your training to become a Litigation Specialist in Corporate Law? You see, our records show you started here on graduation from university.

You have worked here full time ever since. Other than your holidays you have never been away from the office for more than a day or two."

"I have completed in-house training with your staff, who specialise in Corporate Law. I have gold-leaf on my door saying I am a Corporate Specialist in Copyright and Trademark Law. I am recognised as the best in this office and your Billings Department charge out my ten-minute segments at the specialist rate."

"But you are not a specialist are you. You have not done a post graduate Master or Doctorate in those areas have you?"

"No, and you know that I do not need to do that. The regulation states that I must work under the direct guidance of a qualified Corporate Specialist, and after two years the supervisor requests the right to the title for me, subject to Law Society reviewing my work. That was done and the Title was granted. If you wish to come to my office, you will see the certification on the wall."

"But you have not actually done the study have you?"

"With respect Sir, it would appear that you have not done the study. I have the certification; it is not fake, and it is signed off by regulating authorities. Your comments are irrelevant." She could feel her temperature rising, and at this stage she no longer saw James as anything other than a pettifogging arsehole.

"You believe you should receive more remuneration than you currently get.

Why, considering you would earn more money than almost any other woman in London?"

"What other women earn in London is irrelevant. I work for Smith Clyde and Farrow. My billings are the highest in the department, my success rate in court is one of the highest in Britain, and you fellows are getting very wealthy as a direct result of the work I do. I have men in my office getting paid more than me with a much lower caseload, and a dramatically lower success rate. I simply request that my remuneration reflects the work I do and the earnings I put into this company."

"So, if that were true, why do you think they get paid more."

"Sir, it is obvious. For whatever reason you think that a dick makes a Lawyer better. Well frankly I don't, and I would suggest that you move on from the nineteenth century and treat your staff according to their capacity and effectiveness, not according to what is in their underpants."

"Well Miss Hampton, I think we have just seen one of the reasons you are paid less. You are vulgar and uncouth, and that latest outburst would be adequate grounds for dismissal.
Now stand up. I notice you have covered up compared to the apparel you wear to the Office."

"Excuse me Sir, I do wear this to the office, and my other work outfits are similar."

"Really Jane. Your supervisor says you wear skirts so short the men in the office can look straight up to your knickers, and your shirt is often unbuttoned to the third button, exposing your rather ample breasts. You wear stilettos that are designed to make your buttocks stick out."

"Sir, let me tell you we are now getting to a dangerous level of conversation. I am a Lawyer and I have one friend in a rival company that would act on my behalf to sue you for those comments. I hope you have remembered your two stenographers are writing this down, because I will make sure that last comment is included word for word in the transcript. Would you care to ask them to repeat what you just said before I answer those statements? No, oh good.
Let me answer. I never wear skirts shorter than this one. My desk has a modesty panel so no-one can look up my skirt when I sit down. I trained at a deportment school to stand correctly. That certificate is in my top drawer if you want to see it.

I wear a two-button jacket which I am sure you are aware should only be buttoned up on the top button. If it is very cold, I wear a woollen blazer, with a white cotton shirt and a heavy scarf. If that becomes too hot in the office, I take it off and button the shirt up to the neck. This is always done facing my desk where nobody can see my ample bosom. And I wear stilettos. Well Sir, so do most of the female staff and I am fairly sure that your wife wore them to the Christmas party.

I am just wondering if you have anything relevant to say, or do I just leave now? When all is said and done, you offered me thirty minutes and you have wasted twenty of them already."

"Jane, the concern is that you are obviously testing the waters in the office since your separation, and you are making the other staff uncomfortable."

"Well Sir, for you and the other partners let me be very clear. I do not need this office to organise a root for me. I am capable of that outside the office environment, and everyone in my sphere at the Company is married or with a partner. That does not stop them groping me, brushing against my breasts, or patting my buttocks. Maybe I will just call their wives and have a friendly discussion, girl to girl.

So, Sir, let's end the bullshit. I gave you a list of my complaints which you seem keen to ignore. I expect that all staff will be told that this sexual contact stops immediately.

I have also told you that I have several months of accrued leave that I plan to take. If you check Addendum 4 to my documents, you will see the charged billings issued from your office for my work. When you check, you will find that I am doing forty percent of the work in an office with seven lawyers. You will also see that my success rate, even though I am working my arse off for you, is the highest in the office.

As of Monday, I will be away from the office for an indeterminate time.

It will be at least six months, it could be twelve months, and on the other hand I may not come back at all. If I return to London, I will advise you, and you will have two weeks to notify me that you have accepted the details in the attached contract.

Addendum 5 is a list of fifteen other major companies, all your competitors, that I am sure will gladly employ me to take your clients. And in case you missed the period I will be away; I will be returning after the exclusivity clauses of my current contract run out."

She looked around at the other imaginary Partners of the Company and said, "Any questions? Good. Get that transcript to me today and make sure it is accurate."

James sat back in his chair with his mouth agape. "Jane, you bloody scared me. If you handle their questions like that, they will be calling for oxygen. They may tell you to not even bother contacting them on your return, but they will be in no doubt what the rules are if you do return. Have you sent those addendums to them? Yes, I know that technically I should say Addenda but that sounds a bit stupid. Can you prove you do forty percent of the work in an eight-person office? How did you get the billings report, and how far does it stretch back?"

"Yes, Yes, and Yes. It stretches back three years. I know how to scare people when I need to. I went to the junior staffer in the Billings Department, and I told her I had been nominated for an award by the Law Society, and that it would be presented by the Queen.

It was essential that I had the information for my speech, and it was also essential that it remain confidential. Nobody must know about it. I told her that by Royal edict the Queen would invite the Partners of Smith Clyde and Farrow and other senior London Legal Officers to the Palace.

I went back to her on Wednesday and told her the presentation had been delayed for at least six months, due to my mother's illness. She has sworn to tell no-one about the research, under threat of gaol for breaching Royal Confidence."

"Gee-zus Jane, you really do scare me at times. You realise you were sensational today, don't you?"

"Yes, I was good and so were you. Do we need a refresher tomorrow, or is that enough?"

"Listen, if you deal with them like you did with me, you will scare the gargoyles off the fucking building. You don't need any further training; I can assure you."

There was an awkward silence before James asked, "Would you like to go for a little tour around the neighbourhood, and we will call into the Crooked Billet and make a booking for a meal tonight. It is right next to Friar Park, which is owned by the most eccentric old bugger in the town, but the Crooked Billet is a fabulous little place. If you have a warm coat, I suggest you wear it. We could walk there tonight, but it will be cold walking home. We could enjoy a few drinks and discuss some of the water under the bridge since the university days. The place is quaint and very discreet.

It's something of a hangout for some of the current batch of singers. I've seen Mick Jagger, Keith Richards and George Harrison, and several others at that restaurant. The booking desk always requests that you must not be seen to recognise anybody, or they'll ask you to leave. The selling point for the artists is that they can relax and have a private night with friends.

Mick once said hello to me, and it shocked me so much I asked him if Cliff would be there as well. He looked at me for a couple of seconds with a puzzled expression and said, "Be careful what you call him. His name is Keith Richards; if you call him Cliff you are likely to get a guitar smashed over your head."

Jane said that she was delighted she had come to Henley. She wasn't sure whether her answers were too harsh, but she was sick of the rubbish in the office, and she felt it had to be dealt with. He assured her, "Your answers were perfect; so long as you realise the Partners might decide that as good as you are, they can do without you. Just so long as you realise that is a possibility, I would tell you to answer their questions like you answered mine. And if the whole thing collapses, take your holiday and then contact those on whichever addendum it was. Either they fit in with your request, or you go! Do not make a stand and then back-pedal.

James took her for a drive in the Jaguar, and they roamed around the beautiful countryside looking at the cottages and gardens. They went to the River Thames to see where the Royal Regatta was rowed.

They crossed the famous bridge on foot so they could look up the river. Jane slipped her arm through James' arm, and he reached around her waist. They walked along the rivers edge, and found the tunnel that went under the houses to allow the lower classes to get to the river in days of yore. Halfway through the tunnel Jane kissed him lightly on the cheek and thanked him for being so caring. James gently held her head in his hands and kissed her passionately. Her head was spinning as they came back to the car. They drove out of town to a small hill where they could climb and get a picture postcard view of the perfect English village. James held her close and kissed her again, before laying his head on her breast and crying. "You know what Jane? It is a copious bosom."

She lightly clipped him on the ear, but he snuggled in further and just lay there, listening to her racing heartbeat.

James suggested they should make the booking for the dinner, as it was popular and might already be sold out, being Saturday.

They managed to get a dinner booking, but only because there had just been a cancellation. James went to the car and brought it down to the restaurant. "You will have to walk far enough tonight, so I think we should go home for a warming cup of tea and make sure the fire is set for tonight. By the time we get home we will look forward to warming up in front of a fire."

She wondered if he might try to get her into his bedroom before dinner, but he didn't. James recommended leaving home at about half past five, and back around ten unless some singing started.

He had seen some impressive performances in the Billet, but they were never mentioned in the newspaper.

At five o'clock he checked that she was still happy to walk. "The Jag is there if you prefer to be driven, or we could call a taxi. But a walk will be romantic with a bit of a chill in the air. Perfect snuggling weather."

The Crooked Billet was a wonderful venue for a romantic dinner. It felt like it belonged in the Elizabethan era. The ceilings were low with heavy exposed beams. The meals were solid country cooking; nothing pretentious but beautifully presented on fine china, and with silver cutlery. The place was warm and intimate, with enough privacy to allow conversations, but not enough to block out the ambience of a lovely old-world inn.

They talked about their lives since university, their personal disasters and achievements, and their professional successes. They told silly stories about themselves. By the end of the evening, they were talking about their disappointments in life, and the frustration of being obviously successful yet totally fed-up with not doing anything of worth.

"So, I stopped Coca Cola from closing a corner store. Big deal. And I prevented a new company from claiming that their shoes were so good they made your toes curl in pleasure, because someone else had used the line to sell a milk drink. Bloody hell, how is that worth a fortune?"

"Well, I probably financed some large company so they could afford to destroy a small family trying to develop a company that they saw as a competitor."

Their conversation was getting a bit morbid when James suggested they have a warming scotch and walk home. "It will be cold, but it is only a twenty-minute walk, so we won't freeze to death."

James' home was like a warm sanctuary. The fire had gone out, but the heat was still in the air. The walls were thick, and the roof was thatched heavily to keep in the heat. James raked over the coals and found a few embers still burning so he loaded up the fire with old newspaper to get a flame. Using some kindling, soon there was a blazing fire. A few solid logs and a back log ensured the fire would burn for hours. They settled down on the carpet in front of the fire and watched the flickering flames as they both returned to room temperature. James gently rubbed her neck and kissed the top of her head.

"You know Jane, I had made a pact with myself to never let a woman get through my defences again, but I suspect you are dismantling the barricades pretty quickly."

"Well, let's see what develops. I honestly am not looking for a new husband; the last one left too many scars on my brain to want to go there again."

"Ditto. But bloody hell you are different, you fiery little legal warrior, you."

They lay on the carpet in front of the fire for hours. When they went to bed, they lay side by side in total peace, and both went to sleep.

"My God man, you are a surprise packet. I expected that you would test me out last night with some gentle foreplay, but you didn't do anything. Are we still just friends?"

"Jane, I am in two minds with you. You are the most appealing woman I have met in years, but we have been friends for ever. I don't want to lose you as a friend if we start a relationship and it falters. And anyway, both of us had drunk too much yesterday. I hated the thought that you would wake up this morning and tell me that you felt you had been taken advantage of."

"Well, you are sober now, and I am sober now and I am just about to take my pyjamas off, and you'd better get out of that stuff you are wearing, because I am as horny as hell and I plan to take advantage of you whether you like it or not."

"Gee-zus, I love a direct woman!"

Jane returned to the office on Monday mid-morning to find a large bunch of roses on her desk. She smiled as the crazy thought crossed her mind that it was her boss saying sorry for being such a pig.
They weren't. They were from James, asking her if she would like to come back up to Henley next weekend. He normally did not go home every weekend, but the previous three days had been the most wonderful in living

memory, and he wanted more of the same. She sent a telegram to his office. "Thank you for the offer of further study at Henley, your assistance would be appreciated."

She moved the flowers to a vase at the side of the desk and saw the note from John.

'As per your request, you have an opportunity to discuss your grievance at the Partners meeting on Wednesday at 2.30. I have already had some informal discussion with two of the Partners in relation to your disruptive behaviour in the office during the last month. You are requested to provide a detailed statement of your grievance, how you wish this to be addressed, and any further relevant information. You should expect a detailed verbal examination from the Partners. I have been invited to the meeting, along with two of the male staff that you have made some defamatory remarks about.

John
Manager: Copyright and Trademark Department. SC&F'

Jane knew it was written to create a response. She chose to add it to her documents and not comment.

At 1.30 John phoned to check she had received the memo. She stated that she had.

He asked her if she was still planning to meet the Partners.

"Of course, I am. I am delighted that you and two of your posse will be there too. It will ensure that this office is fully aware of my concerns, and the outcome from the meeting. I look forward to the discussion.

John, might I suggest you speak to Harold Smith on floor two. He is our expert on Defamation Law.

I think he will tell you that the truth is the perfect defence against the claim of defamation. I will bring two colleagues along in case I have to prove what I have said."

"They have not been invited."

"Yes, they have; by me. See you Wednesday John, and please do not call to my office before then. I plan to be very busy clearing my desk before I go on a long, well-earned break."

Jane reviewed her notes and the file that had been sent to each of the Partners. She was grateful that James had been such a tough nut with her. She was prepared to deal with the meeting without fear. If it all went pear-shaped, she would quickly get further employment. She briefly considered talking to News of the World but decided that would not help her prospects of employment if the Partners severed her contract.

She would rely on the fact that female lawyers all over London were being treated poorly, and she could expect outrage if the details became known.

James had been good. The meeting was almost a carbon copy of his dress rehearsal, and she answered each question directly and bluntly.

Mr Farrow was the only Partner with one of the original names. He was the grandson of one of the founders and thought of himself as the head of the Group.

The others did not agree but were happy to let him lead the charge at the meeting.

"Jane, as I see it, you are a relatively young divorcee, working in an office that is mainly men. You dress provocatively and use your feminine charms to gain advancement and then complain if the men comment about your looks. If you dressed conservatively, in a way that did not attract attention, there would be no concerns."

"Mr Farrow, that is disgusting. Tell me, what feminine charms have I used on you, or any of the rest of the Partners to gain advancement? Have I sat on your knee? Have I offered you sex in the bathrooms? Have I shown you my tits? Have I exposed my bottom to you? Of course I have not. I wear business suits made in Saville Row that are discrete and well-tailored. If you want me to wear clothes like the tea lady then tell me, but it might not be appreciated by the people who pay this company tens of thousands of pounds to defend their business.

Read the notes provided to you. I can assure you they are accurate. In a department of eight Lawyers, I generate forty percent of the income. For your information you will see that John, who is the Department boss, is paid twenty percent more than me, and generates eight percent of the work. And his two bodyguards do less than ten percent and earn more than I do.

Mr Farrow; take your blinkers off. If I walk out of this Practice, I will take that work and a whole lot more with me and you and your colleagues will see a massive reduction in Company income."

Andrew Costain had been a Partner for forty years. He could never remember the Partners being spoken to like that by one of the staff.

He started to say that he was disappointed with her tone, but he got two sentences out before Jane said, "Listen, all of you. On Friday I am going away for a prolonged period. Frankly, you can decide whatever you want.

If you want to say goodbye to a large amount of your income, send John down to tell me today, and I will pack my desk and start my break this afternoon. If you want to see how the Department works you will have up to a year to check. When I return from getting a life, you can tell me if you want me to work here. In the file you will see a list of all the relevant major Law firms in this area. I would be happy to work with any of them.

Or maybe I will set up my own firm; "Jane Hampton Law. Where we really do give a damn."

She stormed back to her desk, but her office door did not open all day. She left the office in total silence. 'Good, John has obviously told them how the meeting went.'

As she went past the Reception Desk, she sweetly asked the young lass to phone the Senior Secretary to the Partners to request the transcript of the meeting be on her desk by nine tomorrow morning, so it can be signed for filing.

She went to the Red Lion for a scotch on ice.

Bloody hell, she felt good.

14: Hobart Matriculation College. November 1966.

The planning for the Walk was at a critical stage.

Andrew's knee was causing him little trouble, providing he protected it with the brace, but Julie was adamant that the next 'Homage to the Mountain' would be his last, and she was doing the walk with him.

Andrew decided that the walk should be in term holidays, as it was possible that he would be having some minor surgery to the knee in September. He planned the walk for August, as a penultimate event for a small group of the Leavers, and he would do the walk with Pete Smithies and Sonia Johnstone, who would be co-leaders after this year. The school looked like making it mandatory that if there was a mixed group then there should be at least one female leader. This year there would be two.

Andrew told Julie he would be delighted for her to join the walk, but like everybody else, she would have to carry all her supplies.

They would share a tent, but even then, her pack would weigh more than fifty pounds, and she would have to carry it for at least twelve days. Julie was not fit; she could not carry fifteen pounds for a mile, so there was serious training to do.

He had her fitted with a modern pack with a proper internal frame. She started with two bricks in the pack and began a walking regime in the morning and the evening. With her permission he told the students what she was doing. Andrew instructed each of them to start a fitness programme to carry their packs. He set up a schedule which he copied on the old Gestetner machine in the staff offices. It provided an end of month activity list that every student on the walk had to be able to perform. He would allow a student to slip one month behind schedule, but more than that, the student would be removed from the list. Each student was provided with the list of essential supplies that needed to be available for inspection one week prior to the walk. Every backpack would be emptied at the start of the trip and every item checked off against the list. All waterproofing had to be practiced so that the kit was ready to go.

As the students started the long summer break, Andrew informed them that at the start of Term one everyone would be assessed, and those who were not up to standard would be removed from the programme before it started. He told them that the new rules issued by the Education Department were clear.

Outdoor education was for students who could physically and mentally stand the stress of twelve or more days of very trying conditions.

"I promise you; you will hate me, and you will hate my wife. You will hate Mr Smithies, and you will hate Miss Johnson, but when it is all over you will love everybody. This will prove to you that you can do anything if you prepare properly.

I want all of you to do some serious self-assessment over the summer break.

This is not easy. You will have to determine if you are fit enough. We will try to break you in the weeks leading up to the walk, because once we start, we all must finish, and we cannot have any slackers. You will carry your pack and all your belongings. You will walk with blisters and abrasions. You will eat bushwalking food. You will be filthy; you will probably not wash for two weeks. You will stink. Boys, you will do as you are told. There is no room for heroes, or tough guys. There will be no arguing and there will be no fighting.

Girls, you will have to cope with minimal hygiene. There will be virtually no chance to wash. If you have your period, you must cope with it. There are no dump points, so you carry everything out, and that includes sanitary gear. You take nothing but photographs; you leave nothing but footprints.

And there will be no crying, no matter how hard it gets. The sympathy switch is turned off at the start of the track and will not be turned back on till we are back on the bus.

We will decide early next year whether we walk from the north or the south. You will all be given track notes today, so read them over the break because we will be deciding that when we come back.

At the first briefing session in February, you will have the opportunity to change your mind. We will almost certainly be in temperatures of below zero Celsius, and there are likely to be places with snow up to your hips."

They were all provided with the notes and a guide to a fitness programme to get them started over the holidays.

Andrew started the training for the Homage to the Mountain the same way every time. Better to be blunt and have a few decide to opt out, than get to the stage where they must be told that they are not measuring up.

This year was typical; at the moment there were 45 students signed up to go. By the time the walk started in August there would be about twelve. Many would drop out, and the rest weeded out as they proved to be unfit or unsuitable.

As they headed home Julie asked him, "How elastic are your rules? What if a student cannot afford all the items, as some are very expensive?"

"At the start of term, the process will begin and people having trouble getting the kit together will be invited to talk to me or Pete, and we can assist. We know the ones from financially stressed families so we will talk to them individually.

You and Sonia will be on your first trip, so like the students; you will both need to get the kit together or ask for help."

"Sometimes Andrew you can be a supercilious bastard."

"Yes, I know. I have trained hard at that."

15: The Theatre Royal.

The Theatre Royal was the oldest working theatre in Australia.

It was designed as a Music Hall Theatre in the traditions of the grand theatres of England and catered for all kinds of live performances.

The Hobart establishment loved their theatre and attended modern plays, musical comedies, local productions and visiting Theatre Companies at the Theatre Royal. Shakespeare was regularly performed there as well.

When a local production "in the grand traditions of English Music Hall" advertised for performers, Mary suggested Marcus try out as a magician. He was reluctant, but Bill Adams assured him he could easily perform at a professional level, and "it will be good for you psychologically to put yourself out there; get the buzz from blind-siding an audience."

The audition was a breeze, although the producer said that his close one-on-one acts would not work on a stage.

He suggested Marcus come back with a few grand illusions in a couple of weeks, but he had a spot on the bill if he could do that.

The toughest part of the preparation was making the magician's equipment. He needed a magician's table, the stage props to allow him to disappear, and a high revving chainsaw that would not cut. He bought some flash powder for his fingers, so they would throw short flames when he clicked his fingers, and some flash paper that exploded with a tiny flame. He contacted Dr Slash, as he now called Dr Bill Adams, and asked for help. Bill called in some mates for the construction work, and to help him source the props. Mary and one of the smaller framed nurses agreed to be the magician's assistants.

"Marco the Magician" was a hit. He was able to disappear and reappear at the back of the hall, he levitated his assistant and then himself, and then cut her in half with a chainsaw before magically having her reappear. For effect he made sure there was some blood on her clothes. He had the audience totally enthralled. When one of them called out that he knew what Marcus was doing, he just smiled and replied that he knew that he did not. With a flourish he invited the fellow on stage, handed him the wand and said, "Now disappear." The audience roared laughing and the fellow resumed his seat without further interruption.

At the closing of the curtain on opening night, the audience clapped vigorously till the curtain rose for the curtain call. Marco the Magician was greeted to a wild cheer and a call for more.

It is almost impossible to add a further grand magic act to an encore, but during the acknowledgement bows he waved the wand, wrapped himself in his cape, clicked some flash paper, and in the smoke, he disappeared. There was a roar from the audience.

Mary was waiting off-stage. Her eyes were wet from tears of joy and pride as she told him he truly was magnificent.

"I just can't wait for tomorrow when I can do it all again." Every night was better than the previous one. He felt that every part of the act was more professional, and all the moves became slicker with practice. Other members of the cast watched closely and still could not work out how the tricks were done. There was no way that Marcus would tell them; they were the rules of the Magic Circle Club and Marcus was a paid-up member.

Bill was right; there were magic healing powers in being a magician, and Marcus believed he could have walked on water during the theatre season.

The newspaper gave a rave review of his performance as a highlight of a fabulous night of gala theatre. Marcus was elated. Even the small error he made with the chainsaw act had not been noticed; Bill's advice to make sure if something does not go exactly to plan, that it can always be covered if the magician shows no surprise and incorporates it into the act. Nobody noticed the stumble as he added a small skip to the rest of his movements.

The season went for two weeks, and Marcus never faulted once. At the end of the season the producer was quick to ask if he would be available next year.

"Not sure of my plans yet. But I really enjoyed that. I will keep in touch."

Mary asked him to consider doing it again the next year as she could see how much he enjoyed it. "Darling, if they were paying me I certainly would, but it is an amateur show. Some of the things I would like to do would need a decent sum of money for the props and the construction and we can't afford that at the moment. There is no way that I would come back next year and just repeat what I have just done. I will see what happens, but I got a real buzz out of the show and if possible, I would love to do some bigger and better illusions next year."

Hellfire

16: Leuven. November 1966.

University studies were going well.

Marine and Katrien were about to start the examinations at the end of the semester. They had some casual work to go towards funding their big trip, but they knew they were not going to have enough money for their planned adventure. They had decided they would work hard through the Christmas break then put a downscaled plan to their parents and ask for a loan. They both knew that their parents had never asked for a loan to be repaid and would be unlikely to ask for it back this time, but at least they were trying to be responsible.

The exams went well. The culling process saw a significant number of students removed from the course for not reaching the academic standard, but Katrien and Marine were in the top five percent. There was no risk that they would lose their placement if they kept studying hard. The breaks were designed for students to have some free time, and they planned to have a few nights on the town. Katrien invited Marine to visit Antwerp for two weeks before Christmas and then return to Brussels by train just in time for Christmas Day.

202

They were busy planning a night out when Lucas came home from work. He told Marine that he had been talking to her father by phone, and Frederick had suggested that it might be better if Marine only stayed one week. He had arranged a good job for her, and Christmas week paid very well in the retail industry. "It will get you at least a good start to your travel fund."

Katrien was not happy, but her father told her he had arranged work for her with the same company in the shopping centre in Antwerp.

"Dad, have you two been talking and planning this?"

"Well of course. Frederick is an accountant, and he searched around for work amongst his contacts. He found both jobs."

"For goodness sake Dad, we have just finished some really hard exams. We need a break."

"Then have one, girls; but cancel your plans for overseas travel. The gravy train stops at Leuven station unless you fund the airfares.

Frederick and I have decided that you must be able to fund the complete airfares and then we will arrange a bank loan for the rest. You will have to repay it by continuing to work these jobs until all your costs are met. We will provide modest spending money, but that will be the limit of our involvement financially with the trip."

"Oh, Dad, that is unfair."

Really. Well, I can't speak for Frederick and Emma, but your mother and I have never been outside Europe.

We have been paying for all you kids to achieve your dreams. We are proud of you and what you are doing with your studies, but if you want outlandish trips you will have to learn to pay for them."

Marine started to object, but Lucas told her that Frederick had purchased her train ticket, and it was in the mail. He had arranged it for Saturday, so she would be ready to start work on Monday. "Hema has agreed to provide you with uniforms and paid training for three days from Monday. You will work from eight o'clock till six o'clock. Hema is entitled to pay you youth wages because you are temporary student workers, but because of Frederick's contacts you will receive the full adult salary. They will expect an adult work ethic, so get used to it."

As he walked away, he said that they should discuss just one destination, as the airfare would be substantially less than what they were planning.

The next day the ticket turned up in the mail, so obviously Lucas was not joking.

They were heart broken. How dare their parents destroy their dream holiday, when everyone knew study was about to become much harder, and there was little chance of a significant time away over the next five years. "It is just not fair Marine, and I hate that they have discussed us behind our backs. They should have at least been brave enough to talk it over with us before they decided."

Two hours later they went to Antwerp to collect brochures for the USA, South Africa, and Australia. It was the first time they realised how much impact the exchange rate had on the air ticket prices.

Australia was much cheaper than the USA and Africa was cheaper still, but they were told it was not safe for two pretty white girls at the moment. The Prime Minister had recently been assassinated and there was white versus white and white versus black fighting. All the Republics around South Africa were in turmoil and young white females were definitely seen as easy targets for robbery, rape and murder. "Seriously girls, I would leave South Africa out of your plans for now."

They decided that they would look at the brochures, but probably go to the USA because there were more things to do. Marine had lived in Boston for a year and loved it, and they both knew nothing about Australia. "I can speak Dutch, French and English. I don't think I can learn Australian as well while we are studying medicine."

"Actually Katrien, they speak a version of English. It is a bit like your Flemish Dutch, nobody in the Netherlands understands a word you say, but it doesn't take much for you to make yourself known. Australians have a lot of strange words, but once they slow down the accent becomes softer, and you can understand them. I had a couple of friends in Boston from Australia, and they were good fun.

They have some very cute animals and apparently some great cities and some very hot boys, if the ones in Boston were typical."

"Wow Marine, how well did you get to know them?"

"Stop it. I was an exchange student. We signed a pledge of no drinking, no drugs and no dating.
I stuck to it. But I won't say I wasn't tempted. One of them was drop-dead gorgeous."
They read all the brochures about South Africa but decided to accept the advice to not go there. Katrien told her family that they were no longer interested in going to South Africa because it was too dangerous, and Lucas just nodded and said he agreed with their decision. "The newspapers are full of horrible stories about South Africa, and the violence is getting worse. And frankly the United States is getting worrying as well.
The students are becoming unruly and the anti-Vietnam rallies are becoming dangerous. The race riots in the South is a powder keg ready to explode. Frankly, I would give that a miss at the moment too."

"So, are you telling us to go to Australia then?

"Well actually, no. On your budget I would suggest Paris for a weekend and then home to work, but that is probably not your choice."

"For goodness sake Dad, this is ridiculous. Marine and I will go to the pub and go through the brochures and make some decisions."

"All right then but remember every beer you drink will need thirty minutes work at Hema to refill the piggybank so don't be silly."

"Dad, sometimes I think you enjoy being a killjoy."

17: Snug: December 1966.

Colin used his TV segment very effectively.

He encouraged people to clean up around their houses, he warned them that if the days remained dry and the winds continued to blow, that all of Tasmania would have a nightmare bushfire with just one lightning strike, or an arsonist. He certainly did not expect the surge of people claiming that he was destroying the natural environment, or the number visiting their local politicians to demand that the clearing had to stop. Eric Reece called him into the Parliamentary Offices to tell him that there was some concern that the warnings were being exaggerated, and that the consensus of the Parliament was that although it was necessary to keep the population alert, his warning was starting to create panic.

"Eric, if a fire breaks out in any forested area of this state in the next four months, we will not have the capacity to control it. The result will be catastrophic. I would rather frighten them now, than bury them then."

"Point taken Colin, but just ease up on the severity of your predictions.

I am not sure you are making any discernible difference by scaring people to a level where they can't sleep."

Colin checked the trees on his access road and decided he would cut back all the dangerous trees and the ones overhanging the road. He wanted to be able to get out with his family in the event of a forest fire. It would make a very sensible segment on his next TV segment to show some proactive clearing to reduce fuel in case of a major fire. He organised a training exercise with his crews and their trucks to cut the branches and the clear the tinder dry rubbish around the trunks at ground level. He made sure TVT6 was there to film it as a news story, and to get enough footage to highlight his next fifteen-minute segment. Within thirty minutes of it going to air on the evening news he received a phone call telling him that legal action was being taken against him for destroying native vegetation and using publicly owned vehicles without permission or valid reason. By the next morning, he had received a court order to cease and desist the clearing unless there was specific consent signed by both the Minister and the Premier

Colin called his fire crews together and told them there would be a major drill on the Domain with a simulated emergency on Saturday morning. All fire trucks would be called to attend under lights and sirens. He wanted them to coordinate their schedules to make as much disruption as possible to the Saturday morning traffic flow.

If the politicians and the judges were not prepared to listen to reason, then a demonstration of the potential disruption of an emergency would make some people take notice.

All hell broke loose after the emergency drill. Colin was called in to Police Headquarters for not getting permission for the Drill.

"Listen," he said "when we have a big fire this summer, and we will have at least one, I am not running in here to ask your permission to put the fire trucks on the road. If you don't like it, too bloody bad." The politicians were angry, and the local paper called for his head.
Colin went home and cut down another tree.

Marcus was finding the Fire Service a real challenge, but he absolutely adored Colin. This was a man who behaved like a military commander. When a job had to be done, the risks were investigated and mitigated where possible, and then he sent his men in to do the job. He would attempt to walk on water if Colin requested it, and Colin recognised that Marcus was the kind of recruit that every commander needs. He was fearless, a master tactician and a man who instantly saw the strengths and weaknesses of a planned fire-fighting event.
Colin quickly promoted him and told him he needed him to get into training to become brigade captain. It was still a voluntary posting, but he was assured if he wanted to be a salaried fire fighter that could be expedited almost immediately.
Marcus decided his CV was looking better. He could kill efficiently and quietly; he could perform as a reasonable magician and now he was a half-decent fire fighter. Life was looking up.

He was assigned to the volunteer brigade at Glenorchy. It wasn't too far from home if he was called to an emergency, but the group was undermanned and had a large area of forested hills skirting the city and along the Derwent towards New Norfolk, as well as up the major road heading North. Both areas had low populations so there was no effective fire service other than those along the outer border of Hobart. Some of those areas were of real concern. The areas around Bridgewater had a high crime rate, and it was not that far to the new Prison at Risdon Vale. It was set amongst heavily forested areas. A fire there could reduce Tasmania's prison population very quickly or set them loose if it caused a break in the perimeter fence. Neither option was good.

Colin asked Marcus to have a drive around the area and check potential fire risks. "Go up the Highway for twenty miles or so and put a plan together of what we need. We will not get it yet, but at least it can go on the shopping list. I would particularly like a Station and Fire crew out there somewhere, but it is difficult to convince the authorities because every public structure is broken into on a regular basis. The little pricks break into schools and work depots to steal anything not firmly secured."

Marcus stopped in Bridgewater for a Coke and a sandwich.

As he came out of the milk bar there was a group of teenagers around his car. "Nice car mate. Can you give it a rev as you take off? Let's hear if it roars."

Marcus obliged.

Colin headed into the television company for his weekly broadcast, prepared to reinforce his view that the city was at high risk and that everybody needed to clean around their properties.

By the time he got home his wife had received three phone calls. The Premier wasn't happy; the chief of Police wasn't happy, and the environment idiots were making threats.

Linda was waiting for Colin when he got home., "Listen to me; sit down. This has to stop. I am getting harassed continuously, and if you are not careful you will be stood down from your job. Premier Reece phoned today, and he could barely control his temper. I told him we were going on holidays for three weeks from tomorrow. I made a phone call to put us on the boat to Melbourne and we are going somewhere. I don't care where; but you will not be on duty. You will not be inspecting stations, or checking on fire readiness, or anything else. If you say no, then OK it is no. For you. But the kids and I will be on that boat, and I will cancel the return ticket."

Colin was about to speak, but he could see Linda was at breaking point. He phoned headquarters and said he had a family emergency, and he would be away for three weeks. They could sort out rosters and preparations, as well as the television spot.

He went to the bedroom and packed a suitcase, threw in his bathers and goggles, and left it open on the floor. He took off his clothes and clambered into bed. Lying there as rigid as a statue, he started to shake.

Twenty minutes later he was in a cold shiver and was sobbing uncontrollably. He noticed Linda come to bed sometime later, but never moved till daybreak. He got up and had a shower and made a strong cup of tea. He went out to the front verandah to watch the day light up his city. His sense of foreboding just got stronger, but he would follow Linda's direction. They would head north to Surfers Paradise and have a few days away from everything. He intended to return to Hobart just before Christmas, so the kids could enjoy Santa at home.

He decided to spend the day putting up the Christmas tree and shifting the family pets up to his brother's home at Hamilton. He told everybody to have their stuff packed so he could load up the car when he got home. "One more sleep, and then we will go to Devonport to catch the Princess. We are going to have an adventure, starting tomorrow morning."

18: Melbourne. December 1966.

Lizzie and Alison had finished the semester.

Both of the girls achieved Distinctions and High Distinctions in all subjects. They were able to relax knowing had a two-month break before the critical third year of study. At the end of 1967 they would receive their Bachelor of Arts Degrees, but both intended a further year of study to complete their Diploma of Education, where they would learn the skills to transfer their knowledge to students in the classroom. It was a common belief that with the conclusion of the second year, the end was in sight and some of the tension went. Well, they didn't feel it. Alison was tired, and another two years seemed like forever.

"I should have followed Dad's advice and been a hairdresser. I would now have a car and an income. I could be enjoying life instead of studying my arse off and getting nowhere."

Lizzie just laughed and told her to lighten up.

"Why don't we have a talk to Anne and see if the house at Cheviot Beach is available for a few days? A swim and a surf would do us the world of good. We haven't had much time with her in the last few weeks."

The girls went to the Union building at the University to check for some casual work over the summer. There wasn't much on offer, but they filled in an application form and headed down Swanston Street towards the train station. The Toc H Tavern was a favourite spot for university students; it wasn't likely that many students would be there, as the main courses had finished for the year, and most of the students left the area like cockroaches when the lights came on. They decided to have a glass of Cold Duck and a packet of crisps and then go looking for Anne. She was probably back in Ballarat, so it might take a phone call. On the off-chance, Alison decided to use the red phone in the pub and try the number at the beach house. It was worth a try, as Anne had told them that she sometimes went down on her own for some peace and quiet at the end of term. Her family normally headed to the beach after Boxing Day for a couple of weeks, and the beach house was just bedlam.

Anne answered the phone on the third ring. She had been at Cheviot for a week and was considering going home because she was feeling a bit lonely. When Alison told her that she and Lizzie were thinking of coming down, Anne offered to come to Melbourne and get them.

"It takes all day to get here by train and bus, and that only gets you to Sorrento anyway. I have my car with me, so it won't take long."

They arranged to be picked up in the later part of the afternoon, as they both needed to go home and throw some clothing and personals in a suitcase.

Alison volunteered to pick up her stuff from home and then come back to Port Melbourne, which would mean that Alison did not need to drive through the city in heavy traffic.

Lizzie grabbed her mother's shopping cart, and she went to the shops for some essential groceries, as food prices at the beach in summer were very expensive. She picked up a bottle of suntan lotion and a large straw hat. She looked at a new bathing suit, turned over the price ticket and put it back. It was outside her budget so her old one would have to do. For a moment she considered buying a packet of condoms just in case, but she was too embarrassed. Everyone in Port knew her and her family. If it looked like that might happen, she would get some in Sorrento where nobody knew her. She returned home, packed a small bag, and waited for Alison and Anne to arrive. Alison took the train to the city, caught the Port Melbourne train, got off at North Port and had a short walk to Lizzie's house on Ross Street. She arrived at quarter past four, not wanting to be too early as Lizzie's father made her feel uneasy. She didn't dare say that she felt he was mentally undressing her, because she knew that could end the friendship. It was just easier to be cautious.

Anne turned up about five o'clock, so they all bundled into the car and headed to Cheviot Beach. It was starting to get dark as they passed through Sorrento. Anne stopped and bought some pizza and a couple of bottles of Fosters.

"You gotta have beer with pizza, according to my dad," Anne said, as she came back to the car.

It did not take long to get to the beach-house, where the two girls dropped their bags, had some pizza and some beer. The three of them sat in the lounge chairs around the television, and all feel asleep. It was still relatively early when they all headed off to bed.

It was a typical December morning when they woke. The temperature was already in the eighties and the sun was blazing from a clear blue sky. The waves were gentle, and the sunlight ripples on the ocean were stunningly beautiful. Alison stood at the window of the kitchen to make some toast. She watched Harold Holt and his bevy of young admirers playing on the beach. They all went in for a swim, with a lot of splashing and laughter, and seemingly innocent fun. Well, it would be innocent if they were his daughters and all about ten years younger, but it seemed a bit inappropriate.

She was waiting for the kettle to boil when he came out of the water to towel off. She watched him and one of the young women go out of sight over the sand dunes. "None of my business," she said to herself.

"What is none of your business, Alison?"

"Anne, I was just watching the Prime Minister heading into the sand dunes with someone who is definitely not his wife."

"You will see that every morning when he is down here. Dad says he doesn't care, so long as he keeps running the country the right way; what he does in his private life is a matter for him and Zara."

Lizzie planned to get up early to see what happened if she was on the beach when he turned up the next morning. She went for an early swim but kept her head out of the water. She did not want daggy hair. Her bathers clung to her body just enough to let a passerby get a good look at her well-toned youthful body.

Harold came down to the beach with his bodyguards. As he walked past, he told her that she should come in for a swim.

"I already have. It was great."

"You should come in again. We have a lot of fun in the water."

She dropped her towel and headed to the ocean with four other girls. The bodyguards went for their morning coffee as per instructions.

The girls were splashing Harold and giggling, so Lizzie joined in. Harold told them it was time for porpoise diving, so as he stood with his legs open, the girls dived between his legs . Lizzie took her turn and Harold dipped enough so she gently brushed against his crotch. He laughed and told her that she was a bit naughty. He then dived through her legs and his hands gently touched her as he went through. She thought that it was no accident. She decided that was enough and as she left the water, he followed her. "You should see the wildflowers up here in the dunes," he said.

Two others were going with him so she thought not much could happen.

Once out of sight, the girls dropped the tops of their bathing suits and Harold caressed their breasts. Lizzie watched for a short period and started to walk away. "I will give you a hundred dollars if I can lick your boobies, little darlin'. Nothing else, just a taste of those lovely puppies."

It was easier than a week at work, she thought. He spent a couple of minutes sucking on her breasts , telling her that she was lovely and to pick up the money off his beach towel. Lizzie was embarrassed as she told Alison what had happened at the beach.

"My God, I am not sure if that is prostitution, but it was dead easy money. He made me feel a bit squeamish, but if that is all you must do to get a hundred dollars it is pretty bloody easy."

The next morning, they went down together, and they both earned a hundred dollars. This time however, he told one of the others to stay behind. He really needed a shag, and a bit of young blood would tune him up for the day. He had to go into Melbourne for a meeting that would bore him witless, but a bit of pussy beforehand would get him through the day. Alison and Lizzie decided that was a bit too close, so they stayed away from the beach in the mornings for the rest of the time down at the beach. On the way home Alison said quietly to Lizzie, "I wonder what he paid her. It certainly could not be included in the standard one hundred dollars, could it?"

They got back to Port Melbourne at four o'clock. Anne said she was going to drive home to Ballarat, as her mother had phoned and told her to be home for dinner.

Alison started to arrange her bags to walk back to the station, but Mrs Ainsworth said she should stay the night and go home in the morning. "Lizzie talks about you all the time, but we really have not had a chance to get to know you. There is a separate room at the front you can use. I am cooking a roast meal and then we can have a talk for a while."

Dinner went well, and the conversation was about the girls and their ambitions. They had become such close mates over the two years that their plans had melded to being almost identical. They had decided that at the end of their first year of teaching they would go to London during the Christmas holidays, and they talked about that incessantly. London was the hub of music and fashion, and modern culture. They planned to go to Carnaby Street and buy something; a handbag would be perfect if it had the Beatles on it. They wanted to see a concert with the Beatles or the Rolling Stones; and they wanted to go to Buckingham Palace. Alison excused herself and said she was tired. She planned to catch an early train home tomorrow, as she needed to check with her parents if anyone had been in contact about some work over the summer.

The front verandah was fully enclosed with good thick curtains, but it was hard up against the footpath of Ross Street. She was a bit concerned about intruders, so she locked the door and turned off the light. The room had enough space for a single bed and a small bedside cabinet. She pushed her bag under the bed, but it would not quite fit.

She turned on the light to see what was going on. Under the bed were several boxes of Hecla electric blankets. 'My God' she thought, 'they are probably stolen. Who knows, someone might be due to pick them up tonight.' She rechecked the door was securely locked before returning to bed.

About two o'clock in the morning she was woken by a noise outside the room. "Let me in, sweetie. I've got some booze, and we can have a bit of fun before Faye wakes up." She could hear Gus, as drunk as a goose at her door. She did not move but made her breathing as shallow as possible and waited for him to go away. Eventually he staggered away. She heard him kick a chair in the hallway and curse loudly. She heard the fridge door open and the gentle fizz as the top was taken off another bottle of beer. Alison got out of bed and got dressed. She decided to wait till daybreak before going to the railway station for the first train to the city. She would make up a story for Lizzie, but there was no way that she would ever stay there again, unless the lecherous old bastard died.

She thought to herself that if "an accident" happened at the wharf that got rid of him, she would have to fake tears for Lizzie's sake, but she would not miss him one bit. 'Harold is just a gentleman with a sex fetish. Gus, the bastard, is just horrible,' she thought.

19: London.

The transcripts were on her desk when she
arrived at work.

Jane read them as she would any legal documents.
She checked that the transcript was accurate, that there
were no spelling or grammatical mistakes, and there were
no areas where misinterpretation could occur,
intentionally or unintentionally.
Finally, she read it again to be certain that her complaints
were all recorded, that the inappropriate questions and
answers from the Partners were all recorded; and that her
demands to correct the issues were included. Finally, she
checked that the options she had given for the future were
all in the document.

Jane called in her secretary to witness the signing of
both copies. She dated both and asked for one copy to be
returned to the Senior Secretary on the Partners' floor and
the other one to go to the filing office, to be filed as
"Conflict Resolution, December 1966."
Her workload came in as normal, and her day progressed
as if nothing had happened.

John walked in and said, "Good morning, Jane." He walked to his office without further comment.

Jane decided to get a coffee before she went to her desk. She half expected everything to be boxed up, but it wasn't. Her desk was exactly as she had left it the night before. The in-tray was bulging with new correspondence from the mail office.

She had been working on a file for a commodity trader that felt the corporate image was being invaded by a competitor when the phone rang. She picked it up and the voice at the other end said she was the Senior Secretary to the Partners. "Just checking whether your correspondence needs any specific code before filing."

"No. You file it anyway you like, just so long as you can find it if necessary."

"Okay, no problem. Thanks Jane." The line went dead.

"Well that was a bit weird," she said.

"What was?" asked John.

"I was talking to myself, John, but if you must know, the signed transcript was returned to the Partners' floor, and I get the distinct impression that they are making out that the meeting never occurred."

"The Partners decided that it was an aberration, and it was best if nothing was acted on until you had a chance to cool down," John said as he headed back to his office.

Jane phoned James to confirm that she was going up to Henley on Friday, then she called in the stenographer.

She dictated a letter to John, carbon copy to the Partners' secretary, outlining that, as per her statement at the Partners' meeting, she would commence indeterminate leave from Friday at one o'clock.

Her return to the Company would be no sooner than six months and no later than twelve months, following a meeting with the Partners in relation to all matters discussed at the meeting Wednesday last. She told the stenographer to conclude the letter with "Get fucked, Jane." The stenographer looked aghast. Jane told her she was joking, and to just finish it with the normal pathetic "Yours truly," and bring it back for signing today before five o'clock.

Jane worked through the week and at one o'clock on the Friday, she put a note on her desk that said, "Over to you, John;" picked up her personal possessions and her handbag and left the office. As she passed through the outside door it occurred to her that this might be the last time. 'So be it', she thought.

A line in the sand has been drawn, and I will only come back over it on my terms.

As she reached her car, she started to laugh. This was the first time for years that she was not going home with a satchel of files to work on over the weekend. Sure, she had not spent much time on the files last weekend; James had been a pretty serious distraction, but today she did not even have any files with her. Those files felt like they weighed fifty pounds, although it was probably closer to five.

The extra weight was just the amount of effort that was required every bloody weekend to plough through the mountains of meaningless rubbish. She could not remember the last time one of her wins meant anything to anyone other than some corporate bastard feathering his nest. She had no idea what she was going to do for a while, but it was going to be purely for her pleasure.

It was just on one o'clock as she left the carpark. Even that made her smile. 'I pinched a few minutes off the lousy bastards by leaving earlier than I told them.' She wondered if John put his head around the door to wish her well, or to tell her he was disappointed that she was being so bloody minded. She didn't care.

With a bit of luck next week, he won't be able to look over the mountain of paperwork that lands on his desk now that she has gone.

She drove straight to James' home at Henley; she retrieved the key from under the hollowed-out stone in the front garden, and let herself in. She had seen James do that when they came home from the Crooked Billet the previous weekend. She lit the fire and made a cup of tea. James would not be home for a few hours, she thought. She then remembered that there had not been an answer to her message to him that she was coming up, so she hoped he was aware she planned to be there that weekend.

Jane got herself a glass of riesling from the refrigerator and settled down with a couple of dry biscuits and cheese. Anticipating several hours to herself, she ran a warm bath and soaked for what seemed an eternity.

She could not remember the last time she had nothing to do. She got out of the bath and dried herself with one of his man-sized towels and snuggled naked into the bed. It was warm in the house with the fire going, and she planned to stay awake and surprise him when he arrived. Instead, she fell off to sleep and did not even hear the door open. James looked in the bedroom and saw her there, with her clothes in a neat pile on the floor. It was tempting to just slide in next to her, but she looked so peaceful, he decided she needed to have a sleep. He had been given the message that she was heading up to his home, but when he phoned her office at five to one John had sounded really annoyed that he couldn't find her. 'Well not to worry,' thought James, 'I will see her tonight.' He quietly closed the bedroom door to avoid disturbing her and started cooking an evening meal. Chicken was always a safe option when you are not sure of the dietary habits of your guest. He loved steak but there are a million ways to cook steak and people tend to be very fussy. He decided that an Italian-styled chicken dish in a strong tomato-based sauce with fresh vegetables steamed al dente should be acceptable. He had stopped in town and picked up a tub of real gelato. A delightful little Italian restaurant had just opened in town. They only catered for dinner, but served coffee and cake during the day, and had a dozen varieties of gelato to have at the table or to take home. James chose a mix of strawberry and lemon. He bought some fresh strawberries from the grocer in the same block. One or the other, or both, would hit the mark.

The chicken casserole had an hour left when James went into check on Jane. She smiled at him and asked if he had time for an entrée, while easing back the bedclothes so he could see she was naked. "Of course. The chicken is on simmer and you look like you are too. I will turn the chicken to low and hopefully you to full on as soon as I get back." James put some soft music on low as he set the stereo to repeat; He slipped into the bed next to her. "Dinner can wait for as long as it takes," he thought as he gently touched her shoulders and slid his hands down her back.

Dinner was well done by the time it was served, but it was delicious. They ate the gelato in front of the blazing fire; Jane could feel the tension of the last week just easing away. James kissed her on top of the head and asked her what her immediate plans were.

"I hope you are not going to run away on your quest to discover yourself too soon. I am enjoying my quest to discover you and I don't want it to finish any time soon." Jane told him about the weird way the week had finished, and he told her about his conversation with her boss.

"I really think they are in total denial, Jane. They seem to think that you will be back at your desk on Monday, as if nothing has happened."
Jane told him she had consolidated some of the plans of the overseas trip,

"I mean to travel to Africa, and Australia and South America. I want to go to New York and Niagara Falls. I want to wander without any real plans.

I want to have a few months where nothing is planned; I want to be excited, and fearful, and scared shitless. I want to be reckless.

I really want to go to that place in Tasmania where they grow the wool for my favourite clothes. Mind you, I won't be able to afford that with limited income."

"I am half inclined to take some time away from the bank and join you for at least some of the trip; I can't remember the last time I took any more than a few days away from the bank. I must have several months of accrued holidays, but I am not sure I can do it right now. There is too much happening in my office at that moment."

"Well, the Bank has survived nicely without you for two hundred years and will probably not fold up if you are away for a few weeks."

Jane was shocked to realise that she would find it difficult to go overseas without him. Life had taken some very strange turns in the last fortnight, but the strangest of all was finding that she could not live happily without James, who, until two weeks before, had been a buddy that she enjoyed having a drink with after work. Now he was a lover she wanted to be with constantly.

"Let's just enjoy the weekend, and I will have a look at potential time off on Monday when I am back in the office. It would be fun, but I am not as brave as you; I would absolutely need to know what holidays I had available and when I would be returning to the office."

"Well, on Monday I am going to call in to Australia House and some travel agencies to check a few options.

I may have to apply for a new passport, because I don't want to have to rush back to England to renew it, so it will be a few weeks before I can go anywhere really. I want an open ticket if possible so I can move on when I am ready and stay in one place for a while if I find somewhere I love."

James realised that gave him plenty of time to assess his options as well. He was a little frightened to attach himself too strongly to Jane. His ex-wife had kicked him in the guts so hard it still hurt. He really did not want to experience that level of emotional pain again, and he felt he was falling in love so hard there never was going to be a soft landing if it all went wrong. He just wanted to say, 'Hang on, I am coming with you,' and he knew he could do that if he wanted. He was bored witless at work, but it paid well, and it gave him the lifestyle he wanted. What if he went on extended leave and came back to no job, or the same job but with no real prospects of advancement?

James had the week from hell in front of him; he was negotiating the finance of one of the largest corporate takeovers of the decade. It would see a wholesale change on Fleet Street, with some of the most famous mastheads of the British Press changing ownership if it went ahead. The problem with major rearrangements in the printing industry is that all the assets are privately owned, but Governments and the general population claim rights normally left to the owners. The politicians want to protect the public interest, which means they don't want to see newspapers in the hands of people who don't like their side of politics.

Both sides of politics have that opinion, so that is an argument where there can be no winners. The general public like their chosen paper as is, and do not want to see change. The owners want the best deal; the new buyers want the cheapest deal, and the bank needs to be sure that the financial arrangements are viable into the future.

James knew he would need the wisdom of Solomon. The Bank's Board had done the due diligence, and James was armed with the best the bank could offer, but once in the negotiation room there was no one except him and his associates. They had to make decisions that could earn hundreds of millions of pounds for the Bank or could almost destroy it. He told Jane to get lots of material from the travel agents, so they could plan her trip. In his mind he was thinking that maybe it would be their trip, if the negotiations went well. He stood to receive a bonus worth several years' wages if he worked the numbers correctly.

James warned her that he would be so busy that he might not even be able to call her through the week, but promised he would come and stay with her in the city as soon as he had the negotiations wrapped up. She headed back home after Sunday lunch at the Crooked Billet. She had not managed to see any musicians there, but the thought was intriguing. If she did, she knew it would be difficult not to behave like a dizzy schoolgirl, but she intended to impress James by letting him know she recognised them, without their realising she did.

It was odd knowing that tomorrow was a workday and she was not going to be there.

Would there be any reaction from the office, or would she be cut loose, name removed from her door and never mentioned again? Well, she thought, just like Rhett Butler, 'Frankly my dear, I don't give a damn.'

20: The Boys of Bridgewater

Jake and Roly Sturmer were fifteen-year-old twins.

They were street smart but functionally illiterate. They were enrolled at Bridgewater High School but were seldom there; they were suspended regularly for unruly behaviour in class and if one was on suspension the other one wagged school. They were inseparable. They were described as identical twins but there were differences, Jake was a little taller and Roly has a scar on his left cheek from a knife fight. They wore similar clothes but made sure they were not the same. They were noisy and belligerent on the street, and most of the time had a bruise or a cut from a fight in town. The police quickly realised that the normal rules of dealing with kids on the street were doomed to failure, because home was worse than the street. Their father Jim was in Risdon Prison; in their fifteen years, their father had been home for less than two years, and he was in for a long spell currently. He had been found guilty of manslaughter after killing a fellow during an armed robbery.

The police were livid because as far as they were concerned, it was murder, and the sentence was insufficient. The judge had accepted that Jim's judgement was impaired because he had drunk a bottle of scotch and then decided to hold up a service station to get enough money for more alcohol. He had shot the attendant who tried to take the gun from him. He said he never intended to shoot him. He claimed that the gun wasn't loaded when he put it away, but there must have been one bullet in the barrel. He did not know that the twins went out shooting coke cans at night; they waited till he was too drunk to see or hear anything, then took his gun for some fun in the back paddocks.

The Sturmers' mother "had not been sober since the Second World War" according to the local cops. She was a violent alcoholic. She belted the boys with anything she could get hold of, including a steel fire poker on at least one occasion. They had spent time in foster homes, but it was rare that any foster carer could look after the pair of them, and if they were separated, they were impossible to control. Inevitably they were returned to the family home because there was nowhere else for them.

When they were arrested for breaking into a pharmacy, they were sent to Ashley Youth Detention Centre outside Deloraine for a year, but they managed to escape, stole a car, and drove home. They abandoned it in the middle of the Bridgewater Bridge, where they parked it across both lanes of the highway, locked it, and ran away.

They hid in the scrub over the side of the Bridge and laughed at the havoc they created. The traffic was backed up so tight that a tow-truck struggled to get to the car to take it away.

It was so much fun watching the bedlam, they did not notice the police officers who walked up behind them, put them in a headlock and handcuffed them.

They were sent back to Ashley, but this time to the secured wing.

They had been back on the street for six months when Marcus stopped there in his X2. They were hanging around with their best mate, Toby Marshall, just filling in time. Jake was on suspension for swearing at a teacher and had been warned that the next time, he would be expelled. That did nor concern him much. He planned not to go back to school after Christmas anyway. He wanted to be a mechanic; he could leave school at fifteen if he had an apprenticeship.

Toby was sixteen and lived with his mother in the house across the road from Roly and Jake. He had not been to school all year. His father had gone to Melbourne for work but was arrested for armed bank robbery a few months ago. He was doing ten years at Pentridge, but Toby's mother wasn't concerned much; she had an ever-changing array of males at the house. Toby was old enough to recognise the noises at night.

"She's bonking herself silly while the old man is away. He'll kill her when he gets out," he told the Sturmers.

They heard the growl from the X2 and asked the driver to give it a rev as he left. He did and threw gravel all over them. Toby said that he would love to get behind the wheel of that thing, but it was obviously an out-of-towner driving it, and they would probably not see it again. It was Sunday and not much was open except the corner store. Jake went in the shop to distract the girl behind the counter. He eventually bought a packet of fruit tingles, while his mates loaded up two potato sacks with soft drink bottles. They rode away towards their homes and Jake followed ten minutes later. They helped themselves to a packet of Mrs Sturmers' cigarettes and settled down for a smoke in the open paddock near their home, before riding twenty minutes to another corner store and cashing in the bottles.

It was easy money, but they had to be careful; the cops had warned them that they were in their sights, and they would be the first they would pick up, if anything at all happened in the area. "Okay boys you're all still young enough for another trip to Ashley, and then after that you will be sharing accommodation with your fathers. For Christ's sake, behave yourself for a change."

It had no effect.

21: London

Jane had never bothered to check her bank accounts for years.

She earned a great salary but that was not the point. She was being paid less than layabouts in her office because she was female, and they were male. She had an investment account for her retirement that took twenty percent of her salary and was managed by her accountant. She had thirty percent paid into a high interest earnings savings account, and the other fifty percent was for her regular use. It paid her rent, car, food, and entertainment. Her clothing was an important part of the image of a successful corporate lawyer. She dressed well and paid accordingly.

She was surprised to see she had nearly a hundred thousand pounds in her everyday account. Her investment account was much better, and her retirement fund would allow a sensible, if meagre, retirement even if she started immediately. She could afford to have a real break from work and reassess her life and her future.

Did she really want to remain in that job with those obnoxious colleagues? Did she want to stay in London? Did she even want to stay in Great Britain?

It was the first time that she looked at her future and saw options. It was time to look at what she was going to do over the next year or so, and she had no intention of limiting her decisions. James could join her for all the holiday, part of it, or none. That was his call. She was going to do some of the things she had talked about for years. She walked around the inner city and the West End collecting travel brochures about the USA, Australia, and Africa, as well as the Middle East and Asia. Jane had not been to Scandinavia or Eastern Europe, and she had not been to Turkey. But they were close enough to visit during normal annual holidays.

She decided she wanted to travel to Australia as a major part of her time away. She wanted to swim in warm ocean water, she wanted to gaze at the Great Barrier Reef, she wanted to climb Ayers Rock, she wanted to see Cradle Mountain, and she wanted to go to Cynon and meet the people who produced the wool for her favourite clothing. She had seen big cities in Europe, so was not all that fussed about Sydney or New York, but she wanted to see Niagara Falls and the Grand Canyon. She wanted to see the wild animals of Africa and the kangaroos and koalas in Australia. She was not so sure about crocodiles and snakes, unless they were behind a bloody big fence.

For the time being Jane felt she needed to go to the wilds of the world. Hopefully, James would share some of that, but if he chose not to go with her, she would have to make other plans. One thing she had learnt over the last few weeks; she could be a very effective sexual predator if she wanted to be. James was wonderful, but if he was not prepared to travel, she knew she could find high class male company easily enough.

She returned home and laid out the pamphlets. She was intrigued with the around-the-world open ticket. It was a single payment that enabled her to stop as many times as required over a twelve-month period. She could choose clockwise or anti-clockwise but there was no doubling back. With careful planning, the one ticket could be used to visit every place on the hit list.

She could travel to South Africa, and on to Asia; from there to Australia and New Zealand, Japan and on to Hawaii. A couple of stops in the USA combined with some train travel and return via Canada. The more she looked, the more combinations she saw. Even if she needed a second ticket to extend past one year, it would be affordable. And anyhow, she had plenty of money.

Jane decided that she wanted to be in Australia through the winter and Spring. She wanted time in the Outback and in the North. As soon as she looked at the temperature predictions, she realised that temperatures over one hundred and fifteen degrees were insane. She could cope with the colder winter temperatures in the southern parts of the country because she was used to that.

She felt that the summers in the North would literally kill her.so she locked in the months of April till October for Australia, starting in the Outback and moving to North Queensland in June, then arriving in Victoria and Tasmania in the spring. That would probably mean the start of the trip would be in Southern Africa and Asia, New Zealand around November and moving across to the USA for Christmas. She could return through Scandinavia before returning to London. Or not.

Jane decided to tell James she was starting her extended trip in a month; she would ask for his advice, but if he decided not to go that would be fine.

No time like the present, so she grabbed the notes and the tour maps and headed for the phone. She phoned James at his office, requesting his secretary to tell Mr James Pattinson that Jane Hampton, Litigation Specialist needed to see him at the office in Trafalgar Square. It was urgent. She went to the Red Lion Hotel. She was sure he would understand that since she no longer was working, the pub was the closest thing she had to an office. James had a broad smile when walked in. He could see her in the corner seat enjoying the view of the rat-race coming and going near the Square.

"James, I am leaving for Scandinavia tomorrow. I will be away for two weeks. I will then come home for another two weeks to arrange visas and tickets. I am leaving these pamphlets with you, and my provisional itinerary in case you want to join me.

In one month, I plan to be somewhere away from here, at the start of my adventure."

"Oh, hello Miss Hampton. Nice of you to call. Am I part of this discussion or am I just Father Confessor, being told, and asked to forgive?"

"I know you are busy at work, and you have commitments that I no longer have. I would love you to come with me, but I have made up my mind; I am going with you or without you. I don't need you to come to Scandinavia; I am quite happy to do that on my own, but in two weeks you can tell me what your plans are."

James was thunderstruck. He was near the end of a huge financial settlement after which he could take some time off if he wished. He worried that other bank staff would move in on his big cases if he took a break and he might not get them back.

"Well, my hot-tempered little lawyer friend; you take your two weeks in Scandinavia, and I will see what is possible.

I guess you have taken enough time to realise it is pretty bloody cold in Scandinavia at the moment. Like, too cold to go outdoors; so unless you intend to drink gluhwein for a couple of weeks, there are probably better places to go.
Maybe, you'd better keep a couple of these maps and go somewhere warmer." James stood up and left.

Jane punched the top of the table. 'Jeezuz, I am dumb. That made me look stupid, or worse,' She thought with a sense of regret.

She wasn't sure whether James just told her to get stuffed, or whether he was going to think about some travel with her. She decided to go home and get drunk. She would think about it tomorrow.

The phone rang at 9.00pm but she could not be bothered answering it. There was no-one she wanted to talk to and if it was important, they would call back. Jane sat in front of the fire, with a feeling of foreboding. She had effectively resigned her job and nobody at the office seemed too concerned. She had just given an ultimatum to James, and he showed her that her first travel decision was poorly thought through. And he certainly gave her no reason to believe that he was going to throw in his career to chase her around the world.

An hour later her doorbell rang, and James let himself in. "Guess you need some company, since you won't answer your phone." He had the maps under his arm, along with the large travel brochures. "So where are we going first?"

22: **Cynon**

Doris Beech-Jones was ecstatic.

She had just been advised that her breeding rams had been voted the best in the world. Doris had worked tirelessly over the years to improve the bloodlines of her flock. She used her knowledge as a judge, choosing her best rams for breeding. She had six that were magnificent stud animals, and flocks of ewes that were world class. At breeding time her work crew fitted the chalk bags to the rams so that it was easy to see which ewes had been serviced. Her rams had different coloured chalk bags so that she could be certain of the lineage of the lambs. Over the years the flock had been sorted into wool classifications, with the finest kept to be crossed by Ramses III, her champion ram. It started as a joke with Ramses, but his best progeny quickly got named Ramses II. Now, Ramses III received very high stud fees, as well as servicing her prime ewes. High grade sheep were being shipped across Bass Strait to be impregnated by this magnificent animal, or the other quality rams if his service fee was too high. But he was only available after her prime flock were pregnant. Her other rams were used for breeding merino sheep for sale. In her words "these are excellent Merino, producing quality superfine wool," but to her friends, she added that they would never compete with her prime flock. She was happy to get very high prices at the sales for them, but she sure as hell did not want them stealing her market for the best of superfine wool. It was her intention that Cynon would remain the best wool brand in the world.

Doris loved the visits from Marcus and Mary and took every opportunity to make sure they understood the workings of the farm. As they walked around the farm at Christmas time, Doris pointed out the perfectly maintained private church on the property. The Church of England kept it registered as a church if there were four official services a year. Doris made a fuss of having the Christmas and Easter Services, using the Minister from Cressy. He was paid very well to be there, and they were always followed by a sumptuous dinner in the main dining room for the major farmers of the community.

Tom brought in some of the best wines in the world for the dinners, but of late they had mainly been Australian. "This stuff is better than most wines from Europe. It is always good to support great Australian industries."

Doris made it clear that any baby that was christened at her church would receive a christening present every year, so that usually made up the numbers.

"Been a while since we had a wedding though, Mary. We could do something special for you if you and Marcus chose our church."

Mary laughed, "We're not even engaged yet." Doris turned to Marcus and told him to get on with it before someone else snapped her up. "You won't find another one like this Marcus. She's a doll, and you know it."

Marcus started to protest but Doris made her opinion clear; only fools waited when they are certain, and as far as she could see Marcus was certain. "Get yourself sorted and give me a date. I will organise everything. Tell your guests to come for a couple of days. There is a good hotel in Launceston that I reckon I could hire for accommodation for the guests, and I would happily send the pair of you back to The Hotel Windsor for a honeymoon."

23: Snug

Colin and Linda arrived back in Devonport on the twenty-second of December.

They headed south immediately. Colin had promised he was not going to mention anything to do with the fire risk until after Christmas, but he was shocked by how much drier the state was than when he left. He could not see a green shoot anywhere from Launceston to Hobart. South of Oatlands he could see that the cracks in the paddocks had opened to a level confirming serious drought, and all the animals were sheltering in the shadows of the few trees in the paddocks.

"Yes, I know," Linda said, "It does not look good, but you are not going back to work till after Boxing Day." Colin just nodded and bit his lip: there was no point arguing. Linda had made it clear that there was no negotiation about returning to work before Christmas. He was having the time with his kids, and his workmates could wait.

The closer he got to the Derwent the worse the fire risk looked. The countryside from Ross to Hobart was just straw, and the wind was gusting strongly.

The windows of the car were down, and the outside air felt like it was coming off a furnace.

"Close the windows and I will open the air vents and the quarter panel windows to get some airflow. It will still be hot but should be more comfortable." Colin opened the vents and his quarter panel and asked Linda to open the one on her side.

He decided to stop at Constitution Dock for some fish and chips. Hopefully, the air off the Bay would be cooler than in the city, and they could get some water and some food. The fish was fresh and delightful. They certainly had not had fish and chips like that on the trip, but the air was stifling. They ate quickly and got back in the car for the trip home to Snug. At least in amongst the trees it would be cooler, and they could open all the doors and windows and let the air waft through the house.

Colin unlocked the house and started to bring the luggage inside. Jasmine went inside and came straight back out.

"Dad, Santa won't be happy. The Christmas tree is dead, and the leaves are all over the carpet."

"We'll clean it up in a minute and make it look nice again. Santa will be here soon, and then the tree can be put outside on the rubbish pile."

Linda always made sure that at the end of a trip, everything was put away and all laundry was washed. She hated to get up from a sleep to have to wash all the family clothes from a long trip. Colin always cleaned the car; he washed and polished the outside and vacuumed the inside.

When he finished, he was dripping with sweat. He tapped the barometer as he went for a wash.

The temperature was a hundred degrees, and the barometer was rising. That indicated it was not going to cool down any time soon. The air felt as dry as he could remember. The shirt on his back was turning white from the crystalline salt from his sweat. Linda was working overtime on the old Hoover Twin Tub.

She had two loads on the line and one more in the wash. The first load would be dry by the time the next one was ready to be hung out. She planned a good wash down with cold water when she finished, followed by a rest on the bed; she had not slept much on the Princess overnight, and they had driven for nearly five hours to get home. She felt completely worn out.

24: **Christmas with the Sturmers**

It was Christmas Eve and all the shops around Bridgewater were closed.

The boys could not do their usual run to the corner store to steal bottles to get a bit of cash and the mothers were out doing God knows what, probably at the pub. They could not even steal a few cigarettes, as no adults were home.

Jake Sturmer threw two sets of keys on the bed; each set tied with fishing line. They were not complete sets, but they were getting closer. One set was Holden keys, and the others were to fit Ford Falcons. Both companies used a small number of different locks and keys, and it was only honesty that provided any security, as everybody seemed to know that if there were ten cars in the carpark, at least two of them had identical keys.
Jake had started visiting second-hand shops and car junk yards, bringing home any keys he could find. He said to Roly and Toby that he was going down to the shops to see if he could unlock a couple of cars.

If that didn't work, he would drive a screwdriver through the lock with a rubber hammer and hot-wire the ignition. They decided to try to get three cars and drive to Ross for a bit of fun. "We will leave them there and pinch one to come home. We should be home before the owners know their cars have been pinched."

They managed to get a Torana and a Kingswood from the Bridgewater Hotel, and Toby came back with a Police Falcon.

"No-one will stop us. They will think I am chasing you. Just so long as they don't step in to help me, we should have a great trip". They drove sedately to Brighton and then drove at high speed to Ross. Toby kept turning the siren on, until Jake and Roly stopped and threatened to knock some sense into him unless he stopped doing that. They parked the cars in front of the hotel and wandered up to the bakery. While the serving staff were busy, Roly picked out three pies from the pie warmer, and the three car thieves quietly left the Bakery. Jake led his mates to the Ross Bridge, where they sat under a tree and ate the pies in the warm sunlight. A Mercedes pulled into the driveway of the old Barracks across the road, and they watched a couple unpack their belongings from the boot. Jake watched as the driver took two suitcases and a handbag inside, while the young woman grabbed her hat and jacket off the rear seat. They waited for the driver to come back out and lock the car. Jake knew his keys would not get them into that one, but he loved a challenge. He held the screwdriver blade to the keyhole and gave it one sharp rap with the rubber hammer.

The door lock popped up and he slipped into the car. He reached under the dashboard for the ignition wires and cut them with a pocket-knife. He peeled the electrical wire down and wound the wires together. Jake pushed the screwdriver in the key slot to turn the ignition. He signalled to Roly and Toby to push the car out of the driveway before starting the car. In less than a minute, they were heading back to Hobart.

Toby reckoned that the two of them would be shagging for hours so they would be unlucky if the owners realised that the car was missing for quite a while. As the boys headed back to Bridgewater Toby suggested they give the Police an upgrade, by parking the Mercedes in the spot where the police car had been. They laughed at that idea, but decided the cops would know their car was missing and the risk would be too high, so they abandoned it at the Bridgewater Bridge and walked along the river's edge to their homes.

It was New Year's Eve when the police came to the Sturmer house. The boys were inside playing with a slug gun they had managed to get from an uncle. They were planning to go and shoot a few seagulls along the riverbank. Mrs Sturmer had already drunk a bottle of sherry, and the boys knew they had about an hour before she became violent. They were getting a sandwich and some chicken from the fridge when the police turned up.

The police officer asked if Mrs Sturmer was available. "Here – yes! Available – probably not. She's pissed as usual."

"Go, get her. I need to talk to her. And boys, don't try to escape. There are four police officers outside. They are armed and they each have the weapon in their hand. Frankly, I would love the opportunity to put a bullet in you little pricks, so don't even think of doing anything silly. Now get your mother out here now!"

Roly went and shouted that she was needed in the kitchen. She protested, but he told her there were four cops at the house and she should come out now.

"What do you fuckin' want. I am tired after a busy Christmas."

She was told that her two sons, along with Toby Marshall were all being arrested for multiple car thefts, including the theft of a police car.

"You better have some proof; you can't just come here full of accusations just because you don't like my boys."

The Police Officer opened the door and called in the other officers to handcuff the boys. When Mrs Sturmer started to shout, she was politely told there were four sets of handcuffs and only three were currently in use; she would be next if she did not sit down and be quiet.

Sergeant Godfrey was used to dealing with case hardened kids. Bridgewater was a tough neighbourhood, with many kids being raised by single mothers, literally or because the partners were long term prisoners. There was a lot of crime, especially juvenile crime, and a major concern with truancy. It was sometimes difficult to know whether it was school holidays, or the kids were just not attending school.

Between Christmas and New Year, it was horrible. There were hundreds of them running riot; their crimes ranged from stealing returnable bottles from the corner shop to break and enter. They stole cars and motorcycles; but often they broke into houses to steal cigarettes and beer or small amounts of money.

These three were the bane of his life. The first port of call, the first suspects every time something serious happened, Sturmer, Sturmer and Marshall's names went up on the blackboard in the lecture room.

It had not taken long. When the cars were found outside the Man O'Ross Hotel, the licensee told him that one of the patrons of the pub had seen the three kids getting out of the car. He knew that the one driving the police car was not a copper; he was far too young and was dressed in dirty jeans and a tartan shirt. The licensee told him that a tourist in the bar told him about the cars and asked where the police station was. He was going report the location of the police car, as well as the other two that he believed were all stolen.

The tourist had watched them come back and grab a cap out of the police car, and then go to the Bridge to eat something. He saw them head towards the Mercedes. He had taken some photos of them when they had come back to the police car, and he now managed to get a run of photos as they stole the Mercedes.

He went to the Station in the main street, telling them they now had an extra Police car in front of the Man O'Ross Hotel, and another two cars that were almost certainly stolen.

He told them about the Mercedes at the Barracks, and the three young boys that he had photographed. He gave the roll of film to the police officer. "Can you please make sure I get the other photos on the roll? They are some of my holiday snaps." The police took a witness statement and assured him they would forward all the photos to him that did not form part of the prosecution. "Thank you for being so astute; not many people would have bothered." He said that he and his wife were on holidays from Sydney.

"We see crime all the time, but this place was so quiet and beautiful that it caught my attention."
The police officer glanced again at the witness statement and said,

" Jonathon Smythe: is that how you pronounce your surname? We are grateful that you took the photos. It will help us nail them. They will have a police record, and the photos will hopefully be clear enough to identify them."

"Sir, my camera is a top of the range Nikon. You will be able to blow that up enough to see the hairs in the eyebrows. I know what I am doing; I am a professional photographer. The photos will be sharp and high quality; I guarantee that."

"You might have to come back as a witness if they play difficult. Otherwise, we will send the other photos back to the address on the witness statement if that is OK".
The local pharmacy made a phone call to the Kodak Printers and explained the urgency.

They agreed to do a priority print run and said the photos would be back in four days, providing there were no hold-ups in postage.

As soon as the photos were printed, Sergeant Godfrey said that Blind Freddy could recognise those little arseholes from the photos. He pulled in another four officers to go to the two homes. Sturmers first, because that is where the boys always were unless they were out planning something illegal. They could go to the Marshall's after that. He decided that he would send one of the females in first. Let her burst in on the tart. There was a pretty good chance she would be shagging something she had picked up on the street.

"So, you are picking on my boys again because you are too lazy to go chasing real criminals. Every time you have a problem you can't nail down, you come after my boys. I am about to sue you arseholes for harassment."

"Really Mrs Sturmer? Sit down before I knock you down. And for Christ's sake shut up. I have twenty photos here of your boys stealing the four cars. They are good photos taken with a high-quality camera. There is no question that these photos are of your little darlings and their mate. We are taking them to the lockup, and they will be in Court tomorrow. We will oppose bail, of course, but with New Year almost here, who knows what a judge will decide."

"Mrs Sturmer."

"What?"

"When you turn up at Court, I intend to have you tested. If you are drunk, you had better not have driven to the Court, or you will be joining your boys in the slammer. Ok fellows, get these three young pricks to the station, so we can get the paperwork done, and go home.

You lot; say goodbye to Mum. With a bit of luck, you will not be having much time with her for quite a long time."

Toby muttered that she was not his Mum. "I know that you little prick. I will let your lovely mother know where you are, once we can get to her without her having someone on top of her."

It took a few hours to get the charge sheets completed. The boys admitted nothing, and just continued to say it wasn't them.

"Plenty of kids around here look like us."

The Magistrate refused bail and ordered they attend a regular sitting of court in two weeks.

"In the meantime, you can return to Ashley, where you will feel at home, by the look of your record sheet.

I am going to order that the next two weeks gives you some impression of adult jail, as all three of you need to know what your future is if you stay on your current course."

They were put into a secured wing at Ashley Juvenile Detention Centre, and not allowed to spend any time together at all. For two weeks, their day consisted of two hours of recreation, but on differing schedules, eight hours for reading, and fourteen hours of lockdown. They were transported back to court in three separate vehicles.

The court was busy when the boys were delivered from Ashley. They had Legal Aid Lawyers briefed, and they were in front of a young female Judge. Her day looked atrocious, with a string of assaults and an attempted rape case.

"Bloody heatwave; sending all the lunatics troppo," the Clerk of the Courts summed up the day ahead neatly.

The boys were scheduled to appear straight after lunch, but the morning session had been interrupted as lawyers tested the new Judge by requesting delays and legal requests.

Each of the serious cases was dealt with and then a date set for appearance in the Criminal Court. Every case applied for bail, with the lawyers throwing every excuse possible. The Judge refused every one of them, based on the severity of the case and the risk to society.

Jake, Roly, and Toby were called in to the Court in mid-afternoon. The Legal Aid team had supplied some nice clothes and arranged haircuts. They had been briefed to be pleasant and good mannered. And not to show any anger, under any circumstances.

The charges were read out and the witnesses called, except for Jonathon Smythe, the photographer, as he had returned to Sydney.

The boys continued to say it wasn't them; and their lawyers stated that they needed to cross exam the photographer.

"I mean, why would he randomly photograph three boys in the street and then follow them around the town. Your Honour, that seems more than a little odd."

He pointed out that there was a passing resemblance between his clients and the photographs, but that was not definite proof.

The Judge ordered that the photographer be instructed to return for a Court appearance as a witness on February 14th, and that all the photographs be enlarged to the biggest image possible before definition was lost.

The three boys were released on bail under strict conditions. They were not to be seen on the streets together, and they were not allowed to travel anywhere unless in the company of a parent. The Judge was adamant that the court had been full of very dangerous people all day. These "young men are at the lowest level of criminality I have seen today."

"I understand you come from socially disadvantaged families, so applying a significant monetary bail bond will not work. Please understand, that the next four weeks had better be the best four weeks of your life, or I will punish you severely."

The Mercury newspaper ran the story but, of course the names and photos of the three were suppressed. Nobody in Bridgewater was fooled. The three were local heroes to the other street kids, and the shopkeepers just muttered about bloody justice and the waste of space, sometimes called the courts.

25: The Proposal

It was New Year's Eve.

Marcus picked up Mary from work, taking her to Constitution Dock for dinner and to watch some of the slower yachts of the Sydney Hobart Fleet come in. Crowds still greeted every boat, and there was a carnival atmosphere at the Dock. The wealthy boat-owners and their crews joined with the locals in a celebration of a great race, as well as the beginning of New Year. Marcus waited patiently for midnight, and then quietly asked Mary to marry him. He was a no-fuss fellow, but Mary screamed so loud people came running, thinking she had been hurt or assaulted. When they realised what had happened all the other young women started screaming, although none of them knew Mary.

They decided the church at Cynon would be the venue, and that Aunt Doris would be made Organiser in Chief. Marcus wanted to buy a card and send it to Aunt Doris, but Mary insisted that such news had to be personal.

She had a three-day break from work coming up, so she suggested they drive up and tell Doris and Tom personally.

"Do you think Tom would be my best man? I don't know that many fellows, and I can't imagine any that I would ask to travel across the state to my wedding."

"I think he would be honoured. But I was going to ask him to drive the wedding car. He could be a very busy man, considering it is in his church."

Tom and Doris were delighted. Tom chose to be the Best Man, providing his car carried the bride. He would arrange a professional driver.

Marcus agreed but was adamant he and the Best Man arrive in the X2. That made him laugh; Tom was giving up the Rolls Royce to travel in a Holden. "Good swap, I reckon," Marcus said quietly to Mary.

Doris told them that the church could be used whenever they wished but she liked Easter.

"But you better be quick. It is difficult to get a Minister at that time of the year."

Mary instantly agreed. She knew her father normally reserved Easter for family time, so there should not be any major concerns there. Even the Hospital tried to schedule as many staff on leave at Easter as possible, so hopefully many of her friends could come.

Marcus was not concerned. He had no relatives other than Doris and Tom, and a sister he had lost contact with a long time ago.

He had virtually no friends, and a few work colleagues he respected, but hardly knew. His invitation list would be very short.

As they headed home to Hobart Marcus mused how strange life was. He got engaged without any specific plans, but by the time they left Aunt Doris' house the wedding was set, and the honeymoon plans had started.

26: Marine and Katrien

Marine and Katrien were too tired to talk.

They had worked more than fifty hours in the Christmas week, and the similar workload leading up to New Year. The store was so busy that there was no rest time, other than a lunch break.

There has been no free time to spend any of their money, and they had almost raised the airfare to Australia by the middle of January. Katrien told her father that it was unfair; she was working so hard and really there was not a lot of money in the pay packet. Lucas calmly replied that she was earning more money than he earned in his profession at any stage of the first twenty years of work.

"And if you do the mathematics, you will realise that I was supporting a family on that money.

When you must work hard to earn it you will be more careful how you spend it.

Once you are back at school, you will need to start planning your trip. You will be able to top up your bank balance with weekend work."

"Dad, this is horrible, I am losing half the money in tax, so I don't end up with much."

"Well, the next time the students tell you University is free, you can tell them that it is not. And when they tell you all those other things you don't pay for are free, you can tell them they are not. They are paid for by the Government from taxes they take from people who are working. That is another of life's cruel lessons my dear; there is no such thing as a free lunch."

"Dad, Marine and I can't keep working like this through the term. We must study. We will fail our exams if we don't put the time in."

"You will have to manage your time. Work out how much time you have free and allocate study time, work time, and play time. The last one is the easiest to reduce. You just must decide how much time you are prepared to waste on hanging out with friends and getting up to mischief."

"Dad, that is not fair! I have to have some time with my friends."

"Not my problem, young lady. If you want to go to Australia, you have to earn some money. If you don't have the money, you don't go."

"You are being cruel. Marine is not being treated like that."

"Oh yes she is. Frederick and I talk to each other regularly, and we have made a combined decision to make sure that each of you learn the value of money before you head off. We will not be sending you money if you send us messages from overseas saying you are broke.

You will be told to get a job down there.

Don't roll your eyes like that. You will value the lesson one day when you realise the best things don't come easy.

Just remember we are not charging you board at the moment, but that might happen once you return from your trip."

"It won't because Marine and I will get a flat near the University."

"Then you will learn quickly about the cost of living."

27:Daybreak Monday

Mary nudged Marcus, "The phone is ringing downstairs."

He looked at the bedside clock. It was 2.30 am; no decent person rings at that time, he thought to himself. He raced down the steps and grabbed the phone.
It was the Fire Chief at Glenorchy Station.

"Three of our night shift have not arrived. They have decided to move their families to safety and won't be in till tonight. Garry is going ballistic because he says all the indicators say that today could become a complete bloody nightmare."

Marcus pulled on some jeans and a T-shirt and his joggers. He shouted to Mary that he had to go, grabbed his duffle bag with his fire-fighting gear and raced to the car.

He threw his gear in the boot and headed to Glenorchy as fast as he could. He made sure he had his breathing mask close by.

The station was quiet but there was a feeling of tension. All the fire-fighters were off duty except for a skeleton crew that stayed for the night shift.

They were sleeping in the dormitory at the back, wearing everything except the protective fire suit and the boots.

As dawn broke the morning started to heat up quickly. The first two phone calls were from office staff, saying they would not be in for the start of the dayshift as they were on their way back from taking the kids to Launceston. Marcus phoned Mary to tell her he was not sure when he would be home, but she had already left for work. He left a message at the hospital for her and went back to the control room. The building was eerie; it was deathly quiet until the morning staff started to arrive. They had all been told to bring their overnight gear, as Hobart would be lucky to escape an inferno, and they would be on standby through the night. The night crew were sent home but told to stay close to the phone. Garry told them If they received a call to come to work, they had to be at the station in twenty minutes. "This is not the day for you to take the kids to school; or go shopping. Stay at home, stay close to the phone, and stay dressed for duty. If you are not called in before nightfall, sleep in your basic fire-fighting gear."

The phone rang every few minutes from worried people wanting to know whether it was safe to take the kids to school; whether they should leave their homes and what they should take with them. Many remembered Garry on the radio talking about the essentials kit, but they could not remember what he said to take.

Marcus scribbled a note. "Take photos, insurance documents and medication or prescriptions.

Make sure you have a change of clothing for everybody, and put the box in the car, or at the front door of the house. Get the children to pack their own little box, with their favourite toy and a change of clothing."

Nothing happened all day, but the tension could be cut with a knife. The day crew went home, and the night crew returned. They sat around drinking tea, eating biscuits, and playing cards. Most played poker for matchsticks but two fellows played cribbage in the corner. "Oh Mick, would you shut up with your bloody fifteen - two, fifteen-four. We are playing for sheep stations over here and I can't bloody concentrate with that gibberish."

By ten o'clock they were all lying down in the dormitory, but nobody was sleeping. By midnight most of the crew were sleeping restlessly. The toilet was flushed every twenty minutes.

"Sorry mate, you still can't go home. Half the staff have not arrived, and I can't contact most of them. This fuckin' town is completely spooked, and I can't say I blame anybody who has put the family first today. I just wish they had let me know earlier in the day so I could have got some others in. Phone Mary and tell her you will be home as soon as we have someone here to replace you."

28: Bridgewater

"What are we going to do for a month?"

"We can't go to the shops together. The only good thing is we have just been banned from going back to school in three weeks. Can't be seen together you know!"

"I could pinch one of mum's bloody wigs and I would look like John Lennon. And Roly could get a short black one and look like that that Japanese bitch."

Roly rolled his eyes and sang badly; "Yesterday, Ashley seemed so far away. But I suspect we are going to stay. Someday"

"Stop that shit. We are going to be good little boys. Well for a month anyway.

But the wig idea is good. If we nicked a few dollars from Mum's purse we could go to the Salvation Army shop and get a suit each and whack on a wig and spend the time in the city where nobody would recognise us. We could tell anyone who asked that we were on holidays from Melbourne. Just stay out of trouble and keep away from the cops.Toby said he was sure his mother was hiding some money in her undies drawer. He hoped his mother was out of the house so he could get a few dollars.

The Salvos only charged three dollars a suit so if he could get ten, they would have enough. The two Sturmers had to get enough for the bus fares to the city but that should be easy. Their mother was collecting fifty cent coins for a trip when her husband was released from prison. She was keeping them in an old moneybox in her wardrobe. The boys helped themselves regularly. Jake didn't care; "Anyway, that bastard of a man doesn't deserve a holiday. He's having one at the moment at Risdon."

They caught separate buses into town and met up at the second-hand shop. They stepped out looking quite stylish in their suits and wigs. Men's and women's hair styles were so similar that they looked like three members of a band on the way to do a show. Roly decided he needed a feed, so he took the jacket off and gave the wig to Toby before going into a corner shop and nicking a bread roll. He didn't want to take the chance that if he was seen, the police would be told about his new disguise.

Nobody took any notice of them, so the next day they decided to stay closer to home and soon they were back to roaming around Bridgewater and the local suburbs. A couple of their mates had a laugh at them, but they were not noticed by anybody that would report them to the police.

School went back on February 6th, but the boys decided they would obey the Judge's ruling and not be seen together. They did not return to school when the term started.

They got dressed in the suits and wigs and went to Glenorchy for a few hours.

There was no one else at the bus stop when Roly checked to see when the next bus was due. 'Oh, bloody hell; we missed the last bus of the day ten minutes ago. We are going to have to walk home."

They had walked for about half an hour when they decided to find somewhere to have a sleep. It did not take much to get into the Glenorchy Football Club and curl up on the massage couches for a nap. It was about three am when Roly woke them and told them they'd better get moving. The three of them walked around the back streets heading west when Toby said that he thought he had just seen the X2 Holden parked near the Fire Station. "It sure looks like it, and there are a couple of other cars there as well. If we nicked a couple of them, we could hide the X2 and use it for a few days before dumping it back around here. And if we took an old bomb as well, we could get back home and dump it at the Bridge."

There seemed to be a lot of vehicles in the carpark and all the lights were on in the station. "We better be bloody quiet nicking these cars; the station seems to be busy tonight, and we will be in for a long stretch in Ashley if we get caught again."

Toby had the keys and the fourth one he tried fitted the X2. They pushed it out onto the back street while they searched for another car to go home in once they had been for a joyride and then hidden the X2. They found a ten-year-old Ford that would do the job, but they were not lucky enough to have a key for that one.

That did not matter; old Fords were easy to hot-wire. They pushed both cars out to the back street before starting them to make sure they weren't caught. It took about thirty seconds to pull the ignition wires from behind the dash and wind them together. Once the screwdriver was pushed into the ignition, the car started instantly. They drove very carefully until they got out past Bridgewater where the highway speed limit was sixty-five miles per hour. There was a quiet side road with no obvious houses a mile or so past the Brighton Army Camp, so they pulled in there and hid the Old Ford. There was enough fuel in the X2 to get to Campbell Town and back. When they could see far enough ahead to be sure there were no cops around, they planted the boot and felt the wheels spin until the tyres gripped and the car took off like a rocket. They each had a turn before returning to the Ford. They hid the X2 so it could not be seen from the road and drove the old Ford back to the Bridge. Toby said that they would have to nick a car every time they wanted to go for a drive, just so they could get out to the X2.

They turned the lights off as they approached the Bridge, and drifted off the left side of the road, parking the car out of sight of passing traffic. It would be found tomorrow, none the worse for wear, but with a bit of fuel missing. "Jeez we are good drivers. Not a ding on either car!"

As usual Mrs Marshall was with some drunk about half her age. Toby told the Sturmers he was going to stay at their house for the night; he just hated it when his mother brought some new fellow home.

The boys went to bed and were all asleep in minutes.

It was crazy at the Glenorchy Fire Station with minimal staff to handle the unfolding disaster.

Triple-0 calls triggered a special ringtone at the station. The first one was soon after midnight; the alarm triggered in the dormitory. Almost instantly the fire crew were waiting on the truck for instructions. There was a fire burning at the base of Mount Wellington, putting several houses at risk. "Call us on the two-way as soon as you have a specific location," the Captain said, as he raced past the phone desk. The truck left and headed in the general direction of the fire.

In five minutes, every phone was ringing, and all of them were Triple-0 calls.

"Marcus, grab a phone and start answering calls. Get as much detail as you can and call them into Headquarters. Don't send our second unit unless it is close by."

Fires were breaking out everywhere from down the Huon, all around Mount Wellington, along the Derwent, and out into the country. There were so many fires in the suburbs that they had not been counted.

There was a critical shortage of trucks and fire-fighters, and the water supply was not good in some places, due to the ongoing drought. He was told he could not promise, or even insinuate that a fire unit would come out any time soon.

He pulled out the cheat sheet and went through the questions.

Where are you?
How severe is the fire?
Do you feel threatened at the moment?
What have you got for firefighting?
Have you made a plan in case of fire?
Do you have an emergency pack?
Make sure you take your insurance documents, any medications, and prescriptions.

He went through the whole list and then he picked up the phone.
Every call had to finish with a statement to the person on the phone that unless the drive out was blocked, they were to get the family to safe ground NOW.

"Get to open areas where there are no trees, where any grass is stubble, or better still, on a beach, near the ocean or one of the big rivers. Be ready to get in the water." It was meant to frighten people so that they did as they were told. This was not a time to be sensitive.
Marcus looked around the Communication Room.
Harry, the on-duty Station Officer was standing at a large map of the state that was attached to a pin board.
The date, February 7, 1967 was attached to the top of the board.
As fires were notified, a red pin went into the board. When extinguished they would be replaced with black pins.

Roads blocked by fire had bright red tram line pins across them. The fire trucks were marked with big yellow pins. God forbid they had to use them, but they had a box of black crosses if deaths occurred.

The southern half of the state had fifteen red pins in it, and every fire truck in the south was already at a fire or on the road. The Communications Room was flat out with incoming calls, but if there were any moments when the phone stopped ringing, they were to call fire crews in other parts of the state to ask for help.

The North and North West regions were keeping skeleton crews, but everything else was heading south. The weather forecast was for gale force winds, and temperatures over one hundred degrees. That was a perfect storm, a recipe for disaster.

Marcus thought to himself that this was what Chief Fire Officer Colin Anderson had been warning about for months. There will be a lot of people from the Premier down, covering their arses over the next few weeks. This could burn down the whole city and take hundreds of lives, unless we are incredibly lucky and everybody dealing with this does everything perfectly.

The board was becoming a sea of red dots as the phones rang constantly and new fires were called in.

They were burning all down the Huon Valley and along the ocean shores. Port Arthur area and the Peninsula had fires everywhere. House fires in the city and suburbs were being reported every minute.

Then Harry took a message and said loudly, "First one" as a black cross went on the board at the foothills of Mount Wellington.

A call came in that the Cascade Brewery was alight and many of the buildings would not be saved.

"The area is full of convict historical buildings. That area has had enough tragedy over the years. God forbid we lose the buildings as well." A fire crew was doing as much as possible, but it was obvious to anybody that Hobart was going to be changed forever.

The Control Room was notified that Hamilton in the highlands was burning fiercely, as was Bothwell, fifty miles up the Main Highway to the north. "Bloody hell, we will lose some of our best sheep properties in that area. There will be dead animals everywhere." Marcus looked at the map and could see there were not any fires up north near Cressy, so he could assume Cynon was not in danger and Aunt Doris was currently not at risk. He hoped that the fires at Hamilton would not get into the beautiful highlands of Tasmania; "that area is inaccessible and will burn till it rains. There is nothing we can do there."

"For God's sake, get every available person doorknocking houses-at-risk and tell them to get to safety areas. Hopefully some of them will have made some preparations."

The Sturmers were totally unaware of the devastation developing around them. It was still dark when they were woken by lights and sirens everywhere. Someone was bashing on the door and screaming to open it immediately.

The boys looked at each other with amazement. As far as they could remember they had not been seen, and even if they were the witness would have seen three men with longish hair wearing suits.

"Bloody hell Toby I think the full police force is coming for us. This time we will be lucky not to go straight back to Ashley. Thank God neither car is damaged, or we would be dead meat."

Mrs Sturmer opened the door to a fireman who shouted to her to evacuate the area and head north; there was a massive bushfire bearing down on Hobart in all directions, and everybody had to get out of the city.

Residents of Bridgewater and surrounding suburbs were to head north and get to open country. They were told to tune the radio to ABC and follow directions as they came over the radio. They jumped into the car with Roly in the front seat. He turned the dial till he heard grannie music. "This will be it. The ABC. Fantastic! We can listen to Acker Bilk. If we have to listen to this crap for the next few hours you had better put your hair rollers in Jake. This is going to be great."

There was a news break as soon as they got in the car. The fires were coming from all directions. The advice was to get to clear ground or the water. "Don't stay at the house unless you are surrounded and cannot not get out.

If you have put together an essentials pack, put it and the family in the car and go now. Do not go on roads without exits in both directions. Keep well away from trees and tall grass. If you can get to the river or the ocean, then head that way now.

Remember that distance is your best friend. Try to get at least thirty miles out of the city and keep listening to this station." The radio returned to the regular announcer to continue with his programme till the next emergency announcement was scheduled.

"In the meantime, it is back to Mantovani;" the boys jeered their disapproval.

"Hey Mum, can we go to Ross; we know the way."

"Shut up you little pricks. You've caused me enough worries without being smart arses."

"They said to bring the essentials, Jake. Did you get the keys?"

Jake laughed and said they always went with him. Mrs Sturmer was too busy concentrating on driving to listen to that conversation. She would have been angry if she knew what the keys were for. They kept up senseless banter, till Mrs Sturmer told them to shup up as she needed to concentrate. The smoke was difficult to see through, and she did not want to crash and get caught up in the fire.

As they went past the Army Camp and then the road where the X2 was hidden Toby rattled the keys. The three boys all laughed.

The news service said there were more than forty fires out of control now, and the day was looking like a disaster waiting to happen. There was an expectation of gale force winds and temperatures of more than a hundred degrees. There was no stopping that kind of inferno. The fires were all over the place in southern Tasmania, and Bridgewater was one of the early casualties.

There were reports of houses destroyed, and tin roofs being blown around like paper. The power poles and telephone lines erupted in flames and fell across the roads. As they listened, they realised that much of what they knew was now gone. The death toll was rising, and fires had claimed houses on both sides of the river. Glenorchy had erupted in flames just before New Norfolk, much further up the river, became an inferno. Listening to the radio, the Sturmers believed that all of Hobart was alight. They found an area in the middle of a sports ground in Ross and parked there. The grass had been cut to stubble and there had been no rain for weeks, so there was not much fuel for a fire to get a hold. Mrs Sturmer was smart enough to park the car facing the exit for a quick getaway if a fire did start. She knew that she was very low on fuel, so she crossed her fingers and hoped she would not need to move the car till the emergency was over and she could buy some petrol.

Hellfire

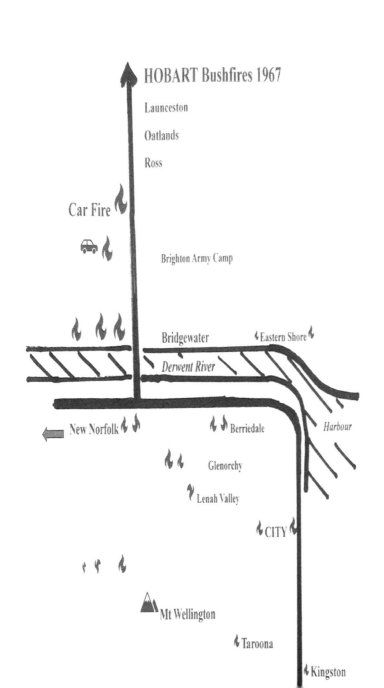

HOBART Bushfires 1967

Launceston

Oatlands

Ross

Car Fire

Brighton Army Camp

Bridgewater   Eastern Shore

Derwent River

New Norfolk   Berriedale   *Harbour*

Glenorchy

Lenah Valley

CITY

Mt Wellington

Taroona

Kingston

By ten o'clock at night, sixty percent of the red pins had been replaced with blue, indicating 'under control,' but the black crosses were growing by the minutes as bodies were found in burnt out buildings and cars. When Marcus was stood down at eleven o'clock, there were 49 crosses where people had died; but everyone knew there would be more. There were close to a thousand people being treated in the hospitals and doctors' surgeries for burns, and many of those were serious. The Army was searching properties all over the South. Dead animals were everywhere, and the veterinarians were putting injured animals down in their hundreds. There was not enough time to help seriously injured animals, so the only feasible course was to shoot them.

When Marcus walked out of the Station to go home there was an empty parking space where he had left his car. He looked around, assuming he was so tired that he had parked it somewhere else. Then he noticed the glass on the ground where the quarter panel window had been broken to gain access to the old Ford. Marcus raced back to the station to tell them his car was missing.

"Look mate, I will call the police, but I suspect that even as special as your car is, the cops will have higher priorities with all the death and destruction around here. Why don't you go home and have a rest, and take the day off tomorrow for a look around? On a day like today there could be a thousand good reasons why someone has taken your car. I will get one of the fellows to drop you home after you have spoken to the police.

If we need you in the morning, I will call you before eight o'clock. Otherwise take the day off and have a look around."

The police were sympathetic and wrote down the details, but the supervisor was correct. It was low on the priority list for a few days as far as they were concerned.

Marcus searched the surrounding area on the forlorn chance that it was parked nearby, but at midnight he decided to head for home and sleep.

Mary had never seen him so angry. He frightened her, although she knew he would not hurt her. But he looked like a wounded animal, one that would strike out at anything nearby.

He did not sleep. He walked the floor, swearing at the low life bastards who would do that when the town was burning down. Not for one minute did he believe that it was taken of necessity.

After a fitful night, he was relieved the phone didn't ring. But he was awake early and was ready to find his car and the people who took it. The cops may not have seen it as high priority; but he did, and he intended to use whatever it took to find out where his car was. He borrowed Mary's car to drive around the area. The town was smouldering, and the smoke was making breathing difficult. He put the smoke mask on as he drove around the town. Crossing the Bridgewater Bridge, he noticed the car parked off the side near the river. One look in the window convinced him that it was abandoned, probably stolen. The wires were hanging below the dash where it had been hot-wired.

They were twisted together, but there was no electrical tape around them. The wiring had been done rapidly. There was something about the car that was familiar. Then he remembered that a car very similar to that had been in the car park near where he parked his car for at least a week. He walked around it, smiling wryly when he saw the number plate. It was WOG 662. He remembered someone in the office saying that he hoped it was not owned by a bloody Greek. It didn't belong to anyone who worked at the Station, and there was some talk of having it impounded because it was in a private parking area.

Marcus tried the door, and it opened. Over the back of the seat was an old cap with the name Sturmer in it.

"Jeezus, that name rings a bell." Marcus tried to remember why that name was familiar. He knew he had heard it recently, but he couldn't remember the context.

The Glenorchy Police Station was closed. Obviously, the police were trying to deal with the fires and the deaths; the paperwork could wait.

He went home so that Mary could take the car to work. The name Sturmer was troubling him. He got out the back issues of the Mercury newspapers and quickly found the story of the stolen police car and the decision to allow the thieves out on bail. There were no names in the story but when he looked at the Court notices for the week, there were the names of two Sturmers to appear before the courts. There was no entry in the phone book, but there were not many phones in Bridgewater. He decided that given half a chance, he would ask the Sturmers a question or two.

He had a few tricks from Vietnam that he knew would get him some answers, once he was sure that he had the bastards who took his car. He took a guess that the thieves had taken both cars at the same time; he would soon know once he spoke to the Sturmer boys. Vietnam had taught him that you could play nice and get nice answers or play bloody rough and get the real answers. He planned on getting the real answers and as quickly as possible.

Marcus was dead tired; it was almost 48 hours since he had a good sleep. He kicked off his shoes and trousers, and lay on the bed, and that was how Mary found him when she came in from night shift.

She cleaned her teeth, had a rinse with warm soapy water and got into bed. She was struggling to breathe in the intense smoky air. It was still hot outside but cooling rapidly.

When Marcus woke, he turned on the radio to hear that many of the fires were under control. There had been a major concern overnight, when a small fire started spontaneously at the Brighton Army Camp, where there were several hundred people who had been evacuated from fire zones. The fire had been quickly controlled, but it had sparked into the bushes to the north and a fierce fire was being fought at that moment.

He phoned the Station to see if anyone could pick him up, as he didn't have a car to get to work. He was picked up soon after, but the boss told him to not get too noisy about his car. Three of his co-workers had lost their houses, and one of the reception girls had both her mother and father killed up around Snug.

"I feel sorry for you mate; I know how much you loved that car, but there are others who have lost much more. At the last count 58 people have lost their lives, and thousands will be unemployed. We are guessing that close to a thousand buildings have gone up in smoke, and about six hundred of those are people's homes."

29: February 7
Snug. 1.am

"Linda, listen to that!"

"We will be lucky if those winds don't bring some of our trees down."
The wind had been gale force for an hour, but it was getting even more intense. The roar was growing louder by the minute when Colin opened the curtains to check on the trees at the back of his block. There was a dull red sky to the west; as he opened the window, the heat and acrid smell of fire drove him back.

"For God's sake Linda get the kids and the emergency box and go! Follow our plan to get to Blackmans Bay, and if necessary, get into the water. I will be there in a couple of hours if I can; I will need to get to Headquarters and make sure everybody is on duty. Grab the cat and Jasmine's teddy and go. Get off these narrow roads, get to the Highway and don't stop."
Linda ran to the Kingswood Station Wagon, throwing everything out of the car into the garage so she had room to put their cases and essentials in the back.

She grabbed the photo albums as she went past, putting them and the emergency pack, as well as the cat cage in the back of the car. The kids were bundled into the back seats with Teddy and a couple of their favourite books. Colin jumped into the Land Rover fire truck, threw his bag of firefighting gear in the back, and raced off to the Headquarters.

Linda headed north to the small development around Blackmans Bay. Finding the access to the beach, she drove towards the water's edge until the sand started to become soft. Parking the car on firmer ground, she had turned it for a quick getaway as soon as the all-clear was given. She could do no more. It was time to sit in the car and wait for a radio announcement to go home.

Three times Colin had to change directions as he headed into the city. Trees were falling across the roads everywhere, taken down by raging winds or all-consuming fires. By the time he reached Headquarters, the Municipality of Snug had been listed as a disaster area. Many houses were burning, and two deaths had been reported. Colin phoned Glenorchy Station but was told that the whole area seemed to be alight. The map was full of red buttons and black crosses. "Mate, you were telling them for months, but no-one was listening."

"I was warning them that it was a possibility, but I was hoping that it wasn't going to happen like this. This is an absolute bloody nightmare."

At five o'clock Colin got a message that his street was alight; by seven he was told it was all gone.

He was distraught when he was told that the remains of his elderly neighbours were being removed from their house and taken to the morgue for identification. Colin let them know that they did not have any relatives, but that he could identify them if necessary. He asked about his house.

"It is just a smouldering mass of burnt timber, Mate. There is nothing salvageable. The land looks as if a giant flame thrower had just blasted the whole area, leaving just burnt remains and the occasional shed", There is not one living animal to see. If they have not been moved, they are dead."

"Thank heavens we got all our animals to Hamilton, and the kids and the cat are with Linda so we will be okay. The house has been a beautiful place to raise our children, but we can rebuild it if we have to."
He had hoped it would survive because it was full of memories, and bits and pieces from all their trips away. Well so be it. The family should be at Blackmans Bay, with the protection of the water.

He thought that the Premier should offer him an apology, but he was unlikely to ever get that. Eric was a good bloke and loved by his community; but he was a successful politician and unlikely to admit he was wrong.

Linda saw the ball of flame racing along the trees and the sand dunes. She grabbed the children and told them they were going for a swim.

"If we have to, we will duck under the water as much as we can. We will be all right."

The flames ripped through the dry grass imbedded in the dunes and snaked towards the cars parked on the beach. The Kingswood erupted in flames and then exploded as the fuel caught alight. Jasmine screamed out for Teddy, but Linda knew the family cat had just been incinerated. She hoped it was instantaneous; at least, that was what she would tell the children.

At Headquarters, the message came in that Blackmans Bay had been decimated. There were deaths there, but the figures weren't known; nor were any of the details, except that the fire had raced along the scrub near the beach and caught many people who had escaped from the city. Colin panicked as he drove towards Blackmans Bay. The smoke was thick and the vision almost zero as he drove into a wall of flame. His Land Rover stalled in the heat. As he drifted to unconsciousness his thoughts were just of his wife and kids. "Lord, keep them safe."

30: Radar.
February 7th

Andrew had a Gladstone Bag full of school records.

He had the details of every-one still registered for the Homage to the Mountains in his bag. He had spent weeks reviewing them and culling the list to twenty-five. The others would be told over the first week back at school that they had not made the final list. Some would have decided during the holidays that they were unsuitable for the walk, but one way or the other, the walking group had to be reduced to about fourteen, fifteen at the very most, plus teachers and assistants. The final cut would reduce the numbers once school resumed. The bag was in the garage behind the car, ready to be loaded once the suitcases and essentials box were in. It was the only work item that he planned to take with him.

He sat in the driver's seat of his Austin 1800 and turned on the radio. The fire notices were continuous – all schools were closed; most roads were closed. It was assumed that there were already deaths. Many suburbs were alight, and it seemed that several houses had been destroyed. He told Julie it was time to grab their essential pack and the kids and get out.

Andrew had decided a month ago to drive straight up the Midlands Highway and stay at least fifty miles ahead of any reported fire. Julie asked him to wait while she fixed her make-up; Andrew yelled at her to get in the bloody car, or she would be finding her own way north. Suzie and Karen thought it was a joke, but Matt wanted to stay and stop the fire getting to the house. "Listen kids, just get in the car. We have done everything we can and now it is down to God, luck, and the fire service. If they can't stop it, then we live with whatever. But we are not staying here to die."

Andrew was twenty minutes into the trip when he remembered the Gladstone bag that he had left in the garage. That work had taken most of his summer's break to produce; he thought of turning around, but he remembered how he had reacted to Julie wanting one minute to fix her makeup and he thought he would never live it down. Best to cross fingers and hope the bag was there when he got back home once the fire danger had passed.

Bridgewater was facing fires from several directions as they crossed the Derwent; there were fires everywhere to Brighton and Pontville. Andrew drove as fast as he could, but visibility was poor due to smoke and ash. The air cleared five miles north of Brighton and Julie suggested they stop at the next little village, but Andrew said they would stop at Campbell Town and assess the risk. If necessary, he would keep going north until there was no risk at all.

Julie turned the radio on to listen to the news spots and fire reports. It was terrible. It seemed that more bodies were being found every few minutes. The fires were all over the city, out past New Norfolk and spreading up the lower end of the East Coast. South of Hobart, it sounded like every town and village had been destroyed.

There was no mention of their area in North Hobart, so they just kept hoping that they would be lucky and would return to an intact house, but it was obvious that was unlikely.

At Campbell Town they knew they needed something to eat but the café sent them to the High School, where a temporary shelter and kitchen had been set up. Volunteers were making breakfast and lunch. Trucks and cars were arriving, with chairs, beds, and bedding. Many people were already asleep, exhausted after a frightening night, and even worse morning.

The volunteer supervisor told them to all turn off their radios and rest.

"If there is anything you need to know, we will tell you. We have a person monitoring the radio and writing notes. If you need specific information, we might have it, but we are too busy to be chasing information that is not essential."

Julie asked Andrew if he was okay. The first couple of times he just said he was rattled by the way this had happened, and he was worried that they might lose the house. Julie told him she had the insurance papers and if the house burnt down, they would have enough money for a new home and modern fittings.

Eventually Andrew told her about leaving the Gladstone Bag in the garage, and that all the work over the summer had been lost. She smiled as she told him that when he growled at her about the makeup, she had picked up his bag and hurled it – into the back of the car. "I think you will find it has the emergency box sitting on top of it, but it is otherwise unscathed."

The three children had found a couple of mattresses and some blankets on the floor and were already asleep when Andrew and Julie decided it was time for some rest. "Hopefully there will be a wind change, or some rain, and conditions will improve."
By daybreak, most people were up and about, after a restless night. The CWA was busy cooking breakfast, and the coffee urn was working overtime.

The ABC morning news lead story was that the death toll had reached fifty, and that the amount of property damage was catastrophic. One of the deaths was a significant member of the fire service but details were withheld until all relatives had been notified. Conditions had eased overnight, and it was expected that some areas would be cleared, to enable people to go back; but they should be prepared for the worst. There was a likelihood that the family home was burnt down or damaged, and that it would not be safe to go onto sites with fire damage, due to the probability of collapsing walls and roof structures. The report finished with a statement of massive stock losses on farms, and domestic pet deaths in the suburbs.

The fire services were trying to clear the dead bodies of domestic pets, to prevent further emotional disturbance to children. But there was a strong chance that some dead pets would be found by families, or that they would not be found at all.

Andrew listened to the details from the police report; their suburb was still closed by police order. There were too many spot fires in the area; the fire crew was operating on skeleton staffing to prevent trees from re-igniting and destroyed houses from throwing embers that could start the main fires again, as most of the crews were still working in the major trouble spots. Half of the fire-fighters had been released for a rest, but many of those were phoning in to tell their supervisors that their own houses had been lost or damaged. They were being sent to the refuges that they had directed thousands to throughout the previous two days.

The three children were making new friends while Julie sat alone and cried. Andrew sat with her for a while, but when she said she needed some time to herself, he went to the car for the Gladstone bag. Starting to read student profiles, he tried to decide who to delete from the walking group.

Julie asked him what he was doing but when he told her, Julie shook her head. "Andrew, for God's sake`, some of those kids are probably dead. Just put the paperwork aside and keep an eye on your children."

He got up and walked over to the girls, who were happily playing Snap with a group of eight other girls.

He asked if they were hungry, but they'd had enough food at breakfast, and did not need a drink. Suzie and Karen were sitting with a group of girls, talking about school, and the toys they had left at home. Matt was angry; he had spent three years nagging his parents for a bike that he got for Christmas. "Now I bet it has been burnt in the fire." Andrew told him that he would get a new one if that was true. "Can I pick the colour Dad, because I would like a red one?"

"That will depend on whether there are any bike shops left in town, Matt. We will do what we can do." Andrew walked to the door; the area was completely clogged with cars, and more were still coming in. He found his car and turned on the radio. Music was playing; he changed channels until he found a news report. The announcer was reading an official report; the death toll was over sixty, but most of the fires were now contained. His street in North Hobart was mentioned as accessible now for emergency returns, but not for habitation. Owners of properties were allowed back in the street with identification that showed they lived there, although some houses were too dangerous to enter. A few houses appeared to have been spared, but most were destroyed or severely damaged, according to the report. No-one would be allowed to return home for a few days, but those who wanted to would be allowed into the street for an hour, to check their homes and belongings.

Andrew and Julie agreed to return to their home, so they could realistically prepare for the next few months.

The city looked like a war zone, with destroyed farmlands and dead sheep and cattle everywhere. They were all bloated as they lay in clusters near fences, where they had been unable to escape. By the time the fences burnt down the animals were dead. Everything was black, with the occasional pristine tree standing alone in acres of burnt grass and forests.

Bridgewater looked like a scene from Dante's Inferno as they approached the Bridge. A single burnt car shell sat forlornly off the side ramp, in a paddock of burnt grass and ash. A blue ribbon of water stretched through the middle of hell, with the city in the distance covered in a pall of smoke. The lower half of Mount Wellington was a grey haze, the upper half of the mountain had vanished into a cloud of smoke.

As Andrew turned into their street, everybody in the car went silent. Their house was sitting in a burnt-out street but appeared to be untouched. All the houses around them were ash and twisted metal, with a few brick fireplaces still upright. What had been a street of timber Edwardian and Federation houses was now just the remains of family dreams.

It was eerie. Andrew was the first to say what everybody else was thinking.

"It would have been easier if our house had burnt down too."

Julie looked at the remains of the houses of their friends and neighbours.

"I don't think I can face them. How can this wooden house still be standing, with slightly blistered paint, and everything else in the street has been burnt to nothing? It doesn't make sense. Look, Mary's brick fence has cracked, and parts have fallen down."

They went inside, to see it much as they left it. The windows were filthy, and there was a strong smell of smoke. The carpet around the chimney had small burn marks and ash covering it for a few feet, but otherwise everything looked normal.

A police officer came to the house to make sure they were the owners. He checked Andrew's driver's licence and said, "You are bloody lucky mate." Andrew told him that they were not feeling lucky; they had lost their neighbourhood and were uncomfortable to still have their house when everybody else had lost theirs.

"Look mate, I am sorry, but even though your house looks fine you won't be able to stay here tonight. The area has been listed as uninhabitable till further notice. You will have to find somewhere to stay. If you need help, there is a command post near Constitution Dock that may be able to advise you."

Andrew thanked him, but they had relatives in the North that were unaffected by the fires. He felt sure they could go there. "Are there working phones there, so I can contact Launceston?"

He was advised that there was a limited phone service there, but it was only available for short phone calls, not long conversations.

"That is all I will need."

31: Search and Rescue
February 7th

Sergeant Garry Rogers had been awake most of the night.

The smell of smoke was overwhelming. From his house he could see a glow in the sky everywhere he looked. He called Headquarters but the initial advice was that the police had enough officers on duty, but to stay ready to go if called.

At five o'clock he answered the phone call from Headquarters that told him that the first death was confirmed. He was ordered to Snug to collect the body and bring it in for an autopsy. Before he got to the address, he had received five messages on the Police radio in relation to deaths. He was warned that he would face bedlam at the Royal Hobart Hospital, as they had more than two hundred people there with burns, ranging from first degree to hands to third degree full body burns. "There will be more deaths. It is not sustainable to be extensively burnt to more than half the body and survive."

Garry started calling in other members of Search and Rescue, to remove the dead from homes and workplaces, and get them to the morgue. Within a few hours the numbers were approaching fifty. But the number of injuries were more than five hundred.

Garry went to Headquarters, where he could coordinate the response; he needed to know who was working and who was available to call in. He phoned every number he had but most of the phones were not working.

"Where the fuck are they?" one of the staff fumed.

"Mate, the lines are probably out, or the house burnt down. He might be fighting a fire on his doorstep, or he might be dead. I bloody doubt that he is sitting in his lounge chair watching the cricket."

Regularly staff had to leave when calls came in about places where they lived or had family. Garry told them all to just go if they had to, but write on the blackboard where they were going, and what time they left.

"I am not checking on you, but I want you to call in on police radio or by phone every hour, so I know you are okay. Please be careful; we have enough dead already. Do not put yourself in unnecessary danger."

It was late in the afternoon when they got a call about a Fire Service Land Rover burnt out just north of Blackmans Bay. There was a badly burnt body in the driver's seat. Garry told them to stay clear but remain at the scene till he arrived. He was certain that it would be someone he knew. The Land Rovers were issued to senior officers of the Fire Service; they often trained with Search and Rescue because their work often overlapped.

Some he knew as Fire Department personnel, some he knew as colleagues, and some he knew as mates. It would not be easy, whether he knew the person or not.

He dreaded the talk to relatives; it was always mind numbingly tough, and it was much harder if he knew the deceased.

He called the Fire Service Headquarters, but they had several Officers out in Land Rovers. He got the name of six of them but was told there were eleven of the vehicles in the fleet, and the other five vehicles could be anywhere. He asked them to start calling on the two-way radios, and then call him with the names of anybody who did not respond.

He was almost at the burnt-out car when he got the call to tell him it was Colin. They had been mates for years. They were about the same age and had been working together for most of their lives.

"That is so bloody unfair. He has been working his arse off for months, to make everybody aware of the risk of fire this year; it is just unbelievable. He would have known the fire was there; why would he drive straight into it?"

Even with the extreme damage to his face Garry recognised Colin immediately. At least he could do that officially, to spare poor Linda from having to make the formal identification. That face would haunt him forever, but it would terrify Linda. He would make sure she did not see her husband like that; it was the least he could do.

He assisted with removing the body for transport to the morgue; then advised he would be in to do the formal identification and not to ask Linda to do that.

He needed to find her first and let her know, before the news media started releasing information. He headed for Colin's house but the whole neighbourhood had gone up in flames. There was nothing left in the street except chimneys and tin roofing, twisted and buckled beyond any recognisable shape.

It took four hours before Garry located Linda and the children in the safety of the hall at Blackmans Bay. He told her what she needed to know, and stayed with her for a couple of hours before the Police Chaplain took over.

Garry phoned Headquarters to let them know he was going home to rest and would come to the station in four hours. An hour later he phoned again.

"Is there a bed available there? My home no longer exists."

32: The Car
February 9

"We have found the shell of a burnt-out car."

"Hey Marcus, we have been up in the hills around the Brighton Army Barracks.There.is a burnt out car there that one of the crew thinks it is the same model as yours." Marcus got his directions and headed out in the service vehicle that had been loaned to him at the station. It took ten seconds to identify the remains from the numberplate, which was severely burnt but still readable. He removed the number plates and took them with him. The ID plate was melted beyond recognition. Marcus walked around the car and checked if from every direction. It was obvious that it had been well hidden, but the fire had removed all the branches and undergrowth. The petrol tank had ruptured and would have significantly added to the fire. There wasn't much left. The body was twisted in the heat, but still recognisable. The seats were burnt down to the springs, the hubs were still there. The bodywork was already orange from rust; there wasn't anything salvageable on the car.

The coincidence that his car was not very far from the other one that had been parked near him at the station and found at the Bridgewater Bridge made him fairly certain the thieves were from around there.

As he headed into town, he saw a small group of teenagers digging through the remains of the fish and chip shop.

Marcus went home and got his first aid kit, plus an extra supply of superglue and gaffer tape.

He returned to the Bridgewater area in his fireman's clothing, and started checking on the burnt houses and vehicles. He took the opportunity to get into conversations with the teenagers hanging around the remains of the little shopping centre. He asked them about the shops, and what the shops had sold. He told them he was looking for anything that might explode, or anything that was dangerous. "If you find anything worthwhile there could be a reward, as we need to clean up the area as soon as possible."

"Do any of you know who owns the car over near the Bridge? The burnt out one. Do you know if it has been there long?"

Four of the boys laughed and said that it had only been there a few hours before the fire. "Probably dumped by someone who was sick of it."

Marcus checked what they had found and made a point of telling each of the boys that they had found something that was useful. He gave each of them a note saying they would receive five dollars reward and a letter of thanks from the Police Commissioner.

He handed them his official report book and asked them to fill in their name and address so he could arrange the letter and reward as soon as the fires were completely under control.

Marcus went back to the station and returned his car to the depot carpark. Two days later Mary was on night duty at the hospital, so he dropped her at work and then drove to Bridgewater. He sat in a quiet street where the four boys lived. There were many houses damaged but most had been cleared to live in. Marcus slipped on his car coat and pulled the hood over his head. He put his sunglasses in the pocket, and his breathing mask in the backpack. With the damage to his lungs, he had become very sensitive around smoke, so he had a rubber mask that fitted over the nose and chin. It had two round canisters either side of the mouth to filter out dust particles. For him it had been essential during the fires. It also conveniently altered his voice. He sounded like an evil character from a horror movie.

The four young males he had talked to earlier in the day had an unexpected visitor. They were woken with their hands tied and gaffer tape over their mouths. The intruder had his eyes covered by reflector sunglasses. He wore a car-coat with the hood pulled up over his head. "Tell me who took the X2 Holden from North Hobart, or I will start pulling your fingernails out one at a time. I will take the tape off your mouth and if you make a noise, I will cut your throat" Each boy talked as soon as the fine point pliers latched on the first fingernail.

They all said it was the Sturmer boys and young Marshall. It took a further ten seconds to get the addresses. Marcus went to their houses; the street had some fire damage, but the Sturmer and Marshall houses were habitable. It was obvious that nobody was at the houses. Marcus put on his uniform and went to speak to the neighbours. Nobody knew where they were.

He left a message that some of their stuff had been recovered after the fire, and the Fire Service was holding it until they returned. "Don't bother troubling them when they show up. I will call around in a couple of days. If they go somewhere else, just drop a note in their letterbox and tell me where they are. It is very important I get their stuff to them soon. The Insurance Company has offered a fifty-dollar reward, so just put your name and address on the note. I will make sure you get the reward. Don't bother telling them about it, because we won't be able to meet them at any set time because of the fires. So long as I can get to them in the next few days it will be hunky-dory."

There were lights on in the street; the electricity was still connected. Marcus drove through the street each night looking for lights from the two houses. On the fourth night the lights were on. "Bingo! Time these little pricks learnt a lesson about the value of private property," Marcus whispered to himself.

He parked the old station wagon in an unlit part of the street. It was cheap, and he'd had cash; he had bought it under a false name.

He had no intention of changing the registration over to his own. He had a job to do, and then he would abandon the car with the keys in it. It would not last long before another group of teenagers took it for a joyride.

Marcus was about to put some of his tunnel rat training to use, along with his magician's skill of vanishing without a trace.

He slipped his car coat on, making sure he had his sunglasses and breathing mask. His thin surgical gloves had been taken from Mary's medical kit; he needed full use of his fingers. He put his sunglasses on and waited, just as he had done in the tunnels. His eyes slowly adjusted to the light, and he could see clearly.

He entered the Sturmer house without making a noise and located the boys' bedroom. They were all asleep. He put his fingers to the throat and gently pressed. The boy passed from sleep to unconsciousness in a few seconds. He picked him up and took him outside the door. He gaffer taped the mouth and eyes closed and tied his hands and ankles tight.

He was dropped into the station wagon. It took a few minutes but soon the old car had three teenagers hog tied in the back. As he drove away, they started to moan.

"Don't worry boys, I am just taking you back to a car you left at Pontville. You remember that car, boys?" He had put the gas mask back on; his voice was a terrifying growl.

Marcus drove past the Brighton Army Camp; he entered a side road to get dressed. He checked he was covered by the car coat and that his sunglasses were on. The gas mask with their bright orange cylinders made him look menacing. He drove with his lights off until the Ballyhooly Road junction when he turned in towards the remains of his car.

He placed the Sturmer boys on the front seat springs and Toby Marshall on the back seat. They were unable to move much because of the way he had tied their arms and legs.

One by one he removed the gaffer tape from their eyes. He had some plastic water-pipe cut to about four inches long. Pulling the gaffer tape off Roly Sturmer's mouth, Marcus growled that this would be glued into his mouth to enable breathing. He coated it liberally with superglue and forced it into the middle of his lips. He pinched the rest of the lips closed and covered them with more glue. The other boys were treated the same.

"We didn't set it alight. We were going to bring it back. We were just having a bit of fun," was all that Toby could say before the pipe was put in his mouth and the mouth glued shut.

He then took the restraints off the hands and glued those to the door frames and the heavy metal bar at the front of the seat.

He walked around the car and spread a gallon of diesel as he said, "If this catches alight you will be incinerated like this car.

That pipe in your mouth will make sure you pull the flames down into your lungs. I guarantee that the world won't miss you at all, you little shits."

They were screaming but there was not much to hear that made any sense. He waved a box of matches at them as he got back in his car and drove away.

Marcus called the police from a phone box on a deserted street. He left the mask on to camouflage his voice. He told the police that a burnt-out car was on Ballyhooly Road in the Mangalore Tiers.

He said that he was not sure if it got caught in the fires or caused the fire. "Be careful not to start another fire. The last one has caused too much damage, and there are three very nasty wild animals nearby that will need careful handling."

When the police arrived, they found three frantic boys. Sitting next to Toby on the back seat was a large bottle of acetone; it had a pharmacy label on it that stated. "Will remove superglue. Treat with care. Will damage skin with heavy contact."

"What the fuck is this about?" He started to lift the hands, and Toby screamed as much as he could through the pipe in his mouth. The police officer stood back to check what to do next, as he reached for a cigarette.

All three boys screamed "No!" That was when he recognised the smell of diesel all around the vehicle. "Jesus, someone has gone to a lot of trouble to terrify these boys."

He went to the police radio to call in the details of what he had found. He asked for help from Search and Rescue and requested a trauma specialist from the hospital. He frankly did not know where to start. He considered just using cutting tools to free the boys, then take them to the hospital for the specialists to break the binding of glue to skin. But the risk of a spark igniting the diesel was too high. Just pulling them free would create massive skin and muscle damage. He had no idea how to use the acetone. He would just wait for help. These three had been there for several hours and survived. It was unlikely they would die in another hour till help arrived.

Marcus drove back to the Bridgewater Bridge. He left the car with the keys in the ignition on the southern side of the bridge, at the opposite end to the remains of the other car stolen on the same night as his X2. The old car near the bridge was a burnt-out shell but there was no evidence of who was responsible. Of course, the police quickly determined that this was the car that was stolen from the Fire Services Headquarters because Marcus' report had included the WOG numberplate. That did not help much but at least the owner had an answer; and could collect the Insurance if he had any.

He had worn a pair of shoes that were four sizes too big. He had a pair of women's shoes on poles that were used to create footprints, before removing the gaffer tape from the eyes of his three thieves. He knew no one had seen him, so his defence would always be that he knew nothing.

He removed his over-sized shoes and the women's shoes from the car and put them in an old shopping bag. He took the women's shoes off the poles and disposed of the shoes in a pile of rubbish that was left for the fire clean up. He put the poles in another pile about a hundred yards down the road.

The bus was on time; Marcus got a ticket to the city but got off two blocks before the Empire Hotel. He walked home and hung his car coat up. He put his sunglasses away, and the mask in his workshop in a drawer with his spray-painting gun and attachments.

Mary was at work at the Repat and was not due home for a few hours, so he went to bed for a sleep. When she came home, he said he had woken with chest pain, and had been in bed all day. He said that the smoky air was causing a lot of trouble to his weakened chest, and he was struggling to do much at all. He managed to cough a few times and sound like an asthmatic when she was near. He must have been convincing because she made an appointment for him with the cardiothoracic surgeon at the Royal.

Forty minutes after the police radio call, a team from Search and Rescue arrived with Doctor Terry Rollins. He had been working with accidents and emergencies since the Second World War. He thought he had seen everything, but the challenge in front of him was a first.

He had seen a few people have fingers stuck together since superglue arrived on the domestic market, but nothing like this.

The boys were frantic and were completely irrational. If he untied their legs, they would be impossible to keep still; if he freed their hands they would lash out with their fists, and if he started working around the mouth, they would not hold their head still.

The only alternative was anaesthetic, then remove enough glue to get them free and safe. It would take days or weeks in the hospital to get the glue off and repair any damage. Psychologically, he feared, they would be damaged for life. Terry determined that he needed to free the airways first. If something went wrong, he had no possibility of resuscitation while the mouth was glued shut with a one-inch diameter pipe for air entry. He started with acetone on cotton buds, wiping it away as quickly as possible to avoid too much damage to the lips. As each area was separated, he added lip balm but left the residue of the superglue on the lips. It was going to be uncomfortable but that could be removed later. His plan was to remove the pipe from all three as the priority and then release the boys one at a time. He asked the police to call for two more doctors and two ambulances. It was essential for the Royal to be ready to receive these boys in three hours.

It was painstaking work. There were a few surface level cuts where scalpels were used to free the buttocks from the wire of the seats, and to get the hands off the door frame.

Terry gave each of the boys a tetanus shot and a heavy dose of antibiotics before putting them in the ambulances. He used the police radio to tell the hospital that these boys would arrive heavily sedated, but that they would need restraints on the beds because they would come out of the anaesthetic in a highly agitated state.

The next morning Marcus noted the old car was no longer at the Bridge. Sometimes thieves are useful, he thought. The morning news gave enough information for him to know the little pricks were alive. Hopefully, they might decide that there is a downside to stealing other people's property.

33: The Sturmers in Hospital

Toby, Jake, and Roly had lost their swagger.

They looked like terrified puppies as they struggled to walk. The cuts in their buttocks made movement painful. Their hands were bandaged from the wrists, and each day the physiotherapists made them work the hands and fingers through the pain. They struggled to talk coherently through swollen lips and tongues, which had rubbed raw on the pipe that had been stuck in their mouths for hours.

The police had tried but were unable to gain much useful information. The description was sketchy but sounded like science fiction.

He was not very tall, but he was super strong. He had a frightening voice that did not sound human. He had weird large eyes that shone in the dark and he had huge round cheeks that were bright orange like a clown. His face just seemed to not be there below the eyes.

The boys said that he had gone to bed and woken up in the back of an old car, with hands and feet tied, and the mouth and eyes taped over. There were no threats, but they were too frightened to call out; and anyway, there was nobody around.

Each was asked why he thought this had happened, and the significance of the location. They all said they did not know. If they admitted they had stolen the car it would certainly mean a very long time in prison. Judges did not look kindly on people committing new crimes while they were on parole.

Three weeks later the three of them fronted court in relation to the theft of three cars, including the police car and the Mercedes. The fires had meant courts were closed and cases delayed for several weeks.

The Judge dismissed the need for the photographer to attend the session after experts verified the photos, and maximum enlargements clearly identified the culprits.

Toby, Jake, and Roly returned to court, still in heavy bandages, and looking like they had been on the losing side of a fight. The Judge asked for some details of their current appearance, and their barrister provided a police and hospital report.

"Have you any idea why you were subjected to this level of brutality?"

The Barrister said that all enquiries had come to nothing. He surmised it related to the matter before her, but he had no evidence of that.

She ruled that the three had been involved in serious crime, with the stealing of three cars, and she ordered that their criminal record be endorsed with the details. As it would appear that they had been subjected to extreme criminal retribution, she would add no further punishment.

Placing them on good behaviour bonds, she stated that she would be less tolerant if the perpetrators of the retribution were brought before her court.

"It is not the duty, or the right, of the public to punish criminals, no matter how much they believe that the criminals deserve to be punished.

But be warned, young fellows; if you return to my court again, this level of criminal retribution will not prevent you from going to gaol. You will almost certainly be adults, and as such, you will go to Risdon Prison. And as much as we try to prevent it, young boys in an adult prison are subjected to some horrible behaviour. It is now time for the three of you to learn your lesson from this; go to school, get an education, and go to work."

34: James and Jane

Jane just started to cry.

She had drunk some wine but not that much. She dared not assume anything; she asked James what he meant, and he just said he was going with her. He had decided initially to use up his accrued leave, and then see where that took him.

"Jane, I understand the economics, I am not sure that the Round the World ticket will work for us. Let's look at priorities, and then decide which is the best season in those areas. From there we can see how we can link the places, and then choose the appropriate flights. It is not worth ruining a fantastic trip to save a relatively small amount of money. At this stage I have four months leave available, but I can take more if I need it. It would make sense for us to visit some of those places together on your wish list, then some of the others if there is time."

"I am not sure I understand what you are planning James?"

"I am not planning anything, and that is the plan. All our adult lives we have lived on a plan. We have got out of bed at a set time and gone to work.

We have worked on the files piled on our desks, until late at night when we have gone home. Once every two weeks we have received a ridiculous amount of money that we have no time to spend or enjoy. We don't take holidays because we are concerned that we might break the connection to the gravy train, then we repeat it the next week, and the next week, ad infinitum. We are the proverbial mice on the treadmill and I ,at least, want to get off. I want to take a plane to somewhere; I do not care where that is. I want to wander around without a plan until I get sick of it; and then I want to get on a plane and do it again. Jane. I looked at my bank account after you left. I would struggle to spend it in ten years unless I was stupid. We can go wherever we want, but I don't want a schedule, and I don't want to be told that I have to fly one way or the other, and that I can't double back. If I feel like doubling back, I want to be able to double back!

Let's look at these brochures and make a starting point; that is all we need. It is late winter/ early spring in the northern hemisphere and late summer/ early autumn in the southern hemisphere. You decide where you'd prefer to be next week, and let's go. Don't even think about what comes after that; just let's go somewhere now."

Jane remembered how foolish she'd felt when James demolished her plan to travel to Scandinavia on her own. The weather was now the priority for decision making. She thought that Scandinavia would be cold yet for months, as would North America, or at least the parts she definitely wanted to see around the Grand Canyon and Niagara Falls.

Canada would be frozen solid for a while yet. Australia reaches much further north than South Africa, and the tropics would be unbearable in Summer.

James challenged Jane to take a two-hour break in another room and make a list of the places she wanted to see as a priority: he said he would do the same and then over a bottle of wine they could create a decision of how to start. After that decisions could be made on the fly.

Jane took her list from previous plans and priorities them according to the weather and the season. James simply wrote a list of places in order of one to six. It was amazing how closely they aligned.

"Okay, let's pick four potential places to go first, then we can do some brainstorming to make the decision where to go. Once we feel like moving on, we can do it again to decide on the second place to visit. An absence of planning, will free us to travel on a whim."

Jane offered, "Australia and San Francisco."

James chose South Africa and Papua New Guinea.

"I'm not going to New Guinea; they are still cannibals there. I read in National Geographic that…."

"Look Jane, you are so tough, they would spit you out. But seriously I only put that forward to test you out. If we leave this week, it will be late summer in South Africa and Australia and late winter in San Francisco. So, Lady Jane; What is your choice?"

"Let's go to Australia, before the north gets too hot. We can fly into Sydney for a few days, and then check local airfares.

We should look at Darwin and the Great Barrier Reef, and head south. Maybe even drive a car. They are not like Europe; they drive on the left like we do."

Jane was excited about no plans. "We'd better get decent suitcases, and a mix of clothes."

"Get the suitcases but forget about the clothes. Take one good outfit. The rest can be stuff you are happy to throw out. We are best buying suitable clothing wherever we are. We are not going to the office. We don't need to impress anybody."

James was right, but once again Jane felt like a goose. She was acting like a person who had never been anywhere; then she realised she never had been anywhere like this. Every other trip in her life was, to some extent, work related.

"Let's not stuff around. We'll go to a travel agent tomorrow, and we will buy the best tickets we can get, providing we leave in less than ten days. We are going to fly into Sydney, or north of that, and we'll have one suitcase each, and it will be less than half full."

James was not missing a beat; he had decided he was going, and he wanted to go now. They checked their passports; both were current, but Jane decided to get a new one as hers only had another six months left. What the hell; she would pay priority fees to get a replacement in a week. They needed to check if Visas were needed, but they would do that tomorrow when they ordered their tickets.

Jane said her preference was to "start in Sydney; explore the East Coast from Sydney to Melbourne, and then go to Ayres Rock before travelling north. It should be getting cooler then. We could go to the Great Barrier Reef, then back to Sydney."

"From what I have read Jane, the only way to get to Ayers Rock is to drive almost to Darwin, then drive down the centre of Australia; or go to Adelaide and drive up. It is thousands of miles, and it is stinking hot and dusty. Maybe we should ask some locals when we get to Australia? We might be able to fly out there; I am not sure. It's a big country Jane. It is like driving around Britain ten times.

Let's not plan. Let's go to Sydney and decide from there. Sometime in your schedule you want to visit that wool place, and I would like to try some surfing. I will look like a long-legged spastic goose, but if you go to Australia, you have to surf. That is the rule according to St James."

"Okay. Start in Sydney, then decide from there. It will be exciting no have no idea and no real plans."

"Let's go to Australia House today to make sure we have all our papers in order and buy some tickets. We can get some practical advice and travel from the staff there and sort out some of the other issues that we will need to know. I would prefer to arrive in Sydney after three in the afternoon, if possible so I can have a decent sleep and not be too travel sick.

The advice in a travel brochure for seasoned travellers was to arrive late afternoon and have at least two nights in a hotel in Sydney.

That will shake off the travel sickness and time lag. Frankly, after that I just want to go with the breeze."

The next day they purchased tickets to Australia with BOAC; the departure was ten days later, to allow time for Jane's updated passport.

They complied with the 'entry with no visa regulation', because of age, financial independence, and the intention to not stay. The best tickets were into Sydney where they had planned to arrive without accommodation booked. But they were told migration would require a booking for the first night, so they chose a room in the city. "That is the only planning I am going to do for the whole trip," James said. "I want to travel free as a bird."

Eleven days later they were in Sydney. The temperature was one hundred and four degrees and there was a powerful westerly wind, making the city feel like a furnace.

"We are heading south!"

35: Leuven, Belgium.

Once New Year had passed, work at the
Department store eased up.

 The workload was easier, with decent breaks during the
day but staff work hours were reduced. Department Stores
in Leuven reduced to skeleton staffing levels for the
month around the return to school and Universities. The
Departments selling school clothing and books remained
busy, but those selling everyday consumables and
discretionary items almost ceased trading. Katrien and
Marine were kept on because their parents had some sway
with management, but most of the student workforce
were laid off until Easter. Katrien and Marine had a few
hours on the weekends when the permanent staff
preferred to be home with their children.

 It didn't take much mathematical calculation to
decide that they would not have enough money to do the
whole trip that they'd planned. Australia was a big country;
they needed to choose a few highlights. and leave the rest
for another time in their lives.

They decided that they would visit Sydney, The Great Barrier Reef, Ayres Rock, and Tasmania; they would see a big city, go swimming in a warm ocean, visit a huge local attraction and follow the convict trail, which seemed a relic of an archaic, barbaric era.

The girls worked up the courage to speak to their supervisors at work for some extra hours of work; they were offered some additional work cleaning the store after closing on Saturdays and Sundays. The pay rate remained the same, so it meant that earnings increased by almost half. The travel budget looked considerably better, but the University social life fell away to almost nothing. Katrien indicated to Marine that she could live with it for a term, if it meant that their big adventure would be better. "We will at least have money for some decent food."

"You will receive a substantial pay increase at Easter time because so many staff request all Easter off for religious observances. You will have about ten days at fourteen to sixteen hours a day, but I am afraid there won't be much more after that before you leave. Unfortunately your income will be severely restricted after Easter."
Both girls asked their fathers to lend them additional money to be paid back later. Both were refused 'a loan' but were promised help to get another job for a few months.

A local tourist company was looking for staff to take people to the war graves and battle fields of Belgium. One of the requirements was that the guides had to speak English.

The fact that Katrien and Marine spoke Dutch, French, English and German, made them strong candidates. They were offered an improved salary but had to be available for long hours on the weekends. Most of the major battlefields required significant bus travel, but Katrien's father told her he could arrange to borrow a car from her grandmother if it was for that purpose. There was an intensive war history training programme, which made them realise how many people died in their country in two separate World Wars.

They were instructed to always express gratitude to those who fought for the freedom of Belgium, but not to show any animosity towards the Germans. Their soldiers were young men fighting for their country, and they had died in huge numbers. Their families had the right to grieve and should be treated with sympathy.
They also proved to be very generous, with the girls receiving very good tips from the Americans and Germans. They noted the Australians were incredibly pleasant but never gave tips. They often were invited to come and stay as guests when they were in Australia; but that would be difficult to do.

Both girls were surprised to see that their study did not suffer. They both submitted their work on time, and their marks remained excellent. They did not go to as many parties, but their relationships with friends that were most important to them remained as strong as ever. They were often asked how they managed to get such cool jobs.

It was difficult to explain that the hardest part was asking for work, and very few of their Uni associates tried; even when they were told who to talk to, and where the recruiting office was.

As Easter approached, they decided to stay with the war graves tours and the battlefields. They were earning good income and gaining great satisfaction from helping ex-soldiers and their families at a very emotional time. The two girls at first struggled with older people whose sons had died, but gradually they took this on as a challenge to unload the burden from some very troubled shoulders. Sometimes parents held them close and wept on their shoulders as they thanked them for their support. They often mentioned that the war graves were of young men who were the same age as their male friends, and that made their work very personal.

Just after Easter Katrien received a registered letter from the United States. In it was a thank you card and five hundred US Dollars 'to make your trip to Australia as rewarding as you made our trip to Belgium. God Bless you both.'

36: Lizzie and Alison.

First term was different than the previous two years.

There were academic studies in the hallowed hallways of the Arts Department, but a large part of the year was on placement at schools in and around Victoria and Tasmania. There were four placements for one month in Hobart, just before the mid-year break. Tasmania needed some teaching students in the Matriculation Colleges, and Lizzie and Alison were quick to apply; they were both outdoor types, and decided if they could get selected, they would stay on after the month and walk the Overland Track. They would take their backpacks with them anyway and they could live in accommodation supplied free by the Education Department in Hobart. When the placement lists were released, they had their option, because no one else applied.

They were confident that they should be able to tag along with a group from one of the colleges, who knew something about the Track but if not, they would do their research and make the walk together.

The months of February and March were dedicated to class-room techniques that allowed the student to learn the art of communication of ideas. This was followed by short placements in local primary schools under supervision, and then two placements into junior high school classrooms in May. For those choosing to teach high school, June was the cauldron. The students were allocated to a school for a full month. Working under the guidance of senior teachers, they designed classes within the curriculum, then presented them while being observed and graded by the school Masters. It was a nerve-wracking ordeal, but it was an essential part of learning how to teach.

July was time away from study. Those who could afford to, used the time for a holiday. The rest found the month useful to work full time, accumulating enough money for the remainder of the year. Alison and Lizzie were on scholarships, so with all their costs met for the month of June they had enough money to take two weeks off to do the Walk. They needed to get the correct gear, but concluded that if they were sensible, they could get jackets that would be suitable for Tasmania in June.

The Melbourne University Ski Club told them that there were plenty of outdoor shops in Melbourne, so they could get advice easily enough. "There are people in those shops who think that walk is a toddle in the park. Your outer gear needs to be able to withstand a blizzard. It is better to be poor and alive than dead for a few dollars. Ask them if it the clothing is good for a hard day in the ski-fields. If not, then don't trust it in the highlands of Tasmania."

Fortunately, they had a great little book about walking in the Tasmanian highlands that had a detailed list of the requirements for a safe walk through the Track. One of the members of the Ski Club told them to treat the list like gold.

"Take everything on the list, and nothing else." They ticked off things as the acquired them, and put them in the little stockpile, with their backpacks.

The term seemed to drag on forever, and they were both becoming frustrated with the course. Lizzie often said that she was terrified of qualifying and being sent to her first school as a teacher. There just seemed to be no connection between the theoretical knowledge they were taught at the university, and what happened in a school when they turned up for their practical sessions.

"Bloody hell, the kids in class should have read the textbooks. They don't act remotely close to what the books suggest." Alison was part way through her first placement with primary students. They were well-behaved but did not seem to have learned anything in her classes. Each morning, she did a brief refresh of the lessons of the day before. Her primary school students had no idea what she had told them. They just looked at her as if she was speaking a foreign language.

By the end of the week, she had concluded that she was not remotely suited to be a teacher, and she should change course before it was too late. Her supervisor asked her how she felt the week had gone. She broke into tears.

"I am hopeless; I have given it my best and they have learned nothing, I think I need to look at other options than teaching."

"Listen to me. You have been great; but students learn very little on a day-to-day basis. Learning soaks in through the pores of their skin. They know and understand virtually everything you have taught them, but they don't want to say so because they are all too concerned that they will get it wrong and look foolish.

On Monday I will play a game with them. You watch; it will require knowledge you gave them this week. They will all pass. Believe me, you did a great job. Feeling like you are failing is just part of being a teacher."

37: Hobart Recovery.

Gradually Hobart started to return to normal

The fire was the worst in Australia's history, with sixty-four dead and almost a thousand injured. Fourteen hundred buildings had been burnt down, and thousands of animals had perished.

There were many recriminations that warnings had not been heeded; the irony being that the warnings had often come from Colin Anderson of the Fire Service, and that he was one to lose his life. Government and authorities promised to do better, but gradually life returned to more or less the same as it had been.

Schools reopened, with some discreet enquiries in relation to losses of life, homes, and businesses. Teachers were instructed to be mindful of students showing signs of stress or anger.

Some schools would never reopen due to the extent of damage. Students had to be relocated to other schools. Temporary classrooms were moved around the state, and some brought in from interstate.

By early March every student was back in school, unless they were injured or suffering psychological problems after the fire.

Andrew Carruthers decided he needed to get his team together to make some firm decisions on this year's Cradle Mountain trip.

"Thank God, Julie saved the Gladstone bag Pete, or I think we would have had to cancel the trip this year. It will be hard enough to see who still wants to go, and who can go, without having to redo all the preliminary planning."

Andrew had organised a few physical tests at the end of term three and written comprehensive notes. He had a detailed fitness plan devised for each of the students, along with maps and the checklist of the walking essentials. Finally, he had a food list, and a list of what not to take.

In week one of term each applicant for the walk would be given their personalised pack, including the exercise regime. Each week, every student had to complete a list of those things on the checklist that they had ready. The supplies were kept in the school storeroom with access twice per week, to add items to the list. Radar could demand to check the pack at any time, and any person claiming to have supplies they did not have, had twenty-four hours to bring them to school or they were dismissed from the walk. The exceptions were the boots, clothing, and the backpack, because they were required for the training programme.

Each person had a monthly fitness target. If they failed to meet the score for two consecutive months, they were removed from the programme. Radar was tough, but he had no plans to have students die in the Cradle Mountain National Park.

He had a target for the other teachers and one for Julie as well. She was annoyed when her programme was provided and her aims were read out, just like all the students. He had assessed she was eighteen pounds overweight, and her endurance was limited to five kilometres per day. She was told to lose the weight and follow the exercise program to be able to walk fifteen kilometres in a full kit. When she protested that his demands were humiliating, he told her that everyone who participated would be ready to deal with anything the mountain could throw at them. He had no intention of losing a student, and even less enthusiasm about losing a wife.

Julie was keen to go, but the challenge was daunting.

After the past month she believed she could cope with anything, and she wanted to prove to Andrew that she could get fit and handle the deprivations of the trip; it would be nothing compared to the fear and frustrations of the last few weeks. She walked every day with her backpack loaded with four bricks, managing to walk four miles without any real concerns. Her legs were sore, and she got cramp in the hamstrings at night, but that was a good soreness. She had lost four pounds, although Andrew reckoned that she had worried that off in the two days of the fires.

Pete Smithies had significant damage to his house, but his insurance was already dealing with that. They had assured him that if the assessment said it could be returned to its previous state, then would commence soon. They were bringing in builders from the mainland. If restoration was not possible, the block would be cleared, and they could design a new house to the value of the insurance. Quietly he hoped for the second option.

Sonia Johnstone was new to the area, and renting. Her unit and belongings were incinerated, as was her motorcycle. Her insurance had already settled her claim, and she had bought a small car and found a flat a bit further from school. She was restocking her wardrobe gradually and enjoying the process.

They all agreed that the Homage to the Mountain should go ahead, and it was time to decide on the students who had qualified to be on the walk.

Twenty students said they could not go, either because of fire damage to their homes and belongings, or they had realised they no longer wanted to do it. No one said that they had concluded they were not fit enough; but it was obvious that some of them weren't.

There were now twenty on the list, plus four staff, including Julie. The student numbers needed to be culled by about five or six. The best outcome would be if the students decided to opt out, but in two months a final decision would be made and if necessary, some students would be told they had missed the cut.

Andrew and Pete arranged for each student to have a gym assessment, but requested they first had a medical assessment of their capabilities. The school needed a medical clearance to take part in the fitness test and challenge.

Two of them were advised not to take part because they had a heart murmur. That was not serious; but should be cleared by a cardiologist before taking part in such strenuous exercise. They decided not to do the walk.

The school scheduled Thursday afternoon for Physical Education for the senior students. Other teachers looked after general sports, but Andrew, Pete and Sonia set aside one month to sort out the walking group. They were each weighed, with results compared to a chart of optimal weight for height and build.

If overweight they were told how much they needed to lose and given a programme and a diet to achieve it. They were provided with targets for two weeks, four weeks and six weeks. It was not negotiable; meet the targets or don't go. They were assessed for fitness on exercise bikes and stair climbing. Again, the challenge was not negotiable; reach the target or stay at home.

Andrew just kept telling them that he was not going to lose students like Scott and Kilvert. Accidents happen, and sometimes were unavoidable; but no one was going to die on his trip because of poor preparation.

Andrew started the briefing session with a list of the applicants.

He emphasised that the list was provisional and would change before the start of the walk.

He gave each of the other leaders the list, along with his impressions. He emphasised that the list was not for distribution, but rather, a reference to be assessed by everyone.

"Tell me if you think I have got it wrong, because the list has to be completed in one month."

Each of the potential walkers were given a check list for supplies, equipment, and preparation exercises.They were all told that their lists would be checked in two weeks, and some basic exercise tests performed. If the applicant was not meeting basic standards of fitness they would be advised to withdraw from the walk.

38:The Wedding Arrangements.
Easter 1967

The Wedding arrangements were almost complete.

Doris sent a message to Mary in early January to advise that all the basic decisions for the wedding were complete. Easter Saturday was the twenty fifth of March; much earlier than usual, so it was necessary to get the final details set.

She needed to know who was on the guest list, who needed accommodation, and which cars would be used as the wedding cars. That made Marcus bristle. Though he had the money from the insurance for his car, he could not buy another one like it, so he just bought a standard car. There were rumours that Holden was about to release a road registrable race car within the next year, so he decided to wait. The dealers had him on an early notification list when details of the car were available, and as an existing client he would be a priority purchaser.

The wedding was planned to be quite small with two of Mary's nurse colleagues as bridesmaids. Her father would be with her to "give her away".

In her opinion, that was sufficient. Marcus had decided long ago that Tom Swinson would be his best man, and one of his mates from the Fire Service could also be in the wedding party. He had no family to invite, and very few friends.

The guest list could be arranged by Doris and Mary. He was happy to just get married and have a few days with Mary on a honeymoon anywhere that pleased her.

Marcus felt like he was not pulling his weight. Mary was looking for a wedding dress he was not allowed see. She was checking flowers and making sure her girls looked lovely. She was checking the guest list, because they were all her family and friends, and she was making sure the wedding breakfast was suitable. Doris was doing everything else. The Church had been repainted, and the pews polished. Arrangements had been made to clean the stained-glass windows during the week of the wedding. The driveway to the church had been spread with new blue-metal and all the grass trimmed. Flower gardens had been planted with white flowers on both sides of the entrance.

Tom took Marcus to Neil Pitt's Menswear in Launceston. Tom's advice was simple. A black dinner suit, white shirt, black bow tie and black patent leather shoes was essential. Once he knew the colour of the bridesmaids' outfits, he would add a fob pocket swatch to match. "Well, that's the main job done!" He and Tom went back around the caryards, but he was flogging a dead horse. There were no X2 sedans for sale, and certainly not one like his.

He briefly wondered if the little pricks had considered another car theft, but he quickly pushed that out of his mind. That bit of madness could have put him in gaol for a very long time. So far no one had put two and two together, but he could bet that more than one person had their suspicions. It was not rocket science.

Marcus and Mary returned to work, with plans to take holidays two weeks before Easter so they could get all the details right. Doris told them there were plenty of rooms in the grand house, and that they would have separate areas in the week leading up to the wedding. Old Tom grinned and said loudly to Marcus that he should be wary of a floorboard near Mary's room that squeaked loudly. "Dead giveaway Marcus. Be careful young man because Doris can be a stickler for protocol."

The weekend before the wedding Marcus and Mary headed north in a hire car. They chose a nice black Holden that should look pleasant with white ribbons. He made sure not to look up Ballyhooly Road as he passed through Brighton; if the remains of the X2 were still there, he did not want to know. Tom told him he was taking his job seriously; he had bought beer and planned to keep Marcus out of the way for a week. Everything was going to plan, and Tom planned to keep it that way.

39: Cynon.

"Bloody Hell, Jane, does this country ever cool down?"

They had been in Melbourne for two weeks. They loved the city; it had the charm of a modern cultured city in Britain, with great theatres and wide streets. The public transport system was fabulous and there was no shortage of lovely restaurants; but the heat was stifling. The days had all been above ninety degrees, and although the news service talked about the unseasonal heat, the locals said it was about normal.

They had bought a second-hand Jaguar in Sydney and driven down the coastal highway. The beaches and ocean views were stunning, but the heat was unrelenting. It was hard to imagine anybody was at work; the beaches were teeming with people, and every decent wave had several surfers searching for the best break.

They found a motel in Carlton where they could park the car, set off to explore the city by tram and train.

After a beautiful day walking around the shops and the parks, Jane suggested that they should spend Easter in Tasmania; it was a cool temperate region, and she could try and contact 'Cynon' and have a look at the fine wool centre.

"Then we can come back here as the temperature starts to cool down; this heat is killing me."
On a whim they stepped into the Tasmanian Tourist Office on Collins Street and discovered they could take the car across on the Ferry. The next evening, they were on The Princess of Tasmania with their belongings and a road map. The temperature was in the mid-seventies with a light breeze when they first sighted land. The morning was crisp, but the sky was like a Turner painting; pale blue with a hint of wispy cloud. They left the docks in Devonport without any plans other than enjoy the relief from the heat. The beautiful morning made them feel like they were about to enjoy a summer's day in the English countryside. "My God, James, it even looks like the English countryside. Look at the Hawthorn hedges and the oak trees. You could swear you were in the south of England."
James headed east while Jane looked at the map to find directions. She saw a road sign to Longford and Cressy, so they decided to see if they could find 'Cynon' and arrange to visit the property. The large grocery shop in Longford was open when they arrived in the town, so they enquired if anyone knew where the farm was.

James was pointed down the road. "About three mile out of town you would see the farm gate. You won't miss the giant statue of Ramses out the front of the farm."

"Why have they got an ancient Egyptian statue on a farm gate?" He was a little embarrassed when it was explained that the statue was a giant Merino ram that was the foundation of the best flock of Merinos in the world.

The first ram was named as a bit of a joke, but the current one, Ramses the Third, was known all over Australia in the superfine wool industry as the finest ram in the country. Multiple champion ribbons from the Sydney Easter Shows were testament to that. James asked if there was anywhere nearby to buy breakfast and a cup of tea but was told there was nothing like that in town. "You can get a counter meal at the pub in a couple of hours, but people have their breakfast at home round here mate." They decided to first find 'Cynon' and then think about food after that.

Doris was busy tidying the gardens when they drove in. There weren't any Jaguars she knew of in the town, so she assumed they were visitors. Jane introduced herself and told Doris they had travelled around the world to see where her woollen fabric came from. She asked if they could arrange to come back, but Doris told her that there was no time like the present. "Give me two minutes to wash my squibs and crackers and put on some clean clothes and I will be with you. Come up to the house with me and I will ask the cook to get you a cup of tea and some scones, and then I will be with you shortly."

Doris was intrigued; Who the hell were these people? As far as she was aware the only people who could afford Cynon cloth were royalty and Lords and Ladies of the realm. She certainly never expected them to drive up her driveway and have morning tea with her.

She happily showed them around the property, proudly displaying her finest sheep and her world-beating rams. The trophy room was full of awards from all over the world and photos of her Ramses I, II, and III. She showed them the wedding chapel that she was preparing for her nephew's wedding on Easter Saturday, then went looking for Tom. James was amazed that the Formula One race was held nearby, and even more so when he realised that Tom was the famous race car driver. He was thrilled, accepting enthusiastically when Tom offered him the opportunity to do a lap of the racetrack. Tom suggested they go in the Jaguar as the Rolls was a little ostentatious.

By the time they returned Doris was trying to convince Jane that they should get married while they were at 'Cynon'. The church was available, and the flowers were all set up. "What could be better, married at the church where your favourite cloth comes from?"

Jane laughed and pointed out that she and James were not even engaged, but Tom reckoned that was easily fixed. "Anyway, you look like you are married already, except you don't argue."

Doris enjoyed Jane and James being around the farm, and they loved the cooler weather. She asked them if they would like to stay for a couple of days. "You can meet my nephew and his fiancée tomorrow.

They will be here for only a few days, and then I am sending them on their honeymoon, after the wedding on Saturday."

"How did that happen? We arrived as perfect strangers two hours ago, and now we are staying here and meeting the family. If we are not careful, I think she might adopt us!"

"This is the kind of thing that I hoped could happen, but never expected too. In London, they'd step over you if you were dying in the street; here you are a long-lost bosom buddy - even if you've never met before. It is extraordinary, but I love it."

Doris told them about Marcus and his troubled life, and how he had been virtually adopted by her. She was shocked by how severely injured he had been in Vietnam, and certainly never expected his level of recovery.

She told them about how angry he was when his car was stolen, and all about the fires in Hobart, and how Marcus had been part of the front-line firemen during the worst of it. She told them about Mary, and how important she was to Marcus and his recovery.
It was a little strange when Marcus and Mary arrived, and even more so as Jane realised that the friendship with Doris and Tom was so recent. They had apparently very little in common with Marcus and Mary, or Doris and Tom but nevertheless becoming friends almost instantly. James had watched the Vietnam War from afar; Britain was not involved, so news coverage was scant.

He had been surprised at the mortality rate, and the rise of the anti-war movement in the United States and Australia. Britain had never been at war in the age of television, so the constant live footage on the evening news in Australia had been disturbing. But now he was talking with a fellow who had suffered incredible injuries, and a nurse that had seen too much.

The nights were like summer in London. Bedding was still required, as the evenings cooled down. Doris arranged for a small fire to be lit in the sitting room, so they were comfortable talking for hours after dinner. James told them how much this visit had meant to Jane; that they would remember this evening with great fondness. They had planned to move on to Launceston the next morning, but Doris insisted they stay at 'Cynon' and come to the wedding. They could come as Marcus' guests because he had no real family, and he obviously enjoyed their company. Jane was honoured but she felt they would be intruders, but Doris insisted. "Anyway, it will help you decide if you want to get married in our little church. A bit like a dress rehearsal for you."

40: The Wedding.

Doris wanted the wedding to be something special for Marcus and Mary;

She had brought in a chef to lead her kitchen staff and had hired a large marquee for the wedding breakfast. Mary was surprised when it was erected; it seemed far too large for her guest list, but Doris said it was necessary. "We don't want people to feel crowded." The church was five hundred yards down the road from the house, and it was agreed that Mary and her entourage would use the master bedroom to get ready. Marcus, with Tom, would use the other side of the house, the guests' quarters. Doris insisted that Tom not deliver Marcus to the church until she was there, and Mary would arrive ten minutes later.

Marcus and Tom conscripted James to drive them in Tom's open-top sports car. As they left the Cressy Main Road to enter the church lane Marcus saw what Doris had done; most of his Vietnam Company were lined up in uniform, to provide a Guard of Honour for him to enter the Church. They appeared in full regalia, including their medals. He walked into the Church under crossed rifles. Inside the door, offering him a salute was Harry Jackson, his mentor and trainer in the Tunnel Rats.

"Looks like you have been captured, Marcus. Sensible advice: Be nice to your captor." Marcus noticed the Captain's pips on the epaulets. He saluted him, and then tapped the pips to acknowledge he had noticed the new rank.

The Church was only small, but it was overflowing. At the end of every pew was a nurse with a single rose. When Mary entered the church, as she walked down the aisle, she was presented with each rose from all her work colleagues and three nurses from her army days. In the front pew were Doris and Tom, with Jane and James. Beside them was a couple he did not know, and a very tall young man and two teenagers; a girl and a boy who might have been twins. Marcus assumed they had to be related to Tom, because he was Doris' one and only relative.

The wedding ceremony was a blur, but once it was over and Marcus had kissed the bride they headed out to the marquee. The whole Tasmanian Symphony Orchestra was set up in the marquee, and as Marcus and Mary entered the area, they played the Bridal March. Doris was grinning like a Cheshire cat; all her plans had worked out perfectly, Mary and Marcus not expecting any of them.
She took the bridal party to meet some official guests, friends that had come to her party, some racing people from Tom's past, and then she took them to the couple who was sitting with her in the Church.

"Marcus, I want to reintroduce you to your sister Elizabeth, her husband Thomas Munster, her eldest son Jonathon, and the twins Michael and Margaret. I thought it was important to reunite the family."

Doris told him that she thought it was important, so she had hired some investigators and found the family in Iowa. Marcus had not cried such tears of joy in such a long time. For the first time in living memory, he hugged members of his family. When he eventually stepped away from his sister Doris whispered that Thomas was the father of all the children; this was the soldier Elizabeth had followed to America in 1948.

They had reunited and fallen in love. They were living on a small farm in Iowa, about fifty miles from Davenport. Thomas came from a large family, so Elizabeth had a strong family network in the USA. She had tried to locate her family but had been told they were all deceased. The Australian Government had officially told her that Marcus had been wounded in Vietnam and had succumbed to his wounds. They even advised her that he was buried in the Melbourne Cemetery.

"What the bloody hell! so, I am officially dead!"

Doris could see that Marcus was agitated to think that his life was so insignificant to a government that continued to pay his wages, arrange his rehabilitation and his pension. Furthermore, an official notification of his death had been sent by some little upstart in the records department to his closest surviving family member.

"Probably some pathetic little low life that Harold Bloody Holt found a job for."

Mary needed to calm him down, so she took his arm and asked him to introduce her to all his Army mates.

His memory of some of them was clear, some vague, but he felt incredibly honoured that they had come from wherever to Tasmania, to be at his wedding. Apparently, Tom had picked every one of them up at the airport in the Rolls Royce and had put them up together at a hotel in Launceston. He had buses bring them to "Cynon" for the service and the celebrations, after which they would be returned to the hotel. Doris had arranged a bus tour of the area the next day, and they would all fly out on Easter Monday. When Mary exclaimed that the wedding must have cost a fortune, Doris simply told her she had too much money, and this would help her get rid of some of it.

A world class Symphony Orchestra as the wedding dance band made for a memorable night for everybody. Mary loved to dance but Marcus was a little stiff and awkward. There had been no reason to learn to dance in his life and, as far as he knew, his wedding was going to be a simple ceremony in a country church with about ten guests.

Walking past Jane, Doris said the offer of the wedding at 'Cynon' was still there if she liked the idea. She would be truly honoured if they ever decided to use her little church for their wedding.

"Maybe not as flash as this, but I guarantee that Tom and I would make it memorable for you."

Doris loved to wear fashion garments made from her wool, but they were gifts from the world's best couturiers; she had never met anyone else who wore them. She had never met anyone else who could afford them.

She could not believe that Jane and James had flown around the world to visit her and see her sheep.

"Tom, that is a bigger honour than any I have received at the Royal Easter Show."

Tom smiled and whispered, "But the Show ribbons are worth more money."

Tom and Doris had slipped an envelope into the pile of wedding presents that included two air tickets to Paris and two weeks at the Hotel Charles V.

A little card said, "Have fun my boy, and look after your darling wife. We love you. Tom and Doris."

Neither Marcus nor Mary had passports. Both had been to Vietnam with the army, but they had not been anywhere else overseas. Mary had very few concerns getting her documents together, but for Marcus it was just one more concern.

A birth certificate was required; he did not have one and did not know where to start looking. He was born in Victoria; that was all he knew, apart from his parents' names. He assumed his birth date was correct, it got him bloody well called up to Vietnam, so that bit had to be right.

He applied to the Army for his records, hoping that would give him some information, but they told him the only Marcus Pigeon that served with the Australian Army in Vietnam had been severely wounded in Vietnam and died on August 28th, 1966. He protested that he had not died; he had been sent to the Repat Hospital in Hobart, Tasmania, and recovered from his wounds.

"Well mate, our records show that Marcus Pigeon died, and as far as we are concerned, he is dead unless proven otherwise."

Marcus went to the Department of Births Deaths and Marriages and showed them his driver's licence, his call-up papers, his discharge papers, and his wedding certificate.

The woman at the counter said, "Hmm; odd. Not sure how you got a wedding certificate when you are listed as dead. The certificate is probably not legal. I am fairly sure that people who are legally dead cannot get married after the registered date of their death."

"Oh, for God's sake woman. Have a look, I am standing in front of you; I am not dead!"

"Nevertheless, the register says you are deceased as of August 28th last year, and you have just got married. Someone will be in trouble for issuing an approval for a marriage involving a person who is officially recorded as deceased." She promised him that she would do everything possible to prove he was still alive, and if so, she would call him in to apply for a birth certificate.

"But I have already applied to you for it."

"Well, you have, but it is in the name of a person who is officially deceased and therefore I cannot process the request. Leave it with me; hopefully, I can prove you did not die, and I will send you a letter to come back here."

"Look I have two tickets to Paris as a wedding gift. We need to get this bullshit out of the way so we can go as soon as possible."

He was cautioned to not do anything about the tickets until this matter was sorted out, as no airline would carry a passenger without a passport, and certainly not one listed as dead.

He had a marriage licence, a driver's licence, and when he checked, he was enrolled to vote. But according to the Government he was dead; and that meant he could not go on his honeymoon. The same people who said he was dead, happily paid him a pension and met his medical bills. And half his battalion came to his wedding and saw that he was alive, including his training officer.

Marcus went to the Federal Parliamentary Offices in Hobart to get the nonsense sorted. He took all his documents, along with his request for a birth certificate, so he could get his passport.

A month later he received an official letter from the Australian Government, stamped with the Prime Minister's signature, advising him that the person he was seeking was listed with the Department as being deceased, killed on active service in Vietnam. The signature on the form was 'Harold Holt.' Below the signature was "Sir Harold Holt, The Honourable Prime Minister, Australia." Marcus became severely agitated. "He has killed off all of my fuckin' family one way or another, and now he has officially killed me off too."

Mary told him to calm down; she would speak to the specialists at the Repat Hospital, and she was sure she could get the error corrected. In the meantime, they could wait for the honeymoon.

It would be better to wait for the European summer anyway; Paris can be cold in winter and spring.

The hospital records office quickly found the problem. He was sent from Vietnam with papers that said, "the body is being returned to Australia for follow up care." Obviously, a clerk somewhere had listed him as deceased, and that was lodged somewhere in the system. Dr Bill Adams contacted the Veterans Affairs Department to advise them of an error in their records. When the clerk at Veterans Affairs started to defend the Department, Bill told him that the Federal Minister for Veterans Affairs was a personal friend; and it would take only one word about the bloody incompetency of their record keeping and all their bloody clerks would be looking for work at the zoo. "Fix this now! And call me back before four this afternoon or I will be speaking to the Minister tonight. Marcus Pigeon was shot but did not die. He was sent to the Repatriation Hospital in Hobart, Tasmania on August 28, 1966, and with the assistance of a pile of great doctors we kept him alive. He is now back living a relatively normal life. I went to his wedding recently. Fix this cock-up today, or I will personally have your guts for garters tomorrow. You got that? Good! Call me this afternoon. The name is Doctor Bill Adams in the post-surgical unit."

At half past three Marcus was again officially alive.

He gave it three days before again phoning the Department of Veterans Affairs to institute his birth certificate search. He explained that he needed the record details for his passport application.

He told them that in error, he had been listed as deceased, but he had been assured that had now been corrected.

"So be it, but you are still officially dead. Providing an error had been found and corrected, the changed information should arrive at the Registry within two weeks. You should contact us again in a fortnight or so."

He did.

"Hi Marcus, I am pleased to advise you that we have located your records. However, because you were reported as deceased, your files had been relocated to the section for service personnel killed in battle, and had all unnecessary paperwork removed. Your file has only the details on your call-up file, your service history, and your injuries. Everything else has been removed and destroyed. I am afraid that personal records are not in your file at all."

"Oh, bloody hell, what more can you bastards do to ruin my life."

Marcus went back to the Registrar of Births, Deaths, and Marriages in Victoria to explain his problem. He spoke to a young woman who told him that they were updating their cataloguing system, in readiness for an attempt to link all the states together she might be able to help. He gave her his full name, date of birth, and his army number. He provided her with the name of his mother and father and the approximate date of their deaths. He was not sure where he was born, nor could he guarantee that he had his mother's name correct. She asked for a day to try to locate his records. He told her that up until a month ago the Army had him listed as deceased, due to a clerical error.

She thought that might help, because although they had pulled the files of people listed as having died in the last five years, they had not been dealt with so that might assist a lot. "It will be a good place to start, and hopefully they will be more or less in alphabetical order."

By the next day she had located the file and was happy to provide a birth certificate. He was provided with a reference number, and an address. He was told to send a cheque with a stamped self-addressed envelope, and the birth certificate would be sent as soon as the cheque was cleared.

He arrived home to find Mary storming around the house, throwing anything she could find. "Look at this Marcus, just look at this!"

She had received an official letter advising her that the Marriage Certificate was being revoked because the groom was listed as deceased. The matter had been passed to the CIB, to investigate whether fraud had occurred or whether "the husband" was an Australian citizen. In the meantime, all banks have been advised to freeze all assets and bank accounts in joint names.

Mary was advised that impersonating a deceased person was a serious crime under Australian Law, and that if she knowingly married a person using the details of a deceased citizen, she would be prosecuted for fraud. If she did not know that the groom was using the details of a deceased citizen, then the marriage would become null and void without cost, and the marriage annulled. The male would be prosecuted under criminal law.

Marcus was furious. He drove into the city with the letter and the reference number from The Department of Births, Deaths, and Marriages, and headed to CIB Headquarters. The receptionist asked him to take a seat until the senior sergeant could see him. He expected to head to an office, but instead was taken to an interview room, where a stenographer and photographer were waiting.

The sergeant did not say hello, or even look at Marcus. He asked the photographer to take a photo, noting the date and time. He instructed the stenographer to title the interview page as : Marcus Pigeon Interview re: Fraudulent use of deceased name.

"Well Sir, how did you get here today?"

"I drove here, obviously."

"Well Sir, unless you can provide a real licence in your own name, you will be charged with driving without a licence; a licence designed to deceive, and anything else we can think up. Because you are not Marcus Pigeon. Who the hell are you, and why are you impersonating a dead man.?"

"Sergeant, I have spent all day dealing with this shit. I am Marcus Pigeon. I am not dead, and I never have been dead. The Army made a mistake, which they have now corrected. Births, Deaths, and Marriages are currently sending me a new birth certificate so if you cancel the wedding certificate there will be hell to pay with my Aunt Doris.

She paid for the biggest wedding in history for the area, and I suspect she is going to be difficult when this becomes public. If you proceed to cancel my Licence, I will make sure that this becomes a major news item."

"Let's get a few things straight. Threatening a police officer is not very bright, whoever you are. I am removing your right to drive temporarily, subject to your providing the documents you claim you will have shortly. If they have not been sighted within the next three weeks by me in this office, I will be issuing a court appearance document for driving with falsified documents. Your car will stay here until it is collected by someone with a valid licence. That means within the next 48 minutes, before the office closes for the day. The other matter of your Wedding Certificate will be stayed also for three weeks; but will be followed through and you will be prosecuted for fraudulently using the identity of a deceased person and a million other things, unless you can prove your cockamamie story, which I absolutely doubt. Of all the dumb-arsed excuses I have ever heard, yours is top of the pile."

Marcus was fuming; "This is stupid. Phone this number at Births, Deaths and Marriages and quote this reference number. They will confirm what I have told you."

"Listen to me. That is a typical public service office. They have been closed since four o'clock. Now I would suggest you use the red phone in the hallway and phone someone with a licence to collect your car. And before you ask, yes, I will need to see their licence."

Marcus decided it was not safe to call Mary; she was livid, and more than a tad upset already. He phoned the Fire Station and spoke to the supervisor, who arranged for two fellows at the Station to come to his aid.

Marcus told Mary that he had three weeks to provide the documentation to the CIB, and in the meantime, they would not take any action in relation to the marriage certificate, or any of the threats relating to fraud. He decided not to tell her about his driver's licence.

Ten days later his birth certificate was delivered by mail; The Defence Department sent an apology for the trouble caused, and Bill Adams sent a detailed statement of his injuries and recovery to the Department for their records.

He took the papers to the CIB, who immediately considered all the documents fraudulent, and phoned each of the senders for confirmation.

"Well, that was a lot of bloody work for no reason. If I could charge you for being a bloody nuisance, I would. Get out of the station, and I will close all this bloody paperwork now. I would prefer if I never hear of you again, even if you really do die."

"Thanks Sergeant. It has been quite an experience dealing with you, so I hope you are right, and that we never see each other again. But if I do die, I will leave instructions that you should be the first to know."

During the next week he received notification that his driver's licence was reinstated, with the normal fee waived as a matter of goodwill; the Marriage Certificate was again valid and that his application for a Passport was being processed, subject to a valid birth certificate and supplementary documents being presented.

Three weeks later Marcus and Mary flew out to Paris for a belated honeymoon.

41: Brighton Melbourne.

Jack Alder felt that he had been sad all his life.

He was born in 1902 to a very happy father and mother who lived in Collingwood, a tough working-class suburb of Melbourne. When war broke out his father, Thomas had been an early volunteer to defend Mother England. There was enough time for basic training and to get a uniform that fitted, then he was off to Britain to fight for King and country, as part of the Dominion Forces of the British Empire. In October 1914, his battalion was posted to Belgium. Thomas died in the slaughter known as the Battle of Ypres. The family received the telegram that was dreaded by every family in Australia, advising that Thomas had died honourably in battle and had been buried on the battlefield near Ypres. His death was listed as November 1st, 1914.

Jack grew up with only a faint memory of his father, and the faded sepia toned photo on the mantlepiece. His mother never talked about Thomas, other than to say he was the perfect husband.

There was never anybody else. She lived alone when Jack left home, and remained in Collingwood until she died in 1958.

Jack was a bright young man, who worked in retail when he left school and had a natural flare for selling. Jack met and married Gillian in 1920, and Maurice was born in 1922. In 1935 Jack decided to open a shop in his own name, specialising in menswear. It was an immediate success, based on high quality clothing and excellent service. Jack made a habit of rewarding employees who provided excellent service and allowed his staff to buy clothing at wholesale prices.

He was successful in business, maintaining a strong family life, but he felt the loss of his father in the War had left a massive hole in his life. He mentioned it briefly on Armistice Day and at Christmas, but he struggled to understand the futility of war. Germany was rising again, and although hundreds of thousands had died in the war to end wars, another looked increasingly likely.

When the Second World War broke out in 1939 Jack was devastated. There would be millions die pointlessly, just like the last time. Jack signed up reluctantly but failed medically due to his asthma. That saved him the trouble of becoming a conscientious objector.

Maurice joined the Army in 1940 against his parents' wishes, but he felt duty bound to protect the Empire. Maurice survived for four years, whilst hundreds of his mates died on the battlefield. But in 1944 he was killed in Belgium, just a few miles from where his grandfather had died in the Great War.

Gillian saw the postman riding to the house on his bicycle. He was carrying mail; but walked past the letterbox to knock on the door. She was crying as she opened the door; knowing she was about to receive the one piece of mail that everybody dreaded. The words were almost identical to the letter in the family file.

"We regret to inform you……." Maurice had been killed in battle and buried on the battleground of Belgium.

Jack returned to work a week later; a shell of his former self. His employees said that the light had gone out in his eyes; there was no laughter, and he seemed completely withdrawn. The business prospered as he concentrated on the essentials; there was no money in the community for luxuries and such stock could not be sourced anyway.

The war ended a year later; the country returned to normal quickly, except for the loss of most of a generation of fit and healthy young men. Those that did return were malnourished, and many would never recover psychologically.

Jack decided to develop the business into a major general store, with many departments selling items the young families setting up homes in the suburbs might need. The baby boom started quickly after the war, so there was a ready market for family orientated retail.

Alders Department Store quickly became an icon of Melbourne. His menswear department became The Alder Men; the Children's Department became Jack and Jill's, and the Ladies' area became Gillian's Fashions.

Jack developed an electrical goods department and a soft furnishing area. The Furniture Department was located in a separate building nearby.

As business was booming, Jack decided to open some smaller suburban stores, and the family business became the biggest retail store in Melbourne.

Jack and Gillian built a new home at the bayside suburb of Brighton, where they could entertain and enjoy a lifestyle with some luxury, but the loss of Maurice was never forgotten. The Alder business empire became a major sponsor of the Shrine of Remembrance and the nearby gardens. Jack arranged a major funding programme from the company to the Australian War Memorial in Canberra. But as much as he wanted to, he could not take himself to Belgium and the graves of his father and son. It was just too raw.

In December 1966, Gillian told Jack that she needed to visit her son's grave whilst she remained fit enough to do so. "Time is marching on", she said, "and who knows what the future will bring? Let's see if there is a way we can go there without fuss, rather than in an organised tour. Just you and me. We can take our time and explore England again, and just take a week in Belgium. I need to do it, Jack."

"All right Love. It won't be easy, but it is time. I will go to the RSL and find out who to contact. If we are going to do this, I want it to be soon. Honestly Gillian, I don't want time to think about it, or I will find a reason not to go."

42: Leuven.

The war graves were no longer work, it became their passion

The girls were surprised how much satisfaction was gained in helping people around the war graves. Their multi-lingual skills proved to be indispensable with tourists travelling from all over the world to the battlefields on the Western Front.

Katrien and Marine worked as a pair whenever possible, taking small groups on personalised visits. When given advance notice they could locate of the graves that were of interest to their group ahead of time. The University had an extensive historical library, but it certainly was not indexed to find individual soldiers. The girls used the details provided to determine which battalion or company was engaged in the battles in the area on the registered date of death. They had become very good at locating specific graves, but they had also developed a reputation for being thoughtful, as well as helpful to grieving relatives of the war dead.

The briefing papers turned up in February, with a request for a guide in mid-March to take a wealthy Australian couple to find two graves. The cost was immaterial, but it was important that the details were kept confidential, and there was to be no media involvement at all. It would be best if the guide spoke English, as the couple were not proficient in a second language. They were searching for the male's father from World War One and their son from World War Two.

Both had died in battle almost twenty-five years apart, but in the same area of Belgium.

When the tour company asked Katrien if she would like to do the work, she suggested that it be in partnership with Marine.

"We don't have much time, and it would be best if we locate the headstones before they arrive. If we have time, it would be helpful to find the war records, so we are able to assist the family through the process. Because they are classed as wealthy, I assume they have waited for this trip till they are ready. It would be perfect if we can get enough information to enable them to return home with some peace of mind about the two deaths."

The girls had enough details relating to the battle in which they had died, and the date of death to work out which town and which cemeteries were likely to be where the two men were buried.

Katrien searched the records of the Second World War and Marine concentrated on the First World War. The Alders arrived in London from Melbourne and after a two-day rest, were ready to face their demons in Belgium.

By the time they met the Alders, Katrien and Marine had the complete details of the battles, and the locations of the graves. They were able to provide the family with a full history of the gallantry of both men, after which the Alders were discretely taken to the areas where each of the men were buried.

The girls stepped away to allow them to find the markers, and to grieve their loss in the way that is only possible when a family stands beside a grave. The two graves were less than 30 minutes apart. Jack and Gillian stood in front of each site and openly wept. Jack was distraught at his father's grave, but a pillar of strength for Gillian at Maurice's grave. They wept together and held each other close, but after an hour it was if a cloud had lifted. They had said their goodbyes and accepted that this was their loved ones final resting place. While travelling over to Europe they discussed trying to repatriate the bodies; but that now seemed wrong. Oddly, they were together in a beautiful, peaceful place, with hundreds of their mates. This was the right place for them to stay.

As they drove back to Leuven, Jack asked the girls how they ended up doing this work. They explained that they intended travelling to Australia in a few months, and that they were earning enough money for the tickets and living costs. Katrien confessed that it had started as a chore, but that they had quickly realised this was an important service to people who'd had relatives fight and die to liberate their country. Being guides to the war graves had started to fund a holiday, had now was an honour.

Jack Alder's eyes welled up again, but this time with tears of joy. He told them that he would provide the tickets and some accommodation in Melbourne, to show his gratitude for their outstanding work. The tickets arrived by courier in the first week of April, along with the contact details of the Alders.

Jack and Gillian told the girls that for the first time in many years they were at peace. They knew their two men were firmly held by people who loved them, in a country that was grateful for their sacrifices. The letter begged the girls to call them when they were in Melbourne, but not to book any accommodation as the Alders would take care of that.All their savings now became spending money, but Marine told Katrien she intended to keep working until it was time to go overseas. She knew that what she was doing was important and Katrien agreed.

The university semester was intense, but somehow the work with the war graves did not seem to interfere. Katrine and Marine spent less time socialising, and much less time on shopping trips and concerts. Their free time was dedicated to study so they could spend work hours on the battlefields.

The university long summer break was from the first of July till the thirtieth of August, so they booked their tickets to Australia from the third of July until the twenty second of August. The only arrangements set in stone were to spend a week in Sydney, and then travel to Melbourne to the Alders. Marine wrote to the Alders and asked their advice about the best way to spend their six weeks in Australia.

Gillian sent a reply almost immediately. They were looking forward to seeing them in July and had a few ideas. They suggested that they stay with them for two weeks and then fly to Brisbane to experience southern Queensland. If they wanted to go to Ayres Rock, it would be best to go just before returning home. "Most people do not realise how cold Central Australia is at night. The nights can be well below freezing point and there are few places to stay, so most people use a tent. By late August the worst of the winter nights will have passed. It will be cool but not cold; and the days are lovely at that time of year. Don't plan to do too much. Australia is a huge country. You are better to have a good look at a relaxed pace and come back again in a year or two to see some more. You could come fifty times and not experience everything, so just take it easy and enjoy our beautiful country."

43: School.

The student group had been reduced to the required number.

Andrew Carruthers, with Pete Smithies, Sonia Johnstone, and Andrew's wife Julie had gradually sorted out the school group. There was room for another two if necessary.

Four of the potential students had not come back to school. One was in hospital with serious burns and unlikely to be returning to school till the next school year. Three had to be relocated because their family homes were uninhabitable. Several had decided that they had endured enough drama for the year and just wanted to go away on holidays during the term holidays, rather than another two weeks of being uncomfortable and under pressure.

Andrew presented the group list with a short summary for discussion. "If you are not happy about taking a particular student, or you believe the summary is inaccurate, then now is the time to say so."

Mary Guard: Very bright dedicated student. Followed instructions precisely but was unlikely to be fit enough yet.

She never stepped out of line. She would be easy to have on the trip if she is fit enough. She will be a good influence on some of the others because she is a thoroughly good young woman.

She has lost a lot of weight over the summer because she wants to be slim. She may not be strong enough to carry a pack and walk the distance. She will need to be forced to comply with the training regime, but she should be fine.

<u>John Ayers</u>: "Stretch" plays footy for Sandy Bay in the ruck. He is a very fit, dedicated football player. He is a good student and follows directions instinctively. Guaranteed a place on the walk. He will be very useful in the event that conditions get tough because he is used to working under extreme pressure.

<u>Marco Caputi</u>: Small stocky Italian lad. Born in 1948 just before parents emigrated to Tasmania. He is a hard-working student, intent on being a doctor. Excellent candidate for the trip. He gets annoyed if people carry on about his Italian heritage, but he will be fine.

<u>Barry King</u>: He is only at school till he can get an apprenticeship. He wants to be a carpenter. He has no interest in schoolwork, except woodwork and welding. He will excel in this environment. He is an outdoors type of fellow and will flourish on the mountain.

He can be difficult at times so may need to be controlled early on the walk to set the rules.

<u>Eddie Travers</u>: Wants to be a mechanic. Does boxing as a sport. He does 5BX exercises twice a day and has a Bullworker to make him strong. There are no concerns about his fitness, but he can be difficult, and starts throwing punches easily. We will need to watch him because he could be a loose cannon. Nevertheless, the trip will be excellent for him.

<u>Jane Armitage</u>: She has been suspended twice for smoking. She has been spoken to on several occasions about her provocative clothing. She had a photo on the cover of her diary of herself in a tiny bikini until she was told to remove it. The staff are concerned that she is often "too friendly" with the boys. She is very fit. Plays netball in the school team. Ladies, this will be one you have to watch. It is not beyond thinking that she could end up in the boys' tents if we are not careful. She will have to learn that she has to obey the rules, or she should be dismissed from the group. However, I expect this will make her grow up if she takes part.

<u>Alex Alexiou:</u> Alex is female of Greek heritage. She insists she is not a wog because she was born in Australia. She likes pies, chips, and refuses to eat European food. Alex is seriously unfit and will need some intense training to be on the Walk.

 However, she is a nice kid and works hard at school. I have a feeling that she will grow stronger mentally from the pressure of this walk.

<u>Jonathon Cowan</u>: Left school in year 9 to work in the family corner store. He is twenty years old and returned to school so he can study dentistry. He is fit and healthy but struggles with the immaturity of his classmates. A well-spoken, intelligent young man who is doing well in his studies. He will be offered a place on the walk without doubt.

<u>Helen Sparkes:</u> Her parents own "Sparkes and Parts", a substantial electrical repair company. Parents want her to go to university to study Law. She wants to study Fine Arts. Her father tells her she has a choice between being a failed artist or a wealthy lawyer. She told him she could always be a teacher. She needs to improve her fitness but will be OK.

<u>Claudette Gameau</u>: "Froggy" is an excellent Science and Maths student. She is small and has never played sport. There is a big concern about her ability to complete the walk, but she is adamant she can get fit and be ready. Andrew mentioned that she has done nothing over the summer break to improve her fitness.

<u>Jim Thompson:</u> The School Athletics Champion. He is very fit. He plans to be a Physical Education teacher. Always helpful during school team events.
In the event of an injury Jim would be capable of carrying two packs, one on the back and one on the front by lashing them together. He should be a certain starter.

<u>Anne Tallow:</u> She is a spoilt brat. She was in London for the school holidays; and had no sympathy for those who went through the fires. The trip is likely to do her the world of good, but I expect she will be difficult. However, this might be the last chance for this girl to grow up and understand that life will never be as easy as she expects. She will change over the Walk, or she will drive us nuts. We will see which it is, but she will be difficult.

Andrew told the others that this was his preferred group. Some would take more work than others but there were another four reserves if any of the initial group failed to reach the markers.

"I realise that Julie does not know any of these kids. That is not really a disadvantage; some of these will be best viewed without too much prior contact. Sonia and Pete, if you think any of the assessments need some tweaking please make sure your concerns are known. It would obviously be best if this list does not end up being seen by anyone outside our group of four."

Andrew said that in previous years Jane Armitage and Anne Tallow would not have been invited on the trip, but with a couple of females in the leaders group, he felt they could control their wild tendencies and might see them grow up a little. Some of the boys will be a handful but some firm direction usually worked.

"Sure, Andrew. Remember, knuckles are no longer a training tool of choice. If they don't fit in, they should be put out."

Sonia was not interested in hearing that the girls could be a problem, when every issue in the past had been caused by male bravado.

"And there are a couple of other students who should be considered. Let's not release this list yet; we should start with our final twenty and see how we go. If there are better students, they should be given a chance."
Andrew was a little shaken by Sonia's reply because this was his baby. He had never had to justify his team choice; he just took who he thought would add to the trip. But it would be Sonia's responsibility after this year, so her opinions were important.

"OK. I am happy with that. Let's start them this week, and Sonia and Pete, how about you produce a small overview of a few more students?
Julie, if you see anyone that you think would be worth considering, let the team know. You are all part of the leadership team now."

44: Ranger Marcus.

"Rangers required for National Parks and
Wildlife" -Mercury"

The Mercury Newspaper had an advertisement from the National Parks Department, looking for permanent Rangers for the Cradle Mountain Park and the Central Plateau. They were looking for young, fit individuals with skills in Fire Fighting, First Aid, and proven experience of working in harsh conditions.
Mary cut it out of the paper at the hospital and gave it to Marcus.

He enjoyed the Fire Fighting, but he was a volunteer; he needed permanent work. Mary had told Marcus two weeks earlier that she was pregnant and would have to leave work for a few months. They would not survive on Social Security, even with the payments from Veterans Affairs that Marcus received. They were keen to buy a house in a nice area of Hobart, and of course, Marcus wanted to get a new car when one turned up that excited him.

The Holden dealers had let him know that a new car was to be released after Christmas that was designed and built to compete with the Falcon GTHO at Bathurst. They were aware of his X2 having been stolen and promised him he would be notified as soon as any details were released.

The downside to the Rangers position was that he would be away from home for a week or so, but there were significant days off that would allow him to have time with Mary, and the baby when it arrived. He was confident he could do the job; nothing could be as difficult as during and after the days that Hobart burned, and dealing with people who had lost everything.

He filled in the application form and obtained a reference from his Fire Chief and a medical clearance from the hospital. He grabbed his medical record that had been updated once he had proven he wasn't dead. The main office for National Parks was in the city so it was easier to hand deliver them than post the forms. At least he could be sure that they had received them.

Two days later he was notified that he had an interview, and two weeks after that he was accepted, subject to his completion of the training programme. It felt strange to be back in uniform, but very satisfying to have a real job with good pay. The training was physically easy for Marcus; he was the fittest he'd been since the days in the army prior to his wounding in South Vietnam. He'd had no trouble with the Fire Fighting training and the First Aid Certificate was simple enough.

He had three weeks in the Mount Field region and then went for a week of orientation to Cradle Mountain National Park. He commenced at Lake St. Clair where he could drive from Hobart in a few hours, and then joined the team patrolling the southern end of the walking track. He was instructed to get to know all the Track, as he could be sent through to the northern end if there were staff shortages or a real emergency. Most of the walkers were very experienced: they knew the dangers and were well prepared. It was the others that caused the problems. Incorrect clothing and boots, poor food or insufficient quantity when the weather turned nasty, walking alone with minimal preparation and becoming lost. The real bushwalkers had a compass and a map and knew how to use both.

Absolute idiots cooked over an open fire, and often just walked away after throwing a small amount of soil on the embers. The vegetation in the central Highlands is fragile; fire destroys it for generations, so the rangers worked to minimise the risk of fires as well as checking walkers on the track. Walkers could cook on fuel stoves but were encouraged to make a fire only in the stoves at the huts.

In his first month as a ranger he caught six people lighting fires in the open. Each time, Marcus told them to walk to the next hut and use the wood stove, after making sure they had extinguished the fire completely. Only once did he have an argument with a walker who refused to put the fire out.

"Listen to me; until recently I was a soldier in Vietnam. If I have to kill you, you won't be in the first one hundred, so why not be a good boy and put the fire out."

That worked.

The incident was reported to headoffice and Marcus was advised that his comments were not appropriate; he needed to think of a more subtle way of getting the same response.

He decided that the discussion was fine; it was just silly to have his name badge on when confronting idiots.

He confiscated some fishing rods, which he usually broke in half and told them to carry them out of the National Park. One night he heard a female in a tent take a couple of serious hits from her male companion, who sounded like he had drunk a bottle of Green Ginger wine. He sobered up instantly when the tent flap opened and a shirtless individual with scars all over him grabbed him by the throat. In one movement he was dragged out of the tent, took two hard hits to the head and one to the stomach, before being thrown backwards into the tent.

"Don't touch her again, you piece of shit. I am watching and listening. Hit her one more time and you won't leave the Park alive."

The front flap of the tent closed instantly. There was no sound of the person walking away. He was there and then he wasn't.

The first week had been eventful and he was looking forward to some time at home.

As he headed south along the track, he heard some light whimpering on a side-track. It did not take long to find a young woman who had fallen over a tree root and broken her leg. She had been walking alone and had been on the ground for several hours when Marcus found her. She had been looking for a waterfall when she fell and then crawled towards the main track until she was beaten by total exhaustion. Marcus quickly realised that she had broken her fibula; he made a temporary splint with a sapling and a bandage before carrying her to the Windy Ridge hut. There he organised food for her and gave her some painkillers. He sprinted back to the Rangers Station at Lake St Clair, where he called the rescue service to come for her. He ran back to look after her till the chopper turned up.

 The sound of the chopper gave him chills and flashbacks, but it served its purpose. Here it was saving lives, not killing them. Marcus returned to the station at Cynthia Bay on the southern end of Lake St Clair to clock off for the week. He felt for the first time that he was back to full fitness and doing something exciting and worthwhile. The drive home was serene; three hours on a windy road to think about his life, and how lucky he was to find Mary when his life was at a low ebb. He thought about his X2 and how much fun it would have been on that road, and he thought about the little shits that had stolen it. 'Amazing', he thought, 'there have been no further reports of them misbehaving'. He was excited to tell Mary about his first shift as a ranger; but he decided that he would keep the episode with the wife basher to himself.

45: Jane and James.

Jane felt like she had accidentally fallen into Paradise.

It was supposedly early winter but compared to London it was quite warm. Most of the days were like London in late spring or early summer. The place was so open and clean, no smog and no traffic. The roads were good and had minimal traffic. Food was plentiful and cheap, and housing was incredible. Most homes in the towns were on huge parcels of land compared to London, and just out of the main cities there were beautiful modern homes on small farms for about the cost of two years' rent in London.

Jane told James that she intended to come back often in the future; so it made sense to buy a property. James had been thinking the same thing. The rest of Australia was just too hot, but this was perfect. They found a beautiful house on five acres near Westbury that was being sold from an estate. It was fully furnished, with quality antique wardrobes and sideboards, The dining room furniture was exquisite, and the lounge area had beautiful leather Chesterfield chairs and lounges.

The beds needed to be replaced and new linen and bedding was also purchased in town. The old beds were donated to the Red Cross, along with old cutlery and crockery. Some smaller pieces of furniture that were cluttering up the house were sent to Armitage Auction House and realised surprisingly good prices.

James bought a new Mercedes that was suitable for touring. He was still spending English pounds, and with the much lower tax regime in Australia the car seemed very cheap. The old Jaguar had served them well; it still looked good, but the engine was tired. James sold it privately to a restorer who told them that fixing the engine would be easy and well worthwhile, as the body work was in such good condition.

"So, what's next Miss Jane?"

Jane said that she would like to spend a month touring around Tasmania, waiting for the mainland to cool down a bit more before exploring "the big Island" as their new neighbours called it. James gazed across their property to the western Tiers and said quietly, "Actually, I was wondering if you wanted to go see Doris about a wedding?"

It took a short while for that to sink in before Jane started shrieking with delight. They selected an engagement ring in town before going straight to 'Cynon' to see if the offer of the church was still open. Doris was so excited she wanted to select a date and get started with the arrangements. But Jane had a few things to check with friends back home that she would like to talk to before making a final decision.

"I would like one of our tailors to make your going away outfit, of course to your design and colour. We can arrange for the measurements to be done in Melbourne, but the outfit will be created in Saville Row."

Jane told Doris that she was thinking of nipping back to London anyway because she wanted to extend the visa. "I am half considering applying for residency so that we can come and go as we see fit."

Doris just laughed and said that it was obvious that Tasmania had bitten her on the bum.

"You won't be the first to come here for a week and stay for a lifetime. Let me know early when you decide on a wedding date. I like to do things properly. I will organise as much, or as little, as you want, and we'll be thrilled to have another wedding in the church. Two in one year would be a record."

Jane loved her home in the country. She did not want horses or other animals, because she was not sure how often they would be there, but for the first time she felt free. She wandered around the property looking at the strange trees and flowers; regularly finding oaks, and beech and maple that had been brought into the state in the early years. They were large, impressive trees that had adapted to the climate. They reminded her of home; even though where she lived, she had to go to a park to see a significant tree.

Jane had discovered Alders Department Store in Launceston. It was her regular port of call. They had clothing to her taste, as well as fine furniture and linen.

They had been very accommodating with the purchase of the beds and the linen, delivering them the same afternoon, and helping to assemble the beds. She had been offered an account and a delivery service, with anything else they needed, as well as a returns policy if she took an item home and it did not suit.

"It is going to be hard to return to the cold and congestion of London, James. This place makes me feel so happy and relaxed that I will really struggle with the Law firm, my flat, and all those bloody people."

The open fire was blazing away in a large fireplace. In London, it was a small oil filled electric column heater that barely raised the temperature past chill point. James laughed and reminded her that they could afford to travel and to buy a house on a whim because of their jobs in London; and that eventually they would have to go back because they would run out of money.

"Well mate, it would take a lot of time to spend my reserve. I am in no rush to go back. In a month or so I want to return to the mainland and have a look around; but this suits me. I am happy. And I feel free."

"Let's tell Doris we will get married at the end of June. It will be summer back home so a few friends might like to come out here. We can send a list of invitations home at least. Most of them won't come so we will have a small wedding here.

In the meantime, we can take the car on the Ferry, and we will drive north for a while and see what the rest of the country is like when it's not baking hot."

Doris was excited by the idea of another wedding. She planned to ask Marcus and Mary to come up, and some local people to make up numbers for a small wedding function. It would be a wedding and a welcome to the district all in one. She would talk to the Minister to find an available date and start the preparations.

"Just let me know who is coming, so I can arrange some accommodation. If they are prepared to come from London, I will make sure they are comfortable around here for a few days." Doris was already in planning mode as James went to get the car.

46: Hobart.

Lizzie felt like she was flogging a dead horse.

Her studies were okay, but she was bored witless. It seemed like she was never going to qualify. Half her high school friends were married, and the rest had been working for two years. Working in the factories and offices around Melbourne, they had enough money to go to the pubs to see all the great bands while Lizzie and her study mates worked at home on their assignments.

Now they were in Hobart without their long-term friends, and Lizzie was finding that teaching was no different in Tasmania than in Victoria. Allison was sitting on the floor reading the same text for the tenth time about how to maintain the attention of a difficult student, when Lizzie announced that she was planning to walk the Overland Track in the July term break.

"What the hell is that about??"

Allison was confused. This had come out of the blue. One minute they were talking about child psychology, and the next, something that she had suggested in Melbourne but never mentioned again.

"We talked about this after that session at Melbourne University. We are here, and Cradle Mountain is close by. We could catch a bus to Devonport and then finish the walk at the southern end of the park. My friends have said that at the end of the walk all you want is your bed; it makes sense to be closer to our digs than finishing in the north. Honestly Allie, I am absolutely bored with this study, day and night. I feel like I am treading water. We study every waking moment to learn how to teach brats to count to ten and say their ABC's. It is not rocket science, but it is taking forever. When we finish this term, we go back to Melbourne; and really, we will have gained nothing. Teaching here is no different than teaching in Melbourne. At least if we did that walk, we would have something to tell the others back home. I read the other day that the walk was the toughest in Australia; more than fifty miles over the highest mountains in Tasmania and particularly challenging in winter with heavy rain and snow. It takes about eight days to do it properly. There are no facilities other than a few rough huts. Most people sleep in tents and are basically wet and cold the whole time."

"Geez Lizzie that sounds like fun. Maybe you could just go and have a bath and sit in the fridge for a week. What the hell would you want to do that for?"

"It is one of the great walks of the world, and it is on our doorstep; Last Tuesday there was a fellow at the school talking about it and he showed some photos that were truly beautiful.

He said he was taking a small group of people through the Cradle Mountain National Park in July. He will provide a list of the clothing and food and has arranged to borrow the back packs from a High School where he works."

"You sure he is not just planning to get into your pants?"

"Don't be silly. We are starting a training regime at the gym next week. I told him you might be interested so he said that you should come along next week and see if it is something you want to try."

"Why go in the middle of winter? It will be cold and dangerous. We could come back in summer and do the same thing, but with less risk and be a damn sight more comfortable."

"That is what everybody says, so the huts are full but the walk is less spectacular. And to tell the truth I need some excitement in my life. At the moment it is an endless cycle; Uni, study, party and start again. I just want to do something, anything, that challenges me physically. I don't have time to play regular sport other than Thai kick boxing when I get the chance, and the holidays just race past doing nothing. I can borrow most of the clothing from the Phys Ed Department and I can afford a good pair of boots. I will take a waterproof jacket that Dad got at the wharf. I will get fit, and I will go."

Reluctantly Allison agreed to meet her at the gym and see what it was about, but she wasn't excited by the prospect. She just wanted to have some down time.

Sleep in on the cold mornings, and wander around the city during the daytime; maybe go and see a few bands and catch up with a bit of study.

One week later they had decided that they would both do the walk, but Allison was far from convinced that it would be fun. "Lizzie, I am doing it to make sure you are safe, and to keep him out of your pants. Did you see the way he looked at you? In his mind he has already had your pants down."

"Don't be bloody silly. He is keen to get new members into the Wilderness Club and that won't happen unless they experience the wilderness."

"We'll see."

Four days later Lizzie caught up with Allison and told her that the walking group had changed the dates of the walk, and they would be on their way back to Melbourne. They would have to go earlier to get home at the end of the semester. "Any way I need to be back in Melbourne for my martial arts competition. We will have to go to Cradle Mountain on our own."

"At least that will at least keep that fellow out of your pants. I was thinking that tent was going to be a little tight if I was sharing it with a love-struck couple."

"For God's sake Allison, sometimes you can be a real bitch."

47: Cynon.

The trip had been wonderful.

They had driven to Rockhampton before deciding to turn around. It was just too hot; and they were running out of time. James planned to fly to Cairns and have a look at the far North Coast after their wedding, and probably go to Ayres Rock if they could get there; but it was time to drive back to Melbourne, and then to Tasmania. They had left the list of invitees with Doris with an RSVP to her address. Thinking they might have one or two guests they would decide on the wedding party once they knew who would be there. Frankly, it did not matter if there were no guests at all. For the moment this was their new life, and they wanted to enjoy it. They knew that sooner rather than later, they would be back at work in London, working under intense pressure, and hating every minute of it. It was time to live for the moment.

Doris gave them big hugs when they arrived, telling them that the basic arrangements were all in order. The Minister was available, the caterers arranged, the flowers were ordered, and the little church had been cleaned, and set up as a wedding chapel.

Smiling, she handed over a satchel, saying that they had better deal with these matters though, and sooner rather than later.

"You seem to be more important than you thought. So far you have forty-two people coming to your wedding from overseas.

Marcus and Mary are coming up, and Tom and I will be there, and I have invited a few neighbours, so it should be a great day. The breakfast and ceremony will be our gift to you, so just plan to enjoy the day, making sure your friends fall in love with our little island.

Marcus is now working as a ranger in the Cradle Mountain National Park. He suggested that maybe after the wedding you might allow him to take you on the walk through there. It would be something to talk about when you do return to London. National Geographic mentioned the walk last month as one of the things everybody should do before they die. A bit late for me; but it would be an opportunity you should not miss."

"My God, we should do that. Let's get some advice on clothing and general necessities. We can leave it at our new home when we head back to London. Maybe we will be able to spend more time exploring some of the wild and isolated areas soon."

They told Doris they would go to town and buy some suitable clothing and decide when they would have their first adventure in the wilderness. Doris told them that she would let Marcus know when they decided so he could look out for them.

48: The Alders.

Marine and Katrien arrived on the third of July

It had been a long flight from Brussels to Sydney, and then onto Melbourne. Jack and Gillian had decided to take them touring the Great Ocean Road with them, and then travel to the gold field cities of Ballarat and Bendigo before the company's Annual General Meeting.

"After the meeting we can take the company's private plane to Ayres Rock. We can stay in Central Australia for a week, so there will be time for a flight to Alice Springs, with a couple of days to explore the Red Centre. That will keep you occupied for the next two and a half weeks"

"We have a dear friend in Tasmania that has agreed to show you around there for a few days, then we will be at your beck and call. Doris has said she would love the opportunity to look after you for a few days while we are busy.

Tell us what you would like to do after your visit to Tasmania, and we should be able to make it happen. Probably not Perth, but we should be able to travel up the East Coast fairly quickly in our plane.

In our Melbourne store we have a specialized tailors' department that measures ladies and gentlemen for Saville Road clothing, made from the finest wool in the world. It comes from a farm owned by Doris in Northern Tasmania.

Her first husband died quite some time ago; he was much older than her. He left Britain to avoid the war that killed my father. I never met him, but Doris has become a good friend over the years. You will like her."

They had no set plans so accepted the offer to travel to Tasmania. Tom was waiting for the girls at the airport; he was still returning wedding guests to the airport, at the end of their holiday. Most had left the state, but a few were still about, having chosen to have a good look around before returning to Britain.

Tom took Katrien and Marine on a short, guided tour from the airport to Cressy, before taking them home to Cynon. Marcus and Mary were heading home later the next day. They had planned to leave earlier but had waited as a matter of courtesy to greet the visitors, maybe offering them a ride to Hobart and a few nights accommodation. Mary still had a week off work, with Marcus due back at the Rangers Station in four days; so there was really no reason to rush home.

Doris promised them that she would arrange some exciting things for them to do around Northern Tasmania, as her way of thanking them for what they had done for the Alders.

"I have been really worried about Jack; he had become so morose. But since you girls looked after him and Gillian in Belgium, he has been a different fellow."

She suggested however, that a few days in Hobart with Mary and Marcus would be very sensible while they had the opportunity.

The girls accepted the offer to travel with Mary and Marcus to Hobart for a few days. The weather was cool, and the air clear as they explored the city with its magnificent harbour. Compared to the European cities they were used to, Hobart was small, and its history short. The stories of the convicts were still very evident, but the city was only about a hundred and fifty years old; very recent compared to Brussels or Paris.

Marcus told them that if they wanted the experience of a lifetime, they could go with him to the National Park for a few days. The rangers worked rotating shifts, so there was always transport back to Hobart. He could arrange the loan of appropriate boots, clothing, and camping equipment. He said that the Park was quickly becoming an experience on the international scene, and they could enjoy it in relative safety in the care of experienced rangers.

Marine said she would enjoy that. It would be hardly a challenge; they had walked the Alps of France and been skiing in Germany and Austria. They had climbed Pilatus in Switzerland.

This was easy, but their friends back home did not have to know that compared to Europe, it was a social jaunt.

They met Marcus in the city and went to the Rangers base where they found mountain boots to fit and the rest of the clothing. They chose a lightweight tent and some sleeping bags, borrowing backpacks and some cooking gear. Their European waterproof jackets and trousers were the best available; no need to look at Australian options in that department. After Marcus helped them choose some appropriate food and some nibble packs, they were ready to go.

Hellfire

49: Hobart Matriculation College

The last week of term was busy for everyone, but particularly for Andrew

The bus was booked for Wednesday morning and the students had all passed their fitness tests. They had returned their checklists, and everybody said they were ready.

They were told to all be at the school by 7.00am on Wednesday. All clothing and supplies would be checked by the leadership team, and anyone without the full kit would not be allowed on the bus. The bags would be checked to ensure everything was waterproof and packed in the right order before they were allowed on the bus. Wednesday morning saw some minor repacking. The waterproof jacket and trousers had to be at the top of the bag to be able to get them on quickly if the weather turned nasty. Some of the meal packs had to be broken down into one day's ration packs, but everything was basically as directed.

"That's a great start, kids. Now we will arrive at the starting point at Cynthia Bay by late morning.

391

It will be dark by 5 pm, we will need to be at our first overnight stop no later than 4 to get the tents up and meals underway. Tomorrow will be a long day, so we need to be ready for bed early tonight."

Sonia Johnstone called the girls together to arrange pairs for the trip.

"You will receive your tent now. One of you will carry the tent itself, and the other will receive the poles, ropes, and pegs. You tie these to the straps at the bottom of the bags. Make sure they are tight because if you lose them, you will be in more trouble than the early settlers."

The girls started to pick someone to share with, but Sonia interrupted that by telling them that the pairings had been organised by the staff.

"Anne Tallow, you are with Mary Guard."

"Miss Johnstone, Jane Armitage and I decided that we would team up."

"Yes, I guessed that, But Jane is with Alex Alexiou."

"Miss Johnstone, I don't want to be with the Virgin Mary."

"OK Anne I have heard enough. If I hear you say that one more time you will face suspension when you return to school. It is not too late for you to decide to not go on this trip."

"Helen Sparkes, you are sharing with Claudette Gameau. When we stop for the night, the girls will assemble their tents near me. Andrew and Julie will be in the centre and the boys will form another group with Mr Smithies beyond them."

"Old Radar is on lookout duties," one of the boys said.

"You guessed it, and you had better believe it. If you leave our area, you will be answerable to me. If you boys cross the line to the girls' tents you will answer to Andrew and Julie Carruthers. And girls, if you are silly enough to venture to the boys' tents you will answer to Miss Johnstone and Mrs Carruthers. You are all on trust, but if you break the trust your parents will be informed as well as the Principal.

Obviously, you will need to go out of sight for toilet stops. Make sure one of the staff knows, so we don't panic. Don't wander too far. If you feel lost don't keep moving. Just stop and call out. We will find you."

Andrew did the same thing with the boys, putting the totally dependable with the potential problems.

"John Ayers you are with Eddie Travers, Marco, you are with Barry King, and Jonathon Cowen, you are with Jim Thompson.

The next few days are going to be hard work; but I suspect it will be one of the most memorable things you do in your whole time at this school. We should all have a great time, but it can be ruined by people not following the rules or just being difficult. There will be times when you are tired, and times when you are sore or unwell. We will try to help, but we are not your nursemaids. You have trained, and we know you are strong enough to carry your pack. Tears won't help anyone, so don't cry unless you have broken your leg. And please don't argue. It does not help."

The bus left at 10 am for the three-hour trip to Cynthia Bay, on the southern end of Lake St Clair.

The plan was to camp around Narcissus Hut at the top end of the Lake. The walk up the side of the Lake was easy, but quite muddy. There were leeches everywhere, so before leaving the bus stop at Cynthia Bay everybody was instructed to do their boots up firmly and fit their gaiters, making sure the sides were sealed.

Peter Smithies said to everybody, "Say goodbye to dry feet, and say hello to smelly armpits. The next few days gets pretty rank, ladies and gentlemen."

They were about to leave when Andrew caught a glance of Anne Tallow putting on her gaiters. "Anne, what the bloody hell are those boots?" They are not the bushwalking boots you showed us this morning."

"I left those back in Hobart. They are heavy and they pinch. These are my Doc Martens, that I got in London at Christmas time. They are strong and waterproof, and they don't hurt my feet."

"OK Anne let me tell you a few facts. By the end of this walk those boots will be ruined. They are not designed for what will happen over the next ten days. The leather is not waterproof, it is water resistant. It is designed for keeping your feet dry in Hobart, not here. The lace holes will let the mud and water straight through. You will be lucky to not have ulcers by the time you get to the other end of the park; you will certainly have blisters as big as dinner plates, and you will get no sympathy.

You will walk EVERY STEP for the next ten days, and if I hear one complaint, I will throw your Doc Martens over a cliff and you can walk barefoot, you stupid girl.

What was the point of telling you all the basics you needed to get through unscathed and then have this irresponsible young idiot put everybody's life at risk."
Anne started to cry. Andrew glared and told her to stop that now.

"If I had seen those boots before the bus left, you would be on the way back to Hobart now. If I hear one word about your bloody feet over the next two weeks, I will dangle you over a cliff by your toenails. You'd better all have a look at her pretty boots, boys and girls, because these fashion accessories will teach you a few lessons about following instructions."

The walk up the western side of the lake was relatively easy. It was flat, but there were large areas of myrtle forest which kept the undergrowth damp and slippery. Moss was everywhere; Peter told everyone to watch where they put their feet.

"Beware of standing on moss covered rocks. There is a high likelihood of falling; and landing on rocks is a recipe for disaster. A broken leg here is a major concern."
After two hours there was a scheduled stop for water and a light snack.

"Be careful where you sit; that area over there that looks like it is small grass moving in the breeze, is actually leeches. Tens of thousands of them.

Check before you sit down, and don't tempt the little buggers. They live on blood and they would enjoy yours."

There was another short rest period at Echo Point.

There was a light rain falling as they rummaged through their belongings for their rainproof jackets. Some sheltered in the emergency hut, but Andrew and Pete stayed outside.

"You are going to be wet for the next ten days; you may as well get used to it."

Anne quietly told Jane Armitage that maybe the boots were a mistake; her right foot was soaking wet and was getting uncomfortable. She could not remember getting into a puddle, and her boots were not particularly muddy, so she did not think that she had got into deep mud. She decided to wait until they reached the proper camp site, when she would take her boots off, dry her feet, and change socks. She had one pair to wear in her sleeping bag and two pairs for walking. She decided that if there was a bit of sunshine, she would tie the socks to the outside of the backpack to get them dry.

Andrew pointed out where he had taken a heavy fall and seriously damaged his knee on the last trip and used that as a lesson for everybody to be careful.

Barry King was sitting beside Eddie in the hut eating some trail mix and drinking some water. He quietly said that he was going to see if he could get in the tent with Mary Guard.

"I haven't had a virgin yet; I reckon she could be fun if you could get her worked up."

"I heard that." Andrew Carruthers knew there would be some boisterous conversations among the boys, and decided an early embarrassment would assist.

"Ladies and gentlemen. I won't embarrass the young woman who was the topic of the conversation, but Barry here is suggesting he might try for some inappropriate contact with one of you girls. I think you all have more brains than that. I am sure, in your lifetime you will get far better offers."

All the girls made it clear he was wasting his time if he happened to be considering them, and all the boys roared laughing. Barry turned scarlet, put on his backpack, and started walking up the track.

"You don't have to leave Barry, just put your imagination into neutral and behave yourself."

Shortly after 3.00 pm they arrived at Narcissus Hut. This was just a large wooden shelter with bench seats around the walls. The tents were arranged as outlined that morning, with the girls closer to the hut and the boys further away. There were plenty of bushes for toileting, with handwashing in the ice-cold lake.

"Two things to remember- you are not the first people to have been here. There is a fair chance that someone else has used your toilet area, so be careful where you tread, and when you finish, please cover it with soil and rocks. Girls- check where you squat. Leeches have a habit or causing real concerns if you squat over them.

"I don't want to embarrass anybody, but I need to tell you that one person died when he was too embarrassed to tell anybody that he was having severe lower abdominal pain.

A leech had got into his penis. If that is possible, then girls, you can also have troubles, so talk to someone if you are having any real concerns."

There was a loud scream from the hut that had Andrew running. Anne was shrieking and speaking incoherently as Andrew arrived. She had taken her boot off and it was full of blood. Her sock was wet, sticky, and deep brownish red in colour. Andrew helped her take the sock off carefully to discover a large, thick, almost black leech attached to the side of her foot. "Don't move and don't touch it" Andrew told her. He reached for his pack and pulled out his Greenlight matches in their plastic pouch. He dabbed the lighted match on the leech, which exploded and dropped off, leaving a trail of blood everywhere.

"Okay, young lady, that was a leech. Almost certainly he got into your fancy English boots via their delightful brass edged lace holes. I would expect you will get at least one every day. Maybe a whole family of them. They won't kill you, so enjoy the experience that you get by totally ignoring your instructions. The leeches inject you with blood thinners to help them feed on your blood. You will bleed for a while. Roll your trousers up and go soak in the ice-cold lake. Wash your sock out at the same time, and make sure you get all the blood out or it will act like sandpaper tomorrow, because those are the socks you are wearing tomorrow.

So, there you are boys and girls, Anne's pretty little English boots have already created their first problem. Tonight, young lady, your foot is going to itch like all hell broke loose. If you scratch it, there is a fair chance you will get an infection, and in 10 days, we might have to amputate your foot. Aren't you glad you did not wear the approved boots, Miss Tallow?"

"And if you continue crying, I will throw you in that bloody lake. Stop it now!"

After water and some food from their supplies, everybody headed to bed. The area was relatively level, and all were tired. Sleep came quickly.

"Don't bother talking to me; I don't need preaching at," Anne said to Mary as she dried her legs and put her dry bed socks on.

Mary just rolled on her side, saying that she did not waste time on lost causes.

"If you need someone to talk to just let me know. Otherwise, I won't waste my time or energy."

"Oh, the joy. The Guardian Angel will look after me if I only ask. How bloody sweet."

50: Marion's Lookout.

Lizzie and Allison arrived on the bus from Hobart.

The trip had taken more than five hours, with the bus stopping at every little town. Devonport was the normal kick off point to Cradle Mountain, but there was only one bus service per day to Cradle.

Allison had a brochure about Cradle Mountain that included details of the bus company that took walkers from Devonport to the start of the Overland Track. The street map was basic, but with some help they found the bus depot; only to be told that the next bus was midday the next day. It was the only way to get there from Devonport without private transport so there was nothing to do but wait. They managed to get overnight accommodation at the local backpackers, where they left their packs and went for a walk to find a pub. There was a lovely old pub on Formby Street, with a roaring log fire and very cheap meals. They decided to sit in front of the fire, read the newspaper and sit on a local beer. There was a lot of local gossip, but nothing serious in the paper.

Allison moved to the weather forecast but was not happy to see a forecast of very cold weather with moderate winds and some heavy snow at times. They were going to start the Overland Track tomorrow, no matter what, but if it became too difficult, they would stay one night and get the bus out the next day. They had a cheap counter meal, and then went back to their accommodation.

The chairs were old but comfortable, and the fire was warm, as they talked about the next few days. Two young men came to the fire and tried to start a conversation. They were obviously from Germany or one of its neighbours; the accents were unmistakeable.

"Hi, I am Friedrich Schmidt, and my friend is Karl Daertmundt. What are you girls doing here at this time of night?"

They said they were catching the early bus to Cradle Mountain the next morning and planned on walking the Overland Track. Karl said they were also going to walk the Cradle Track, so maybe they could walk together. Allison was uncomfortable with the idea; her father had warned her that he would kill her I f she got tangled up with a bloody Kraut. He had been a prisoner of war and was totally unforgiving, "Bring a German home and I will personally kill him and bury you with the bastard."

Lizzie suggested that they start out together and see if the pace was okay, and whether they enjoyed each other's company. "If we find that difficult, then we can split up and walk at our own pace."

The bus from Devonport weaved its way up the winding narrow road to Waldheim Chalet, where Gustav Weindorfer first settled in the 1920's. The bus emptied all the bushwalkers for the start of the long walk to Lake St Clair, although some were planning on returning to Devonport in three days.

That gave them time to explore the northern end of the famous park; to see Dove Lake, and climb Marion's Lookout, probably walking across the face of the Mountain or even climbing to the summit.

The first part of the walk from Waldheim was easy, but as they approached the base of Marion's Lookout it became hard work. It was a serious climb to reach the top of the plateau with a full pack and not much training. As Allison lifted her leg to gain a foothold she felt a very firm hand on her buttock. Karl was directly behind her with his hand pushing hard into her rear. "Get your hand off me, and keep it bloody well off me." "I was only helping you."

"Don't you touch me, or I will kick you in the nuts. If I need help, I will ask."

The four of them reached the lookout, with its majestic views over Dove Lake, and Crater Lake behind them. Allison was fuming. She told Friedrich and Karl that as far as she was concerned the trip together was finished already. "You can piss off now. I am not being mauled by you anytime that I am vulnerable."

Lizzie told the men to get on their way; she had seen what had happened to Allison and she wanted no more of it.

"Just get moving and keep well away from us. We don't need help, and we have no interest in either of you. Just get going."

They watched them walk away, heading to the base of the Cradle Mountain summit track. Lizzie said that their map indicated that there was a rest hut called Kitchen Hut along the way. A good place for a cup of tea and some nibbles, and a few minutes with the back packs off, according to the guidebook.

The snow was about six inches deep, and the sky was blue. Kitchen Hut looked like a postcard, sitting off the side of the track. It was double storey, with two doors, one directly above the other. Sometimes the snow was so thick that you walked in through the top door and climbed down a ladder to the floor, but today it was easy. They stepped into the hut before they realised the two Germans were in there. One of them moved close to Allison and the other one approached Lizzie. "Just give us a kiss to celebrate the mountain." True to her word, Allison gave him a short knee lift into the groin. He moaned as he dropped to the dirt floor, "I was not serious, I was just having a bit of fun."

"Just get your packs and get going. I've studied martial arts for years. If I see you again, I will break a bone; manhandle me again and I will break your fucking neck. Now get out of here."

They decided to take their time with the cup of tea to let the two jerks get away. The next regular stopping point was around Cirque Hut, but they chose to leave the track and head down to Waterfall Valley Hut.

It was a bit of a walk, but in a sheltered area with a spectacular view of Barn Bluff. The chances were that the two creeps would probably camp next to the Track around Cirque. It would probably mean they would not see them again on the Track.

The pot belly stove was cold; no one had been there for a while, but they found some branches down near the creek and lit the fire. It was a simple process to prepare dinner on the woodstove and settle in for the night. The hut was small but there was no one else around. They were tired and dropped off to sleep quickly.

They woke at daybreak to the sound of the birds, had an early breakfast, and were cleaning up the cooking gear when Allison saw a note on the outer step. It said 'Good morning from your German friends. We decided to let you sleep last night.'

"Jeezus Lizzie, that is frightening. We had better stay close to the major stopping points from now on. I am going to keep this note; if I see them over the next few days, I will make sure they know that this is not funny."

There were still walkers around the Cirque Hut when Allison and Lizzie climbed up out of Waterfall Valley. Some were packing up to walk either north or south, and some were keeping the camp intact, as they planned to explore the northern end of the Overland Track. Some were going to climb Barn Bluff, some would spend the day exploring the waterfalls, and some were planning to climb Cradle Mountain via the Summit Track.

Allison asked a couple if a pair of male German backpackers had stayed at Cirque overnight but was rather shaken when she was told that the pair had walked up from Waterfall Valley less than an hour ago. Lizzie went pale. Had the sleaze buckets camped close to the Waterfall Valley Hut overnight? They talked about turning around, walking back to Waldheim, and getting the hell out of the Park. They decided they would not allow a couple of jerks to ruin their trip but would only stay where there were plenty of people around.

The weather was deteriorating as they headed towards the hut at Lake Windermere. The Lake was freezing cold, but many walkers took the opportunity to hop in and wash in the mountain water. It was basically snow-melt, and cold enough to make fingers and toes instantly ache.

Most people left their underclothing on, washing it as well as their body before heading into the hut to dress in warm clothing for the night. The girls had been in the lake for less than a minute when Friedrich and Karl stepped out from behind the hut, still wearing their backpacks.

"Hey girls, that will make your nipples stand out. Come on, hop out and give us a look. We can hold your towels for you in the hut so you can get nice and dry if you like."

Allison came out of the water like a striking cobra. She lashed out with a round kick to the back of the knees that sent one of the arseholes into the lake. Karl dropped like a stone with the kick and screamed in pain.

Friedrich backed off. He promised he would get his friend, and they would head south out of the Park.

"You won't see us again. We will keep going to Pelion and then one major hut a day. You won't see us again." His mate crawled out of the lake and towelled off as much water as possible. He was dripping wet and limping severely as he moved away. His backpack was full of water, and almost too heavy to lift. The two of them left without looking back. Lizzie said that although he deserved it, but he could die of exposure out there. Alison just said, "Good!"

Within an hour there were twelve people at Windermere Hut. One of the new arrivals said they were quite worried because there were two fellows heading towards Pelion Hut about an hour from Windermere.

"They have another five hours at least on the track, and Frog Flats are terrible at the moment; the bog is half-way up your gaiters, and there is no way they will get to Pelion Hut before night fall."

Allison briefly told them why those fellows were moving on.

"I hope it is uncomfortable for the filthy mongrels. If we never see them again it will be too soon."

Dawn was cold and bleak as Andrew and Pete walked through the tents, waking up the students.

"Everybody up and put something warm on. Come into the hut and bring your cooking gear and your first day breakfast ration pack. Make sure you put your boots on, and your warm top."

There were groans from the tents, but not much movement until the second call. Mary called out to Sonia Johnstone to come to the tent; there was a problem with Anne Tallow. She was sitting in her sleeping bag sobbing. Her foot was stuck to the inside of the bag, where she had continued bleeding from the leech the night before. "I am going to bleed to death," she wailed.

Sonia reassured her that it was not much blood really, and that she was at no risk. "You best be quiet, or Andrew will really rip into you. You purposely broke a major rule, and it will be a nuisance for the whole trip, but you will be safe. Now get out of bed, give it a little rinse, put yesterday's socks on and your boots, and get to the hut for breakfast or you won't get any."

They were all ready to leave the campsite by eight thirty. Andrew and Pete had long-johns and singlets, shorts, boots and gaiters and a broad brimmed hat. The others all looked like Mawson of the Antarctic, with all the heavy clothing they owned, and their waterproof outer gear. "We will stop in thirty minutes to let you take most of the clothing off," Pete said. "Unless it is blowing a blizzard, you don't need any more clothing than Mr Carruthers and I have on. In thirty minutes, you will feel like you are in a sauna; we will stop then, but don't try to remove clothing till we call a break. We don't need the excitement of looking for lost students."

The walking groups quickly returned to their own pairings. There was a lot of chatter for the first twenty minutes, when it gradually became quieter, as they all started to sweat profusely.

It was weird; the sweat was freezing on the skin. They felt they were overheating at the same time as they were shivering with cold. When a break was called, they all started removing clothing. "Just remember that clothing goes inside sealed plastic bags, except your weatherproof stuff. Leave that on during the break, then put it in the top of your bag for easy access just before we leave."

51: Cynthia Bay.

Katrien and Marine were unsure where they would go.

Maybe they would catch the bus back in three days; or if they really enjoyed the trip they would walk through. Marcus had told them there was a bus from the southern end that went to Hobart every day, and they knew it was easy to travel from Hobart to Launceston. They had a phone number to call Doris Beech-Jones when they were back in Launceston, and Doris had said she would send a car for them. They would decide on the track, depending on how much they enjoyed it. If it worked out that way they would walk to the northern end of the Park and get a bus to Launceston. At least they had a lift to Cynthia Bay, and Marcus had helped them with a few supplies. He gave them good maps and a lot of advice. "Be cautious. This park can be deceptive, and deadly when it turns nasty." He told them that he would be up and down the Track so if there were concerns, he would sort it out for them.

There was a light dusting of snow in the air as Marcus drove in with Marine and Katrien. He told them he had some work to do at the base, but he made sure they had their map of the Overland Track, and he got them orientated to walk up the western side of the lake. The plan was to stop at Echo Point for a cup of tea and a light snack, then a good rest, and a meal at Narcissus Hut at the top of the Lake.

"You should get on the move from there no later than one o'clock, so that you get to Windy Ridge by four in the afternoon. If there is room, claim a space in the hut, otherwise look for a flat area close to the hut and put your tent up.

Do your boots up firmly and make sure the gaiters are closed because the leeches here can be very aggressive. They won't really hurt you, but a boot full of blood is not that pleasant. If things go to plan, I might meet you at Windy Ridge later today, or tomorrow morning."

Marcus told them to fill in the Visitors Book in each hut and make a note where they were travelling the next day. "I will be up and down the track all the time and I will keep an eye out for you. If you have any concerns just wait at the hut till I find you. If you don't write your plans down, I won't know where you are. Be careful and make sure you keep an eye on the track markers."

He told them to start slowly and just keep walking. Make breaks fairly short as the first day, though relatively easy terrain, is more than eight hours of walking, and it's best to arrive before dark.

They had brought their outdoor clothing from Europe, so they were probably the best dressed walkers in the Park. The wind and the snow was not a concern for either of them, and the walking was easy. Marine and Katrien agreed that this was even easier than expected.
They were surprised by the stunning beauty and the feeling of isolation. In Europe there is no space to turn around without hitting somebody, but here there was no one at all.

The old hut at Windy Ridge was made with split shingles that were covered in moss. The welcome pot-belly stove was already alight. Despite the four people in the hut, there was space to claim a bench. Marine laughed at the sign to hang backpacks on the hooks, until one of the others said it was no joke; the rats would eat into your bag if you left it on the floor. They decided to make an early meal before any more people turned up, as there was not much preparation space. It was warm and pleasant in the hut, and great to get out of the chill air.

Daylight was fading fast when Andrew and his school group came around the ridge. One of the girls was limping badly and crying about her swollen and painful foot.

"Talk to someone who cares," the teacher said. "Just keep bloody moving and we'll have a look at it in the hut. Maybe Doc Marten has got some medication that will help."
There was another very fat leach attached to the middle of her foot.

Andrew again burnt it off and it started to bleed heavily. Andrew pressed his thumb down on the bite and held it for a few seconds, so the bleeding eased to trickle. A walker heading south had a styptic pencil, which he used to stop the bleeding. He told Andrew to keep it. "It won't be the last time she gets a leech through those lace holes". One of the others pulled out a roll of gaffer tape and cut two short strips. "When you put your boots on tomorrow, put this tape on the boot over the lace holes. It won't stay all day as it will be bloody wet on the track for the next few days, but it will be somewhat useful."

Another woman in the group took some antibiotic cream out of her First Aid kit and smeared the top of the foot. Yesterday's bite looked a little infected and swollen.

"Don't spoil her too much. This young specimen of female vanity left her approved boots in Hobart, having switched them for these Doc Martens because she wanted to rub it into the others what a precious little rich girl she is. If we had known that she would now be walking around Hobart in her ox blood fashion boots. Well now they are ox blood on the outside and idiot blood on the inside."

Gradually the others came in as they finished getting their camp set up. Mary had some help from Jonathon to set up the tent. She quietly picked up Anne's backpack from the floor and put it in the tent. Jonathon had his metho stove set up, and his food out. He told Mary to get her food pack so they could cook it together.

"Anne can look after herself tonight. She has had enough attention for one day."

There were strange dynamics amongst the students. They walked in groups similar to how they wanted to be placed in the tents, but they tended to cook and eat with the person they were sharing the tent with. Often, they were in groups of four, with a blend of friends and tent mates.

The conversation got quieter as the tell-tale signs of tiredness started to become obvious.

"I am sorry that I was a bit of a goose back at Narcissus." Barry said, almost too himself. " I was trying to sound macho, but truthfully you all frighten me a bit. To be honest, I am too tired for anything other than sleep anyway. You are all tough young women. Even you Anne, with your prissy boots. I reckon in another ten days we will be mates for life.

You know that mateship through adversity rubbish? well I am starting to believe it."

"Just as long as you are not thinking bed mates, Barry." Alexiou said. The others all laughed, and Barry just said sorry again.

Goodnight Philosopher King. See you down the track," Helen Sparkes said as she headed off to cook some food.

Food was cooked and eaten quickly. There was the all-pervading smell of wet clothes drying out in the warmth of the pot belly stove, and the dank aroma of wet socks at the end of two days of walking. That smell would get worse. Everybody was in the set of dry clothes that doubled as sleep wear.

The clothing hanging up would still be very damp in the morning but would be back on for another tough day of walking.

There was a lot of talk in the hut; there were several people that had one more night before finishing their walk at Cynthia Bay, and several who had most of the walk-in front of them. Marine and Katrien were pleased they had a bunk in the hut, with the warmth of the stove. The students were all in tents to sleep but they were in the hut to cook. It was an opportunity to talk about the day, and to meet the other backpackers. Marine and Katrien enjoyed some general conversation, but the students were several years younger than them and seemed a bit immature. The teachers were very interested in Belgium and their work with the war graves was of particular interest. There was a growing interest in the history of both World Wars as Australia seemed to be getting too deeply involved in Vietnam. Andrew introduced the girls to his students and encouraged a short history lesson about the war graves in Belgium. Andrew was pleased that Katrien and Marine told the kids that the people in Belgium absolutely revered the Australian and New Zealand soldiers who had died fighting for their freedom. Marine told them that her father took the family to the war graves every year to make sure they realised that those young men died to ensure they were freed from Nazi oppression. The night was getting cold when Andrew told everyone to go to their tents and get a good sleep.

"Tomorrow will be wet, cold, and quite severe walking conditions for several hours. Other than that, it will be a fun day!"

The school group went to their tents as everyone settled down to sleep. There was some mild whispering for a while, then the whole area became quiet.

There was a light drizzle at daybreak, as everything was packed in plastic and sealed; the sky looked bleak, with a bluish colouration that meant snow was not far away. The waterproof clothing was put at the top of the backpack, and some nibbles into the side pockets.

The girls decided that they would spend the next day exploring the area, to let the school party get at least one hut ahead of them. The map showed they were close to The Acropolis and Pine Valley and the guide notes sounded wonderful. They unpacked the bags, repacking them with the essentials for a tough day walk. They made sure they had wet weather gear, food, and a billy to make a hot drink. They reserved their sleeping area in the hut by laying out their sleeping bags, and their indoor dry clothes. Setting their tent on top of the sleeping bags, they prepared for the day ahead.

'We'll have a good breakfast, and get moving in an hour or so,' Katrien thought. The weather was not looking good; the temperature was below freezing, and there were fine snow particles floating in the air as the girls left the Windy Ridge Hut. They pulled their wet weather gear on and covered their ears with their beanies.

The wind was howling, and it was bitterly cold, but the walk was easy as they headed west towards the Acropolis.

They could see the mountain in the mist, Mount Geryon to its right, but the Narcissus River was high and flowing rapidly. They walked along the river for an hour looking for a crossing but decided to return. The wind became a blizzard, with snow hitting them in the eyes and face. They pulled their coats up pulling the hoods over their beanies, but they were still cold. Visibility was a few feet, and there were no obvious landmarks. The Acropolis and Mount Geryon had vanished into a wall of white. Katrien was the first to say that she thought they were lost.

"OK, let's stay next to the river and look for a recognisable landmark. Once we find the track we came in on, we'll back track to the hut at Windy Ridge. God, Marine, if we had brought the tent, I would be putting it up and waiting this storm out, but I don't want to be out here without shelter any longer than I need to be."

Each time they found anything that looked like a track, one of the girls would stay still while the other one looked for a yellow marker on a tree. The foliage was too dense for snow poles. Three times, Marine headed down a track while Katrien kept talking loudly. Each time she came back without having seen a marker. Marine suggested they should find some shelter to have a cup of tea; and eat some trail food and a piece of chocolate before looking again. There was an indent in front of them with a good cover of overhanging tree branches. This allowed some break from the wind and the icy wind driven snow.

They sat for about thirty minutes before Katrien caught a brief glimpse of Mt Geryon to her right.

"I think that is similar to what the mountain looked like when we came out of the bush, on the way in. The track must be close."

It took half an hour to locate a yellow marker, before they could start walking back towards the hut. The fog was still low, but the wind was blowing from behind; they were no longer battling stinging ice in the face.

They were careful to follow the yellow markers, and just before nightfall they saw Windy Ridge Hut, smoke billowing out of its chimney.

The hut was full of walkers all getting a meal together. Their clothing was hanging up, and the smell of warming sweaty socks was strangely welcoming.

But Marcus was not impressed. "I was about to alert the Search and Rescue team. I spoke to every person that arrived here, but nobody had seen you on the track. Where the bloody hell were you all day?"

The girls explained that they had decided to take an extra day to separate themselves from the school group. They had planned a moderately short walk along the track to the Acropolis and Mount Geryon. They told him they had tried to find a track across the river, but when they gave up, they had struggled to find the track back to Windy Ridge through the fog and the sleet.

"The weather out there is awful, but you left your tent and your sleeping bags here to reserve your bunks.

That silly mistake would have killed you if you had not found the track. Lesson learnt, girls. This area is dangerous.

You never leave your backpack, and you never leave your tent or your warm clothing. Thank God you followed the rules in the guidebook and looked for the markers, or we would be out there in a few hours trying to get to you before the blizzard killed you."

After a quiet meal and a hot drink, the girls decided to rest in their sleeping bags.

Marcus was on the far side of the hut when Katrien confided to Marine that she was glad they had reserved the bunks. "I would hate to be out there in the tent tonight."

Marine giggled, saying to not say that too loudly.

The Kia-Ora site had been swamped with people and the hut was full to overflowing when the school group turned up. They were told to set up tents quickly and "make sure that there is a little channel cut in the ground that was fairly deep on the prevailing side, going either side of the tent, and rejoining below the toe of the tent. Don't lift the soil out. Just leave it as a bank, so tomorrow you can just lay it back and tread it down. Make sure your tents are staggered, so if we get a heavy rain the run-off doesn't enter the next tent."

The tents went up quickly, and they all cut the water channels.

Barry and Marco were laughing as they warmed their food and arranged the kettle for a hot tea. "We'll be safe if it floods. Protected by the angels."

Julie did her normal walk around the tents, observing their handiwork.

They had produced a beautiful anatomical design of the female reproductive system around their tent, with the outlet being a very large vagina. She was furious. She ordered them out of the hut to fill in their work and do it as they were told. They were told they would have that recorded; the details handed in to the Principal at the end of the trip. It took thirty minutes in the rain to fill in the offending trench and dig out one that satisfied Julie.

It was freezing cold as they headed to their tents and off to sleep. The wind howled, and the rain fell heavily. It was close to midnight when Barry was heard swearing loudly. "I am absolutely fuckin' drenched. The useless trench did not keep the water out. It is pouring through the tent."

He and Marco were out with their torches, trying to fix the water flow when they realised their trench was not there. Instead, their anatomical diagram was back, but all of it in front of the tent with the vagina facing straight at the tent where they were sleeping.

Waterproof crayon had been used to write on the side of the tent, "Looks like you have been pissed on."

The sun rose late, as it always does in July in Tasmania. The rain had stopped, but the day was bleak and very cold. Barry was having breakfast, furious about the night before.

"Who did that? It is not funny.

419

Marco and I now have no dry clothes, and our sleeping bags are full of water. We could freeze to bloody death if this weather does not let up."

Andrew told them they had two days coming up at Pelion, where they would be allowed to put their gear up to dry near the heater.

In two days, it should be OK. For the first night they could sleep in the hut to stay warm. "But you deserve what you got. I have asked everybody, and they all claim they were asleep, but obviously you upset someone with your tasteless stupidity."

"Why, what happened?" the ranger asked. "I came in late last night and all was quiet when I got here." He turned to the teacher and said, " Sir, could you please make sure when your group breaks camp this morning that all those trenches are filled in? It is important to not interfere with the normal runoff for any longer than necessary."

Pelion had the pot-belly stove glowing cherry red when Friedrich and Karl walked in at about two o'clock in the morning. Their torches were no longer working, and they were both badly distressed.

They were freezing cold. One was dripping wet and struggling to walk. "I had a fall and wrenched my knee. I landed in a pool of water, and everything got wet." An experienced walker told him to sit in the far corner. He said it was important that he warmed up slowly or he could die of gas embolism. "Let's see if your sleeping bag is dry. We need to get you warm naturally, with warm food and drink.

You need to get into dry gear, or you will go into shock." The toe of the bag had become a little wet but basically it was ok. He had enough clothing in the bag that had been packed properly to get him clad warmly, but he was shivering like a wet dog. The food and drink helped, and he dropped off to sleep.

The next morning, he was very unwell. He was still shivering, coughing constantly, and struggling to stand on his injured knee.

"If you see a ranger you might have to ask for help. It is still a long way out, and I really don't think you are well enough to walk that far. You should stay here rugged up for another day and if you are no better tomorrow get someone to call for help. There is normally a ranger you can find if you have to."

The night had seemed to take forever to pass but with daylight, Marine and Katrien were up for breakfast before packing the bags and getting ready to head out for the day. They planned to search for some waterfalls before reaching the next hut by about three in the afternoon. After the trouble the day before, they made sure they had everything packed properly, leaving a note saying that they were planning a few short sidewalks but would be at Kia-Ora by mid-afternoon. The track was poorly marked, but with care and attention it could be followed safely. In the forested areas the track was marked with yellow triangles nailed to the trees, but in the open areas there were metal snow poles. Marcus had told them they should be always able to see the next marker.

If they lost sight of the track, one should stay still while the other looked for the marker. That made progress very slow; but at least it was safe. It had got them out of trouble when they got lost near Mt Geryon.

It was just after three o'clock when Katrien saw Kia-Ora hut up ahead.

There was no smoke coming out of the chimney so they guessed they might be the first to arrive. That would mean that they would be able to sleep in the hut again, and not put the tent up.

There was no one there, so they quickly chose a bunk area, claiming it with the backpacks and unrolling their sleeping bags. They found some kindling and some small firewood and lit the fire in the pot-belly stove. A pristine stream was running near the hut, so within minutes they were drinking hot tea and getting a meal ready. Another couple of local Tasmanians arrived at the hut; The fellow walked the track every year and tried to take someone e very year to introduce them safely to bushwalking. He took a couple of weeks each year, exploring some of the isolated areas. His partner was an experienced bushwalker, but this was her first time in Cradle Mountain. They had been in the Labyrinth for six days and were heading north; they planned to get to Dove Lake in three days by bypassing a couple of the huts.

"We'll head off at daybreak tomorrow and plan to be at Windemere tomorrow evening. We want to climb Barn Bluff on the way out if the fog is not too bad, but we won't have time if we don't bypass Pelion and get to Windemere by tomorrow evening.

It's a long day, but I have done it before. The penalty for overstaying in the Labyrinth, I guess, but it was so peaceful and beautiful in there. We have to be at work on Monday, so we have to catch up a couple of days on the way out."

Katrien remarked that this was their first experience of Cradle Mountain, and they had found it much more difficult than they had expected.

The young woman said that although she had walked many tracks in New South Wales, this was her first time too. She had recently moved to Tasmania to commence nursing in Hobart and her work colleague, who was very experienced in Tasmanian highlands had invited her to join him. She had been advised that the safest way to do the walk was with someone who had done it before, and he had been on this track on many occasions.

"It is a pity we can't walk with you, but we want to spend a day here, and go out to Mt Oakleigh, if the fog clears when we are at Pelion?"

He told them to savour the moment. "There is not much point in rushing through and seeing nothing. It is the isolation, the quiet and the extreme beauty you need to experience, to get the most out of the walk. I come back every year. I must have walked every square inch of the place, but it drags me back. Don't rush.

We are going to have an early night and be gone as the sun rises in the morning.

If we are lucky, we will get to Windemere in the evening light, but the chances are we will do the last mile or so by torchlight."

Karl and Friedrich came in as it was getting dark. Karl was limping badly and was soaking wet. He looked very unwell, and his breathing was quite shallow.

The Tasmanian fellow said he was a doctor and was concerned that Karl was hypothermic. When asked what had happened, he said he had slipped at Windermere, and had fallen in the Lake; they were moving as quickly as possible to get to help. He was told to get into warm dry clothing and then his sleeping bag. And stay away from the fire. "If you warm up too quickly, we will have some serious issues to deal with." Karl did not say that he had heard that advice the day before. The doctor found some dry clothes in the fellow's pack and got him into the sleeping bag. "We will get some warm food for you, so you just snuggle down in that bag till we tell you otherwise. If you get any worse, we will have to look for help. You need to be out of the Park tomorrow, so hopefully we'll find a Ranger and get some help."
The girls climbed into their sleeping bags and were almost asleep, when Friedrich crawled up close and said he was cold. "Would you two like to warm us up? Karl needs a warm body next to him to raise his body temperature and I could do with some company." Katrien screamed and the doctor was out of his bag almost immediately.

"What the hell happened?" the doctor asked.

Katrien was shaking as she told him what one of the boys had said.

"I don't care if you die of exposure. . You! Get the tent and get it up. You will sleep in your bloody tent. You, you little prick can stay here in the hut but if you do anything like that again you will be outside in the tent as well. And if you are dead in the morning, so be it."

Marcus had left Kia-Ora early and headed for Pelion. He was concerned for a couple of the students who were struggling in the wet and the cold. He had almost suggested that they stay at Kia-Ora for a day to allow them to recover, altering the last couple of days for an easier walk. Andrew had assured him that they were doing okay, plus several of the students needed a chance to extend themselves. Some of them have been spoilt up until now and this would make or break a couple of them. The four leaders were not concerned with the group, other than the constant whinging from Ann about her Doc Martens, and a couple of boys because they were very cold and wet. They were being watched, and if necessary, they would have a rest day near the fire.

As it was, they were going to have two days at Pelion, so there would be an opportunity to get warm and dry around the pot belly stove.

The school group arrived at Pelion Hut in the mid-afternoon. The wind and rain stopped, the sky a clear pale blue. The jagged skyline of Mt Oakleigh looked like a post-card across the open plain from the hut. Once the tent site was established and everyone started preparing a meal, the hut filled with chatter.

The gaffer tape kept falling off the Doc Martens, much to Ann's annoyance, but she had not seen a leech for two days and her foot was becoming less sore each day. She admitted to Pete that she was an idiot to leave her good boots behind to make a fashion statement. Pete responded, "Yep, I second that motion."

Allison and Lizzie had climbed Oakleigh before they arrived at the hut.

Several students asked them if it was worth the effort to climb it. Allison said "It was the highlight of the trip so far, as it was the first clear blue sky, and the view was uninterrupted for miles. We could have sat there for hours but I would not want to be coming down from there in the dark."

Allison asked if the group had seen two fellows on the track, with one of them limping badly. Julie said she had spoken to them at about midday. They were several hours from Kia-Ora and were struggling. They wanted to get out of the park, so they were heading for the hut for a rest, after which they wanted to be at Cynthia Bay in two days.

Allison described the trouble they had had on the first two days with those fellows. Lizzie told them that she thought Allison had broken Karl's leg, with her kick that put him in Lake Windemere. Barry King muttered to no-one in particular that this was one woman he was not going to say anything to.

Marcus asked Allison and Lizzie to describe Karl and Friedrich, as he realised they would be in the same hut as Katrien and Marine.

Allison said that she doubted they would be much trouble as they would be cold and wet, and very tired. Karl would be very sore and probably unwell. Marcus decided he would have a bite to eat, and a hot drink then go back to Kia-Ora to make sure the girls were OK.

Marcus was having a mug of tea as Allison and Lizzie started talking about football in Melbourne.
Allison was a strong supporter of Fitzroy, because her brother played for the team. He was playing consistently and seemed to have a real future with the club. He was earning "a few bob" to supplement his wage and hoped he would be able to do so for a few years.
Pete Smithies asked Andrew if he knew the boy, but Andrew had stopped following the VFL closely when his simple knee injury ruined his career. Lizzie laughed as she had her regular dig at her best mate. "Everybody knows Jumpin' Jack; the next Brownlow medallist from F-F-F-Fitzroy Football Club."
Marcus blanched. He had a flashback to Vietnam when his mates walked into a minefield. Three of them were ripped to pieces by land mines that jumped just far enough to tear soldiers to pieces. He was there when they picked up body parts and tried to put them together, so there was something to bury back home. Jumping Jacks were feared by every foot soldier in Vietnam; they were the stuff of nightmares.
Marcus was close to screaming at the girls that they were totally insensitive bastards, but he bit down heavily on his lip and headed for the door.

He walked towards Mt Oakleigh; and in the dark found a spot near a tree where he could sit and wait it out.

The horrors came flooding back; the deaths, the blood, the gore, and the fear. He trembled uncontrollably until it passed, then he slowly returned to the hut.

"Are you OK? You look like you have seen a ghost."

"Yes, I am OK. I spent too long in Vietnam and saw too much. Occasionally it hits me like a train, and I have to take time out. But I am alright now.

Tell me what brought you both here to my Park? What do you do back home?"

They told him they were University students from Melbourne, but they had just finished a placement in Hobart, and decided to do the walk before returning next term at Melbourne University.

Lizzie and Allison were in high spirits as Marcus asked them about university and their plans. "When we get through this term, we will be past the half-way mark of the course. We'll have a break at the beach for a couple of weeks, and then return to Melbourne for some summer work to fund the next year." Lizzie laughed and said that there was a chance that Harold Holt would fund their next year if they were kind to him. Marcus immediately was intrigued. "You mean the Prime Minister?"

The girls told him about Cheviot Beach and Harold and his bevy of young women and the rumours about how he threw his money around.

"You sure about that?"

"Well, it is a rumour, but there seems to always be plenty of young company for him at the beach, and he throws his money around if it suits him." Allison laughed, "Yes, he is down there from mid- November till about the second week of January. Well, he has been for the last couple of years, so I doubt if it will be any different this year. He goes to the beach every day and swims a lot of the time. He often uses a snorkel and loves to swim through the legs of the young women. He always manages to brush against vital parts. You could say he is very flirtatious with the young women. It is no secret that he enjoys their company if you know what I mean."

Lizzie wondered how much she should say. When all was said and done, he wasn't hurting anybody, and his behaviour seemed to be a well-known secret around Cheviot Beach.

Marcus just smiled; "Nothing would surprise me with that mongrel."

It was a clear, cloudless night as Marcus headed back to Kia-Ora. He sat in a sheltered area to let his eyes accommodate to the dark before he set off without the torch. It was easy compared to the tunnels; he could see clearly where he was going, as his eyes adjusted quickly to the low light. He had told one of the other rangers that the shrubbery glowed with a light phosphorescence, so that he could walk safely at a fast pace across the broken track. No one else could see that. The walk from Pelion was listed as a three-hour walk, but Marcus was supremely fit and was not carrying a backpack.

There were multiple huts for rangers tucked away from the tracks if things got difficult, but none of this was like pitch black darkness with armed Gooks trying to kill you. He just ran effortlessly at a moderately fast clip, jumping over tree roots and rough ground, arriving back at Kia-Ora an hour after Karl and Friedrich had been put out of the hut into the tent.

Katrien told him what had happened. He immediately left the tent and could be heard whispering to Karl and Friedrich. It did not take much to recognise that it was a very angry whisper.

He came back into the hut and told the girls that he would get Search and Rescue to get them out the next day, before they died. He had no sympathy for them, but he was not keen on the paperwork with deaths, so on balance it was better to get them out.

"Geez, Marcus; you are looking good." In the dull light of the hut Marcus had noticed other people, but he was concerned for Katrien and Marine, and was initially looking for the German lads.

"How is the magic going?" It was Dr Bill Adams from the Repat. It seemed like years, but it was only a few months. Bill had initially kept him alive, and then his magic had given Marcus a purpose.

"Wow, Dr Slash. It is fantastic to see you. I don't remember you ever saying anything about being a bushwalker in our conversations at the Repat. The performance at the Theatre Royal was fantastic. I would like to do some more if I have the opportunity.

You would be surprised how useful being able to disappear is; and I have found a lot of uses for superglue and pulling rabbits out of hats, so to speak."

"What is your opinion of those two idiots? They have been annoying several women on the track, and although they don't deserve any sympathy, I don't want dead bodies on my watch. Both of us would end up with too much paperwork if that happened."

"They are both unwell, but one is much worse than the other. They need to be out of the Park as soon as possible."

" I will have a couple hours' rest, and then I'll see if we can get some help from Search and Rescue. If the lads are up to it in the morning, they'll need to start walking towards Windy Ridge, and I will get help as soon as possible."

Three hours later Marcus checked in with Bill Adams to tell him he was heading back towards Windy Ridge where hopefully he could make radio contact. But if he could not make contact he would have to run to Cynthia Bay, which was going to take several hours. Bill was prepared to walk back with them; he had walked the Overland Track many times and lives were more important than recreation. He told his friend that they would do the walk again, but she needed to return with him for her safety as well as the fact that he might need help if either of the young men became critically unwell.

"Well, the pricks are sleeping soundly at the moment. They are breathing normally; hopefully they have learnt a lesson about respect."

The morning was crisp but clear, with no sign of rain or wind. Bill made sure Karl and Friedrich had plenty to eat and drink, before getting their tent down and the backpacks ready. Taking a bandage from his First Aid kit he wrapped it firmly around Karl's painful knee to give it some stability, before he and his partner, started escorting Karl and Friedrich back south.

Karl was limping and breathing hard as they slogged through the mud towards Ducane Hut, where Bill had said they would stop for a hot drink and some trail food. Two hundred yards from the hut, some of Karl's belongings started to fall out of the base of his backpack; the stitching had started to come undone. Friedrich helped pick up Karl's belongings, but it was difficult to avoid falling face first into the mud with a heavy backpack. Bill used some sutures from his kit to make a temporary fix to the base of the bag, "That should get us to Windy Ridge, and hopefully you will have help from there."
After a light lunch Friedrich grabbed his pack and slung it round to land on his back. The shoulder strap detached from the top of the bag which then slid off his back and down onto the dirt floor.

"Well, chaps; I am not sure where your bags came from, but I reckon you should be looking for a refund."

"They are falling apart, almost by magic." He put a few sutures in the strap, advising Friedrich to loosen that strap and tighten the chest strap. "Hopefully it will hold together for another couple of hours."

The bags were difficult to carry, but by mid-afternoon they were at Windy Ridge. Bill checked out the boys. He decided that they should not walk any further as Karl was showing severe signs of distress, but hopefully Marcus had made radio contact and Search and Rescue would arrive so they would be safely evacuated.

Late in the afternoon Marcus arrived, slightly breathless and with a few slash marks on his legs from running through shrubs.

There was enough reception for his two-way radio at the Narcissus Hut, so he was able to talk to Search and Rescue. They were on their way.

Bill was concerned about Karl, who was hallucinating and shivering like a wet dog. He made up some chicken noodle soup from his food pack and handed it to Karl, who almost spilled it with his violent shaking. "OK Buddy. I will feed you. Where is your mummy when you need her most?"

Marcus stoked up the fire, but they kept Karl and Friedrich well away from it. They were tucked into their sleeping bags with every bit of dry clothing they owned. They were then covered by surplus clothing from the others in the tent while some hot food was prepared.

Marcus said he was going on a scavenger hunt to get more wood for the fire before it got dark. He came back after thirty minutes and asked why the boys had some of their belongings scattered on the track. He gave them a pair of socks, shorts, and a small bag with their passports. "You pair would have been in trouble without these," he said.

"You'd better put them somewhere safe so you don't lose them again, or you will have trouble getting home."

The Search and Rescue Squad arrived at lunchtime, along with a medic with some emergency gear. He put a line into both of them and hooked up a saline drip. Karl was seriously unwell, but Friedrich was in no condition to walk. They were placed on lightweight stretchers to be carried out to Narcissus, where a boat would take them to Cynthia Bay. An ambulance would take them straight to the Royal Hobart Hospital.

Dr Bill decided he would go with the boys in the ambulance. His told his partner to go with him in the ambulance as well. He asked Marcus to arrange for his car to be stored safely until he could come back in a few days to get it.

The boys were almost stabilised by the time they reached the hospital. They were warm in the ambulance and dry. Their bushwalking gear had been removed and replaced with clean and dry transport gowns. They continued to receive saline via the drip and by the time they were in the admissions area they were joking about their big adventure. "Well Karl, I think you will need to practice your lady skills, because you were not very successful on this trip."

The admissions department asked for some ID, so they handed over their passports. Their names were checked twice as the clerk examined their passports carefully. "OK, get them to a ward, and I will be back shortly."

Thirty minutes later she came into their ward with two police officers.

One of the policemen asked Karl for his name. He then asked Friedrich for his name. He looked at the passports again, and then instructed the nurse to move them to the secured ward.

"I don't know what is going on, but we will be calling immigration to come here shortly."

Friedrich was becoming apprehensive as more and more staff came in to check them. "What is your problem Sir?"

"Immigration can sort that out. You two have forged passports and you know it. Whatever you paid was too much; you will be lucky if you are just deported. There is a fair chance you will be held in immigration detention."

"What do you mean, forged? My passport was issued four years ago in Germany, and Karl's is much the same. We have travelled all around the world together without any issue, and here we are in hospital, and you are carrying on about our passports. Most of you would not have a passport, and I doubt if many of you have seen a German passport, so why do you think they are forgeries?"

"Well, smartarse, maybe you can tell us why your passport has Karl's photo, and his passport has your photo in it? I doubt that the Fatherland normally makes that mistake. And I am sure that our Customs people won't be impressed."

"That is ridiculous; we don't look remotely alike. Let me see my passport; I think you are all having a very poor joke with us."

"That just does not make sense. I know that it had my photo, and I have the other copies in my luggage. That is not possible."

Looking at the passports, Bill Adams suggested that it was just magic that the photos had changed.

"Weird things happen in our mountains, boys; particularly to visitors that abuse the hospitality of the locals."

Marcus had two more days before the end of his shift. He checked his supplies before heading out again along the Overland Track. His snack packs and his weatherproof clothing were in his daypack. He had his first aid kit. The scalpel was still sharp, but the superglue was getting low. He made a mental note to restock before returning to the mountain. "You never know when that stuff will come in handy."

He planned to walk through the Track and see if he could find James and Jane. Aunt Doris had let him know that they were planning on spending a few days on the northern end of the track; and if it proved to be something they really enjoyed, they would come back and do the full track in a year or so. Marcus realised that there were a lot of people in the park that he knew, and most of them were through his association with Aunt Doris. It was amazing how many people Aunt Doris had introduced him to. She somehow attracted interesting people, like bees to pollen.

He was an hour north of Narcissus when he saw the familiar appearance of Lizzie and Allison, walking towards him. He told them that the Germans had been taken out of the Park by Search and Rescue.

"They'll be all right, and well enough to leave the country in a few days. At the moment, they are a bit confused; they are probably not sure who they really are, but I guess they will figure it out. Hopefully by then they will have learnt some manners; and figured out how to treat women."

Allison laughed as she said that they apparently had a damn lot of learning to do, but they had received a few sharp lessons in a week.

"Exactly how do I get to Cheviot Beach, if I decide to try a bit of Christmas surfing?" Marcus asked. The girls laughed, directing him to head from Melbourne down to Mornington Peninsula and follow the signs.

Marine had decided at six o'clock in the morning that she and Katrien would have another day at Pelion. They had spent the night again with the students, who were noisy and annoying. Most of them had climbed Mount Oakleigh, and the boys particularly wanted everybody to know how easily they had conquered the mountain. Anne again discovered she had leeches in her boots; but now she burnt them off without help, albeit still complaining that it wasn't fair.

"Mr Carruthers should have told us about the leeches, and then I would have worn the horrible old walking boots. How was I to know the bloody things could get through the lace holes?"

The school group were so sick of her and her bloody boots that there was a chorus of boys and girls telling her to shut up. Mary Guard leaned across to her, quietly telling her that if she got the chance, she would throw her bloody boots into Dove Lake at the end of the trip, "with you still in them." Ann went quiet and snuck back to her tent to cry herself to sleep.

Two days later Andrew, Julie and the students were at Waterfall Valley Hut. Andrew told Julie that his knee was really causing him some concerns.

"I think it is time I handed the reins over to Pete and Sonia. They will be leading this event next year anyway. I can't climb Barn Bluff tomorrow, or the Summit of Cradle Mountain either. They can lead the students from here on; I will be the oracle that knows everything and does nothing."

"I think that is smart Andrew; but I will be walking with them. The girls come and talk to me before Sonia, and I think she likes an adult to talk to. Some of those girls are annoying brats."

The sun rose to a bright blue sky, but the day was freezing. Barn Bluff looked like a badly broken shard from the valley, unrecognisable by its appearance from any other direction in the Park. The climb was hard, but Pete made sure they carried everything.

There was too much risk of rapid weather change to allow them to leave their packs at the base of the climb. Regularly, he would stop and teach a short geology lesson, pointing out the rock formations, the scree, and the plants. Everyone took the opportunity to do some deep breathing and have a stretch before they set off again. The view from the top of Barn Bluff was pristine clear, but the wind was below freezing. Pete made sure that the most tired students lead the group back towards camp. They stopped for a warm drink on the way back, when John Ayers asked if any of the girls needed a hand with their bags. He offered to take a bit of weight if anyone was really struggling. It was obvious that several of the girls were completely exhausted, so the strongest of the boys took the tents and sleeping bags, adding them to their own. The group was ready for some food and a very early night when they reached Cirque Hut, where Andrew was waiting for them.

For the first time in their married life, Julie had achieved a physical challenge that Andrew was unable to do. She never mentioned it but smiled till they crawled into the tent to go to sleep.

The next day was even more exhausting. Andrew had planned to climb Cradle Mountain to the Summit, letting his kids feel the majesty of the mountain. He loved to tell them that they shared a uniquely rare experience; that only a minute fraction of Australians had ever seen that view; and that Australians were a miniscule fraction of the world.

Pete had heard it before. He quietly told Andrew that he would give them the message about how privileged they were.

By the time they returned there were two distinct camps; those who revelled in the experience, and the others, who were too tired to care.

Ann started complaining about her boots and her sore feet again. Andrew was about to scream at her, when he got the look from Julie that told him quietly to back off and be quiet.

Julie went over to Ann and picked up her boots. She looked at them slowly, from the crystal soles to the badly scarred patent leather uppers. She felt the brass eyelets and the totally saturated tongues of both boots. The inner soles were spongy and breaking up.

"Well Anne, we have all learnt lessons on this trip. A couple of the boys found out their vulgarity was not appreciated, and someone made sure they took a soaking. Most of us have been pushed to our endurance levels, but we have coped. Andrew has discovered that his knee is completely buggered, and he can no longer do this. I have discovered I can do this, and I am pretty bloody proud of myself. The girls have learnt to make new friends, and the boys have learnt that there is much more to women than just playthings. And hopefully Ann, you have learnt that experienced people give you advice for very sound reasons. These boots are totally fucked, and your feet won't be much chop for a few weeks either. And don't bother reporting me to the school for my language, because I don't work for the school.

Why don't you ask the Ranger over there what he thinks of your boots, your lovely little London fashion statements?

Hey Ranger, this stupid girl left her real boots in Hobart, and brought these after everyone was checked that they had the right gear. She thought it was so clever to show off the boots she had bought in London at Christmas time. Rich daddy's spoilt brat can have anything she wants, and most of all she wants all the other students to see what she has. Should we just leave her up here for a week or two, or do we persist and hope she has learned her lesson?"

Marcus looked at the boots, and then at Ann and shook his head. She started to tell him that it was an honest mistake, when he told her she was a spoilt brat that deserved to be uncomfortable.

"How much did they cost? You know there are people in Hobart still living in huts because they lost their houses in the fire? And you are overseas spending a month's rent on a pair of purple boots."

"The colour is ox blood."

"Very appropriate for someone who is as thick as an ox. Let me give you a suggestion. Stop whinging; and put up with the result of your stupidity. Learn the lesson, and in future listen to people who know."

He retreated to his corner and read his track notes.

He needed to put in a report that Frog Flats was getting worse, and maybe they need to lay some timber in it to stop it becoming a total bog before the weather cleared for the summer. Cirque Hut was showing its age, needing serious repairs or replacement.

As he continued writing, Ann continued complaining that everybody was ignoring her. She wanted to borrow some dry socks. She wanted some lotion for her feet to stop the itching, and she wanted to know how to dry the boots out a bit to make them better for the final long day coming up.

"Put them near the fire," Alex suggested.

Marcus called out that was what you did with real bushwalkers' leather boots. "Put those shitty things near the fire, and they will split all over the place. Wrap them up in clothes that you won't be wearing again and put them in the bottom of your sleeping bag. In a plastic bag, so they don't make your bedding wet.
Pack socks or whatever in them, and they will steam, so some of the water will come out of the purple shit into the clothing. It won't be perfect, but it will be better."

Ann had a restless night. She kicked the boots several times and woke with a fright. They were up to get breakfast and pack their bags with the daylight. Andrew told them they would walk behind the mountain, and down the Goat Track to the new Scott Kilvert Hut. "It's new and quite weatherproof. Just completed this year as a memorial to those two who died up here.

If we get there early enough, we will sleep in the Hut rather than the tents, and then tomorrow we walk out to the bus."

Ann took her boots out of the bag and immediately complained they were still wet. Marcus told her that he had said they would be better, not perfect.

"Put your feet into them and lace them up tight. And while you're at it, do the same thing with your mouth. Try giving everybody's ears a rest young lady. In a couple of days, you can be back with Mummy and Daddy and be their little princess again. Until then, try to be an adult for a change."

52: Farewell to the Mountain.

They were tired but the walk had been an amazing experience.

"Let's have one more night here, and then we can head out to get the bus to Launceston. We can have a couple of days with Doris and then head back to Melbourne."

"You know Marine, this has been extraordinary. We have been in one of the world's great wildernesses, and we did not even include it our plans."

"Probably because we'd never heard of it; but it will be something to remember and talk about for years."

"Mr and Mrs Alder should be finished all the work stuff they had to do, so we can have that trip with them, and then off to Sydney. After all this cold I am looking forward to some hot weather. I want to swim at Bondi Beach and go up to Queensland before we go home."

Cirque Hut was full when they got there, so they continued to Waterfall Valley Hut, where they were able to find a bunk to share. There was room for eight indoors, with plenty of room for camping outside.

The stream was snow melt; it was so cold it made the mouth tingle, but it was pristine.

She had heard a local say it was sweet, which was a strange description because there was no sugar taste, but it made the most beautiful cup of tea, and there was something about the taste that was cleaner than any water Marine had ever tasted. "I will never forget the taste, and yet I have no idea how to tell my friends why it was different."

"Let's just tell people that it is sweet. In an odd way, that is an accurate description."

There were eight people in the hut, from six different countries: but no Australians at all.

"Isn't it strange that the locals don't seem to realise what a jewel they have here?" a young fellow from Canada said to nobody in particular.

"Goodnight everybody. It is amazing how the aroma of wet, smelly socks puts me to sleep," one of the others said with a laugh.

It was chilly when they woke. The girls organised a quick breakfast so they could start the walk out of the Park. The bus departed mid- afternoon, and they did not feel like another night in a tent. It was time to return to civilisation. A short stop at Kitchen Hut for a warm drink and some chocolate before the long walk around the edge of Cradle Mountain in deep snow.

It was hard packed and easy to walk on, but there were occasional areas that were undercut by running streams.

More than one person had fallen through or gone in deep enough to wedge tight.

But the well-marked footprints were easy to follow, eventually leading to Marions Lookout. The sky was azure blue, and Dove Lake was stunning. There were a couple of cars, but no bus parked in the carpark.

It was a deceptive walk, with a near vertical descent off Marions Lookout, and a track covered in scree. "A heavy fall would ruin our day," Marine said to Katrien, "so let's take it easy on the way down. We have at least two hours before the bus leaves, so there is no need to rush."

Sonia decided to lead the group around the back of Cradle Mountain, with Alex and Helena reading the maps and the compasses. Sonia and Andrew knew the way, but it was important to teach some outdoor skills, without it looking like lessons.

Claudette twisted her ankle when she walked on a loose stone that was buried by snow. It rolled and she fell heavily. Her boots saved the ankle from serious damage, but she had a heavy bruise on her upper thigh, and some nasty abrasions. Pete made everybody take a break as he packed her thigh with hard-packed snow. Checking her ankle, he told her to do her boot up tight and not to take it off to sleep.

"It is better for your feet to be a bit cold and wet, than to be too swollen to walk out tomorrow."

Jim Thompson told her that he would carry her pack for her. He lashed the two packs together, and had Jonathon lift them onto his back.

He tied the straps tight around his waist and chest, and then called out, "Hi, ho Silver! Away!" as he set off down the track.

He had to lean a lot further forward, so he did not overbalance backwards, but he kept up with everybody. When they stopped for a break, he left the bags on, asking for some help getting back on his feet.

Claudette called him Superman; he responded that as Silver belonged to the Lone Ranger, she could be Tonto.

"OK Kemo Sabe, to the hut then."

Ann continued to complain all day until they reached the Scott Kilvert Hut.

"Oh, for God's sake Ann. You have a leech bite. Claudette has a badly sprained ankle, with some serious damage to her thigh, and you are making a noise like a wounded banshee, while she is just getting on with it. Would you just shut up for a while?" Jonathon had become totally sick of her, her bloody boots, and her sore feet.

He had loved this trip and the time with the other students even though at times he was aware that some of them needed to grow up a bit. Ann was such a pain in the arse that in an off moment he thought that it was a pity her house was not burned down in the fires; it may have improved her sense of proportion and consideration of others.

Jonathon had enjoyed the company of the others most of the time.

Most of the girls had proven to be very strong, physically and emotionally.

They coped with the deprivations and the lack of hygiene without complaint, and they managed to maintain their dignity when things got difficult. The boys had all coped well physically.

Their emotional maturity was a stumbling block, however, that drove him crazy. Their idle chatter about the girls, the bravado and bull dust about their sexual experience annoyed him, because he was sure that very little of it was true. He'd overheard Eddie Travers at the Scott Kilvert Hut, bragging to Barry about his conquests, and Barry boasting even bigger stories. Jonathon told them twice to tone it down. 'That rubbish is not appropriate in mixed company, so cut it out." They persisted till Jonathon yelled that the pair of them would be like a dog chasing a car. "If you caught it you would not know what to do with it." The girls cheered when Alex said that there was no chance that it would happen with them; nothing would make her run faster than being pursued by either of those two."

"That's a bit harsh, Jonathon. I guess you have had so much experience in your years away from school, have you, big boy."

"Well for a start, if you ever listen you will notice that is not something I talk about. And for good reason; it is not your business, and I don't have to justify my life to you."

Andrew cut the conversation there by organising a drinks break. He told them that tonight would be a celebration, the last night of the trip.

They could eat their extra rations if they wished, providing they kept one day's portions as an emergency. They could choose any place on the floor, providing there was no mixing of girls and boys. "The four staff will sleep in the middle of the hut. Boys on that side and girls over there. But you don't have to be with your tent buddy tonight." Ann put her boots back in the bag with the spare clothes and stuffed them in the bottom of the sleeping bag. She complained that the boots made the sleeping bag uncomfortable, and that she planned to never sleep on the floor again. She hated camping and planned to tell everybody next year not to do the trip. One of the boys called out that she would be useful if she told everybody to listen to the teachers' instructions, and make sure they followed the rules. There was a burst of applause. The room gradually became silent, and all that could be heard was the sounds of exhausted sleeping.

No one stirred when the door gently opened, and a shadowy figure came into the hut. It moved around for a little while, settling on the floor for about an hour before silently leaving again, without disturbing anybody.

The Scott Kilvert Hut was modern compared to every other hut in the Park.
It even had glass windows; so as the sun came up, sleeping students started to wake and move around. The pot belly stove was red hot by the time most of the students had got out of bed. Andrew had a kettle boiling on the stove, and others were getting hot food ready on their personal fuel stoves for breakfast.

Some had slipped their boots on, but most were just in the dry socks that were kept for sleeping. It was time for the final pack, and preparation for the return to civilisation. Andrew called them all together to stress the importance that there were no shortcuts today.

"Make sure everything is packed properly, and everything is weather-sealed. We have several hours to walk out today. And remember this hut is named after two people who died on the walk we are doing today. If the weather turns foul and we have to make camp, you will be grateful that your sleeping bag and emergency clothes are dry. So do not wear your dry socks today. They go back in your backpacks."

"What bastard did this! This is not funny," Ann screamed at everybody and nobody in particular. She had pulled the bag out of her sleeping bag to get her Doc Martens, only to find that the soles were not attached to the uppers any longer. Every yellow stitch had been surgically cut through, and the sole totally separated. In the bottom of her bag was a full roll of gaffer tape, with a note showing how to tape the soles on so they would not leak.

"Sir, someone was in my bag while I was sleeping. The bottom of the bag does not open, but whoever it was got to my boots in the bottom of my bag.

Whoever did this managed to not wake me while they got into my bag I was sleeping, and then put them back."

She sat on the plinth near the pot belly stove and cried hysterically. "How could anyone do that and not wake me up?"

There was no logical explanation to offer. There was nothing that made sense; there was no one in the hut that would, or could, do that. The stitches had not rotted; they had all been surgically cut though. And the boots had been in the bottom of her sleeping bag.

Julie and Sonia had a quiet talk to her to settle her down, but also to ensure that she had not been sexually assaulted. They asked everybody in the group if they had brought sleeping tablets with them, or any alcohol that may have been a reason for Ann to sleep through the intrusion. There was nothing that made any sense.

Julie followed the instructions, and the gaffer tape worked well. But on the sharp rock on Hansons Peak, it started to wear through. There was plenty on the roll, so Julie just kept wrapping it until they got off the mountain and onto the flat near Dove Lake. Julie had a little laugh as she said that at least the arse-hole left enough tape for the job. Ann burst out laughing as she said the boots were the most comfortable they had been on the whole trip. It was nice to hear her having a good laugh.

The school bus was waiting for them at the car park at Waldheim Chalet.

'It's time for some luxury. We will sleep on real beds, and have a real hotel meal. and a hot shower, boys and girls."

There was a loud cheer from everybody, students and staff. The bus driver said their bag on the seats had a full change of clothes and spare shoes.

"Tonight will be a celebration; you have all completed the Homage to the Mountain, and over time you will understand how this trip has changed you for the better."

Andrew was feeling a bit disconsolate.

"I am unlikely to be able to do this walk again, unless my knee surgery is a success, but we have discovered a great new leader for next year, with Miss Johnson proving totally capable. The only problem I might have, is learning to cook at home if Julie decides she wants to do it again. They have been a great team. And Mr Smithies has been superb, as usual. You girls have been the best surprise.

You have been amazing; tough, strong, and absolutely resilient. You have all exceeded our expectations. Ann, even you have got to the end; imagine how easy it would have been in the correct boots. I am sure that you, like everybody else will look back on this as a life changing experience, and possibly a shoe preference changing experience as well."

Andrew took Ann's sleeping bag to the police to report what had happened. One of the female officers took the bag over to the window to get better light; she came back and said that whoever had done it was clever, but that the girl had not been at risk.

"Whoever did this, unpicked the bottom seam of the bag and resewed it perfectly, with surgical stitches. The bugger was good. How the hell that could be done at night with no artificial light is staggering. You can assure the girl that no one touched her. But whoever it was, sure as hell wanted to frighten her."

James and Jane had hired some equipment and but bought some boots and jackets from Allgoods in Launceston. They were pretty sure that three or four days would be enough, but it would be something to add to their brag album when they returned to London. They had driven to Devonport but decided to take the bus to the Mountain. James was worried about leaving his new car in such an isolated area, and for some reason bush walking shops liked to talk about cars having the wiring chewed out by rats; or other disasters that probably never happened. The bus company had a lock up area for cars, that was cheap and secure. The price made them laugh. In London that amount of money would get a secured carpark for about three hours.

They got off the bus at Waldheim, as Marine and Katrien climbed on.

"How far have you walked? You look exhausted."

"We have been on the track for ten days. It has been exhilarating, and tough. The weather has been sometimes beautiful, and sometimes bleak. We have been wet and cold for ten days, and I would not swap a minute of it.

There were times when we had conversations that don't happen in the normal world, and sometimes they were with complete strangers. We seemed to meet so many lovely people."

"With two exceptions" Marine added.

"We will come back better prepared. We will climb to the top of Cradle Mountain and walk across the front of the mountain and down through the ancient forests. We will be back sometime, but it is time to see some more of the mainland."

"So how far are you going?"

"We only have four days this time, but we have bought a house so they can come back to Tasmania when we wanted to."

"Well actually when we need to. Frankly, I am not too sure how I will cope in London after this pure serenity." Jane smiled. James had never said that before.

"Have fun! Make sure you go down to Waterfall Valley. That was my favourite place."

They had drawn a rough mud map, and carried a beautiful little book, as well as the map of the Overland Track they picked up in the bushwalking shop.

Preferring to avoid backtracking, they decided to walk up the eastern side of the lake and climb to Hanson's Peak; they'd spend the first night in the Scott Kilvert Hut, then walk behind the back of the Mountain to join the Overland Track where they would head south to Cirque Hut.

From there it was a simple walk to Waterfall Valley, before walking out along the Facetrack.

They planned to walk down through the Ballroom Forest. The big climbs could wait for another day, having concluded that would allow them to experience the area broadly.

Jane remembered that Marcus suggested that he might catch up barring emergencies. He had their basic plan but it had changed since they had talked..

Originally, they had planned to walk up Marions Lookout, but they had decided at the last minute to go up the Eastern side to the Scott Kilvert Hut.

The weather was mild, with no fresh snow and only a light breeze. They were in a warm sweat by the time they reached the hut. Jane stated that as she could smell herself already, she expected to be pretty rank by the end of four days.

"So be it. I will still love you, smelly or not."

They were not used to that level of exertion. Making a quick meal and preparing to sleep on the floor, Jane snuggled down in the sleeping bag. The thin roll of foam under the bag was barely noticeable. "This is the most comfortable bed I have slept in since the Dorchester," Jane joked. She was struggling to find any position that did not hurt. "God, I wish I had a bit more fat on my bum and hips."

"I will remind you of that when we are back home."

"I wonder if anyone ever thought of making softer wood?"

"Go to sleep Princess; or I will slip a pea under your mattress."

The morning sun rose to an azure sky. The air outside was freezing but the hut was reasonably warm.
For breakfast they mixed powdered milk into warm water and added some cereal, before repacking for a hard day's walk.

They walked up the Goat Track, with a little stream finding its way through the stones and the rubble in the middle of the track. The foliage along the track was coarse to touch, but it smelled magnificent. Some of it was very citrus and other bushes were fragrant. There were some that smelled and tasted like pepper, some that were quite nutty. Their guidebook listed which to taste, so there was not much risk.

The back of the mountain was extraordinary. The view through Fury Gorge was stunning, and as they came out towards the Overland Track, they could see Barn Bluff in the distance. Turning south they headed to Cirque Hut. It was nearly full, so they quickly found space on a bench to claim as a bunk, placing their backpacks there. To make sure, they unrolled their sleeping bags.

"I need to change into some dry clothes, but not in front of all these people."

"The guidebook says if you tell everybody, they will discretely look away. If that does not work Princess, I will hold up some of my clothes.

"Hey folks, Jane needs to get some dry clothes on. Could I ask you all to look away for a moment." They all did.

"Looks like the rules of the mountain actually works Princess. Sorry; I had a peep, but nobody else did." She gently punched him on the arm. "Save that for when we get home."
The environment in the hut was like a fabulous party. Some were regulars, some had never been before.
Most were from overseas and had travelled extensively. This was on the list of things to do before they died. No one was disappointed; the place was even better than they had hoped.

There were professionals from all over the world, and lots of young people on their first overseas trip. They came from everywhere except Tasmania and the rest of Australia.

"How can these people have this on their doorstep and not come here?"
They shared tea and coffee, jokes, and conversations about far flung places, but within an hour of darkness most were asleep. The bunks here were appreciably more comfortable than the floor the night before.

The hut was empty by eight o'clock the next morning. Some were walking north, some south. Some were planning to climb the summit of Cradle Mountain, and some were heading off to climb Barn Bluff. For some, the trip was finishing today, and for others it was just starting.

James and Jane were heading to Waterfall Valley; and hoping to be there on their own for their last night in this beautiful part of God's Kingdom. As Waterfall Valley Hut was out of the way, most stayed at Cirque to be ready for the next day.

It added an extra hour and a half to start at Waterfall Valley, but this hut was becoming more popular as people learnt about the beauty of the place.Arriving in time for a cuppa before lunch, they sat on a large rock near the babbling stream and talked about their future.

Where would it be? London was such a magnificent city; it was the centre of the known world as the 1970's approached. Music, fashion, and theatre, commerce, and trade, all centred in London, but this little island was going to be hard to leave. Here they had tranquillity and open space, and time for each other. They had enough money to live comfortably.

"We could keep your lovely home at Henley, and we could go back as often as we wanted."

"Or we could keep our lovely home at Longford and come out here as often as we needed." James was thinking that unless they went back to London in the next few months, they might not have a choice; their jobs may have vanished.

The light breeze off the water was bone chillingly cold as Jane snuggled into James and he put his arms around her. Two wallabies hopped up along the stream. There was no sign of fear as they came right up to Jane.

She put her hand out, and one of them nuzzled the palm, looking for food. She gently stroked its soft fur, and it just sat looking at her as if they had known each other for years.

James watched the pair of them. It was so foreign to a Londoner, but it now seemed perfectly natural to him.

"Whatever happens, this has been the most extraordinary time of my life."

"Me too," was all Jane said.

"Oh my God; look at you two lovebirds." Marcus roared from thirty metres up the track. "You look like you have just found nirvana."

"Feels like it, Marcus. We are just so lucky that you told us to come here. If there is one place on earth that makes you reassess your priorities, I think this would have to be it."

They sat and talked about nothing in particular, and then Jane fetched a billy of water from the stream and lit their little gas stove to make a cup of tea.

"What are you doing from here?" Marcus asked James.

He and Jane explained their plan to head out the next day by walking along the Facetrack and down through the Ballroom Forest to Dove Lake. "We'll get the bus back to Devonport, pick up our car, and head back home."

"Hmm. I note that you call it your home. I think this little island has grabbed you by the short and curlies, Mate. What does Jane think about that?"

"She would stay in the blink of an eye, but we really need to go back to London and reassess our lives with some perspective. Whichever way it goes, we'll be back sooner, rather than later.

What about you Marcus? What are your plans? You happy to stay a Park Ranger, or have you had other thoughts?"

"I'm planning on having a break over Christmas. I thought we might go to Victoria for a few days. Mary loves Melbourne, and the city does Christmas so well. I don't think she has seen the shopfront of Alders at Christmas time, but everyone should do that at least once. We will stay at the Windsor. I have some people to catch up with, and Mary is comfortable exploring the city on her own. I'll see a couple of medical specialists to make sure all my war wounds are behaving well, and I will visit Mum's grave to put some flowers on it for Christmas."

Marcus thought to himself,

'And I just might go down to Cheviot Beach. It would not take much of a magician to make Harold Bloody Holt disappear.'

THE END

– maybe.

Milton Keynes UK
Ingram Content Group UK Ltd.
UKHW020756231024
450026UK00001B/52